Stradella

F. Marion Crawford

Alpha Editions

This edition published in 2024

ISBN : 9789362996978

Design and Setting By
Alpha Editions
www.alphaedis.com
Email - info@alphaedis.com

As per information held with us this book is in Public Domain.
This book is a reproduction of an important historical work. Alpha Editions uses the best technology to reproduce historical work in the same manner it was first published to preserve its original nature. Any marks or number seen are left intentionally to preserve its true form.

Contents

CHAPTER I .... - 1 -

CHAPTER II .... - 15 -

CHAPTER III .... - 23 -

CHAPTER IV .... - 30 -

CHAPTER V .... - 39 -

CHAPTER VI .... - 50 -

CHAPTER VII .... - 68 -

CHAPTER VIII .... - 81 -

CHAPTER IX .... - 87 -

CHAPTER X .... - 98 -

CHAPTER XI .... - 112 -

CHAPTER XII .... - 123 -

CHAPTER XIII .... - 127 -

CHAPTER XIV .... - 135 -

CHAPTER XV .... - 146 -

CHAPTER XVI .... - 152 -

CHAPTER XVII .... - 162 -

CHAPTER XVIII .... - 170 -

CHAPTER XIX .... - 182 -

CHAPTER XX .... - 195 -

CHAPTER XXI .... - 213 -

CHAPTER XXII .... - 227 -

CHAPTER XXIII .... - 233 -

CHAPTER I

The Senator Michele Pignaver, being a childless widower of several years' standing and a personage of wealth and worth in Venice, made up his mind one day that he would marry his niece Ortensia, as soon as her education was completed. For he was a man of culture and of refined tastes, fond of music, much given to writing sonnets and to reading the works of the elegant Politian, as well as to composing sentimental airs for the voice and lute. He patronised arts and letters with vast credit and secret economy; for he never gave anything more than a supper and a recommendation to the poets, musicians, and artists who paid their court to him and dedicated to him their choicest productions. The supper was generally a frugal affair, but his reputation in æsthetic matters was so great that a word from him to a leader of fashion, or a letter of introduction to a Venetian Ambassador abroad, often proved to be worth more than the gold he abstained from giving. He spoke Latin, he could read Greek, and his taste in poetry was so highly cultivated that he called Dante's verse rough, uncouth, and vulgar— precisely as Horace Walpole, seventy or eighty years later, could not conceive how any one could prefer Shakespeare's rude lines to the elegant verses of Mr. Pope. For the Senator lived in the age when Louis XIV. was young, and Charles II. had been restored to the throne only a few years before the beginning of this story.

Pignaver was about fifty years old. There is no good reason why a widower of that age, robust and temperate, and hardly grey, should not take a wife; perhaps there is really no reason, either, why he should not marry a girl of eighteen, if she will have him, and where neither usage nor ecclesiastical ordinances are opposed to it, the young lady may even be his niece. Besides, in the present case, the Senator would appear to his peers and associates to be conferring a favour on the object of his elderly affections, and to be crowning the series of favours he had already conferred. For Ortensia was the penniless child of his brother-in-law, a scapegrace who had come to a bad end in Crete. The Senator's wife had taken the child to her heart, having none of her own, and had brought her up lovingly and wisely, little dreaming that she was educating her own successor. If she had known it, she might have behaved differently, for her lord had never succeeded in winning her affections, and she regarded him to the end with mingled distrust and dislike, while he looked upon her as an affliction and a thorn in his side. Yet they were both very good people in their way. She died comparatively young, and he deemed it only just that after enduring the thorn so long, he should enjoy the rose for the rest of his life.

When Ortensia was seventeen and a half her uncle announced his matrimonial intentions to her, fastened a fine string of pearls round her throat, kissed her on the forehead, and left her alone to meditate on her good fortune.

Her reflections were of a mixed character, however, and not all pleasant. The idea that she could disobey or resist did not occur to her, of course, for the Senator had always appeared to her as the absolute lord of his household, against whose will it was useless to make any opposition, and she knew what an important person he was considered to be amongst his equals.

But in her inmost heart she knew that he was not really what he made people think he was. She had a ready sense of humour, and she felt that under his ponderous disguise of importance he was quite a ridiculous person. He was miserly to meanness; he was as vain as an ape; he was a man who had flattered himself, and had been flattered by others, into a sort of artificially inflated doll that imposed on many people and deceived almost all. And yet Ortensia was aware of something in him that frightened her a little, though she could not quite tell what it was. Possibly, like many externally artificial people, there was a cruel side to his character. There are men who become ridiculous as soon as they cease to be dangerous, and who are most dangerous when they fear that they are just going to become a laughing-sk.

Ortensia reflected on these things after her uncle had given her the pearls and had kissed her on the forehead. The pearls were very beautiful, but the kiss had been distinctly disagreeable. The Senator waxed his moustaches to make them stay up, as many men did then, and she thought that if a cold hard-boiled egg, surrounded with bristles like a hair-brush, had touched her forehead, the sensation would have been very much the same, and she shook her delicate shoulders in disgust at the thought, and slowly rubbed the offended spot with two fingers, while her other hand played with the string of pearls in her lap.

It would be a great thing, of course, to be a senator's wife and the mistress of such a house as the Palazzo Pignaver, which she had first entered as a little orphan waif ten years ago. But to be kissed daily, even on the forehead, by her Uncle Michele, would be a high price to pay for greatness. She supposed that he would kiss her every day when she was married, for that was probably a part of marriage, which had always seemed to her a mysterious affair at best. Young girls looked forward to it with delight, and old women seemed to look back on it with disappointment, while those who were neither old nor young never said anything about it, but often seemed to be on bad terms with their husbands.

But Ortensia was a fatalist, like most Venetian maidens of her time. Whatever the master of the house and the head of the family decided would be done, and there could be no question of resistance. In due course she would marry her uncle, she would hold her tongue like other married women while he lived, and when he was dead she would be at liberty to tell her friends that her marriage had been a disappointment. Of course Uncle Michele would die long before her—that was one consolation—and the position of a rich widow in Venice was enviable.

Happily she had six months before her, during which time her education was to be completed; happily, too, a large part of it now consisted in music lessons, for she had a sweet voice, and the Senator meant that she should astound Venetian society by singing his own compositions to them, accompanying herself. She had great beauty, as well as some real talent, and he judged that the effect of his verses and music, when rendered by her, would be much enhanced by the magic light in her hazel eyes, by the contrasted splendour of her auburn hair and ivory complexion, and by the pretty motion of her taper fingers as they fluttered over the strings. He looked forward to exhibiting the loveliest young woman in Venice, who should sing his own songs divinely to an admiring circle of envious friends. That would be a magnificent and well-deserved triumph, after his long career as a gifted amateur and critic—and it would cost nothing. Why should a wife be more expensive than a niece? His first wife's brocades and velvets could easily be made over for Ortensia; and for that matter the young girl expected nothing better, since she had no family of her own to give her a great carved chest full of beautiful new clothes and laces.

Uncle Michele did not condescend to honour her with another kiss, after the formal occasion on which he had announced her betrothal to himself. But he showed a growing interest in her music-lessons as the weeks passed, and he frequently made her sing pieces of his own to him, correcting each shade of expression most fastidiously, and occasionally performing the more difficult passages himself, with many affected gestures and self-approving waggings of his head, though his voice was tuneless and harsh, and his ear anything but perfect.

'Of course,' he would say, 'it is only to give you an idea!'

The idea which he conveyed to Ortensia was that of a performing bear eating strawberries; but she managed to keep her countenance, and not to mimic him when she repeated the passage herself, profiting by his instruction. It was the sort of music that rich amateurs used to write by the ream, subject to the unacknowledged 'corrections' of a well-paid professional; but the girl's sweet voice and genuine talent made the airs sound passable, while her dreamy eyes and her caressing pronunciation of the trivial words did the rest. It was mere talent, for she hardly understood what she was saying, or singing, and she felt not the least emotion, but she seemed to kiss the syllables as they passed her lips.

The first bloom of young womanhood was already on her cheek, but the frosts of childhood's morning had not melted from her maiden heart.

One day she was sitting just at the edge of the sunshine that poured upon the eastern carpet from the high loggia. The room overlooked the garden court of the palace, and the palms and young orange-trees, in vast terra-cotta pots, laden with yellow fruit, had already been brought out and set in their places, for it was the spring-time; the sunshine fell slanting on the headless Ariadne, which was one of the Senator's chief treasures of art, and the rays sparkled in the clear water in the beautiful sarcophagus below. The lilies had already put out young leaves too, that lay rocking on the ripples made by the tiny jet of the fountain. There were long terra-cotta troughs full of white violets, arranged as borders along the small paved paths, and red flower-pots were set symmetrically in squares and rings and curves with roses just blooming, and mignonette, and carnations that still lingered in the bud. It was a formal little garden, but in the midst of its regularity, neither in the centre, nor at any of the artificially planned corners and curves, but out of line with all, one cypress reared up its height. Even as Ortensia saw it, looking out from her loggia, it overtopped the high wall that divided the garden from the canal and the low houses on the other side, showing its dark plume sharp and clear against the sunlit sky; but when the morning and the evening breezes blew in spring and summer, it swayed lazily, and the feathery top waved from side to side, and bent to the caressing air like a live thing. Ortensia loved the tree better than anything else in the garden; even better than the beautiful Greek Ariadne, which her uncle had himself brought from Crete in one of his ships.

She was watching it now, and where the sunlight played in the tip, she could see the golden and reddish lights of the cypress twigs through the deep green. On her knees she held a large musical instrument all made of ivory, and inlaid with black, a lute with eleven strings, but of the shorter kind with the head of the keyboard turned back at a right angle. It lay in her lap, in the ample straw-coloured folds of her silk skirt, and its broad white ribband was passed over her shoulder, and pressed on her lace collar on the left side of her neck.

At a considerable distance from her, a small, middle-aged woman in grey sat in a high chair, bending forward over the little green pillow on which she was making bobbin lace.

There was a good deal of furniture in the large room, and it belonged to different periods; some of it was carved, some inlaid, some gilt in the new

French fashion. A great Persian carpet of most exquisite colours softened and blended by age lay on the floor, and the curtains of the doors were of rich old Genoa velvet, with palm leaves woven in gold thread on a faded claret ground.

The time lacked about an hour of noon, and in the deep stillness the trickling of the tiny fountain came up distinctly from the garden.

Something had just happened which Ortensia did not understand, and she had let her lute sink in her lap, to lean back and think, and wonder, watching the familiar outline of the dark cypress against the open sky.

She had been learning a song by a new composer, of whom she had never heard till now, and the manuscript lay open on a cushioned stool beside her. For a time she had followed the notes and words carefully with her voice, picking out the accompaniment on her lute from the figured bass, as musicians did in those days. At first it had not meant much to her; it was difficult, the intervals were unexpected and strange, she could not find the right chords, the words would not quite make sense, and some of them were unfamiliar to her.

But she was patient, and she had talent, and she had tried again and again, very soft and low, so that the woman in grey had nearly fallen asleep over her lace, nodding visibly and recovering herself each time with a little grunt.

Then, all at once, the breath of spring came in, like the breath of life, with the warm scent of the garden below, and the sunlight had stolen across the Persian carpet to her feet. She turned from the manuscript she had been studying, and without it her fingers suddenly found the chords, and her lips the words, and the melody floated out with them into the stillness, low, trembling, and passionate as the burden of a love-dream, a wonder to hear.

But she scarcely heard it herself, for it came unconsciously. The meaning had dawned upon her unawares, and she understood without ears, as if the music were all in her heart, and much nearer to her life than it could come by hearing alone.

It stirred delicious depths within her; the spring and the sun and the melody waked that in her which had slept the long sleep of childhood, while her beautiful outward self was maturing to the blossom.

She understood, and yet she did not; it was a bewildering joy, but it was a longing; it was an exquisite satisfaction, yet it was also a secret, unspeakable wish; it was the first thrill of a feeling too exquisite for words to describe, but with it there came a mysterious forelightening of something unknown that troubled her maiden peace.

Her lips quivered, her voice died away to a whisper, while her body vibrated still, like the last string she touched on the lute; a sudden warmth came to her face then, and sank suddenly away, and all at once it was all past, and she was gazing at the dark top of the cypress, and a strange, listless, half-sweet loneliness had come upon her, wherein nothing mattered any more, nor could anything ever matter again.

That was what had just happened. But the woman in grey had not noticed it, though she was wide awake now and busily plying her bobbins.

Then the heavy velvet curtain before the door was lifted, and a man's footstep was heard on the marble floor, and there was another step after it. Ortensia turned her head carelessly against the back of the chair to see who was coming, and then rose quickly to her feet.

The Senator had entered and was ushering in a man she had never seen, a handsome young man of five-and-twenty or so, with a thoughtful face and deep-set eyes, of a rather dark complexion, as if he came from the south; his manner was grave, and he was soberly dressed in a black velvet coat with purple silk facings, and wore a plain broad collar of linen instead of the fashionable lace; he was a man of middle height and well made, and he moved easily. In his left hand he carried a musical instrument in a purple bag.

'"This is the celebrated Maestro Alessandro Stradella of Naples"'

He bowed very low as soon as the Senator stood still before Ortensia.

'This,' said the master of the house, 'is the celebrated Maestro Alessandro Stradella of Naples, by far the greatest musician and composer in Italy, who has very kindly consented to hear you sing, and to give you a few lessons if he finds you sufficiently advanced.'

Ortensia was surprised, and anything but displeased, but she showed no emotion. The young man before her was the composer of the song she had been studying, the very one that had so strongly disturbed her a few minutes ago; this of itself would have been interesting, even if he had not been such a singularly handsome young man.

The woman in grey, who was her nurse, had risen too, and was looking at the musician with more curiosity than might have been expected in a sober person of her years.

Ortensia bent her head a little, in acknowledgment of the introduction, but said nothing. She saw, however, that Stradella had already noticed the manuscript of his own music on the stool beside her.

'You may sing "Amor mi dice" to the Maestro,' said the Senator, taking a seat. 'A little composition of my own,' he added, with a self-satisfied smile, for the musician's information. 'I have taught it to my niece myself.'

For one instant Stradella's eyes met the young girl's and she returned their glance. It was enough; they already understood each other. Doubtless the composer had met his patron more than once and knew his weakness and what to expect now. Ortensia resumed her seat, and drew her full skirt into folds on her knee, for her lute to rest on. Stradella sat down at a little distance and looked at the Persian carpet, and she could not help seeing that he had remarkably well-turned legs and ankles, and wore very well-made shoes of soft purple leather with handsome chiselled silver buckles. She felt inclined to raise her eyes to his face again, but resisted the temptation, and turned resolutely towards her uncle as she struck the opening chords of the accompaniment.

The musician now looked up and watched her. At first he put on the amiable smile which professionals keep especially for amateurs, and as a matter of politeness he listened attentively, till he had convinced himself that the song, as he had expected, belonged to that large class of which the chief characteristic is a general resemblance to everything of the kind that was ever written before, and will ever be written hereafter. This being settled after hearing a few bars, Stradella quietly gave himself up to the pleasure of looking at the young girl, though he often turned towards the Senator, who expected admiration at every full close, and meant to get it.

He thought he did; for the effect of watching Ortensia was to bring to the musician's own face an expression of such genuine delight that Pignaver could not fail to be pleased, since he attributed it to the charm of his composition. He was in the seventh heaven. Here, at last, was a true genius, able to appreciate his talent as it deserved. Here was a master fit to teach such noble music, as it should really be sung. Ortensia should profit by the opportunity, even if Stradella asked a silver ducat for each lesson. For once, money was no object to the Senator. The triumph his young bride would certainly bring him, in singing his songs after being taught by Alessandro Stradella, would be worth much more than gold.

She sang the stuff as creditably as it deserved, her voice was fresh and true, and her touch on the lute was at once light and sure. With such a face, what did it matter that the song was exactly like a thousand others? The musician praised it so enthusiastically that the Senator was almost satisfied for once.

'You flatter me,' he said, bowing a little in his chair, spreading out his hands in a gesture of deprecation and grinning like a pleased monkey.

'Not in the least, my lord, I assure you,' answered Stradella with great emphasis. 'If I were capable of flattering you, I should not deserve the confidence you place in me, in desiring me to give this gifted young lady a few lessons.'

Ortensia pretended to be busy with her lute, bending over it and softly trying the upper strings, though they were already perfectly in tune. But she was listening to the young master, and she thought she had rarely heard a voice that had more winning tones in speaking, or an accent that pleased her better. And as she bent down she could just see his well-turned ankles and purple leather shoes.

'It would be my wish,' the Senator said, 'that you should give her some hints as to the performance of a number of my songs. Yes, I have devoted much time to your art as well as to poetry. Hitherto I have written ninety-seven songs, both words and music. Yes, I have been industrious. If my niece had my industry she would know them all by this time.'

Ortensia bent still lower, till her face almost touched the frets of the instrument, and she was biting her lip; but Stradella was imperturbable.

'I trust you may be spared to contribute many more beautiful compositions to the art treasures of our country,' he said politely.

'I hope so,' answered Pignaver with gravity.

And then—Ortensia looked up, and for the second time her eyes met the musician's, and she felt that he and she already understood each other.

With many patronising smiles on the Senator's part, and many flattering expressions of admiration and respectful salutations from Stradella, the two parted and Pignaver took himself off, leaving his niece to take her first lesson under the guardianship of the nurse, who moved her chair so that she could watch the pair while she was busy with her lace.

For a few seconds neither spoke, and they looked at each other in silence as if making better acquaintance through their eyes alone, by which they had quickly reached a first degree of understanding. Stradella's face was quite grave, while Ortensia's lips were just parted, as if she were ready to smile, if he would. But he would not, and he was the first to speak.

'How shall we begin?' he asked.

Ortensia hesitated and touched the strings of her lute idly, as it lay across her knee, just kept from slipping down by the broad ribband.

'When you came,' she said at last, 'I had been trying to learn a song of yours. It is beautiful. Will you show me how to sing it?'

She blushed faintly, and he smiled; but he shook his head.

'I saw it lying there as soon as I came in,' he said. 'But I understand it to be the Senator's wish that we should study his music rather than mine.'

She was disappointed, and did not try to hide it; but she was not used to asserting her own will, and her uncle's word had always been law in his house, to be obeyed whether he were present or not. As for Stradella, he would have sung his own song for her with delight, but he distrusted the woman in grey, who might be a spy for all he knew. He carefully withdrew his lute from the purple bag and began to tune the strings. It was a fine instrument, made in Cremona, but by no means so handsome in appearance as Ortensia's ivory one. It was differently designed, too, being much longer, with a double fret-board and no less than nineteen strings.

'Let me see,' Stradella said, when he was ready. 'That song of the Senator's you just sang—how was it?'

He struck chords, bent low over the lute, softly hummed a few snatches of the melody, and then, to Ortensia's surprise, he began to sing the piece as if he knew it well. He sang softly, without the least effort, and his voice seemed neither high nor deep, but there was a tone in it that the young girl had never heard before, and that sent a thrill to her heart at the very first note. She bent forwards, watching him with parted lips and eyes full of wonder, scarcely breathing till he finished the stanza and spoke to her again.

'Is that it?' he asked quietly, and he smiled as he looked at her.

'But you know it!' she cried. 'If I had ever heard you I should not have dared to try to sing before you!'

'I never heard it before,' Stradella answered, 'but I catch any tune easily. Shall we study it a little?' he went on, before she could speak again. 'I will accompany you at first, and I will stop you now and then, where I think you might do better. Shall we?'

Again he smiled, but this time it was by way of encouragement, and he at once began a little prelude on the lute.

'You will sing better if you stand up,' he suggested.

She rose, took her own lute from her neck, and stood resting one hand on the high back of her chair, turning her face from him; for she was afraid, now that she had heard him. It was as bad as the worst stage-fright; her tongue was paralysed, her limbs shook under her, she shivered with cold in the sunshine, and her forehead was damp. Yet she had not felt the slightest shyness a quarter of an hour earlier, when she had first sung the piece.

'Sing with me,' he said quietly, and he began the song again.

Presently she took courage and the notes came, unsteadily at first, but then true and clear; and Stradella's own voice died to a whisper, and she went on alone, to the accompaniment he played.

'You see,' he said, as she paused, 'it is better to stand. Now I will show you how to make one or two little improvements.'

So the lesson went on, and she conscientiously tried to do exactly what he taught her; and their eyes met often, but that could not be helped, for he showed her how to vary the quality of her tone by movements of the mouth, and to do this she had to watch his lips and he was obliged to look at hers, which is sometimes a dangerous exercise for young people, even at a first meeting. For acquaintance grows and ripens precociously when two people are busy together so that they depend on each other at every instant, as teacher and pupil, or as the chief actor and actress in a play, or as a man and a woman who are suddenly thrown together in adventure or danger.

When Stradella put his lute back into the purple bag at last, telling Ortensia that she had sung enough for one morning and that she must not tire her voice, she felt as if this could not possibly have been her first meeting with him. His face, his tone, his gestures, the way he held his lute, were all as familiar to her already as if he had given her half-a-dozen lessons; and when he was gone and she sat once more in her chair looking at the top of the cypress tree against the noonday sky, she saw and heard all again, and then again; but she neither saw nor heard her nurse, who had laid aside the lace-pillow and was standing at her elbow telling her that it was time for the mid-day meal and that her uncle did not like to be kept waiting. The nurse spoke three times before Ortensia heard her and looked up.

'They say well that music is a thief,' observed the middle-aged woman in grey, enigmatically, as she stood with her hands folded under her black apron, gazing intently at Ortensia's face.

The young girl laughed as she rose.

'Poor old Pina!' she answered, tapping her forehead with one finger as if to say that the nurse was weak-minded.

But Pina smiled, and made three gestures, without saying a word: first she pointed to herself, then she shook her forefinger, and lastly she jerked her thumb back in the direction of the door that led to the Senator's apartments. The weak-minded body was not Pina, but her master, since he had brought that handsome singer to teach Ortensia, who had never before exchanged two words with any young man, handsome or plain, except under the nose of the Senator himself; and that had always been at those great festivals to which the Venetian nobles took their wives and daughters, even when the latter were very young, to show off their fine clothes and jewels, though it meant comparing them publicly with quite another class of beauties.

For the Venetian maxim was that women and girls were safe in public or under lock and key, but that there was no salvation for them between those two extremes.

But, in the eyes of Pignaver, a musician was not a man, any more than a servant or a gondolier could be. Where a Venetian lady was concerned, nothing was a man that had not a seat in the Grand Council; that was the limit, below which the male population consisted of sexless creatures like domestics, shopkeepers, and workmen.

Furthermore, the vanity of Pignaver raised him above all other competitors as high as the Campanile stood above Saint Mark's and the Ducal Palace, not to mention the rest of Venice, and the idea that Ortensia, who had been informed that she was to be the wife of his transcendently gifted and desirable self, could stoop to look at a Sicilian music-master, would have struck him as superlatively comic, though his sense of humour was imperfect, to say the least of it.

Even if the great man could have set aside all these considerations for a moment, so as to look upon Stradella as a possible rival, he would still have believed that the presence of Pina during the lessons was a trustworthy safeguard against any 'accident to Ortensia's affections,' as he would have expressed the danger. He had unbounded faith in Pina's devotion to him and in her severity as a chaperon. On the rare occasions when the young girl was allowed to leave the palace without her uncle, Pina accompanied her in the gondola, and sometimes on foot as far as the church of the Frari, where she went to confession once a month; but, as a rule, she had her daily airing with the Senator himself, meekly sitting on his left, and pretending to keep her eyes fixed on an imaginary point directly ahead, as he insisted that she must, lest she should look at any of the handsome young nobles who were only too anxious to pass as near as possible on her side of the gondola.

For, though she was not eighteen years old, the reputation of her beauty was already abroad; and as it was said that she was to inherit her uncle's vast wealth, there were at least three hundred young gentlemen of high degree who desired her now, since no one knew that the Senator had determined to marry her himself. Their offers were constantly presented to him, sometimes by their fathers or mothers, and sometimes by ingenious elderly friends who undertook such negotiations for a financial consideration. But Pignaver always returned the same answer, politely expressing his thanks for the honour done his niece, but saying that he had 'other views for her.'

Pina, however, hated him for reasons of her own, which he had either forgotten, or which he disregarded because, in his opinion, she was under the greatest obligation to the house. Pina's hatred of her master was more sincere, if possible, than her affection for Ortensia, and her contempt for his intelligence was almost as profound as his own belief in its superiority over that of other men.

These facts explain why Pina acted as she did, though they could not possibly excuse her evil conduct in the eyes of righteous persons like the Senator and others of his class, who would have thought it a monstrous and unnatural thing that a noble Venetian girl should fall in love with a music-master, though he were the most talented and famous musician of his day.

This was what Pina did. In the middle of the fourth lesson she deliberately laid aside her lace-pillow and left the room, well knowing that her master would have her thrown out of the house at once, and ducked in the canal besides, if he ever heard of it. But he was a man of unchanging habits. Each time that Stradella came he led him in, sat down, listened while Ortensia sang one of his own pieces, and then went away, not to return that morning. So when Pina was quite sure that his coming and going had settled to a habit, she boldly ran the risk, if it was one, and left the two together.

Alessandro Stradella was a Sicilian on both sides, though he had been born in Naples, and he wasted no time when his chance came. He tried no little trick of word or glance, he did not gaze into Ortensia's eyes and sigh, still less did he boldly try to take her hand and pour out a fervid declaration of his love; for by this time, without the exchange of a word, the girl had taken hold of his heart, and he saw her eyes before him everywhere, in the sunlit streets and canals, and at night, in the dark, and in his dreams.

He did none of these things. He was the master singer of his age, and he himself had made divine melodies that still live; he knew his power, and he trusted to that alone. The velvet curtain had scarcely fallen behind Pina as she went out, when he bent over his lute, and with one look at Ortensia began to sing. But it was not one of those ninety-seven compositions on which the Senator prided himself: it was a love-song of Stradella's own that he had made within the week in the secrecy of his own room, and no one had heard it yet; and it was his masterpiece.

Ortensia felt that it was hers. That strange voice of his that was not deep, yet never seemed high-pitched, breathed softly through and through her being, as a spring breeze through young leaves, more felt than heard, yet a wonder to hear. The notes vibrated, but did not tremble; they swelled and grew strong and rang out fiercely, but were never loud; and again they died away, but were not quite silent, and lingered musically in the air, though a whisper would have drowned them.

The girl's eyes grew dark under their drooping lids, and her face was luminously pale; her delicate young lips moved now and then unconsciously, and they were icy cold; but she felt a wild pulse beating at her throat, as if her heart were there and breaking to be free.

She felt his look on her too, but she could not answer it, and when the song ended she turned from him and laid her white cheek against the high back of the chair, looking out at the cypress against the sky. She could not tell whether it was pain or pleasure she felt, but it was almost more than she could bear, and her hands strained upon each other, clasped together just on her two knees.

In the silence the velvet curtain was lifted and fell again, and Pina's step was heard on the marble floor.

'I have brought you some water to drink,' said the nurse quietly; and speaking to both, 'Your throats must be dry with so much singing!'

Ortensia took one of the tall glasses and drank eagerly before she turned her face from the window.

'Thank you,' she said, recovering herself and smiling at Pina.

'And you, Maestro?' asked the latter, offering Stradella the drink.

'Thank you,' he said, 'but it is too much. With your permission!'

And then, with the effrontery of youth in love, he deliberately took the almost empty glass from which Ortensia had drunk, poured a little into it from the other, and drank out of it with a look of undisguised gratitude on his handsome face. Thereupon a little colour came to Ortensia's ivory-pale cheek, and Pina smiled pleasantly. Instead of setting down the salver, however, she took it away, leaving the room again.

'How beautiful that song is!' Ortensia said in a low voice, and glancing at Stradella almost timidly, when they were again alone. 'How more than beautiful!'

'It is yours,' answered the musician. 'I made it for you—it is not even written down yet.'

'For me!' The exquisite colour deepened twice in her face and faded again as her heart fluttered.

'For you,' Stradella answered, so softly that she barely heard.

The nurse came back just then, having merely left the salver outside to be taken away. In her judgment things had gone far enough for the present. Then the mid-day bells clanged out, and it was time to end the lesson, and Stradella put his lute into its purple bag and bowed himself out as he always did; but to-day he kept his eyes on Ortensia's, and hers did not turn from him while she could see his face.

CHAPTER II

Love-dealings and Deceit, says an ancient poet, were born into the world together, daughters of Night; and several dry-hearted old critics, who never were in love and perhaps never deceived anybody in their lives, have had so much trouble in understanding why these divinities should have made their appearance in the world at the same time, that they have suspected the passage and written pages of learned trash about what Hesiod probably wrote instead of 'Love-dealings,' or the pretty word for which I can think of no better translation.

Pignaver was not a particularly truthful person himself, but he exacted strict truthfulness from others, which is good business if it is bad morality; and Ortensia had been brought up rigidly in the practice of veracity as a prime virtue. She had not hitherto been tempted to tell fibs, indeed; but she had always looked upon doing so as a great sin, which, if committed, would require penance.

Yet no sooner had she fallen in love with Alessandro Stradella than she found herself telling the most glaring untruths every day, with a readiness and self-possession that were nothing short of terrifying. For instance, her uncle often asked her to tell him exactly what she had been studying with the music-master, and he inquired especially whether the latter ever sang any of his own music to her. To these questions she answered that she was too anxious to profit by the lessons she was receiving, through her uncle's kindness, to waste the precious time in which she might be studying his immortal works.

She used those very words, without a blink, and Pignaver swallowed the flattery as a dog bolts a gobbet of meat. She added that the Maestro himself was so enthusiastic about the Senator's songs that he now cared for nothing else.

Yet the truth was that Stradella had summed up his criticism in a few words.

'They are all so much alike that they almost produce the impression of having been written by the same person.'

That was what he had really said, and Ortensia had laughed sweetly and cruelly; and even Pina, busy with her lace-pillow, had smiled with evil satisfaction in her corner, for she was a clever woman, who had been educated above her present station, and she understood.

Further, the Senator asked whether Stradella ever attempted to enter into conversation with his pupil, between one piece of music and the next.

'Conversation!' cried the young girl indignantly. 'He would not dare!'

If Pignaver noticed the slight blush that came with the words, he set it down to just anger at the mere suggestion that his future wife could stoop to talk with a music-master. Yet, being of a suspicious nature, he also made inquiries of Pina, whom he unwisely trusted even more than Ortensia herself.

'Conversation, Excellency? Your Excellency's niece in conversation with a fiddler, a public singer, a creature little better than a mountebank! My lady Ortensia would as soon talk with a footman! Shame, my lord! The suspicion is unworthy! I would scarcely answer to the young man himself, if he spoke to me, though I am only a poor servant! A fiddler, indeed! A lute-strummer, a catgut-pincher, and a Neapolitan into the bargain!'

Thus did Pina express herself, and while her rather hard grey eyes seemed to flash with anger, her mouth, that had once been handsome, curved in lines of scorn that were almost arisratic.

It is as easy to deceive a very vain person in matters where vanity has a part to play as it is to cheat a blind man, and Pignaver was hoodwinked without difficulty by his niece and her nurse, and the love that had sprung up between the two young people almost at first sight grew at an amazing rate while they sang and looked at one another over their lutes.

But the first word had not been spoken yet, though it had been sung many times by both, separately and together. It was not that Stradella doubted how it would be received, if he spoke it when Pina was out of the room, nor was Ortensia not eager for it long before it came. Yet she could not be the first, and he would not, for reasons she understood so little that at last she began to resent his silence as if it were a slight. Few Italian girls of her age have ever known that sensation, which is familiar enough to many women of the world.

Stradella found himself faced by a most unexpected circumstance. He was not only in love; that had happened to him at regular intervals ever since he had been barely fourteen years old, when a beautiful Neapolitan princess heard him sing and threw her magnificent arms round his neck, kissing him, and laughing when he kissed her in return; and she had made him the spoilt darling of her villa at Posilippo for more than three weeks.

Since then he had regarded his love affairs very much as he looked upon the weather, as an irregular succession of fine days, dark days, and stormy days. When he was happily in love, it was a fine day; when unhappily, it was stormy; when not at all, it was dull—very dull. But hitherto it had never occurred to him that any one of the three conditions could last. Like Goethe, he had never begun a love-affair without instinctively foreseeing the end, and hoping that it might be painless.

But to his amazement, though he had been prepared to be as cheerfully cynical and as keen after enjoyment as usual, he now felt, almost from the first, that there was no end in sight, or even to be imagined. The beginnings had not been new to him; it was not the first time that beauty had stirred his pulse, or that a face had awakened sympathy in that romantic region of feeling between heart and soul which is as far above the brute animal as it is below the pure spirit. Before now his voice had brought fire to a woman's eyes, and her lips had parted with unspoken promises of delight. That was what had happened on the first day when Pina had left him alone with Ortensia and he had sung to her; that had all been normal and natural, and only not dull because the fountain of youth was full and overflowing; that might have happened to any man between twenty and thirty.

He had gone away light-hearted after the first lesson, with music in his heart and ears. Was not every beginning of new love a spring that promised summer, and sometimes a rich autumn too, all in a few weeks, and with only a dull day or two to follow at the end, instead of winter?

But the next time he saw Ortensia it was a little different, and after that the difference became greater, and at last very great indeed, till he no longer recognised the familiar turnings in light love's short path, and the pretty flowers he had so often plucked by the way did not grow on each side within easy reach, and the fruit of the garden seemed endlessly far away, though he knew it was hidden somewhere, far sweeter than any he had tasted yet. For it was a maiden's garden in which no man had trod before; and the maiden was of high degree, and could not wander along the path with him, yielding her will to his.

His light-heartedness left him then, his face grew grave, and his temper became melancholy, for the first time in his life. He was only to give her a few lessons, after all, and Pina would leave him with her for ten minutes, scarcely more, each time he came. One minute would be enough, it was true; if he spoke she would listen, if he took her hand she would let him hold it. But what would be the end of that? A kiss or two, and nothing more. When the lessons were finished he would be told by the Senator that his teaching was no longer needed, and after that there would be nothing. He might see her once a week in her gondola, at a little distance; but as for ever being alone with her again in his life for five minutes, that would be out of the question. Could he, a musician and an artist, a man sprung from the people, even think of aspiring to the hand of a Venetian senator's niece?

In those days the idea was ludicrous. And as for her, though she might be in love with him—and he felt that she was—would she entertain for a moment the idea of escaping from her uncle's house, from Venice, to join her lot with a wandering singer's? That was still greater nonsense, he thought. Then what could come of it all but a cruel parting and a heartache, since this was real love and could not end in a laugh, like the lighter sort he had known so well? She was a mere child yet, she would forget in a few weeks; and he was a grown man, who had seen the world, and could doubtless forget if he chose, provided there were never anything to be forgotten beyond what there was already.

But if he should speak to her in one of those short intervals when they were alone, if she stretched out her hand, if he clasped her to him, if their lips met, things would not end so easily nor be so soon forgotten. He had the careless knowledge of himself that many gifted men have even when they are still very young; he knew how far he could answer for his own coolness and sense, and that if he allowed himself to cross the limit he would behave like a madman and perhaps like a criminal.

Therefore he set himself to be prudent till the lessons should be over, and he even thought of ending them abruptly and leaving Venice. His acquaintance with Ortensia would always be a beautiful recollection in his life, he thought, and one in which there could be no element of remorse or bitterness. He was not a libertine. Few great artists have ever been that; for in every great painter, or sculptor, or musician there is a poet, and true poetry is the refutation of vulgar materialism. In all the nobler arts the second-rate men have invariably been the sensualists; but the masters, even in their love affairs, have always hankered after an ideal, and have sometimes found it.

When the Senator ushered in Stradella one morning and quietly announced that the lesson was to be the last, Ortensia felt faint, and turned her back quite to the open window, against the light, so that the two men could not see how she changed colour. The nurse's hard grey eyes scrutinised Pignaver's face for an instant, and then turned to Stradella; he was paler than usual, but grave and collected, for the Senator had already informed him that his services would be no longer needed after that day.

Everything was to take place as usual. As usual, Ortensia was to sing one of her uncle's ninety-seven compositions to him while Stradella accompanied her; as usual, Pignaver would then go away; lastly, at the customary time, Pina would go out for ten minutes and reappear with water and sherbet.

Ortensia was shaking with emotion when the ordeal began, and for a moment she felt that it was hopeless to try to sing. Some sharp discordant sound would surely break from her lips, and she would faint outright in her misery.

She was on the very point of saying that she felt a sudden hoarseness, or was taken ill, when her pride awoke in a flash with a strength that amazed her, the more because she had never dreamed she had any of that sort. Stradella should not guess that she was hurt; she would rather die than let him know that her heart was breaking; more than that, she would break his, if there was time, and if she could!

She stood up by her chair and sang far better than she had ever sung before in Pignaver's hearing; she threw life and fire and passion into his mild composition, and she remembered every effective little trick Stradella had taught her for improving the dull melody and for emphasising the commonplace verses it was meant to adorn.

The Senator was surprised and delighted, and Stradella softly clapped his hands. She hated him for applauding her, yet she was pleased with the applause.

'What music, eh?' cried the Senator, with a grin of satisfied vanity.

'It is music indeed!' answered Stradella with a grave emphasis that gave the words great weight. 'It has been my endeavour to do justice to it, in instructing your gifted niece.'

'You have succeeded very well, dear Maestro,' Pignaver answered with immense condescension. 'The world will be much your debtor when it hears my melodies so charmingly sung!'

With this elephantine compliment the Senator nodded in a patronising way and took himself off, while Stradella bowed politely at his departing back.

When the curtain fell before the door, the singer turned to his pupil and sat down in his accustomed seat, with great apparent self-possession. Ortensia watched him, and her new-born resentment increased quickly.

'What will it please you to study to-day?' he inquired, just as easily as if it were not the very last time.

She felt much inclined to answer 'Nothing,' and to turn her back on him, but somehow her pride found a voice for her, as indifferent as his own, though she avoided his eyes and looked out of the window.

'It does not matter which song we take,' she answered. 'They are very much alike, as you have often said!' She even laughed, quite lightly and carelessly.

It was his turn to be surprised. Her tone was as natural and unstrained as a child's. At the sound of it, he asked himself whether this slip of a thing of seventeen years had not been acting emotions she had not felt, and laughing at him while he had been singing his heart out to her. Any clever girl could twist herself on her chair, and lay her cheek to the back of it, turning away as if she were really suffering, and twining her hands together till the little joints strained and turned even whiter than the fingers themselves.

At the thought that she had perhaps made a fool of him, Stradella nearly laughed, and he came near being cured then and there of his latest and most serious love-sickness. His lute was lying on his knees; he began to strum the opening chords of Pignaver's dullest composition, in the dull mechanical way the music deserved. He thought the effect might be to make Ortensia laugh and to change her mood.

But, to his annoyance, she rose, laid one hand on the back of the chair, and proceeded to sing the song with the greatest care for details, though by no means with the dashing spirit that had made him applaud her first performance that morning. She was evidently singing for study, as if she meant to profit by his teaching to the very last moment.

He accompanied her mechanically, wondering what was going to happen next, and when she had finished he eyed her with curiosity, but said nothing. She seemed completely changed.

'Why do you look at me in that way?' she asked with great calmness. 'Did I make any bad mistake?'

He smiled, but not very gaily.

'No,' he answered, 'you made no mistakes at all. You are admirable to-day! I quite understand that my services are no longer needed, for I can teach you nothing more!'

'I have done my best to improve under your instructions,' answered Ortensia primly.

She rested both her elbows on the back of the chair now and looked calmly out of the window at her favourite tree. Stradella pretended that his lute needed tuning, turned a peg or two and then turned each back again, and struck idle chords.

'When you are rested,' he said, 'I am at your service for another song.'

'I am ready,' Ortensia answered with a calmness quite equal to his own.

Pina, watching them from a distance and neglecting her lace-pillow, saw that something was the matter, and got up to leave the room at least half-an-hour earlier than usual; but because the Senator might come back unexpectedly during this last lesson, she went out through the other door beyond which a broad corridor led to his own apartments, and she stood where she could not fail to hear his steps in the distance if he should return.

Ortensia was still standing by her chair when Stradella left his seat and came towards her, holding his lute in one hand. It did not suit his male dignity to take leave of her without finding out whether she had been playing with him or not, though half-an-hour earlier he would not have believed it possible that vanity could enter into any thought he had of her.

He stood quite near her, and she met his eyes; she was rather frightened by his sudden advance, and shrank back behind the chair.

'You will find me in your loggia to-night, outside that window,' he said, pointing as he spoke. 'I shall be there an hour before midnight, and I shall wait till it is almost dawn.'

He paused, keeping his eyes on hers. She had started back at the first words, and now a deep colour had risen in her cheeks; he could not tell whether it meant anger or pleasure.

'I shall be there,' he repeated; 'I shall be there to say good-bye, if you will have it so, or to come again if you will. But if you do not open the window, I will come twice again at the same hour, to-morrow and the night after that, and wait for you till dawn.'

Ortensia turned from him without speaking and went out into the covered loggia. It was her instinct to look at the place where he was to be, and for the moment she could not answer him, for she did not know what to say; she herself could not have told whether she was angry or pleased, she only felt that something new was happening to her. Her mood had changed again in a few seconds.

He followed her to the threshold of the window, and stood behind her in the flood of sunshine, so near that he could whisper in her ear and be heard.

'There is love between us,' he said. 'We have seen it in each other's eyes ever since we first met, we have heard it in one another's voices every day! I will not leave you without saying it for us both, just as much for you as for myself! But I must say it all many times, and I must hear it from you too. Therefore I shall be here an hour before midnight to wait, and you will come, and you will open the window when you see me standing outside, and we shall be together! And if you will, we need never part again, for the world is as wide as heaven itself, for those who love to find a safe resting-place.'

She raised one hand as if to stop him, without turning round. While he spoke, she had turned pale again by soft degrees, and she drew her breath sharply once or twice, with an effort. He caught the hand she put out and kissed it slowly three times, as if he would leave the print of his young lips on the smooth white skin for a memory. She let him have his way, though she shook her head, and would not turn to him.

He was so near her that he could have bent and kissed her, just above the broad lace collar, behind her little ear, where the strong auburn hair sprang in silken waves from the ivory of her neck. The scent of lavender and violets rose from her dress to his nostrils in the warmth.

'You will come,' he whispered.

'How can I?' she asked, very low.

Then they heard Pina's voice behind them, not loud, but sharp and imperative.

'The Senator is coming back!' she called to them, as she dropped the curtain after entering and hastened to her seat.

Stradella crossed to the other side of the window in an instant, raising the lute he still carried in one hand.

'Sing!' he commanded, and he was already playing the accompaniment to one of Pignaver's everlasting songs.

As pride had helped her before, sheer desperation strengthened her now, and, without moving from her place, she began to sing, not very steadily at first, for her heart was beating terribly fast, but carefully, as if she were studying.

A moment later Pignaver noiselessly lifted the velvet curtain and looked in, confident that he had surprised them, and perfectly satisfied with the result. Beyond the fact that they were standing in the sunshine to sing and play, on opposite sides of the great window, everything was precisely as he had expected. When the song was ended, he revealed his presence by a word of approbation, and he installed himself to hear the rest of the lesson. When it was over, he himself accompanied Stradella to the stairs.

CHAPTER III

Ortensia heard the bells strike midnight. She was lying on her back, her eyes wide open, and staring at the rosette in the middle of the pink canopy over her head. She could see it plainly by the dim light of the tiny oil-lamp that hung above the kneeling-stool at which she said her prayers. She had said them with great fervour to-night, and had gone to bed with the firm intention of repeating the last one over and over to herself till she fell asleep.

But in this she had not succeeded. She had heard the bells at eleven o'clock and had been wide awake; at that moment Stradella was stepping over the marble balustrade into the loggia. She tried to say her prayer again, but it was of no use at all; she knew that he was standing there just outside the great closed window, waiting, and that to see him she had only to pass through her dressing-room, where Pina slept on a trestle-bed, which was taken away every morning. There was only one door to Ortensia's bedroom, which was the last on that floor of the house; for it was proper that a noble Venetian girl should be safely guarded, and every night the Senator locked both the outer doors of the sitting-room where she had her lessons, and he kept the key under his pillow. Pina and Ortensia were in prison together from ten o'clock at night till seven every morning, and the girl could not leave her own room without passing Pina.

To the Senator's insufficient imagination two things were out of the question; he was convinced that no one could get up into the loggia from below, and he was persuaded that Pina, unswerving in her devotion to his interests and honour, would guard Ortensia as jealously as the dragon guarded the Golden Fleece. Moreover, as to getting in by the window, a man would first have to get access to the walled garden below, which Pignaver regarded as another impossibility, for the wall was high, he himself kept the key of the postern that opened on the canal, and the gardener entered through the house.

Nevertheless Stradella was standing in the loggia at eleven o'clock; Ortensia was sure he was there, and at midnight she was still lying on her back, staring up at the canopy, with outstretched hands that clutched the edges of the bed on each side. Her idea of what was possible was quite different from her uncle's; the one thing which seemed to her out of the question was that she should lie where she was much longer, and she only succeeded by giving herself the illusion that her own hands held her down by main force. By and by they would be tired, she supposed, and then she would have to go to him.

She held fast and listened, hoping to hear the bells again, as if an hour could slip by as in a moment while she was awake; and suddenly she started, and one hand left its hold, for she heard a noise at her own window, a sharp tap, followed by another and another. Then there came a sharp rattling, and she knew that it was only raining, and tried to laugh at herself. The first big drops of the squall had struck the panes like little pebbles. Her hand went down to the edge of the bed again and clutched the mattress desperately, while she listened.

He was in the loggia, and the rain was driving in upon him as it was driving against her window. He would not move; he would wait there in the wet till dawn, for he had said so and she believed him. It was hard to hold herself down now, knowing that he was being wet through. He must have left his cloak behind, too, for he could not have been able to climb if hampered by the folds.

It was pouring now, and there was wind with the rain, since otherwise it could not have made such a noise against the glass. She had often stood inside the closed window of the sitting-room when it was raining from the same quarter, and she had seen how the gusts drove the water in sheets against the panes, till it ran down and made a river along the loggia and boiled at the grated gutter-sinks through which it ran off. He was perhaps nearly up to his ankles in the little flood by this time, but he would not go away for that. She knew he would wait.

Her hands let go and she was suddenly sitting on the edge of the bed, feeling for her slippers with her bare feet; with bare arms raised, she instinctively put up both hands to her hair at the same time, to be sure that it would not come down, for Pina always did it up at night in a thick coil on the top of her head.

She heard the rain even more distinctly now; it was coming down in torrents. She looked up at the little lamp burning quietly before Robbia's blue and white bas-relief of the infant Christ, and she thought of her prayers again; but it was positively wicked to let any one stand outside in the rain for hours, to catch his death of cold.

She slipped a silk skirt over her thin night-dress and put on her fur-edged dressing-gown over that, for those were the days of wonderful dressing-gowns, quilted with down, bordered with sable or ermine, and trimmed with lace. She drew the cords tightly round her slim waist, and she was ready.

For a moment she hesitated; there was no night-light where Pina slept, nor in the day-room beyond; the stormy night must be so dark that she would not be able to find her way to the windows. That thought decided her, and she stopped to light a small hand-lamp. Then she cautiously opened the door, shaded the flame from Pina's face with one hand, and passed quickly through the dressing-room. The nurse lay in her trestle-bed, well covered up, and did not move, and Ortensia shut the next door noiselessly.

She hastened to the window, and when she got there she started; his dripping face was flattened against the pane, so white and ghostly that it was like a vision of him dead, but his eyes were alive and were watching her, and when she was quite near the window he smiled. She set down her lamp on the floor at a little distance and began to undo the fastenings with the greatest caution, fearing to make any noise; but as soon as the bolt was drawn the wind forced the frame open so violently that it almost knocked her down. Stradella sprang in with the driving wet and only succeeded in shutting the window after several efforts, during which the lamp was almost blown out.

He stood before her then bare-headed, and the water ran down upon the marble floor from his drenched clothes. He had neither hat nor cloak, and his dark hair was matted with the rain; but his face was radiant.

'You are frozen! you are soaked through and through!' she cried anxiously. 'You will get an illness, and I can do nothing! There is not even a little wine here to warm you.'

He smiled and shook his head.

'Never mind me,' he answered. 'Or let me take your hand in mine for a moment and the chill will pass!'

He put out his own, and when she felt that it was cold and wet, she took it in both of hers and tried to dry it, and chafed it between her palms, till he drew it away rather suddenly with a low laugh.

'Thank you,' he said. 'That is enough!'

'No, let me warm it better, or give me the other!'

'There is too much fire in your touch,' he answered. 'It burns through cold and wet. It would burn through ice itself!'

His tone made her forget her first anxiety for him; but she felt that she must explain why she was there, if only to quiet her own conscience.

'I would not have come if it had not rained,' she said, avoiding his eyes, 'and now I must not stay with you. As soon as it stops you must let yourself out and go away. It was only when I heard the rain——'

'Blessings on the rain!' answered Stradella devoutly. 'I never loved it before!'

'You should not have come on such a night—I mean——'

She stopped and he saw her blush in the faint light that came up from the lamp on the floor.

'I had no choice, since I had promised,' he answered. 'And I promise you I will come to-morrow again———'

'Oh, do not promise—please!' She seemed distressed.

'Yes, I will come to-morrow and every night, until you come away with me. I will bring you a disguise in which you can travel safely till we are over the Venetian border and free.'

'But I cannot—I will not!' she protested. 'You speak as if—as if———'

'As if we loved each other, heart and soul, for life or death,' he said, not letting her go on, and taking her hand again. 'I speak as if we had been born into the world only for that, to love and live and die together! As if there were no woman for me but you in all the earth, and no man for you but me! As if our lips had promised and had met!'

She was drinking his words, and her eyes were in his as he bent to her face. But then she started, in returning consciousness, and tried to draw back.

'No, no!' she cried, in sudden maiden distress. 'Not yet! It is too soon!'

He drew her nearer to him in spite of herself, with both her hands in his, till he could speak close to her ear.

'Tell me you do not love me, love! Tell me you will not feel one little regret if you never see me again! Come, say it in my ear, sweetheart! Say that if I fall and am killed in climbing down when I leave you, it will make no more difference to you than if a dog were drowned in the canal! Is it not true, dear? Then say it quickly! Only whisper it in my ear, and I will go away and never come back. But you must say it———'

'Yes—please go!' she answered faintly. 'Go at once———'

'No, you must say the rest first,' he insisted, and his lips were almost touching her ear. 'Say it after me: "I hate you, I despise you, I loathe you, I do not care whether you live or die." Why do you not begin to repeat the words, heart of my heart?'

She turned suddenly in his hold, holding her head far back, wide-eyed and very pale. But she could not speak, or would not, foreknowing what must happen now that had never happened to her before.

He smiled faintly, and when he spoke again it was a sweet breath she felt, rather than a sound that reached her ear.

'Will you not say it?' he said, and his face came slowly nearer to hers. 'Would it not be true? No? Then say "I love you, love," or speak no word aloud but let your lips make syllables on mine, and, like the blind, the touch will tell me what you say.'

Her eyes closed of themselves, the speaking breath came nearer, and then, as lightning flashes through a summer's night, flame ran from her lips to her feet, and to her heart from her hands that lay in his and felt his life stirring.

It was innocent enough, a girl's first love-kiss, and the kiss of a man who loved in earnest for the first time, but it seemed a great and a fearful thing to her, irrevocable as lost innocence itself; and he, whose masculine light-heartedness made not much of mere kisses, and laughed at the thought that love could do much wrong, felt that he had given a pledge he must redeem and a promise he must honourably keep.

It was innocent enough. He held her by the hands as he bent and kissed her, for the water was still trickling down his drenched clothes, and her pretty dressing-gown would have been spoiled if he had even put one arm round her waist. There was a dash of the ridiculous in that, which would have made them both laugh if they had not been so simply and utterly in earnest. And then when he let her hands go and she sank upon a chair, he could not even sit down beside her, because the velvet seat would have been ruined. So he stood bolt upright in the midst of the little puddle the water had made round his feet.

She covered her face with her hands for a moment, not in any shame, but trying to make herself think.

'You must go now,' she said presently, looking up at him. 'It is enough to make the strongest man fall ill, to be drenched as you are. You will lose your voice———'

'What does that matter, if I have found you?' he asked. 'But I will do as you wish, for it has stopped raining at last, and it is growing late—you will lose half your sleep to-night.'

'Or all of it!' she answered softly, thinking of his kiss. 'How did you get up to the loggia? Have you a ladder?'

He had none. He had got over the outer wall by means of a rope with a grappling-hook fastened to it, which he had thrown up from the canal. Thence he had reached the loggia without much difficulty, for in the short intervals during the lessons he had more than once looked down and had seen that it was quite possible, and more a question of steady nerves than of great strength and activity. At the level of the loggia a stone ledge ran round the palace, and along this it was easy to creep on hands and knees. He had drawn himself up to it from the top of the wall, which joined the building at the corner of the garden.

'It is easy enough,' Stradella answered. 'And now good-bye. To-morrow night again, love, an hour before midnight.'

She rose and they joined hands again.

'I ought to tell you not to come,' she said in a weak voice, like a child's. 'But how can I say it—now—now that——'

If any other word would have followed, it could not. Once more her closed eyes saw sweet summer lightnings, and the thrill of the flame ran from her lips through every vital part.

He turned from her at last to unfasten the window, and for a moment she was too dazed to stop him, though she would have kept him still. Then she tried to follow him out into the loggia, but he would not let her.

'No, love,' he said, 'your wet shoes would tell tales.'

'But there is danger!' answered Ortensia, holding him by his drenched sleeve. 'I must know you are safe!'

'When I reach my boat I will whistle softly,' he said.

He was gone in the dark, and she was listening by the open window, her heart beating so that it seemed as if it must drown any other sound. But he made no noise as he crept along the ledge to the corner, and then cautiously let himself down upon the top of the wall, dropping astride of it then to pull himself along in that position by his hands till he found the grappling-hook of his rope. The wall rose perpendicularly from the canal, and he had moored his little skiff to the only ring he could find at the base of it, some distance from the corner.

Ortensia listened anxiously for the promised signal, and peered into the darkness, her hand on the window, ready to close it as soon as she knew he was safe.

But suddenly she heard the sound of oars striking the water, and a yellow glare rose above the wall from the other side.

'Who goes there?' asked a deep voice.

No one answered, but instantly there was a heavy splash, as of a body falling into the canal.

Half-an-hour later Ortensia was lying on her back again, staring up at the rosette in the canopy. But her face was distorted with horror now, and was whiter than the pillow itself.

In the day-room, by the light of Ortensia's little lamp, Pina was on her knees, carefully mopping up the water that had run down from Stradella's clothes, and drying the marble floor.

CHAPTER IV

Soon after sunrise the Senator came and unlocked the doors of Ortensia's day-room. That had always been his custom, for he kept the key under his pillow, as has been said, and he would as soon have thought of sending a servant to liberate the girl and the woman in the morning as of letting any one but himself lock them in at night.

'The master's eye fattens the horse,' he said to himself, quoting a Spanish proverb without much regard for metaphors.

It was his wont to open the door, and to look into the large room before going away, for he was sure that his eye would at once detect the slightest disarrangement of the furniture, or anything else unusual which might warrant suspicion.

But this morning he did more: he entered the room, shut the door behind him and looked about. He went to the window and examined the fastenings carefully, opened it wide, went out into the loggia and looked down into the garden. Everything was in order there, not one flower-pot had been upset by the squall, not a branch of the cypress-tree was broken or even bent.

Then he came in again and tapped sharply at the door of the dressing-room where Pina slept. She appeared instantly, already dressed; but she laid one finger on her lips, to keep him silent, and came out into the room before she spoke.

She said that Ortensia had been kept awake half the night by the storm, and was now sound asleep.

'A thief tried to get into the house after midnight,' said Pignaver. 'Did you hear any noise?'

'I should think I did!' cried Pina promptly. 'I was going to tell your lordship of it. I was up with the young lady, and when the first squall was over and she was more quiet, I thought I would just come in here to see if any water had run in under the window as it sometimes does. Just then I saw a glare of light beyond the garden wall, and I opened the window at once and heard the Signor of the Night challenging a thief, and directly afterwards there was a splash in the canal, and then silence, and the light went away slowly. I hope the man was drowned, my lord!'

While she was speaking, Pignaver had nodded repeatedly, for her little story bore the stamp of truth.

'I grieve to say that the villain got away,' he answered. 'At daybreak an officer from the Signors of the Night was waiting downstairs to inform me of the attempt. The Signors' boat searched the canal for the body of the man during more than an hour, but found nothing. He must have been on the garden wall when he was seen, and he threw himself into the water to escape, leaving the rope by which he had climbed up.'

'Mercy!' cried Pina. 'We might have all been murdered in our beds!'

'No one shall get upon that wall again,' answered the master of the house. 'I will have the coping stuck full of broken glass from end to end before night.'

'Would it not be well to set a watch in the garden, too, my lord? We should sleep soundly then!'

'We shall see, we shall see,' answered Pignaver, repeating the words slowly, as he went off. 'We shall see,' he said once more, as he went out.

As soon as he was gone, Pina hastened to Ortensia's room.

'He is safe!' she cried as she entered. 'They searched the canal for a whole hour, and could not find him!'

Ortensia uttered a little cry and sat up in bed suddenly; but she could scarcely believe the news, till Pina had repeated all that the Senator had said. When she heard that the wall was to be crowned with broken glass, however, her face fell, for she saw in a flash of imagination how Stradella would climb up confidently in the dark and would cut his hand to the bone when he grasped the jagged points on the top.

'You must warn him!' cried Ortensia. 'You must go out and find him, and tell him not to come again!'

'I will find him,' answered Pina.

They had never spoken of Stradella before the night that was just past. Day after day, while the lessons were going on, Pina had left the two together, and Ortensia had silently accepted the nurse's conduct without understanding its cause; she was too proud to speak of it when they were together, or too shy, but she was sure from the first that Pina would stand by her, though it was the woman's sole business never to let her be out of her sight for a moment.

'And what shall I tell him?' Pina asked. 'What message shall he have from you? I will faithfully deliver your words.'

Ortensia covered her eyes with one hand, leaning on the other behind her, to steady herself as she sat up.

'Tell him that—that we must wait—and hope——'

'For what?' asked Pina bluntly. 'For the end of the world?'

Ortensia uncovered her eyes and looked up, surprised at the change of tone.

'Will you wait till you are the Senator's wife?' Pina asked, her grey eyes hardening suddenly. 'Will you hope that by that time the broken glass on the wall will have softened in the rain till it will not cut his hands? Or that you will be more free when you are married? You will not be. That is not the way in Venice. I am a serving-woman, and, besides, I am neither young nor pretty—I was once!—so I may go and come on your business and walk alone from the Piazza to Santa Maria dell' Orto. But you noble ladies, you are born in a cage, you live in bondage, and you die in prison! Will you wait? Will you hope? What for?'

'What do you mean?' asked Ortensia in a frightened voice. 'Am I never to see him again? Is my message to him to be a good-bye?'

'Good-bye is easily said,' Pina answered, shaking her head enigmatically.

The young girl let herself sink back on her pillow, and turned her face against her bare arm, so that at least her eyes were hidden from the nurse.

'I cannot!' she whispered to herself, drawing a breath that almost choked her.

'Yes,' Pina repeated harshly, 'it is easy to say farewell; and as for any hope after that, the devil lends it us at usury, and if we cannot pay on the day of reckoning he takes possession!'

'What cruel things you say!' Ortensia cried in a half-broken tone, turning her head slowly from side to side, with her face hidden in the soft hollow of her elbow.

'What hope will there be for you, child, when you are your uncle's wife? The hope of dying young—that is all the hope you will have left!'

The woman laughed bitterly, and Ortensia felt that she was going to cry, or wished that she could, she was not quite sure which.

'Therefore I say it is folly to send a man such a message. "Wait and hope," indeed! How long? His lifetime? Yours? You are both young, and you may wait and hope fifty years, till your hair and teeth fall out, and you discover that there is nothing in hope after all! Better say good-bye outright, though it kill you! Better try and forget than make a martyrdom of remembering! Better anything than hope!'

The grey-eyed woman's voice shook with an emotion which Ortensia could not have understood if she had noticed it, for she was dreadfully miserable just then. Pina bent down over her, smoothed her hair and patted her bare arm softly.

'Why hope for what you can take, if you have the courage?' she asked, dropping her voice to a whisper, as she glanced behind her towards the door.

Ortensia lifted her head and looked up, her lips parting in surprise.

'Why should you waste time in waiting?' Pina asked, still whispering. 'That is the message I would send if I were you,' she added. 'Shall I take it?'

'But how?—I do not understand—he cannot come to me here.'

'We can go to him,' answered the nurse. 'Is it not easy? The next time you confess at the Frari he will meet us. It is simple enough. Two long brown cloaks with hoods, such as old women wear, a few hundred yards to walk from the Frari to the Tolentini, his gondola there, and out by Santa Chiara to the mainland and Padua—who shall catch us then? You are young and strong, and I am tough; we shall not die of the fatigue; and by the next morning we shall all three be out of Venetian territory. What is easier?'

Ortensia listened to this bold plan in silence, too much surprised to ask why Pina was so ready to propose it, and a little frightened too, for she was a mere girl, and all the world beyond Venice was a mysterious immensity of Cimmerian gloom in the midst of which little pools of brilliant light marked the great and wonderful places she had heard described, such as Rome, Florence, and Milan, and royal Paris, and imperial Vienna.

'But my uncle would send men after us,' Ortensia objected. 'The Council of Ten will do anything he asks! They will give him soldiers, ships, anything! How can we possibly escape from him? We shall be caught and brought back!'

Pina smiled at such fears.

'Beyond the Venetian border they can do nothing,' she said. 'Do we mean to rob the Senator or murder him, that Venice should send an ambassador to claim us for trial under the laws of the Republic? Is it a crime for young people to love, and to run away and marry?'

'You do not know how powerful my uncle is,' Ortensia said.

Pina's face changed at once, and her expression became stony and impenetrable.

'You are wrong,' she answered in a hard voice. 'I know he is powerful. But if you fear him, as I do not, then wait and hope! Wait and hope!'

She laughed very strangely as she repeated the words, and her voice cracked on the last one, with a discordant note that frightened Ortensia, who was weary and overwrought.

'What is it, Pina?' asked the young girl quickly. 'What has happened?'

The nurse was already herself again, and pretended to cough a little.

'It is nothing,' she said presently. 'Something in my throat, just as I was speaking. It often happens. And as for what we were speaking of, there is no hurry. I will find the Maestro Alessandro before noon, and warn him not to come near our garden wall again, and I will tell him from you anything you wish, except that you do not care what becomes of him, for that would not be true!'

She laughed again, but quite gently this time, and began to busy herself about the room, making preparations for Ortensia to dress. The girl had laid her head on her pillow again, looking up at the little pink silk rosette in the middle of the canopy, and she was sure that it had a much less sad look now than it had worn in the small hours by the flickering night light. This seemed quite natural to Ortensia, for the familiar little objects in a girl's own room have a different expression for every hour of her life, to sympathise with each joy and sorrow, great or small, and with every hope, and surprise, and disappointment.

But Ortensia herself could not have told what she felt just then, for it was a sensation of startled unrest, in which great happiness and great fear were striving with each other to possess her; and she knew that if she yielded to the fear, she would lose the happiness, but that if she opened her heart to the happiness, the fear would at once become a terror so awful that she must certainly die of it.

She did not ask why her nurse was so ready to help her to run away. The fact was enough. The plan looked easy, and Stradella was the man to carry it out. She had only to consent, and in a week, or less, all would be done, and she would be joined to him for ever. If she refused, she must inevitably become the wife of Pignaver in a few months. She writhed on her pillow at the mere thought.

Two hours later she was standing before the big open window, watching three masons who were working on the top of the garden wall; they spread thick layers of stiff grey mortar over the old coping, and then stuck in sharp bits of broken glass, patting and pressing down the cement against each piece, to make the hold quite firm. The murderous splinters gleamed in the sunshine, and the men set them so near together that one could hardly have laid a finger anywhere between them.

Ortensia watched the work, and now and then she looked at the top of the cypress-tree, half-unconsciously wondering how many days would pass before she saw it for the last time. But in the broad daylight she lived over and over again every instant of that short night meeting that was the greatest event in all her life. If she only drooped her lids a little she saw Stradella there before her in his dripping clothes by the rays of the little lamp, his face was close to hers again, her lips touched his, and a delicate thrill ran through all her body and reminded her faintly but very sweetly of what she had felt when he kissed her.

Meanwhile, Pina had found the musician's lodging, near Santa Maria dell' Orto, which was a long way from the Senator's palace, for that quarter lies on the extreme outer edge of Venice, looking across the lagoon towards Murano. The door was opened for her by a hunchback, with a large, intellectual face, beardless and strongly modelled, such a face as Giotto would have taken as a model for a Doctor of the Church. The sad blue eyes looked up to Pina's with cold gravity; but when she explained that she came from the Palazzo Pignaver with a message, they brightened a little, and the man at once stood aside for her to enter.

She touched his hump lightly for luck in passing, as every Italian woman will to this day if she finds herself close to a hunchback in the street, and this act is rarely resented. Pina thought it a piece of unexampled good-fortune and of the best possible augury that the door should have been opened by a 'bringer-of-fortune,' and the deformed servant smiled gently at her touch, quite understanding. As he led the way in, after shutting the outer door, Pina saw that nature had meant him for a man of large proportions, and that his short stature was chiefly due to the terrible deformity of his back and chest, for his slightly bowed legs looked as sturdy as a street porter's, and his powerful arms were so long that his hands swung well below his knees when he walked. He wore plain brown clothes, and a broad white collar, and Pina, who was observant, noticed the neatness of his dress.

Stradella received her with a politeness to which, as a serving-woman, she was little accustomed, and he made her sit down in a comfortable chair before asking for news of Ortensia. He himself was none the worse for his wetting. The hunchback waited a moment as if expecting some order, but Stradella only nodded to him, and he went out.

'My young lady is well, and greets you, sir,' Pina said in answer to the Maestro's question, when the door was shut. 'She bids you be warned and not try to climb the wall again, for it is already being crowned with broken glass, which would cut your hands; and, moreover, the Senator will probably set a watch in the garden, since you were fortunately mistaken for a thief last night.'

Stradella listened to this business-like statement attentively, and watched Pina's face while she was speaking. Her hard grey eyes met his with perfect frankness.

'I see that you know everything,' he said. 'Tell me, then, how can I see the lady Ortensia? Surely you are not come to tell me that I am not to see her again.'

Pina unfolded her plan with a clearness and precision that first surprised him, and then roused his suspicion. For a few moments after she had ceased speaking he was silent, and examined his left hand with thoughtful interest, gently rubbing with his thumb the callous places made on the tips of his fingers by playing on stringed instruments. The woman puzzled him, for he understood well enough from her tone that she was not moved to help him merely by affection for her mistress, and she could certainly not be supposed to be actuated by any sudden devotion to himself. Besides, she must be aware that he was not a rich man, and could not requite with any large sum of money such a service as she offered. Her motive was a mystery. At last he spoke.

'Listen to me,' he said, watching her eyes. 'Your plan is good, and perfectly feasible. If you are in earnest, it can be carried out to-morrow, or whenever the lady Ortensia is ready. I will reward you as well as I can, but you must remember that I am a poor musician and not a Venetian senator——'

Pina's grey eyes were like steel, and her tone was cold, and not without a certain dignity.

'Have I asked money of you, sir?'

'Oh, no!' answered Stradella readily. 'I only wished——'

She interrupted him, as if she were his equal.

'Even a servant may love something better than a bribe!' she said.

'I beg your pardon,' Stradella found himself saying, a good deal to his own surprise, for he had not expected to hurt a serving-woman's feelings by speaking of money. 'I misunderstood you.'

'You did indeed, sir!' answered Pina. 'All I ask of you is that you will take me with you in your flight, for the Senator will certainly have me murdered if I am left behind. Afterwards, if my lady does not want me, I will look for another place, or live by lace-making.'

Stradella did not like the answer. The Sicilian character has grave defects: it is revengeful, over-proud, violent, and sometimes cruel; but it is generally truthful, and it is, above all, direct.

'You talk lightly of leaving your mistress,' said the musician. 'It is not for love of her that you are ready to help us.'

Pina faced him fearlessly.

'You are right,' she answered. 'And yet she is the one living being I love at all. Affection is not the only motive one may have, sir.'

'Nor love of money either,' Stradella said thoughtfully. 'The third is hate. Last of all comes charity!'

'I am not a saint, sir,' said Pina. 'So you are answered. I hate my master, and I have the right to hate him. That is my affair. If I dared kill him, I would, but I should not have the courage to bear being tortured if I were arrested and tried. I am only a woman, and I fear bodily pain more than anything. That is why I did not kill the Senator twenty years ago.'

The musician watched the cold, resentful face that had once been so handsome, and though he could not guess her story he partly understood her.

'You are frank,' he said. 'I see that you are in earnest, and that I can trust you.'

'Trust me for anything, sir, except to resist torture,' Pina answered. 'I know what it is,' she added in a low voice, and avoiding his eyes as if she were suddenly ashamed. 'As for my master,' she went on, turning to Stradella again a moment later, 'I believe he would rather die than be made a laughing-sk. I know that he yesterday announced to his friends his betrothal to his niece, which has been a secret for several weeks. I can hear the fine ladies and gentlemen laughing at him when they learn that she has run away with her music-master on the eve of her marriage! I can fancy the jests and the sarcasms the Senator will have to put up with!'

She laughed herself, rather savagely, and Stradella smiled. Provided he could carry off Ortensia, he did not even object to becoming the instrument of a serving-woman's vengeance.

They agreed upon the details of the flight. On the next day but one, being the feast of one of the many Franciscan saints, Stradella was to sing an air at Vespers in the Church of the Frari. It was therefore arranged that Ortensia and Pina should go to the church at that hour on pretence of confession. At the monument of Pietro Bernardini, near the main entrance, Stradella's hunchback servant would be waiting for them with two brown cloaks and hoods, which they were to put on immediately. They were then to kneel down quietly in the shadow and to wait till Stradella had finished singing, when they were to leave the church without waiting for him; his man would lead them through by-ways to the gondola, which was to wait on the farther side of the Tolentini. Stradella himself would slip away from the loft as soon as the Benediction began, after Vespers, just when all the other musicians would be very busy. He would probably reach the gondola almost as soon as Ortensia and the two servants, and in five minutes they would be well out of the city.

'And pray, sir,' asked Pina, 'what is your man's name?'

'Cucurullo,' Stradella answered.

'What a strange name!' Pina exclaimed.

'It is common enough in Naples.'

CHAPTER V

The Benediction was over, and the music had died away; the deep colours of the ancient windows already blended into luminous purple stains, like red wine spilt on velvet just before dusk; on the altar of the Sacrament and all about it hundreds of wax candles were burning steadily, arranged in dazzling concentric rings and shining curves. A young Dominican monk had prostrated himself before the shrine, a motionless figure, half kneeling and half lying on the steps.

The service was ended and the priests were gone. Some five hundred feet shuffled slowly away from the blaze of light into the gloom and out through the western door, and the brighter part of the church was already deserted; but the young monk remained motionless, prostrate upon the steps.

Two men stood by the choir screen, the broad-brimmed black hats they held in their hands hanging so low that the draggled feathers swept the pavement, their eyes directed towards the retiring crowd. They were two shabby gentlemen of thirty years or under; though their clothes were not yet actually torn or patched, most of their garments were already in that premonitory state which warns the wearer of old breeches to sit down with deliberation and grace, rather than with rash haste, and to make no uselessly quick movements whereby an old sewing may rip open, or the silk or cloth itself may split and gape in an unseemly manner, furnishing a cause for mirth in better-clad men.

These two poor gentlemen were very unlike in appearance, except as to their well-worn clothes and in respect of their rapiers, which were so exactly similar that they might have been made for a duelling pair. Each had a beautifully chiselled and polished bell-guard, with the Italian cross-bar for the middle finger; each was sheathed in a good brown leather sheath, with a chiselled steel shoe to drag on the pavement, and each weapon hung from the wearer's shoulder-belt by two short chains of well-furbished steel. The weapons looked serviceable, though they made little pretence to beauty, in an age when most things worn by men and women were adorned too much rather than too little.

But the men themselves were not alike. The shorter of the two was very fair, with the complexion of a Saxon child, and unnaturally pink cheeks; his nose turned up to a sharp point in the most extraordinary manner, so that the pink openings of the nostrils seemed to stand upright above the flaxen moustache, reminding one of the muzzles of certain wild cats. His blue eyes were large, perfectly round, and often aggressively fixed, and the long yellow lashes that bristled all round them might have passed for rays. He wore a short pointed beard, and his very thick fair hair was parted exactly in the middle and hung down below his dingy collar on each side, perfectly straight and completely hiding his ears. There was something both comic and disturbing in his aspect.

His companion was much less extraordinary in appearance, though any one would have noticed him in a crowd as an unusual type. Instead of being fair, he was as dark as a Moor; instead of turning up, his immensely long and melancholy nose curved downwards over his thin lips like a vulture's beak as if trying to peck at his chin. His eyes were shadowy and uncertain under his prominent forehead and bushy eyebrows. His beard was a mere black wisp, and the points of his scant moustaches were waxed and stood up stiffly. He was the taller of the two, but his hat hung lower in his hand than his friend's, for he had unnaturally long arms, with a long body and short legs, whereas the fair man with the turned-up nose was remarkably well-proportioned.

'Who says we have no good music in Venice?' inquired the latter at last, fixing his round eyes on the other's face angrily, and pressing down the hilt of his sword so as to make the point stick up behind.

His mouth looked ridiculously small, and his pink cheeks were very large and round. His companion had long ago come to the conclusion that he was very like one of those rosy cherubs that roll about the clouds in the religious pictures painted in those times, blowing their trumpets till they look as if their red cheeks must burst. Accordingly, he had nicknamed his friend 'Trombin,' short for 'trombino,' a 'little trumpeter.'

The dark man had always gone by the name of Gambardella, and seemed quite satisfied with the appellation. The two had been companions in their profession for several years, but neither knew much of the other's antecedents, and both were far too proud, or too tactful, or too prudent, to ask questions. They wore the dress and weapons of gentlemen, and were extremely ticklish as to the point of honour; but they did not now sit in the Grand Council of the Venetian Republic, though each perceived that the other had once enjoyed that privilege, and had forfeited it for the good of his native city. They travelled a great deal, always together, and their friends knew that they met with frequent and sudden changes of fortune. Their clothes were shabby now, yet scarcely six months ago they had been seen strolling arm in arm in Florence, in the Piazza della Signoria, arrayed in silks and satins and fine linen. Only their weapons were never replaced in prosperity by handsomer swords with gilded hilts, nor exchanged in adversity for others of less perfect balance and temper.

'This Stradella sings like an angel,' said Gambardella after a moment. 'I hear that he composes good music himself, and that his new oratorio will be performed before the Doge in Saint Mark's next Sunday.'

'If we had any money,' observed Trombin regretfully, 'we would hire a house and ask him to supper.'

'Yes,' answered Gambardella in a melancholy tone. 'Our Venetians do not understand these things. To them a man of genius like Alessandro Stradella is just a music-master, and nothing else, a mountebank or a strolling minstrel, to be hired and paid for his work, and dismissed with a cool nod, like a servant. Trombin, let us leave Venice.'

'After we have heard the oratorio on Sunday——'

'Of course! Do you think I would miss that? But there is nothing for us to do here just now, whereas in Genoa, or Florence, or even Rome, we should not be always idle.'

'Venice is a dull place, compared with what it used to be,' Trombin admitted, and he raised his right forearm, turning it till he could examine the threadbare elbow of his coat in the glare of the candles. 'Another week will do it,' he added, after a careful examination. 'I can already perceive the direction which the split will take.'

'I never sit down, if I can help it,' said Gambardella mournfully.

'It is a strange fact,' answered Trombin thoughtfully, 'that only those nations that wear breeches sit upon chairs; the others squat on their heels, though they have no breeches to save. This is a most contradictory world.'

'I never could see any sense in it myself,' returned the other. 'Shall we go to supper?'

'It pleases you to be humorous,' Trombin observed, and they moved away from the great choir screen.

As they passed the blazing chapel of the Sacrament, each bent his knee and crossed himself devoutly. The young monk was still prostrate before the altar. Trombin looked at him sharply, and the two went on towards the open door, through which the fading twilight outside admitted barely enough light to distinguish the great pillars and tombs.

The two shabby gentlemen left the church and strolled slowly along the edge of the canal. In the open air it was quite light still, and the warm afterglow of the sunset had not quite paled yet.

'Supper!' said Trombin presently, dwelling on the one word in a musical tone, and with the deepest feeling.

'That is the worst of Venice,' answered Gambardella, gloomily pulling his soft hat over his eyes. 'One cannot even eat here without paying. Now in Florence or Rome the people are more simple, and when you have made your necessary debts, and creditors talk of imprisoning you, why, then, you need only appeal to the Venetian Ambassador for protection, and you are perfectly safe! But here! On the word of a gentleman, it is enough to drive a man to highway robbery!'

Trombin laughed softly.

'Supper!' he said again, as musically and feelingly as before.

'You will make me mad with your whining!' cried Gambardella angrily. 'You will drive me to commit a crime!'

'One more will make no difference,' returned Trombin, with great coolness. 'After the first, which sullied the virgin lustre of your spotless soul, my dear friend, it is of no use to count the others, till you come to the last—and may you enjoy many long years of health, activity, and happiness before that is reached!'

'The same to you!' answered the melancholic man morosely, for he was hungry, and in no humour for banter.

They stopped where a wooden bridge spanned the narrow canal, for all bridges in Venice were not yet built of stone in the year 1670.

They had only one thought, and Trombin had already expressed it twice with longing and regret. So far as mere hunger and thirst went, they could satisfy themselves with bread, salt fish and cheese, and a draught of water. They were not such imprudent gentlemen as to risk absolute starvation in their native city, where they could get no credit, and though they often lived riotously for months together, they invariably set aside a sum which would furnish them with the merest necessities for a considerable time. There was a system in their way of living, and they stuck to it with a laudable determination which would have done honour to better men. Enough was not as good as a feast, and since their income was always uncertain, the only way to get any real enjoyment out of life was to feast recklessly while they could, though only for a few days, and then to pay for extravagance with the strictest asceticism, till a rain of gold once more gladdened the garret to which they had retired to fast.

They stood by the end of the bridge in silence a long time while it grew dark, Gambardella gazing sadly at the dark water of the still canal at his feet, while Trombin, who was of a more hopeful disposition, looked at the evening star, just visible in the darkening west, between the long lines of tall houses on each side of the canal. The reason why they stopped just then with one accord was that to cross the bridge meant to go home to their wretched lodging, though it was still so early; and the prospect was not attractive. But they knew their weakness, and long ago had bound themselves together by promises they would not break. If they turned away from the bridge and followed the narrow street, they would come in time to Saint Mark's Square, and they would breathe the intoxicating air of pleasure that hung over it as the scent of flowers over a garden at evening, and temptation would assail them in one of at least twenty delightful shapes; and then and there the little sum that stood between them and starvation would melt away in a night, leaving them in a very bad way indeed.

Yet now they lingered just a few moments by the wooden bridge, dreaming of riotous nights and glorious suppers, before going home to bread and cheese and cold water. And just then fate sent to them the young Dominican monk they had left prostrate before the altar in the church when they came out; at all events it seemed natural to suppose that it was he, though they had hardly caught sight of his youthful face before and now could not see it all, for he had pulled his white hood well down over his eyes.

He was evidently about to cross the bridge, when he unexpectedly found Trombin in front of him, stopping the way. The street and the canal were deserted, and not a sound broke the stillness. The monk stood still. He was short and slight, and could have slipped through a very narrow space, but Trombin seemed to swell himself out till he filled the bridge from side to side, and kept his hand on the hilt of his rapier.

Gambardella looked on indifferently, supposing that his companion meant to indulge in some witticism or practical joke at the expense of the young monk.

'Your reverence must pay toll at this bridge,' said Trombin.

'Toll?' cried a youthful voice from under the cowl.

'The decree has just been passed by the Ten,' answered Trombin. 'My friend and I are stationed here by the Signors of the Night to exact payment.'

Gambardella did not clearly understand, but he moved up behind the monk, so that the latter could not get back.

'I understand,' said the Dominican in his sweet voice, after a moment's hesitation. 'But I have no money. I am only a poor monk——'

'The Fathers of the Order of Preachers do not take vows of poverty, your reverence,' said Gambardella in deep tones, behind the youth.

'That is true, but I have no money with me,' protested the latter.

'That emerald ring you wear on your left hand will do quite as well,' answered Trombin. 'We shall not ask you for anything else this evening.'

Now the monk's hands were thrust deep into the two slits in the front of his frock, as in a muff; but Trombin's eyes were good, and they had caught sight of the jewel unwarily exposed while the young man was performing his devotions in the church. He seemed disturbed, hesitated, and hung his head.

Standing behind him, Gambardella laid a heavy hand on the slight shoulder, while Trombin, in front, grasped his left wrist roughly, to draw it out of his frock.

At this the young monk suddenly burst into a flood of tears under his cowl, and began to sob bitterly.

'What fish have we caught here?' asked Gambardella, laughing for the first time that day, and he seized the point of the hood at the back to pull it off the head and face.

But instantly the monk's right hand went up and held it down in front desperately.

'No, no! Please—you shall have the ring—anything—only let me go!'

There was no mistaking the feminine voice now, broken as it was with sobbing, and Trombin made one step backward on the bridge and bowed to the ground.

'Madam,' he said, with a grand air, 'we are not ruffians, but Venetian gentlemen. We will respect your disguise, and shall be delighted and honoured to see you safely to your own door. For this little service we shall be more than rewarded if you will leave us your ring in recollection of our auspicious meeting!'

'As a further return for your kindness,' added Gambardella, speaking over the disguised lady's shoulder, 'we are at your service, to rid you of any obnoxious friends or relations.'

'I see that you are Bravi,' the lady said, keeping her face closely concealed under the hood. 'I am the less unwilling to part with my ring since I may have need of you. But where can I find you in that case?'

'When we are unoccupied, you will find us at our devotions in the Church of the Frari during the Benediction, any day,' answered Trombin, receiving the ring from the delicate white fingers that held it out to him.

He bowed as he took it, and flattened himself against the rail of the wooden bridge, hat in hand, to let the disguised lady go by.

'Shall we follow you, Madam, for your greater safety?' asked Gambardella.

'No, I pray you! I will go alone. I live near here.'

'We wish your ladyship a very happy night,' Trombin answered.

'The same to you,' said the young voice.

She was out of sight in a few seconds in spite of her white monk's frock, which might have been seen at a considerable distance even in the gloom of the narrow lane beyond the bridge. Trombin, who tried to follow her with his sharp eyes, was sure that she had turned into a cross alley that led to the large court in which the Palazzo Pignaver then stood.

But that was a matter of speculation, whereas the emerald ring was a matter of fact, and could be converted into a number of things which the two adventurous gentlemen very much wanted just then. Their vow of economy now no longer bade them cross the bridge and return to their wretched lodging and frugal supper. The ring would pay for many suppers, and for good clothes too. They did not even exchange a word as they turned in the direction of the Rialto with a light step, and they felt that delightful sensation which fills the being of a man who loves eating at the moment when brutal hunger, that has expected only prison fare, turns into keen appetite at the sudden vision of boundless good things to eat in half an hour.

Gambardella's melancholy face relaxed in the dark, and the lines that had before turned down now all turned upwards, except those of his long hooked nose; and the formidable beak seemed to stand sentinel over his thin lips, so that no good thing should enter between them on the way to his stomach without sending up its toll of rich savour to his nostrils.

Trombin's small pursed-up mouth also widened to a set smile, and he softly hummed snatches from the beautiful air Alessandro Stradella had sung during the Benediction service. It was a mere thread of a squeak of a falsetto voice, but it had at least the merit of being perfectly in tune, and his musical memory was faultless.

'You are a great man,' said Gambardella thoughtfully, when they had walked some distance and were nearing their destination.

'You flatter me!' laughed Trombin. 'What is easier than to guess that a Dominican monk with a small white hand and an emerald ring may be a lady in disguise? Besides, my dear friend, with your exquisite sense of all that is feminine, you must surely have noticed her walk as she came up to the bridge. I am not a judge of women myself, but as soon as I saw the monk walking, I was sure of the truth.'

'I did not see her coming, but she has a delicious voice,' answered Gambardella thoughtfully. 'I wish I had seen her face.'

'Perhaps you may, some day. Here we are.'

They stopped before a low arched door not fifty yards from the Rialto. A large dry bush, sticking out of a narrow grated window beside the forbidding entrance, showed that wine was sold within. The faint yellow light from the lamp of a shrine, built in the wall on the opposite side of the street, just overcame the darkness. Trombin tried the door and found it ajar; both men entered, and Gambardella pushed it back to its original position.

It was quite dark within, and the place smelt like a wine-cellar, but the two evidently knew their way and they walked quickly forward, half a dozen paces or so, till a wide space suddenly opened on the right, and a wretched little earthenware oil-lamp appeared, high up, dimly lighting the first landing of a damp stone staircase. The friends began to mount at once.

As they went up the air became drier, the smell of the cellar turned into a complex odour of grilled meats, savoury sauces, rich wine, and spring fruits, which the companions snuffed and breathed in with greedy delight; sounds of laughing voices were heard, the stairs were better lighted, and now and then the idle tinkling of a lute or of a deep-voiced, double-stringed guitar made an improvised accompaniment to the cheerful echoes.

Gambardella and Trombin entered a brightly lighted vestibule at the head of the stair and were greeted by the host in person, a broad-shouldered, black-haired Samian with brilliant red cheeks; he was showily dressed in blue cloth trimmed with gold braid, wore a tall fez and spotless linen, and had a perfect arsenal of weapons stuck in his belt, all richly ornamented with silver work, in which were set pieces of coral, carbuncles, and turquoises. He had a look of tremendous vitality and health, and the tawny light danced and played in his eyes when he laughed. He spoke the Venetian dialect fluently, but with a strong Greek accent, and an evident difficulty in pronouncing the letter B.

'Welcome, young gentlemen!' he cried in a formidably cheerful voice, as he rose from the little table at which he had been busy with his accounts. 'Here is old Markos, your faithful friend! What can Markos do for your lordships to-day? Do you desire money of Markos? It is yours, all his poor store! Or do you come for supper, to taste a real pilaf and a brace of quails roasted in fig leaves, with a jar of old wine of Samos and a sweetmeat, and some liquor brewed by the monks of Mount Athos? Markos is here to serve you!'

He looked as broad as he was long as he stood there bawling out his noisy greetings, his thumbs stuck into his broad red leather belt, his legs apart, and his white teeth gleaming like a young boar's tusks in the midst of his shiny black beard.

Trombin nodded gravely at each phrase, keeping his hat on his head, and making his rapier stick up behind him. From the rooms beyond the vestibule the rich steam of good things floated through the half-closed door, and the ring of merry voices, clinking glasses, and tinkling strings was delightful to the ears of men who had supped in a garret on bread and salt fish for three weeks.

'Markos,' said Trombin, 'apply your excellent sight and your money-lender's intelligence to this marvellous ring, with which unfortunate circumstances now oblige me to part. It belonged to my sainted aunt, the Abbess of Acquaviva, who left it to me with her blessing when I was young and innocent. It was once blessed by His Holiness Saint Pius the Fifth, who thereby endowed it with efficacious power to protect the virtue of those who should wear it. My sainted aunt wore it for forty years, and she was indeed virtuous to the end of her life. I remember that she was cross-eyed and had bad teeth and a sallow complexion. For my own part, I must confess that I have not always———'

'How much do you want on it?' interrupted Markos, who had been examining the stone as well as he could by the light of the oil-lamp, while Trombin was talking in his grand style.

'A hundred ducats down, and no wine,' answered Gambardella, without hesitation, in his deep voice.

'We would accept half a dozen jars of Samos, to be drunk here,' suggested Trombin, 'if we sealed them ourselves.'

Markos grinned from ear to ear.

'Twenty ducats,' he said quietly, 'and a hogshead of "rezinato," worth ten ducats more! That is all I can give.'

'Rezinato at ten ducats!' sneered Gambardella.

'It costs me that,' retorted the money-lender, 'so it must be worth it. Possibly I might make the cash twenty-five ducats, but that would only be out of old friendship. I shall lose by it if you do not redeem the ring.'

'I wish you might lose something for once!' cried Trombin devoutly.

They bargained long. In those days, and long before and afterwards, the money-lenders of Venice were Greek and Eastern eating-house keepers and sellers of wine, and it was impossible to pawn any object with them without accepting at least one-third of the advance in the shape of wine more or less sour, or watered, or both.

But the two shabbily-dressed gentlemen who had taken the emerald ring from the disguised lady were not ordinary customers. Trombin inspired present terror, and Gambardella apprehension for the future, and though Markos was as broad as he was long and had a dozen pistols and knives in his belt, his courage was not equal to his ferocious appearance. From a business point of view, the Venetian Bravi were children in his hands; but when they came quite near to him, one on each side, and spoke slowly and clearly in their determined way, the tremendous Markos felt his bravery shrink within him till it seemed to rattle like a dry pea shaken in a steel cuirass, and the amount of money he actually advanced on the ring was considerable; he even consented to let Gambardella seal the six jars of Samos wine, which formed part of the loan, with the heavy brass seal ring the Bravo wore, on which was engraved the Bear of the Ursuline Order of Nuns, with a few words in Gothic characters. One of many things which Trombin did not know about his companion was the story of that ring and how Gambardella had become possessed of it.

So the transaction was duly terminated, and when Markos had at last parted with his money and his fine old wine, his jolly face cleared once more; for, after all, he had not lost by the bargain, though he had not made much, and the good-will of the two most famous and dangerous cut-throats in all the Venetian territory was worth something to a man who always lived more or less on the outer edge of the law.

Half-an-hour later bliss descended upon the companions as they sat at table in their favourite place, a sort of alcove or niche in the general hall of the eating-house, whence they could see and hear all that went on, without being too much disturbed in their enjoyment of the good things set before them. The place was brightly lighted by several scores of lamps fed with mingled oil, tallow, and camphor, and fastened on large wooden rings that hung from the high ceiling. The smoke floated up to the blackened beams, and found its way out through a small clere-story window at one end, and the light below was clear and soft. Thirty or forty guests were seated at tables of different sizes, and amongst them was a fair scattering of handsome women, mostly dressed in silks and satins of bright colours, and wearing jewels that sparkled when they moved. The men were of all sorts: there were a few good-looking young Venetian nobles, who had laid aside their cloaks and outer coats, and sat in their doublets and lace collars; there were two rich English travellers, in dark velvet, their long fair locks carefully combed and curled in the manner of the cavaliers, their hands conspicuously white, and their fingers adorned with magnificent rings; with them sat two auburn-haired Venetian beauties, radiant and laughing, and sipping Eastern wines from tall goblets of Murano glass. At one long table near the wall a serenading party was installed, their pretty instruments hanging on pegs behind them, together with their hats and cloaks. Beyond, in a corner, a pale young Florentine, with a spiritual profile, was supping with a lady who turned her back to the hall, and whose head and shoulders were almost hidden in a cloud of priceless lace. These two spoke little and ate delicately, and now and then their dark eyes met and flashed upon each other.

The air was hot, and heavy with the fumes of Greek wines and savoury dishes. At the farther end of the hall a large door opened now and then, and showed the bright kitchen where the host's wife presided, and whence neatly dressed youths brought dishes to the guests. Considering what the place was, an eating-house kept by a foreign money-lender, there was an air of luxury about it, and an appearance of orderly and temperate behaviour among the guests, that would have surprised a stranger who knew nothing of Venice, if he had been suddenly introduced by the gloomy entrance from the street through which Trombin and Gambardella had made their way.

CHAPTER VI

The lady who chose to go about Venice at dusk in the disguise of a monk encountered no further adventures after the loss of her ring; but she met with a very grave disappointment, of which the consequences directly concern this tale. After leaving the Bravi who had robbed her, she threaded the narrow ways northwards with a quick step till she came to a point near to the Fondaco dei Turchi on the Grand Canal. There she took the gondola that waited for passengers at the old traghetto, and she was quickly ferried over to the landing by the Palazzo Grimani. A few minutes later she was knocking at the door of Alessandro Stradella's lodgings near Santa Maria dell' Orto.

She knocked firmly and confidently, like a person quite sure of admittance. But no one came to open, and she heard no sound from within; so she knocked again, and after a shorter interval a third time. There was no answer, and nothing broke the stillness. With small regard for her disguise, the lady stamped twice in a most feminine way, then tried to shake the solid door with her hands, and finally turned away in disgust. It was almost dark in the staircase, and she descended the two flights slowly, drawing her hand along the wall to steady herself. The exercise of some caution, to avoid a fall, momentarily cooled her anger a little, and when she reached the entrance of the house she reflected that she had perhaps been hasty, and that the Maestro had possibly been detained by the other musicians, and would come home before long. She waited some time under the shadow of the archway, though several persons passed her, some going in, others going out. No one is ever surprised to see a monk waiting at the door of a large house. The disguised lady walked slowly up and down, her hood drawn well over her eyes, and her hands hidden in the slits of the frock.

But when the clocks struck the hour, and it had grown quite dark, she gave up all hope, and went away, returning in the direction whence she had come, and revolving plans of vengeance on the ungrateful singer as she walked.

She could not call him faithless, even in her mortification, for she had never exchanged a word with him in her life; and if that seems strange to any who read this story, let them learn something, if they can, of what constantly happens nowadays to popular operatic tenors. The disguised lady was of a romantic disposition; she was the respected wife of a rich citizen, by no means noble; her husband was absent in the East, and she had foolishly fallen in love with Alessandro Stradella's voice. She had written him the most silly letters he had ever received, setting forth the searing passion that devoured her, and apparently certain that he already shared it and only wanted an opportunity in order to tell her so. As he never answered her letters, she made up her mind that he feared her husband, though she had repeatedly assured him that the latter was absent and had left no Argus-eyed relation in charge of her and responsible for her acts. She wrote again and again, and even descended to promising that she would make him a rich man if he would only take courage and answer her pressing invitation.

Still he did not answer; and at last, despairing of any other means of moving him, she had written that she would come disguised to his dwelling on that evening, after the music in the Frari. For she always knew where he was to sing, and she never missed an opportunity of hearing him. She had accordingly gone to the church, and before leaving it she had prostrated herself and offered up the most sincere prayers for the success of her amorous enterprise, as if Saint Francis and Saint Anthony of Padua had power to suspend the rule of the Ten Commandments for her benefit during the evening.

These, in few words, are the facts which had preceded her visit to Stradella's lodging, and which resulted in the maddening disappointment and humiliation she felt when she turned her steps homewards.

At the same hour no one at the Palazzo Pignaver had yet noticed the absence of Ortensia and Pina. The gondolier waited by the landing at the Frari till it was dark, and then returned to the palace, supposing that the two had walked home and had forgotten to dismiss him, for this had happened once or twice already. He ran his gondola in between the painted piles by the steps of the palace, without inquiring whether his mistress and the nurse had entered by the postern; for almost every Venetian palace has two entrances, the main one being on the canal and approachable only in a boat, while the other opens upon the street at the back.

Ortensia was not missed till supper-time, and that was fully two hours after sunset; for it was the Senator's custom to leave his niece to herself or to Pina's company from the time when he brought her home, if she had been out with him in the gondola, until the evening meal; and if she asked leave to go to confession, as she had to-day, she returned before dark and retired to her own rooms without seeing him until she joined him at supper.

He required the most extreme punctuality of her and of all his household. Excessive exactness in regard to time is often the delight and the torment of people who have nothing to do of any importance. The time which some punctual persons waste in waiting for others would be enough to make them notable men if they used it better.

The Senator waited for Ortensia at least two minutes with equanimity, but after that his brow darkened, he paced the room impatiently, and he began to compose the scolding he meant to give her as soon as she came. This occupied him satisfactorily for at least five minutes, for he was always very nice in the choosing of his words on such occasions. His scoldings were administered in classical Italian, and not in the Venetian dialect of everyday life; they were constructed like short orations, with an exordium, an exposition of the fault committed, and a peroration, and they were followed by a long silence, during which they were supposed to work and take effect on the mind of the delinquent. Pignaver mentally reached the end of the intended admonition, and yet Ortensia did not come.

'The footman came back at last with a white face'

Then he lost his temper and sent one of the two servants to call her; and at the same time it occurred to him that he was making himself ridiculous in the eyes of the others by waiting for a mere chit of a girl. He therefore sat down rather hastily at the supper-table in the middle of the room and attacked the preliminary appetisers, shrimps, caviare, and thin slices of raw ham, and the chief butler poured a light white wine of Germany into his large glass; for the Senator was fond of good eating and drinking.

But to-night he was not to enjoy his supper, though the caviare had arrived that very day from Constantinople, and the shrimps were precisely of the right size, which is very important to a true epicure. The footman came back at last with a white face and said, in a trembling tone, that neither the young lady nor Pina were in the house.

The Senator dropped his two-pronged fork, his jaw fell at the same time, and at least four seconds passed before he recovered his breath. Then he sprang up, overturned his heavy chair in his excitement, and rushed from the room, followed by both the servants.

He searched the palace himself, he stormed, he raved, he cursed, he threatened, but Ortensia was not to be found. Everything in her rooms was in order, just as usual; she had gone to confession with her nurse as she had gone scores of times before, but she had not come home. That was all there was to be said about it.

At first no suspicion of the truth crossed Pignaver's brain. He believed she had been kidnapped either for her beauty, or by miscreants who would hold her for a ransom. Then he remembered the gondola and asked if it had come back. Yes, it was below; the old head gondolier had taken Ortensia to the Frari as usual, but he said she had returned on foot. The Senator sent for him, but no one could find him now, though the porter had been talking with him only ten minutes ago.

Nothing remained but to search Venice, and to inform the Signor of the Night that the girl and her nurse were missing from the palace. Pignaver forgot his supper altogether in his anxiety to lose no time.

The Signor was in his office, and was a distant cousin of the Senator's; for the Signors of the Night were noblemen who served in turn, superintending the police from sunset to sunrise. Only forty-eight hours had passed since this same gentleman had sent word to Pignaver of the attempt made by a supposed thief to get over the garden wall.

'He was not a burglar, my friend,' the Signor now said with conviction. 'If you will allow me to say so, with the most profound respect for your honour, I am sure that the man was your niece's lover, and that he has now succeeded in carrying her off, with the help of the serving-woman.'

Pignaver groaned and turned pale. But the Signor, who knew his business, asked him questions, and elicited enough information about Stradella and the singing lessons to convince him that the famous singer was at the bottom of the mischief. He said so plainly.

'A music-master!' cried Pignaver in a black rage, for he saw that the other was probably right. 'A singer! A catgut-pincher! A villainous low lute-strummer! No, sir, no! A thousand times no! The niece of Michele Pignaver is incapable of demeaning herself with a mountebank, sir! I must assure you——'

'The young lady,' interrupted the Signor, with a faint smile, 'is not your own niece, Senator, but the daughter of your late wife's brother.'

'No matter!' cried the Senator. 'Do you mean to imply, sir, that my late honoured wife would have been capable of demeaning herself with——'

'Heaven forbid!' ejaculated the other, interrupting again. 'You might as well suggest that Eve was herself a murderess because one of her sons killed the other. I suggest nothing, Senator—certainly nothing in the least derogatory to the honour of your house.'

'What do you advise me to do?' asked Pignaver, suddenly appeased.

He had changed his tone and spoke almost calmly, for his anger, like most things he did, was a matter of acting. The Signor understood, and again he smiled faintly. Before he answered he carefully snuffed and trimmed the three wicks of the tall brass lamp on the table. It had a big metal shade in the shape of a butterfly, which he turned so that it screened the light from his eyes and reflected it into his visitor's face.

'You will naturally wish to avoid a scandal,' he said, watching the Senator. 'Yes, I thought so. Very well, if Stradella has carried off your niece, as I am almost sure he has, they are beyond pursuit by this time. They have reached the mainland and are riding away as fast as they can towards the frontier. There is not the slightest chance of catching them. You must say that you have sent the young lady to the country for her health.'

At this Pignaver made a dramatic gesture. He raised both his hands on each side of his head, clenched his fingers, turned up his eyes, and pretended to be trembling with almost uncontrollable fury. The Signor knew his weakness and looked on with quiet amusement.

'I will have the city thoroughly searched during the next few days for two persons resembling your niece and the woman,' he continued. 'But if they have already fled, and if you insist upon finding them, you will have to employ private agents.'

'Yes, yes,' answered Pignaver thoughtfully. 'That will be best. Can you recommend any person to undertake such a delicate business, sir? I suppose that, in your position, you are acquainted at least with the names of some such men.'

The Signor, who was an amiable man, smiled pleasantly now.

'The truth is,' he said, 'we have some of them under supervision, and I chance to know of two who would suit your purpose well, and are unemployed at present, and badly in need of money. I have no doubt but that they will be glad to serve you. They have earned the reputation of being conscientious in carrying out their engagements, and intrepid in danger.'

Pignaver had listened attentively, and at once asked for the names and the address of the Bravi.

'They are known as Trombin and Gambardella,' said the Signor; 'they are now in Venice, and are generally to be heard of at the eating-house of Markos, the Samian money-lender and wine-dealer. I dare say you know where his place is? Not far from the Rialto, on this side——'

'In what is left of the old Quirini Palace, where they sell poultry downstairs?' asked Pignaver.

'Precisely. I see you are acquainted with the resort. I have, in fact, been there myself—on a matter of duty, of course.'

'Of course,' echoed the Senator. 'I have only heard of it, but I think I can find it.'

'I am sure you can,' assented the Signor, without a smile.

Pignaver had not only heard of the eating-house, but he had been there more than once, and knew the taste of the famous pilaf and the flavour of the old wine of Samos as well as anybody. He had even sat in the recess where the two gentlemen of fortune were at that moment supping. He had worn a mask, it is true, and by some mistake a lady had sat down at the same small table a moment after he had come, and he had fallen into conversation with her. But it was not necessary to tell this to the Signor.

The latter promised again to have a thorough search made through the city for Ortensia and Pina, and wrote down the descriptions Pignaver gave him. The nurse was described as 'a serving-woman, with grey eyes, and black hair turning grey at the temples, whose manners were rather above her station, and who had once been handsome. Age: forty-three. Mark: the thumb of the right hand had been broken and was distorted.'

'By the thumb-screw, I suppose,' observed the Signor in a business-like tone.

'It certainly looks like it,' answered the Senator indifferently.

He took his departure after a few more words and went out by the back door; he then walked in the direction of the Rialto, muffling himself in his great cloak, of which he threw one corner over his shoulder, so that it almost covered his face. He had left his gondola waiting in the narrow canal, and if he chose to come back and take it again, he could reach it without going through the low building in which the Signors of the Night had their office, and the city watch its headquarters.

The Signor had promised to continue the search during three days, and to inform him of any clue he found. Meanwhile, Pignaver thought it would be as well to find the two gentlemen who had been so highly recommended to him, and he hastened to the half-ruined Palazzo Quirini. He went in by a more convenient entrance than the two Bravi had chosen for reasons of their own, but he found Markos where they had found him, still busy with his accounts in the bright little vestibule. When the Senator entered, he had already slipped on the little velvet mask which most Venetians carried about them in the evening, but the Samian either recognised his voice or knew instinctively that his visitor was a person of quality, for he bowed to the ground, rubbed his large hands as if washing them before serving his guest, and answered the Senator's brief salutation in a profoundly obsequious tone.

Pignaver now laid one finger on his lips and spoke in a whisper, asking whether Markos was acquainted with two honest gentlemen named respectively Signor Trombin and Signor Gambardella.

By an almost miraculous coincidence the two honest gentlemen were at that very moment supping within. Markos offered to call them out.

'Unless,' he added, 'your lordship is in need of supper, and will join them.'

The Senator remembered that he had eaten only a few mouthfuls since dinner, and the savoury fumes from the hall further sharpened his appetite.

'The gentlemen are eating together at the little table in the recess,' Markos added, as he detected signs of hesitation. 'You can turn your back to the room, my lord, if you do not wish to be watched.'

Pignaver nodded and followed the host, who at once led the way in. Some of the people who had been supping when the Bravi had entered were gone away, but others had taken their places. The young Florentine and his beautiful guest had disappeared, and their table was occupied by a noisily gay party, of whom more than half wore masks. The two fair Englishmen in velvet were still gravely drinking with their laughing companions, but their eyes were growing rather dull. The serenaders had finished their meal, and were making soft music in their corner, trying over the songs they were going to sing.

'Gentlemen,' said Markos to the Bravi, 'allow me to introduce a highly respectable personage who has business with you, and would like to join you at supper.'

Trombin and Gambardella rose with a courtesy which showed where they had been bred, in spite of their present profession. Though they had been at supper two hours and had done well by a jar of old Samian, they were as cool and steady as when they had sat down, a fact which predisposed Pignaver in their favour.

'Will you do us the honour to be our guest, sir?' asked Gambardella at once.

'But you have already supped, gentlemen,' answered the Senator.

'That is a trifle, sir,' Trombin said. 'We have not quite finished, and if you will join us we shall be delighted to begin again from the beginning. A clean cloth, Markos,' he went on at once, turning to the host, 'and the same dishes over again!'

'Your hospitality confounds me, sirs,' protested the Senator. 'I can but accept your gracious invitation.'

He sat down at the end of the small table, turning his back to the hall. Markos was already making preparations, and in a few minutes the board was set again, and with the very same delicacies which the Senator had just begun to taste at his own supper when Ortensia's flight had been discovered. He ate in silence, with solemn greediness, while his two companions each took one shrimp and a taste of the caviare, and exchanged an occasional glance. When he had consumed everything except the bread, Pignaver spoke.

'I believe I am not mistaken in thinking that you two gentlemen occasionally undertake little matters of private business,' he began. 'If I am wrong, pray correct me.'

'You are rightly informed, sir,' answered Trombin; 'we do, though only on certain conditions, which, again, so far as they are favourable or unfavourable, depend on circumstances; and these circumstances themselves, as your experience of life has made you well aware, sir, are often the result of that element of chance, which, under Providence, plays such an important part in the affairs of men.'

This was rather vague, and Pignaver, who read the classics and prided himself on his memory, was reminded of those Lacedæmonians who answered the wordy fugitives from Samos by saying that they had already forgotten the first half of their speech and did not understand the second. When Trombin had finished speaking, he waited for an answer and looked steadily at the Senator, opening his eyes wider and wider till they were perfectly round and the lashes stood out in a circle like yellow rays, and he puckered his lips in the most ridiculous manner, as if he were just going to whistle. Gambardella, on the other hand, took a minute quantity of caviare on the end of his fork and tasted it delicately, looking unconcernedly at the guests in the hall.

Pignaver reflected a moment and drank wine before speaking.

'I attribute my presence here,' he said, 'to the direct intervention of Providence.'

'We share your view,' answered Gambardella with gravity.

'In fact,' added Trombin, 'the elements of acquaintance all agree admirably well—the circumstances, the conditions, chance, and Providence itself. For if, as I gather from your own words, sir, you stand in need of a little friendly assistance from us, we, on our side, are weary of wasting our wits in conversation and our strength in luxurious idleness. It is our mission to benefit mankind both here and hereafter, by despatching useless persons to Paradise and thus cheering the lives of the friends they leave on earth. Assured of this, as we are, all inactivity is unbearable to us. At the present moment we are, so to say, unemployed philanthropists; we are but a potential and passive blessing to our fellow-creatures, though we burn to be doing good to all! I appeal to my friend, Count Gambardella, here. Is this not the exact truth?'

'Absolutely,' answered the other, toying with a shrimp. 'What my friend, Count Trombin, says is always strictly true.'

'How could it be otherwise?' asked Pignaver. 'But I must apologise for not having addressed you gentlemen by your proper titles, which are foreign, though I had taken you both for Venetian nobles.'

'We are, sir,' Trombin answered, 'but it pleased his Majesty the King of France to confer titles of French nobility on us, after we had rendered him a trifling service. We should likewise esteem ourselves your debtors, sir, if you would inform us of your own name, since we are fortunate enough to be entertaining you as our guest.'

Again the round eyes opened wide, like those of an angry cat, and the mouth was all puckered in the midst of the cherubic face, while Trombin waited for the answer. The Senator saw that he had no choice.

'My name is Pignaver,' he said slowly, and dwelling proudly on each syllable, 'and I am a Senator. You will understand at once why I wear a mask here. I am well known by sight to many, and I have many friends——'

'One too many, I presume,' suggested Gambardella, interrupting softly.

'I shall communicate my business at once,' said Pignaver, 'for the person in question could never have been my friend any more than he could be my enemy.'

'We understand your meaning,' said Gambardella; 'he is of low birth. Shall we say that he is "superfluous"?'

'A weed,' suggested Trombin, 'a parasite, a wart, an overgrowth, a thing to be eradicated before it does greater harm! Do you take me, my lord? Have I fitted the word to the definition and suited the definition to the man?'

'Admirably, Count,' assented Pignaver. 'Your command of language fills me with envy. "Eradicate" is good, very good!'

'Does the weed flourish in Venice, my lord?' asked Gambardella, who was bored and wished to settle the preliminaries of the business at once.

'If I did not detest false metaphors,' said Pignaver, 'I should say that the weed has just flown, or, as I might say, fled, taking with it the finest flower of my garden. But since elegant speech must not be submitted to such outrages, I will speak plainly.'

At this point the conversation was interrupted by the appearance of the steaming pilaf, brought on by a neatly clad youth, whose companion set down beside it a dish of quails roasted in young vine leaves, and emitting a deliciously aromatic odour. Trombin and his friend helped the Senator generously, and filled his glass again. He was so hungry by this time that he ate several mouthfuls before he spoke again.

'I have always found the emotions to be great appetisers,' observed Trombin, watching him. 'Men feast at a wedding, and gorge themselves after a funeral. A fit of anger whets the appetite, for I have seen a man fly into a towering passion with the cook and then immediately devour the very dish he has found fault with, to the last scraping. As for the passion of love, a French proverb says well that happiness makes an empty stomach. I can only hope, my lord, that in a week's time you may enjoy your supper as much, with satisfaction for a relish instead of annoyance. As for me, the mere thought of doing some good in the world makes me hungry.'

And as he spoke he began to eat another quail which he had already taken on his plate. But Gambardella was more and more bored, and went to the point, as soon as the Senator looked up from his plate.

'We understand,' he said, 'that some low-born fellow has carried off a lady of your lordship's household. Do you know where they are?'

'No. I know nothing, except that they have either left Venice already or will escape before morning.'

'That means a wide search,' said Gambardella.

'But an easy one,' the Senator replied. 'The man is Alessandro Stradella, the singer, and may the devil get him!'

'He will be safer in our hands, my lord. The lady's name, and some description of her, if you please.'

'Ortensia is her name. She is only seventeen years old, but is very beautiful, for she is fair, and her hair is of a true auburn colour, such as the lamented Titian often painted. Indeed, the young lady much resembles that master's "Bella," though younger and thinner. With her is fled also her nurse, a woman called Filippina, of middle age, with grey eyes and greyish hair, once not bad-looking, and whose manners are above her station.'

'I suppose she is commonly called Pina,' observed Gambardella. 'Let us understand each other, my lord. I presume you wish the young lady and the woman to be brought back to you, when the singer is dead.'

'Precisely. I shall say that she has been spending a week with a relation of her mother's who is the Abbess of the Ursuline Nuns in Ravenna.'

'Did you say the Ursulines in Ravenna, my lord?' asked Gambardella slowly.

'Yes,' answered Pignaver, at first a little surprised by the question, for he had spoken clearly, although the whole conversation was carried on in low tones. The Bravo saw his expression, and hastened to explain.

'My left ear is a little deaf,' he said, turning his head so as to present the other. 'Nothing remains but to agree on the price of the service,' he continued in a business-like tone. 'When we are told exactly where we shall find our man, it is simple enough. But in this case we may have to travel far. We shall require two gold ducats daily for our expenses till we find the opportunity we need for such a difficult business, and five hundred gold ducats when we hand over to you the young lady and her nurse. One hundred gold ducats must be advanced before we start, on account of expenses.'

Pignaver's sour face twitched at the mention of such sums.

'You set a high price on your services, gentlemen,' he said.

'"Service" is not precisely the word, my lord,' said Trombin, desisting from picking the leg of a quail, and staring intently at the masked Senator. 'It is, as I may say, a false metaphor, which is an outrage upon elegant speech—forgive me for borrowing your own expressions!'

And suddenly Trombin's eyes glared in such a way that the Senator was cowed.

'I assure you, I had no intention of giving you offence, Count,' he said. 'If you will, choose the word you prefer; I will use it with pleasure.'

'"Benefit," my lord, or, if you prefer the longer form, "benefaction." Either will do very well.'

Trombin thereupon resumed operations on the leg of the quail, and when his absurd little mouth showed his teeth the Senator observed they were as white and sharp as a cat's. It was clear that he was the talker in the partnership, and left all business arrangements to his companion.

'I have named the sum we require, my lord,' the latter said calmly, 'and we are not accustomed to argue such matters. You would give ten times as much for your own life any day, and Alessandro Stradella would certainly find a thousand or two to save his, if the matter were laid before him.'

Pignaver saw that he must agree to the demand, for if he refused and sought help elsewhere the Bravi would warn the musician and offer the latter their protection. The Senator was uncomfortable in their company, as many of his friends would have been; for if a born coward ever comes into contact with such men, he regards them much as a timid woman looks on a loaded gun. Though the two cut-throats behaved with the outward courtesy of gentlemen, there was something terrifying in their looks which it would have been hard to define, and the highly refined Venetian noble, who admired the elegant works of Politian and composed scores of polished inanities, shuddered from time to time as he glanced at Gambardella's sinewy brown hand or Trombin's strong pink fingers and thought of the stains that must often have been on both.

A silence followed the Bravo's last speech, during which Trombin consumed more pilaf, and his companion thoughtfully salted a small bit of bread-crust, ate it slowly, and then sipped the old Samian wine from the blue and white glass beaker which he kept constantly quite full. And immediately, though he had only drunk a few drops, he re-filled the glass exactly to the brim. Trombin drank at much longer intervals, but always emptied his tumbler before replenishing it. Nor were these opposite habits of the two men mere matters of preference or taste; for the nose of the one turned up in such a convenient manner that he could drain the smallest glass or cup with ease, but the other's portentous beak turned down and then hooked itself in towards his lips, so that wherever his mouth went, there it was also, always in the way; and if he ever tried to drink like ordinary people, its tip was wetted before he had tasted the wine.

The Senator was reflecting before giving an answer which must be final. Was Ortensia worth the six or seven hundred ducats which the whole affair would cost him? That was really the question, for he looked upon the murder of Stradella merely as a necessary and just consequence of his niece's capture, and though the thought of vengeance was agreeable to his nature, he would not have been willing to pay such a price for it. Ortensia herself was certainly not worth so much, in his estimation, for the sake of her beauty, seeing that he could buy a Georgian girl almost or quite as pretty, in the Fondaco dei Turchi, for much less. Besides, though Stradella would be dead and buried, it would always be humiliating to feel that she had belonged to him first, though the truth need never be known in Venice.

But there was another consideration, which turned the scale in her favour. Pignaver had heard her sing his own compositions, after having been taught by Stradella, and he had dreamed of electrifying Venetian society at last by her rendering of his immortal works. Hitherto, even his most industrious flatterers had not given him the very first place among living poets and musicians; but he was sure that when they heard Ortensia they would exalt him above all his predecessors and all his contemporaries; at last he would enjoy that absolute supremacy which is the prime birthright of genius in all ages, and to which he firmly believed himself entitled. Ortensia alone could assure to him that final victory, and beside it all objections, all scruples, all petty questions of technical honour sank away to nothing. He must marry her himself, of course, so that he might order her to perform his works whenever he pleased, and she must be a married woman before propriety would allow her to sing to his assembled friends; but marriage was a detail and of no consequence compared with the triumph he expected to gain by it; the girl's flight with the musician was a childish escapade of little importance, since it could be kept quite secret, and she might be supposed to have been spending a few days in a convent in Ravenna to complete her education. As for any resistance on her part, it was absurd to think of such a thing; no doubt she would cry her eyes out for a few weeks, after Stradella was despatched to a better world, but she would soon see the error of her ways and be only too glad to accept the magnificent position the Senator offered her, instead of being murdered herself, or forced to spend her life in a convent.

The two Bravi did not hurry their new acquaintance to a decision, though Gambardella had flatly declined to discuss the terms of the bargain; they only made it clear that their offer must be accepted or declined as it was, and they seemed quite indifferent as to Pignaver's decision. Trombin continued to eat pilaf in a leisurely way, as if he could go on for ever, and Gambardella sipped his wine, filled his glass again, and ate several little morsels of salted crust, while the Senator turned the matter over in his mind and plied his knife and fork in silence.

'The truth is,' he said at last, 'I should not wish you to start till the city has been thoroughly searched by the police. As you wisely observed, I think, a man of Stradella's reputation cannot remain long concealed, and will be more easily found next week than to-morrow.'

'I believe,' answered Gambardella politely, 'that the remark was yours, and it is a wise one. Are we then to understand that if the Signors of the Night do not find the pair, you desire our help on the terms I have stated?'

'Exactly so,' said Pignaver. 'That will give you time to make your preparations for the journey at your leisure. Where shall I find you three days hence, gentlemen?'

'At Benediction in the Church of the Frari, my lord, for the day will be a Sunday. If you desire it, we will call for paper and pen and set down the terms of our agreement at once.'

'That will not be necessary, sir,' replied the Senator, who did not care to put his name to such a document. 'I have confidence in you.'

Trombin at once raised his head and fastened his eyes on Pignaver.

'As between gentlemen, my lord,' he observed, 'it would be more fitting to say that we have confidence in each other. With your permission I shall complete your statement by saying that we are willing to trust you without any written promise. We will leave such sordid dealings to the lawyers and notaries. You give your word, we give ours, and the matter is safer for accomplishment than if a contract were engrossed on a dozen sheepskins and sealed with the Fisherman's Ring!'

'Certainly, certainly,' assented the Senator, who did not like the Bravo's eyes. 'You have my word, I have yours, and that is enough.'

'My lord,' said Trombin, his manner suddenly becoming extremely affable, 'I have the honour to drink your health!'

'Your health, Count,' responded Pignaver, raising his glass.

'Your health,' said Gambardella, bowing politely, and then sipping his wine with all the caution required to keep his long nose out of it.

Having settled matters in this way and, moreover, satisfied his appetite with a good supper, Pignaver took leave of the Bravi with considerable ceremony, for he perceived that they were as exigent and punctilious as to all points of courtesy as any noble in Italy, France, or Spain; and it would not be good to fall out with such touchy gentlemen on a point of manners. Indeed, as he retraced his steps to the office of the Signors of the Night, where his gondola was waiting, he really congratulated himself on having escaped without a quarrel, and hoped that the next interview would pass off as well.

The three days went by, and at noon on Sunday he received a note from the Signor of the Night informing him that the runaway pair and the serving-woman had been in Padua early on the morning after they left

Venice, and had immediately taken an extra post to Rovigo and Ferrara. They had excited no suspicion, and the spy who had brought the news had not obtained the information without considerable difficulty, for many travellers were going and coming, and in a time of peace like the present more attention was bestowed by the authorities on foreign travellers than on Italians. But Stradella had brought some of his belongings with him, which his man had carefully concealed in the gondola, and amongst other things there was his favourite long lute; the instrument had been noticed by the ostlers at the postern-house in Padua on account of its unusual size, and they remembered the four travellers after hearing the spy's description of three of them, for he knew nothing of Stradella's servant.

There was therefore no doubt but that the fugitives were now far beyond the Venetian border in the States of the Church, and Pignaver resolved to keep the appointment at the Frari, taking with him the hundred gold ducats which were to be paid in advance.

The Bravi were already there indeed, but he did not see them at once, and as Vespers were over and the Benediction was about to begin, he selected a spot a little apart from the common herd and knelt down to his devotions, for it was of no use to waste time that could be so profitably employed.

But while he was thus engaged, it being already sunset and the light in the church failing, the men he sought were earnestly conversing in low tones with a young Dominican monk in a distant corner; and the monk, it is needless to say, was the lady whose ring they had taken, and who had knocked so long in vain at Stradella's door three days earlier.

'Madam,' Gambardella was saying, 'the search may be a long one, but we will do our best. We shall require two gold ducats daily for our expenses in travelling, and the payment of five hundred gold ducats in cash when we deliver to you Master Alessandro Stradella, bound hand and foot, at your villa on the Brenta.'

'But the woman must die!' protested the lady earnestly.

'That goes without saying, madam,' answered Gambardella. 'You may regard her as already dead and buried, for you have our word for it. Nothing remains but that you should place in our hands a hundred gold ducats on account, which we shall require in order to start.'

The lady was evidently prepared for such a demand, and produced a small leathern bag from within her monk's frock. But she was evidently a woman of business.

'Since we are now friends,' she said, putting the bag into Gambardella's hand, 'you ought to give me back my ring when the thing is done!'

'Madam,' said Trombin, in his grand manner, 'you have our word for that. In fact, we only meant to borrow it for a day or two, and for your great kindness in allowing us to do so we have the honour to tender you our sincerest thanks.'

'It is impossible to be more polite, sir,' answered the lady.

So they parted, for she slipped away into the dusk and soon left the church by a side door. But Trombin and his companion went forward, and finding the Senator on his knees, they knelt down, one on each side of him. He glanced to the right and left, and was surprised at the improvement in their appearance since he had seen them at supper. They had been distinctly shabby then, and he would not have liked to be seen in their company by his friends; but to-day they were dressed with excellent taste and neatness, in perfectly new clothes. Gambardella wore a suit of dark purple cloth slashed with velvet of the same colour; but Trombin wore black velvet and silk, which he considered most becoming to his infantile complexion and yellow hair. Both had new hats, too, and their feathers, purple and black respectively, were nothing short of magnificent. Only their rapiers were unchanged, the same serviceable, business-like weapons that Pignaver had seen before.

The three men knelt side by side, putting on an air of devotion; and no one else was very near them.

'*Tantum ergo* ...' began the choir, somewhere out of sight.

'I presume you mean business, my lord,' said Gambardella so that the Senator could just hear him.

'They passed through Padua, and took post to Rovigo and Ferrara,' answered Pignaver. 'You cannot miss them if you go that way.'

'A very convenient place, Ferrara, if they would wait for us there,' observed Trombin.

'... *veneremur cernui*,' the choir sang, and many of the people were joining in the ancient hymn.

'When can you start?' inquired Pignaver.

'As soon as we have funds for the journey,' answered Gambardella promptly.

'You said one hundred ducats, did you not? Your expenses are to be counted at two ducats per day, and as much of the first hundred as is left when you have finished is to be deducted from the final payment of five hundred. Is that it?'

'Precisely,' said Gambardella.

'It is impossible to be more accurate,' observed Trombin, without turning his head, and preserving the expression of a devout, fat-cheeked seraph, which he always put on when at his prayers.

'I have the money with me, gentlemen,' continued Pignaver. 'As soon as the Benediction is over I will hand it to you, and I hope you will find it convenient to start at once.'

'We are ready,' Gambardella replied. 'To-morrow night we shall be in Ferrara, and if your friends are still there, we may be here again on the third day.'

'Heaven grant us all its favours and a speedy return!' prayed Trombin.

'Amen,' said the Senator, calculating that if only three days were consumed, the Bravi would have ninety-four ducats in hand, and he would have to pay them only four hundred and six.

In his pocket his hand grasped the heavy little bag containing the gold, and he wished that private vengeance and justice were not so dear; but he was not a miser, though he had a real Venetian's understanding of the value of money, and did not like to part with it till he was sure that he was to receive a full equivalent. For the rest, what he was doing was perfectly justifiable in his eyes: if the couple had been caught within the territory of the Republic, Alessandro Stradella would have had to answer to the law for the atrocious crime of carrying off a Senator's niece and affianced bride who was a minor, and the law would not have been tender to the Sicilian; the least penalty he would have suffered would have been to be chained to an oar on a government galley, and it was quite possible that he might have been hanged. Most people would prefer to be run through with a rapier, and it was therefore clear that Stradella ought to be satisfied. As for such weakness as a qualm of conscience, Pignaver was as far above such childishness as the Bravi themselves.

He gave them the little bag of ducats and took leave of them by the monument of Pietro Bernardini, almost on the spot where Ortensia and Pina had put on their brown cloaks three or four days earlier.

When he was gone, Trombin and Gambardella looked at each other in silence; the dark man's thin lips, visible on each side of the point of his nose, but quite shaded by it in the middle, were smiling faintly, but Trombin's cherubic countenance expressed, or caricatured, the utter beatitude of one of those painted angels to which his friend always compared him.

They walked slowly up the church towards the sacristy, and at the door they met the sacristan, a lay brother, coming out with his long extinguisher in his hand. They stopped him politely.

'We desire to offer two candles to Saint Francis,' said Gambardella, 'one for each of us. We also desire to leave a gold ducat for masses to be said for the soul of a departed friend.'

'I will serve you at once, gentlemen,' answered the sacristan. 'What was your friend's baptismal name, if you please, that I may write it on the list?'

'Alessandro,' answered Gambardella.

'Do you wish to mention the date of his death, sir?'

'No. It is of no use.'

The lay brother took the money and went into the sacristy to deposit it, and to fetch the candles, which the Bravi then lighted and put up themselves.

CHAPTER VII

Trombin had rightly guessed that the fugitives would rest themselves in Ferrara, where they would be safe within the Pope's dominions, and beyond the reach of Venetian law. By the old road the city was nearly a hundred miles from Padua, and it was only by a lavish use of money that Stradella succeeded in reaching it at midnight, after leaving Padua soon after sunrise. Ortensia was utterly exhausted, and even Pina, who was very strong, was beginning to be worn out. They had trouble in getting into the inn at that hour, and when they at last succeeded, they found that there was only one room to be had, although, as the sleepy servant who had let them in added, they might have the whole house to themselves the next day, for all the travellers would be gone again long before noon.

Pina slept with her mistress, while Stradella and his man rolled themselves in their cloaks and lay down outside the door, with valises for pillows; for they expected to be pursued, and though they had made good time, they knew that mounted men, with frequent relays of horses, might overtake them before morning. It was not Stradella's first adventure, though it was his last, and he fully realised that Pignaver would use every means to wreak his vengeance. It could not have occurred to the runaways that three days would be wasted in searching Venice before the pursuit actually began.

Even that knowledge could not have made Alessandro sleep more soundly, since the fear of danger to Ortensia could not keep him awake, and he slept as peacefully on the stone pavement of the corridor as ever he did in the most luxurious bed.

But his man was awake and was watching for all the four, though he lay quite still, rolled up in his brown cloak. For Cucurullo was one of those people who sleep little at the best of times, and generally have to content themselves with resting their bodies by lying motionless, while they deaden thought as best they can with those melancholy devices that are familiar to the sleepless.

The hunchback rested now, but was glad to lie awake, though he was well aware that he deserved no especial credit for watching while his young master slept soundly by his side. But he did not try to cheat time by fancying that he was counting a flock of sheep that crowded through a narrow gate into a field, or by saying the alphabet backwards, or by repeating all the prayers he knew, which were many, for he was a religiously inclined person, nor did he laboriously reckon how many Apostolic florins there were in seventeen hundred and sixty-three and a half Venetian ducats.

On the contrary, he concentrated his mind to the best of his ability on a problem which it seemed to him of the very highest importance to solve at once; for it involved nothing less than the salvation of Alessandro Stradella's soul.

Now Cucurullo, as I have said, was religiously inclined. He was not devout in the same sense as the two cut-throats who lighted candles before the image of Saint Francis for the success of their murderous enterprise, and paid beforehand for masses to be said for the soul of the man they were going to kill. He would not have denied that this was a form of piety too, if any one had asked him his opinion. Everything, he would have argued, was relative; and if you were going to stab a man in the back, it was more moral to make an effort to save his soul than to wish to destroy it with his body. He would have admitted this, for he was charitable, even to such people as professional murderers. But his own religion was quite of another sort; he was devotedly attached to his master, he was deeply concerned for the latter's future welfare, and it looked just now as if Stradella's chances of salvation would be slender if any accident carried him off suddenly. Moreover, such an accident might occur at any moment, for, like Stradella himself, he anticipated that Pignaver would seek a speedy revenge.

Like the early Christians he was a pessimist about this world and an optimist about the next; for that is usually the state of mind of those who labour under any material or bodily disability, from slavery, which is the worst, to blindness or deformity.

As a pessimist, therefore, Cucurullo thought that his master, Ortensia, Pina, and himself had a most excellent chance of having their throats cut within twenty-four hours, and he was rather surprised that it should not have happened already.

As an optimist, on the other hand, he trusted that by his own exertions he might so dispose matters as that his master and Ortensia should be murdered while in a state of grace, and not in mortal sin; to be plain, he was determined that they should be duly married before Pignaver's agents despatched them. For he had been constrained to aid and abet his master in more than one romantic adventure before now, and nothing had come of any of them that was at all conducive to the young man's salvation.

Poor Cucurullo knew the whole process of those affairs, as the conjurer's assistant knows how the tricks are done. Even when Stradella was at home, in his own room, his man had always been able to tell whether he was in love or not. When he was not, he industriously composed oratorios, or motets, or some other kind of serious music; but when he was, he sang to himself, as a bird does in spring, improvising both the words and the melody; or else he would sit still for an hour at a time, doing nothing, but dreaming with open eyes and slightly parted lips; or he would pace the floor impatiently, and go to the door every five minutes to listen for a light footfall on the stairs. All this Cucurullo had observed frequently; often, too, he had carried letters and tokens, and had brought others back; and not a few times, by night, he had held cloak and lute and rapier, while his master climbed up to a balcony or a window high above. Many such things had Cucurullo done, and had confessed them afterwards as misdeeds. Wretched sinner that he was, he had even paid flattering compliments to a chambermaid to sweeten her humour till she promised to take a message to her lady. This had seemed to him particularly wicked, yet he had done it and would do it again, if Stradella required such service, simply because he could not help it.

Now, however, all former adventures sank to nothing in comparison with the present one. So far, the musician had lightly loved and ridden away; but this time he had not ridden away alone, and, moreover, he was not carrying off the buxom wife or daughter of some meek citizen who would appeal in vain to the law and could do nothing without it, and who would probably let the erring lady return to his home at the trifling price of a sound beating when Stradella was tired of her. That would have been bad enough, in all conscience; but this time the hare-brained singer had done much worse, even from a worldly point of view; and looking at it from another, Cucurullo thought that the irreparable nature of the deed made it more wicked, besides the fact that all the persons concerned might lose their lives by it. He was a very simple person in some ways. Under the circumstances it seemed necessary before all things to convert moral wrong into moral right by the simple intervention of a priest and a wedding ring, after which the question of civil right, as the law would regard it, would take care of itself well enough.

In the grey dawn Cucurullo's large unshaven face emerged from the ample folds of his cloak, and his mild blue eyes seemed to review the situation by daylight as he looked from his master's half-muffled figure to Ortensia's closed door, and then towards the window at the end of the passage. Then he sat up cautiously and drew his heels under him, and because his body was so short and so completely covered up, he looked as if he had none at all, and as if his big head were lying in a nest of brown cloth on a pair of folded legs. Then, from just below his chin, an immensely long arm stole out quietly, and his hand drew up Stradella's cloak which had slipped from his shoulder; for the morning air was chilly, though the spring was far advanced. Any one, coming on him suddenly as he sat there, would have been startled as at the sight of a supernatural being, consisting of a head, legs, and arms, all joined together without any body.

The dawn brightened to day, and all sorts of noises began to come up from below, echoing through the staircase and long passages of the house; a distant door was opened and shut, then some one seemed to be dragging a heavy weight over a rough floor; far off, some one else whistled a tune; and then, all at once, came the clatter of many horses' feet on the cobble-stones in the yard.

Cucurullo sprang up and ran on tip-toe to the window, instantly fearing the arrival of mounted pursuers; but he only saw the stablemen leading out the post-horses to be watered and groomed. When he turned to come back he saw that he had waked Stradella, who was sitting up, yawning prodigiously, and rubbing his eyes like a sleepy boy. He raised his hand to stop his man, and then got up without noise and joined him near the window.

'What is it?' he asked in a whisper, not without some anxiety.

'Only the post-horses, sir, but I was afraid of something else.'

'I wish we were already in Florence. This is too near Venice!'

'Better still in Rome,' said Cucurullo, gloomily. 'Still better in Sicily, and altogether much better in Africa; but best of all in heaven, sir, if you can manage to get there!'

'It is not the first time you and I have run a risk together,' observed Stradella, slowly moving the back of his hand up and down against his unshaven cheek.

'It is the first time you have risked the life of a lady,' answered Cucurullo quietly, for he understood his master very well.

'We had better go down and see about getting horses,' Stradella answered, and he led the way to the stairs, his man following in his footsteps.

The sun was rising now, and there was much bustling and clattering in the yard, and sousing and splashing of cold water about the fountain; a dozen horses were tied up to rings in the wall on one side, and the stablemen were grooming some of them industriously while others waited their turn, stamping now and then upon the cobble-stones, and turning their heads as far as they could to see what was going on behind them and on each side. Three men were washing the huge coach that ran to Rovigo one day and back the next, and several smaller conveyances stood beyond it in a row, still covered with dust from yesterday, for the weather had been dry.

As in many inns of that time, the innkeeper was also the postmaster. Stradella found him under the arched entrance to the yard, giving instructions to the cook, who was just going to the market accompanied by a scullion; the latter carried three empty baskets on his head, one inside of the other.

'You can have no horses to-day,' said the host, in answer to Stradella's demand, and he shook his head emphatically.

'No horses! It is impossible! It is absolutely necessary that we should go on at once.'

The innkeeper was a square-shouldered Romagnole with grey hair, red cheeks, and sharp black eyes. He shook his head again.

'I have not a horse to give you,' he said. 'Everything in my stable was engaged beforehand for the Nuncio. I cannot give you the Government's horses from the Rovigo coach, can I? Patience! That is all I can say.'

Stradella began to ask questions. The Nuncio, on his way to Verona and Austria, had spent three days in the inn, both to rest himself and also to be sure of having enough horses ahead to go on with, and word had been sent to Mantua to make all the necessary arrangements. He should have gone by Modena, but the road was in a bad state. A bridge had broken down, and he had been forced to pass through Ferrara.

'But surely,' said the musician, 'I can hire a pair of horses of some sort in the town, by paying a good price for them!'

No. The Nuncio had hired everything. Did the gentleman suppose that a Papal Nuncio could travel with as few as eight or ten horses? He needed about fifty in all. That was why he proceeded so slowly. There was not another animal to be had in the town, horse or mule, that could be put to a wheeled vehicle—not one! The gentleman might hire a riding-horse or two, but the innkeeper had been told that he had a lady and her tire-woman with him. Patience! A day would soon pass, Ferrara was a fine town, well worth seeing, and he could go on to-morrow morning in the Bologna coach, which would arrive from that city at noon to-day.

Clearly there was not the smallest possibility of being able to get on during the next twenty-four hours. Stradella's face was very grave as he turned away, and Cucurullo was paler than before.

Upstairs Ortensia had wakened just then and had called Pina, who got up and opened the window wide, letting in the air with the morning sun. Utterly unprovided as the two women were, they had slept half-dressed, and as Ortensia rose the nurse threw one of the two brown cloaks over her bare shoulders and fastened it round her neck.

For a few moments after she had opened her eyes the young girl had not quite understood where she was, for she had lain down exhausted, and sleep had come to her as her head touched the pillow. Now, in the broad daylight, when she had plunged her face into cold water, she realised everything, and the colour rose slowly to her throat and cheeks. She went to the window and stood there, turned away from Pina and looked out. Below her lay the chief public square of the city; on the left rose the huge castle, the most gloomy and forbidding she had ever seen. She had never heard of Nicholas Third of Este nor of his wife Parisina, fair, evil, and ill-fated, nor of handsome Ugo, who died an hour before her for his sins and hers, in the dark chamber at the foot of the Lion Tower; but if Pina had known the story and had told it to her in all its horror, Ortensia would have felt that it must be true, and that only such tragedies as that could happen within such walls. They were so stern, so square, so dark; the towers rose so grimly out of the black waters of the moat! It was of bad augury to look at them, she thought, and she drew back from the window and sat down where she could see only the sky.

Pina was making such preparations for her mistress's toilet as were possible. Being a prudent woman she had brought in her pocket three objects of the highest usefulness, a piece of white Spanish soap, a comb, and a shabby little old rolling work-case of yellow leather, in which there were needles and thread and pins. The figure of a wild animal, which might have been meant for a bear, was embroidered in black thread on the outer flap of the case. Pina had used it ever since Ortensia could remember, and seemed to value it as much as any of her few possessions. It was a very useful little thing, and she kept it always well filled with sewing materials.

As the young girl did not move and showed no inclination to dress herself, Pina came behind her and began to let down and comb her hair, which she had not even taken down on the previous night, being far too much exhausted to think of such a thing. She submitted her head willingly to the skilled hands of her nurse.

'Where is he?' she asked after a time, and she felt that she was blushing again.

'They slept on the floor in the passage,' Pina answered. 'Perhaps they are asleep still. You shut your eyes as soon as you lay down, but I opened the door again and looked out before I went to bed. Signor Alessandro asked me if we needed anything, and then said good-night.'

'Will you go and see if they are still there, please?'

Pina crossed the room, drew back the bolt, and put out her head, looking up and down the passage. There was no one to be seen, and she shut the door again without bolting it. She came back and again began to comb out the girl's hair.

'They are not there,' she said. 'Probably Signor Alessandro is ordering the horses. He will come in a few minutes and tell us at what time we are to start.'

A short silence followed.

'Have you ever been here before?' Ortensia asked presently.

'Yes,' Pina answered, 'I have been here before. I do not like Ferrara.'

'Why not? Have you any particular reason for not liking it?'

'It was here that my thumb was hurt,' said the nurse. 'That is a fair reason, is it not?' She laughed rather harshly. 'To hate a place because one has had an accident in it! The men would say that is just like a woman!'

'I hope I may never come here again, either,' Ortensia answered. 'How did you hurt your thumb?'

'That is a long story, my lady. But why do you also dislike the place already? You have only looked out of the window once.'

'I saw the castle, and I thought it was of bad augury, for it looks like a great prison.'

'There are prisons in it without any light, very deep down,' said Pina quietly. 'The Pope's Legate lives in the upper part. The Legate is the Papal Governor, you know, my lady.'

'I did not know. But the ugly castle is not the real reason why I do not like Ferrara. I could not tell any one else, but I think I can tell you, Pina.'

She turned her head half round under the nurse's hands, looked up sideways, and then hesitated. It was not easy to explain.

'What is it, my lady?' asked the serving-woman. 'You can tell old Pina anything.'

'It is all so different from what I thought it would be,' Ortensia said in a rather low voice, and again a blush rose in her cheek.

'I think I understand,' Pina said, steadily combing out the heavy auburn hair.

'You see,' Ortensia explained, 'we all four got into the gondola together, and there was that long row to the land, and that dreadful night in the cart on the road to Padua—and then the half-hour at daybreak, while he was getting the carriage, and then the journey here—and last night—and now——'

She did not finish the sentence, hoping that Pina would really understand.

'Yes,' the woman said quietly. 'You have not been alone together for a moment since we left Venice, and that is not what you expected.'

'No,' Ortensia answered in the hurt tone of a disappointed child, 'I thought it was going to be quite different! And now we shall start again and drive all day and half the night, and then it will be just the same, I suppose!'

'Once in Florence, or even in Bologna, there will be no more hurry,' said Pina in a consoling tone. 'Besides, my lady, you can be properly married then.'

'Of course, of course! We shall be married as soon as we can, but all the same———'

'All the same, it would be pleasant to spend half-an-hour together without old Pina always listening and looking on!'

The nurse smiled and shook her head, but Ortensia could not see her, and did not think her tone was very encouraging; it sounded as if 'old Pina' thought it was going to be her duty to play chaperon two or three days longer, which was not at all what Ortensia wished.

'If he had even shown that he was a little disappointed, too———' the girl began, and then she stopped.

'That would not have been good manners, my lady,' Pina said primly. 'When a gentleman has carried off a young lady, with her own consent, the least he can do is to look pleased, I am sure!'

'I thought you would understand better,' Ortensia answered in a tone of disappointment.

Some one knocked at the door, not loudly but sharply, and as if in a hurry; Pina went at once to see who it was, and found Stradella himself outside.

'May I come in?' he asked quickly.

Beyond Pina, as he looked in, he saw Ortensia in her brown cloak, with her hair down and all combed out over her shoulders, and without waiting for an answer he pushed past the nurse and went to her. Instinctively she drew the cloak more closely round her, but she looked up with a bright smile, which vanished when she saw his expression in the strong light. He spoke anxiously, without even a word of greeting.

'There are no horses to be had,' he said. 'I have done my best, but the Pope's Nuncio is passing through and has engaged everything there was. There is not even a public coach to Bologna till to-morrow morning. I am more distressed than I can tell you! I have sent my man out to see if he can find anything, and he will if there is a beast to be had. If not, we shall have to wait here.'

While he was speaking, the door had closed softly and Pina was gone. Ortensia saw her go out and put out one hand timidly between the folds of the cloak, for her arm was bare, and she tried to cover it. At the same time the glorious colour rose in her face, the third time since she had opened her eyes that morning.

'I am glad,' she said simply, as soon as her hand was in his.

He glanced behind him and saw that Pina had disappeared. Then without a word he drew the lovely girl up to him, and for a while they stood clasped in each other's arms; and she forgot that hers were bare, and he scarcely knew it; and if their faces drew back one from the other for a few seconds, it was that their eyes might meet in one another's depths; and the broad morning sun shone full upon the two through the open window, making the girl's auburn hair blaze like dark red gold, and a white radiance glowed in her pure forehead and snowy arms.

Stradella shivered a little, even in the sunshine, as he let her go, and she sank upon her chair, finding his hand again and holding it fast as if she feared lest he should leave her. It had been a strange wooing, in which song had played a greater part than words; and as for anything else, he had kissed her twice on that night when he had climbed into the loggia, and not again till now. Had he loved her less, he would have laughed at himself for the innocence of such a love-making; but it was all unlike anything that had ever happened to him before, and, moreover, he had no time for such reflections at the present moment, since every hour of delay might mean the nearer approach of danger, not to him only, but to Ortensia herself.

'We are not far enough from Venice,' he said, when he spoke at last. 'I would give the world to have you safe in Florence!'

'My uncle will not even try to catch us,' Ortensia said calmly. 'You do not know him. When he finds out that we are gone together he will fear a scandal, and he fears ridicule still more. He will tell his friends that he has sent me to the country, or to a convent, and by and by he will tell them that I am dead. He dreads nothing in the world so much as being laughed at!'

She was so sure that she laughed herself as she thought of him, and almost wished that he might hear her, though he was certainly the very last person she wished to see just then. But Stradella thought otherwise.

'No one would laugh at him if he had you assassinated,' he said.

'I am not afraid of that!' Ortensia smiled at the mere idea of such a thing. 'Why are you standing? Come, bring that chair and sit down beside me, for we are alone at last!'

He was well used to women's ways, but the ways of grown women of the world are not those of innocent maidens of seventeen; her perfect simplicity and fearlessness were quite new to him, and had a wonderful charm of their own. He drew a chair to the window and sat down close to her, and afterwards he was glad that he had done as she wished.

It was all very strange, he thought even then. As yet, a love-affair had mostly meant for him a round of more or less dangerous adventures by night, such as climbing of balconies, unlocking of forbidden doors with stolen keys, imprisonment in dark closets and wardrobes, and sometimes flight in break-neck haste. That had usually been the material side, whereas now, reckoning up his risks, he had only climbed once to a loggia at night, and once he had been taken for a thief and chased, and that was all, excepting the actual escape from Venice, which had been without danger until now. On the other hand, there had stood to love's credit, as against those insignificant perils, only two kisses and no more, exchanged when he had been so drenched with rain that it had been quite out of the question to put a dripping arm round his lady's waist.

And now, for the first time in his life, he was suddenly alone with an innocent girl of seventeen who loved him, and whom he loved even to the point of having carried her off out of her house; he was alone with her, in her own room, when she had but just risen from sleep, and she was sitting beside him in the early sunshine, that wove a blaze of glory round her young beauty, and her soft white hand held his; and he was not satisfied as she was, but wished it were night instead of day, and wished the sun were the moon, and that there were sweet silence without instead of the thousand cries and echoes of a waking Italian city. For all he had ever known of joy on earth, or ever hoped for, he would not have wished that Ortensia's face could change into any that had once been dear to him under the summer moonlight of the south; yet he felt strangely constrained and awkward, like a schoolboy in love, not knowing what to do or say in the overwhelming daylight.

'You are not glad, as I am,' Ortensia said after the long silence.

At the sound of her voice he found himself again, and he lifted her hand and pressed it to his lips.

'I am afraid for you,' he answered. 'When a man has taken the most precious thing in the whole world, and carries it with him through an enemy's country, he may well be afraid lest some harm come to it on the way.'

'But this is not the enemy's country!' laughed Ortensia, too happy to be serious. 'Are we not a hundred miles from Venice and my uncle?'

'They say the Republic has long arms, love, and the Senator can count on every one of the Ten to help him. The law cannot touch us merely for having run away together, it is true, but what if he invents a crime? What if he swears that we have robbed him? The Pope's Government will not harbour thieves nor shelter criminals against the justice of Venice! We should be arrested and given up, that is all, and then sent back! This is what I fear much more than that he should have us tracked and murdered by assassins, as many Venetians would do in this civilised age!'

'But we have taken nothing,' Ortensia objected, quite unable to be afraid of anything while her hand was in his. 'How can he accuse us of robbing him? Pina and I have a comb and piece of soap between us! As for money, she may have a little small change, for all I know, but I have nothing.'

'I have a good deal,' Stradella answered; 'quite enough to justify such an accusation as that. But, after all, nothing can hinder such a thing, if it is going to be. I dare say you are right—it is my anxiety for you that makes me think of everything that might happen.'

'Nothing will happen,' Ortensia said softly, 'nothing will happen to part us!'

Still holding his hand, she gazed into his eyes with an expression of ecstatic happiness, and she could not have found another word, even if she had needed speech; then suddenly her bare arm circled his neck like a flash of white light, for he was very close to her, and she took him unawares and kissed him first.

She laid her head upon his breast a moment later, and he pressed her to him and buried his face in her sweet auburn hair. His heart overflowed in many soft and loving words.

The door opened while he was speaking, and both started and sat upright, expecting to see Pina, and ashamed to be surprised even by her. Then Ortensia uttered a sharp cry and Stradella sprang to his feet.

Two big men in rusty black and long boots had entered the room, and were advancing. They were broad-shouldered men, of a determined bearing, with sinister faces, and both wore swords and kept their slouch hats on their heads. Stradella was unarmed, and could only stand before Ortensia, awaiting their onset, for he had not a doubt but that they were Bravi sent by Pignaver to murder him. To his surprise they stopped before him, and one of them spoke.

'You had better come quietly with us,' the man said.

Stradella understood at once that the two intruders were sbirri, come to arrest him, and he was sure that Pignaver had pursued precisely the course he had explained to Ortensia, and that he was going to be accused of robbery.

'I am a Sicilian and a Spanish subject,' he said. 'By what right do you dare to arrest me?'

'We know very well that you are a Sicilian, Master Bartolo,' answered the man. 'And as for the rest, it is known to you, so come with us and make no trouble, or it will be the worse for you.'

'My name is not Bartolo!' cried the musician indignantly. 'I am Alessandro Stradella, the singer.'

'Any one can say that,' replied the man. 'Come along! No nonsense, now!'

'I tell you, I am Stradella——'

But the man glanced at his companion, and the two had him by his arms in an instant, though he struggled desperately. They were very strong fellows, and between them could have thrown a horse, and though Stradella was supple and quick, he was powerless between them.

During the short exchange of words Ortensia had leaned back against the window-sill in frightened surprise, but when she saw her lover suddenly pinioned and dragged towards the door, she flew at the sbirri like a tigress, and buried her fingers in the throat of the nearest, springing upon him from behind. The fellow shook her off as a bull-terrier would a rat, and, while keeping his hold on the prisoner with one hand, he tripped her roughly with his foot and the other, by a common professional trick, throwing her heavily upon the brick floor. Before she could rise, the men had got Stradella outside, and as she struggled to her feet she heard the key turned, and knew that she was locked in. In wild despair she beat upon the solid panels with her small fists, but no one answered her. Stradella's man was scouring the town for horses, and Pina was not within hearing.

Meanwhile the singer had submitted, as soon as he realised that he had no chance of escape, and that, unless the men were acting a part, he had been taken for a man called Bartolo, and would be able to explain the mistake as soon as he was brought before a responsible officer or magistrate. Indeed, when this view presented itself to him, he was only anxious to facilitate the course of events as much as possible, and spoke civilly to his captors, while walking quietly downstairs between them; but they did not let go of his arms for that reason.

Below, in the arched entrance, the innkeeper was waiting, in conversation with three other sbirri, dressed and armed much in the same manner as the two who had made the arrest.

'It is a mistake,' Stradella said to the host. 'I am taken for another man, and as soon as I have explained who I am, I shall return. I shall be obliged if you will attend to the wants of the lady and her serving-woman.'

'Guests who quit the house without paying their score generally leave their luggage as security,' answered the host with an insulting sneer, and pointing towards the entrance.

There, to his surprise, Stradella saw two sturdy porters, laden with his valises, his cloak, and his lute, and evidently waiting to accompany him.

'What are you doing, you scoundrels?' he cried. 'Put down my things!'

But they only grinned and began to move on, and as he was hurried out of the door into the square, they jogged across the square at a trot with their burdens. A few moments later he followed them across the drawbridge of the castle and in under the great gate where a papal soldier, armed with halberd and broadsword, was pacing up and down on guard.

Just as he disappeared, Pina emerged upon the square from a narrow street at its northern end, and hastened to the entrance of the inn. The host was standing there, his legs apart, his arms crossed, and his small black cap on one side of his head. He stopped Pina.

'Your master has changed his lodgings,' he said in a jocular tone, and pointing with his thumb towards the castle. 'His Excellency the Legate has just taken him in free.' Pina understood instantly, and drew back a step in consternation.

'If you mean to stay here, you must pay in advance,' continued the host, 'for your master has taken all the luggage with him. Perhaps he expects to spend some time with the Legate.' 'But we have no money of our own!' Pina cried in great distress. 'What are we to do?' 'That is your affair,' answered the innkeeper. 'You have had your night's lodging from me, and that is all you will get for nothing; so, unless you can pay, take your mistress somewhere else.'

Pina bent her head, and went upstairs without more words. A quarter of an hour later she and Ortensia left the inn, with the hoods of their brown cloaks drawn over their heads. The young girl leaned on her nurse's arm, and walked unsteadily.

Their worldly possessions, besides the clothes they wore, consisted of a piece of Castile soap, a comb, and Pina's work-case.

CHAPTER VIII

The Nuncio departed amidst a tremendous clatter of hoofs and rumbling of wheels, after being accompanied to his coach by the Legate of Ferrara himself. The second coach was occupied by his chaplains, and a third by his body-servants; in his own he took only his secretary; each vehicle carried a part of his voluminous luggage. After the coaches rode the footmen, mounted on all sorts of beasts, such as could be had, but wearing good liveries and all well armed. A dozen papal troopers commanded by a sergeant brought up the rear.

The wizened little Legate bowed to the ground as the noisy procession started, for though he wore a clerical dress he was only a layman, and the Nuncio was Archbishop of Kerasund, 'in partibus infidelium,' and returned the Governor's salutations with a magnificent benediction from the window of his coach. The papal halberdiers of the castle, all drawn up in line outside the moat, saluted by laying their long halberds to the left at a sharp angle.

The Legate put on his three-cornered hat as the escort trotted away after the coaches, and he stood rubbing his hands and watching the fast-disappearing procession of travellers, while the guard formed in double file and awaited his pleasure, ready to follow him in.

He had scarcely reached middle age, but he looked like a dried-up little old man, with his wrinkled face, his small red eyes, and his withered hands. No one who did not know him would have taken him to be the tremendous personage he really was in Ferrara, invested with full powers to represent his sovereign master, Pope Clement the Tenth; or rather the Pope's adopted 'nephew,' who was not his nephew at all, Cardinal Paluzzo Altieri, the real and visible power in Rome. The truth was that the aged Pontiff was almost bedridden and was scarcely ever seen, and he was only too glad to be relieved of all care and responsibility.

Monsignor Pelagatti, for that was the Legate's name, was a man of no distinguished extraction; indeed, it would be more true to say that he had extracted himself from his original surroundings. For it was by dint of laudable hard work as well as by virtue of certain useful gifts of mind and character that he had raised himself above his family to a really important position. It was commonly said in Rome that his father had been a highway robber and his mother a washerwoman, and that his brother was even now a footman in service; but it is quite possible that the Roman gossips knew more of his people than he did, seeing that he had declined to have anything to do with his family ever since he had got his first place as assistant steward in the Paluzzo household, before that family had been adopted and had received the name of Altieri from the Pope; and this is all that need be said about his beginnings for the present.

In due time he went upstairs again, installed himself behind the long oak table in his office, and took up the business of the day. A brown wooden crucifix stood before him, and at the foot of it was placed his large leaden inkstand, well provided with pens, ink, and red sand for blotting. At each end of the table sat a clerk; of these two, one was an untidy old man with a weary face and snuff-stained fingers, the other was a particularly spruce young fellow, with smug pink cheeks and carefully trimmed nails. The room had one high window to the north, from which a cold and dreary light fell upon the table and the three men.

The Legate proceeded to transact current business, receiving in turn a number of officials and citizens who came of their own accord, or were summoned, for various reasons, mostly connected with the revenue. When he had dismissed them all, more or less satisfied or dissatisfied, as the papal interests required, he ordered the officer at the door to send for the prisoner who had been taken at the inn that morning.

'Let us see this famous Sicilian coiner,' he said, rubbing his hands and screwing up his little red eyes. 'Bring up his effects, too, and send for a goldsmith with his touchstone and acids.'

He leaned back in his high chair to wait, and mentally ran over the questions he meant to ask. The shabby old clerk took snuff, and sprinkled a liberal quantity of it on his spotted black clothes and on the edge of the paper before him. His colleague at the other end occupied himself in improving the point of his quill pen. In the silence, a huge spotted cat sprang upon the table and calmly seated itself upright beside the crucifix, facing the Legate, who paid no attention whatever to it. From time to time it blinked and slowly moved the yellow tip of its tail.

Presently Stradella was led in by the gaoler and his assistant. On his wrists there were manacles, joined with each other by a strong chain which was highly polished by constant use. He was bare-headed, of course, and he seemed perfectly cool and self-possessed. Immediately after him, two men entered bringing his luggage, which was set down on the floor before the table. The cat did not even turn to look at the people who had entered.

'What is your name?' asked the Legate, eyeing him sharply.

'Alessandro Stradella.'

Instead of writing down the answer the two clerks looked at their superior for instructions.

'His name is Bartolo,' the Legate said, in a decided tone.

'By your worship's leave, my name is Stradella,' protested the musician.

'You may note that this fellow Bartolo persists in calling himself Stradella,' said the Legate, looking first at one clerk and then at the other.

'I am not Bartolo!' cried the musician indignantly. 'I am Alessandro Stradella, the singer, well known to hundreds of people in Rome.'

'You see how he persists,' answered the Legate with an ironical smile. 'Write down what he says as correctly as you can.'

Stradella saw that it was useless to protest, and that vehemence might be dangerous.

'By your leave,' he said more quietly, 'if you will loosen my hands and let me have my lute there, I will prove what I say, by singing and playing to you.'

'Anybody can sing,' retorted Monsignor Pelagatti with profound contempt, and without even looking at him. 'Write down that he has insulted this tribunal by offering to sing to the Legate and his clerks—which low jesting is contempt of court, and nothing else. The man is either drunk or insane.'

Stradella was speechless with anger and disgust, and his face grew very pale.

'Open his effects,' the Legate said, when the clerks' pens stopped moving.

Two of the sbirri at once unstrapped the valises, and laid out the contents on the long table on each side of the Legate, neatly and in order. One of the bags contained clothes and personal effects, but the other was almost entirely filled with manuscript compositions and a supply of paper ruled for writing music. It also contained a leathern pouch stuffed full of gold ducats.

'There we have it!' exclaimed Monsignor Pelagatti. 'Is the goldsmith come?'

'He is waiting, your worship,' answered the officer at the door.

The goldsmith was ushered in, a grey-haired man, who still stooped when he had finished his bow to the Legate. The latter ordered him to sit at the table and test the gold coins one by one.

'This fellow,' said Monsignor Pelagatti, by way of explanation, 'is the famous Sicilian coiner of counterfeit money, Bartolo. Push the good ducats towards me, if you find any, and the false coin towards the clerk at your elbow.'

The goldsmith glanced curiously at Stradella, and then took his small block of basalt and a stoneware bottle of nitric acid from a leathern bag he carried, slung on his arm. The spotted cat seemed interested in these objects, and after having gazed at them placidly for half a minute, rose with deliberation, walked along the edge of the table, and sniffed at the stone and the goldsmith's fingers. It then crossed to the Legate and sat down on his left, surveying the prisoner with apparent satisfaction.

The Legate's eyes followed with keen interest the operations of the expert, who took one coin after another from the pouch, rubbed it on the basalt, poured a drop of acid on the yellow mark made by the gold, and then examined the wet spot closely to see how the colour changed; and he shook his head each time and pushed ducat after ducat towards Monsignor Pelagatti, but not a single one towards the clerk. The Legate's crooked fingers played absently with the coins as they came to his side, arranging them in little piles, and the piles in patterns, almost without glancing at them. The goldsmith worked quickly, but the ducats were many, for Stradella had supplied himself plentifully with money before leaving Venice, and had drawn the whole balance of the letter of credit he had brought with him from the banking-house of Chigi in Rome.

The sbirri and the two clerks eyed the gold longingly. Stradella stood motionless between his keepers, wondering what would happen next, and never doubting but that the whole proceeding had been inspired by Pignaver.

But what had really happened can be explained in a dozen words, and will show that the sharp little Legate was acting in perfectly good faith. The truth was that a notorious Sicilian counterfeiter who was described as a pale young man with black hair, and who went by the name of Bartolo, was really travelling in the north of Italy, and had been heard of at Vicenza, whence it was reported that he had set out in haste for Padua. The spies who were in pursuit of him learned in the latter city that a dark young man with a pale complexion had hired an extra post for Rovigo, in a very great hurry, and was spending money liberally, and after that it had been easy to trace Stradella to the inn at Ferrara. One of the spies had ridden in before daybreak and had warned the innkeeper not to let the musician have horses at any price, and had then given information at the castle, which the Legate had received before sunrise, for he was an early riser. For the rest, he always followed the time-honoured custom of considering every prisoner guilty till he was proved innocent. In his opinion any criminal could call himself a singer, and could very likely sing, too, if his life depended upon it. Moreover, a hundred gold Apostolic florins had been offered for the capture of Bartolo, and the Legate meant to have a share of the prize money.

By the time the goldsmith had tested all the coins and found these good, Monsignor Pelagatti had also counted them over several times.

'Three hundred and ninety-one ducats,' he said, dictating to the clerks, 'were found amongst the criminal's possessions, and were confiscated to the Papal Treasury.'

'But they are all good,' objected Stradella.

'Precisely,' answered the Legate. 'If anything was wanting to prove you guilty, it was this fact. Could any one but an expert counterfeiter have in his possession three hundred and ninety-one ducats without a single false one, in these dishonest days? But a coiner, whose nefarious business it is to exchange counterfeit coin for genuine, is not to be deceived like an ordinary person.'

'But I drew the money from an honest bank in Venice——'

'Silence!' cried the Legate in a squeaky voice.

'Silence!' roared the gaolers and the sbirri with one accord, all looking at the musician together.

The spotted cat rose sleepily at the noise, arched its back and clawed the oak table, by way of stretching itself.

'The counterfeiter Bartolo is duly committed for trial and will be sent to Rome in chains with the next convoy of prisoners,' said the Legate, dictating. 'Till then,' he added, speaking to the officer, 'put him into one of the cells at the foot of the Lion Tower. He is a criminal of some note.'

It was worse than useless to attempt any further protest; the gaolers seized the singer by his arms again, one on each side, and in ten minutes he was left to his own reflections, locked up in a pitch-dark cell that smelt like a wet grave. They had brought a lantern with them, and had shown him a stone seat, long enough to lie down upon, and at one end of it there was a loose block of sandstone for a pillow, a luxury which had been provided for a political prisoner who had passed some months in the cell under the last of the Este marquises, some eighty years earlier, and which had doubtless been forgotten.

After he had been some time in the dark, Stradella saw that a very feeble glimmer was visible through a square grated opening which he had noticed in the door when the gaoler was unlocking it before entering. Even that would be some comfort, but the unlucky musician was too utterly overcome to think of anything but Ortensia's danger, and his own fate sank to insignificance when compared with hers; for he was sure that Pignaver's agents must have seized her as soon as he himself had been taken away, and he dared not think of what would happen when they brought her back to Venice and delivered her up to her uncle. That they would murder the defenceless girl he did not believe, and besides, it was much more likely that Pignaver would prefer to torment her to death at his leisure, after assassinating her lover. Stradella guessed as much as that from what he knew of the Senator's character.

As for himself, when he was able to reflect soberly after being several hours alone in the dark, the singer came to the conclusion that he was in no immediate danger of his life, though he owed his present imprisonment to his enemy. It looked as if he stood a good chance of being sent to Rome, as Bartolo the counterfeiter, to be tried; but once there, he would have no difficulty in obtaining his liberation, for he was well known to many distinguished persons, including Cardinal Altieri himself. Pignaver had cleverly cut short his flight in order to take Ortensia from him, but to accomplish this the Senator had been obliged to put off the murder he doubtless contemplated. Stradella's life would probably be attempted in Rome, as soon as he was free, but meanwhile he could not but admit that the Senator had succeeded in making him exceedingly uncomfortable, merely from a material point of view. It was not likely that prisoners were sent to Rome more than once a month, and the last convoy had perhaps left yesterday. He might have to spend thirty days in the cell.

As the hours passed he forgot himself again, and thought only of Ortensia. In his imagination he fancied her already far on her way to Rovigo in the jolting coach with her captors; in the very coach, perhaps, in which he had brought her to Ferrara only last night. He called up her face, and saw it as pale as death; her eyes were half closed and her lips sharp-drawn with pain. He could hardly bear to think of her suffering, but not to think of her he could not bear at all.

He did not know how long he had been locked up, when he noticed that the faint glimmer at the grated hole was almost gone, and suddenly he felt horribly hungry, in spite of his misery, for it was nearly twenty-four hours since he had tasted food. The gaolers had brought a little bread and a jug of water, and had set them down on the ground at one end of the bench. He felt about till he found them, and he gnawed the tough crust voraciously, though it tasted of the damp earth on which it had lain since morning.

After a long time he fell asleep with the stone pillow under his head.

CHAPTER IX

Cucurullo came back to the inn in less than an hour after Pina and Ortensia had left it. In spite of the asseverations of the innkeeper, he had found that there were horses to be had in plenty in the city, and that it was merely a question of choice and of paying well for the accommodation. He was hastening upstairs to tell this to Stradella when he was stopped by the host himself, who informed him that Stradella was imprisoned in the castle, and that the lady and her serving-woman had just gone away on foot.

'You had better melt away yourself,' the innkeeper concluded in a confidential tone, 'unless you wish to be clapped into prison too.'

Cucurullo had betrayed no surprise at what the host told him, and he did not seem inclined to pay any immediate attention to the latter's advice, though it was distinctly friendly. He was used to that, for few Italians would care to incur the hatred of a hunch-backed man, who is supposed to bring good luck to those who treat him well, and to dispose of the mysterious curses of the Evil Eye for wreaking vengeance on those who injure him. Cucurullo stood still on the stairs, in deep thought, after the innkeeper had ceased speaking.

'What is the name of the Legate?' he inquired, looking up at last.

'Pelagatti,' answered the other. 'He is from the South, they say; though, between you and me, he looks more like a rat than a Christian. Monsignor Luigi Pelagatti, that is his name.'

Again Cucurullo was silent, apparently more absorbed in his thoughts than ever.

'Come, come!' cried the innkeeper in an encouraging tone. 'You need not be so down-hearted! I will have a good meal cooked for you, and if you need a little ready money for your journey, it is at your disposal. A clever fellow like you will soon find another place.'

By way of laying in a sk of luck for the day, he patted the deformed man's hump as he spoke, but he awaited the answer with evident concern, for it was fortunate to have a hunch-backed man eat and drink in one's house; a hunch-backed woman, on the contrary, always brought evil with her, and should be driven from the door.

Cucurullo's reply was not only of favourable omen, but announced a piece of unexpected good-fortune.

'You are very obliging,' he said, 'and I shall be glad of a mouthful at noon. As for your kind offer to lend me money, I thank you heartily, but I am well provided, and wish to pay my master's bill here before accepting your friendly offer of a dinner. My master always trusts me with a few ducats to pay his small expenses.'

The innkeeper congratulated himself on having patted the man's hump, for it was clear that the good luck which at once befell him could be traced to no other source. He now inwardly cursed his haste in turning Ortensia and Pina out of the house, since Cucurullo was perhaps in a position to have paid their score for some time. Of this, however, the host could not be quite sure, for the serving-man did not show his purse, but only produced some loose silver from the pocket of his wide brown breeches.

'I shall charge nothing for the lady's use of the room,' said the innkeeper magnanimously. 'You came with three horses from Rovigo, I believe; there is their feed, and the supper of the postillion, who left in an hour. That is all. Three pauls will pay for everything.'

'You are very obliging,' Cucurullo said again, as he paid the money. 'Your charges are very moderate. Since you act in such a friendly manner, I will tell you something.'

Thereupon Cucurullo laid one of his large hands gently on the innkeeper's sleeve, and looked up earnestly into the latter's face; and when he was very much in earnest, his large blue eyes had a peculiar expression, which lent great weight to what he said.

'A friendly act deserves a friendly return,' he said, 'for, as we say in the South, "one hand washes the other and both wash the face." My master has been arrested by mistake. He is really and truly the famous Maestro Stradella, and is a great favourite with the Roman Court, for he has sung to His Holiness himself and often to His Eminence Cardinal Altieri. Therefore, if any harm comes to him in Ferrara through the ignorance of Monsignor Pelagatti, there will be trouble for you, since the Legate will be severely reprimanded, and will make those persons who gave him wrong information pay for his scolding. As you have shown me kindness, I tell you these things beforehand, because I know them for certain. Do you understand?'

The innkeeper not only understood, but began to feel uncomfortable at the thought of being called to account even for his small share in Stradella's arrest. As for the spy who had made the mistake, his lot would not be enviable if he was within the Legate's reach when the error was discovered.

'Pardon the question, my dear friend,' said the host in an extremely gentle tone, 'but are you quite sure of these things?'

'Altogether sure,' was the answer. 'I have been in the Maestro's service since he first began to be famous. He saved my life at the risk of his own, and I have served him five years come the Feast of Saint John. I therefore know that he is not a Sicilian counterfeiter! If you have any means of reaching the Legate, therefore, it would be well to set him right at once in this matter. He will be the more grateful, or, at least, the less angry, if my master is detained in prison for a few hours only.'

The innkeeper saw the wisdom of this, on the supposition that Cucurullo was speaking the truth, but of that he was not quite sure. It was a bad world, he reflected, and the counterfeiter might have a clever hunchback for a servant, with a knack of fixing his eyes as Cucurullo did, and of putting great earnestness into his tone. So far, the innkeeper had only done what the law had required of him, except in the matter of turning out two women who could not pay for their lodging, and in doing this the law would support him. Monsignor Pelagatti was a tremendous personage, who ruled the whole Marquisate of Ferrara in the name of the Pope; he knew his business, or believed he did, and it was absurd to think that a humble innkeeper and posting-master could influence him to act upon the mere word of a serving-man.

On the other hand, it was unsafe to doubt a hunchback openly, and it would be fatal to quarrel with him, because he could cast the spell of the Evil Eye.

'I shall do my best,' the innkeeper replied, 'and far more readily for your sake, my dear friend, than for my own, I assure you.'

Cucurullo smiled quietly, and seemed quite satisfied with this answer. He now went on to ask questions about Ortensia and Pina, but the host knew nothing, except that they had left the house together, immediately after the arrest of Stradella. For obvious reasons he said nothing of his interview with Pina. He declared that they had simply left the inn, and that he had not hindered them. He had not seen them go out, and could not tell whether they had turned to the north or the south. He suggested that since they had gone away at once and without the least hesitation, they probably had friends in Ferrara to whom they could turn for protection and help in their difficulty. He was ready, he said, to help Cucurullo to find them out; he would be only too happy to be of use.

What he suggested was not unlikely. During the flight from Venice, Cucurullo had observed Pina closely, and had come to the conclusion that she was a woman of resources, who had travelled much at some time or other, and who could hold her tongue. She would certainly think of some expedient, and would succeed in placing her mistress under some sort of protection. His own mind always instinctively ran in the direction of an ecclesiastical solution of any difficulty in life; if he himself were starving and friendless in a strange city he would knock at the door of a Franciscan monastery and beg for shelter and work. He therefore concluded that Pina would naturally have taken Ortensia directly to a convent, where they would both be cared for; the serving-woman would take care to be informed of what happened to Stradella, and as soon as he was let out she would communicate with him.

Moreover, as compared with the fate of the musician, Cucurullo cared little what became of Ortensia; for his devotion to his master filled his whole life, whereas the young girl's only claim to his attachment was that Stradella was in love with her. On the other hand, the pious serving-man saw in the present separation of the two a special intervention of Providence for the purpose of keeping the lovers apart till they could be duly and properly married. From this point of view to putting Ortensia out of his thoughts altogether was only a step, and he devoted every energy to the liberation of his master.

Having come to this conclusion in a much shorter time than it has taken to explain his reasons, he again thanked his new friend, promising to come back for dinner at noon, and adding that he would go over to the castle gate and gather such information as he could. He was hindered from doing so at once, however, by the preparations for the Nuncio's departure, which has been already described. He mixed with the crowd that had gathered to see the sight, and waited till some time had elapsed after the Legate and the guard had gone in before he approached the drawbridge.

The single sentinel had now returned to his beat, but half-a-dozen of the halberdiers were loitering about the door of the guard-room within the deep archway, at some distance from the gate. The sentry stopped Cucurullo and asked his business.

'I am the servant of the gentleman who has been arrested by mistake at the inn,' the hunchback answered humbly. 'My master had sent me out on an errand, and when I came in I learnt the news. So I have come to wait for him.'

'I am afraid you may wait long,' answered the sentry, with a friendly glance at Cucurullo's hump; 'but you are welcome to sit in the guard-room, if you like.'

'Thank you,' Cucurullo answered, and as he passed he felt the soldier's light touch on his crooked back.

The other halberdiers received him with equal kindness, and there was not one of them who did not believe that he would have a stroke of luck before night, if he could by any means touch the magic hump without offending its possessor. Cucurullo took off his hat civilly as he stopped before them.

'Good-morning, gentlemen,' he said. 'The sentinel was kind enough to say that I might wait here for my master, who has been arrested by mistake and will soon come out.'

'And welcome!' cried the sergeant on duty, who had lost money at play on the previous evening.

'At your service! Pray sit down! Bring out a chair!'

The men all spoke together, and gathered closely round Cucurullo to touch his hump, so that he almost disappeared amongst them. Then they got a chair from the guard-room and made him sit down at his ease, and some remained standing beside him while others sat on the end of the stone seat that ran along the wall. He thanked them warmly, and at once entered into conversation, asking for news of Stradella, and explaining the strange mistake that had led to his arrest. In a few minutes he had learned that his master was in all likelihood at that very moment before the Legate.

'And what sort of person is his worship, the Governor?' asked Cucurullo, anxious for information, and lowering his voice.

The sergeant was a jolly, red-faced, merry-eyed man from the March of Ancona, and he laughed before he answered.

'We used to call him Pontius Pilate, because he does not know what truth is,' he said, 'but we gave that up because he never washes his hands!'

Cucurullo smiled at the rough jest, but he looked curiously at the speaker.

'I see that you are familiar with the Scriptures, sir,' observed the hunchback.

'I come by the knowledge honestly,' answered the soldier. 'I did not steal it! My father, bless his soul, was killed in battle, and so my mother tried to make a priest of me. Eh? You see me as I am! This is the kind of priest my mother made! Neither more nor less than a poor sergeant of halberdiers. But a little of the Latin stuck to me, for indeed it is sticky stuff enough, and the priests laid it on with a stick!'

The men roared with delight at their superior's elegant wit, and Cucurullo laughed a little too, more out of politeness than because he was amused.

'You may yet die a saint, sir,' he said with a grave smile when the general mirth had subsided. 'Many of the saints were soldiers, you know. There was the blessed Saint Eustace, and there was Saint Martin, and Saint Sebastian, and Saint George——'

'But there never was a Saint Hector, and that is my name, at your service.'

At this retort the men again showed their delight, laughing in chorus.

'Do you think you have no chance of being the first Saint Hector in the calendar?' asked Cucurullo pleasantly. 'Why not? You have a good heart, sir. I see it in your face, if you will pardon me for saying so. Gentlemen'—he smilingly appealed to the other men—'has not Sergeant Hector a good heart?'

'A heart of gold!' cried one of the soldiers.

'A heart as big as a pumpkin!' another chimed in.

'A lion's heart!'

'There is not another like him in all the Pope's army!'

'And God bless him!'

The sergeant stood back, pretending to put on a terrible frown, and cutting the air in carte and tierce with his handsome tasselled stick.

'You ruffians!' he roared. 'You know well enough that I would beat you all black and blue if you did not praise me seventeen times a day, four times for each watch and once more for good luck! Eh?' He glared ferociously about him, and his stick flew round in his hand like lightning, through a whole series of cuts, feints, and round parries. 'Have I trained my men well or not?' he asked, desisting at last, and turning to Cucurullo.

'You have trained them to tell the truth about you, sir, I have no doubt,' answered the hunchback.

'And we will make a bad day of it for any man who says a word against him,' said the biggest of the halberdiers with a grin.

The rest confirmed his statement with a variety of asseverations, according to their several tastes, calling to witness indifferently both heathen deities and Christian saints.

'Very well,' said Cucurullo. 'It is proved that you have a very good heart, sir, and that is the chief thing needed to make a saint. For to say that a man is kind-hearted is only another way of saying that he is charitable, and Charity is the greatest of the three Theological Virtues, as you must have learned at the seminary.'

'Good friend,' answered the sergeant, 'if you are going to open the "Process" concerning my Beatification this morning, the Devil's Advocate must be appointed to argue against you and try to prove me the worst of sinners, for that is the rule in Rome.'

'Very well, sir,' laughed the hunchback. 'Appoint him yourself, sir!'

'He is upstairs just now,' retorted the other, 'sitting in judgment on your master! But I will promise that if you argue with him about me, he will prove that my soul is rotting in original and acquired sin, and that nothing can save me but cutting my pay!'

Again the gloomy archway rang with the soldiers' hoarse laughter, which was by no means the expression of obsequious flattery. The sergeant was more than popular with the whole company of halberdiers that garrisoned the castle; he was beloved for his inexhaustible good-nature and respected for his undoubted courage. Cucurullo had guessed this in a few moments, and in view of possible complications he was resolved to make an ally of the sergeant and friends of the men.

He felt amongst the loose silver in his pocket and jingled it in a manner agreeable for poor soldiers to hear.

'It is still early,' he said, 'but talking always makes me thirsty. If you would allow some one to fetch some drink, sir, I should be grateful.'

The sergeant assented to the proposal with alacrity, and at his nod a young soldier stepped briskly forward to take the piece of silver Cucurullo was holding up.

'How much shall I fetch?' asked the man, grinning.

Cucurullo counted the company quickly before he answered.

'We are nine,' he said. 'I think you had better get nine pints in a stoup.' A little murmur of approval and anticipatory satisfaction ran round. 'I do not know whether that is right,' he added, in a tone of hesitating interrogation.

'You speak the wisdom of all ages,' answered the sergeant. 'Solomon never said anything better. "Take a little wine for the good of the stomach," says Saint Paul.'

So the time passed pleasantly for the soldiers down there under the great gate, while Monsignor Pelagatti was conducting his singular judicial proceedings upstairs. A couple of horn cups were produced from the guard-room, and the men drank to Cucurullo's health in turn, while he himself swallowed a little; for he was tired, and he was terribly anxious, in spite of his cheerful manner and jesting tone.

They were all laughing and talking together when the old goldsmith appeared from within, on his way home. The sergeant hailed him and asked what news of the counterfeiter there was from the Legate's court.

'Three hundred and ninety-one good gold ducats confiscated to the Treasury,' answered the grey-haired crafts-man, 'and the prisoner to be lodged under the Lion Tower till he is sent to Rome for trial.'

The sergeant looked at Cucurullo, and saw that he grew paler, and dead white all round the lips; but the hunchback showed no other sign of emotion, and the goldsmith nodded gravely and went out.

'This is bad news, gentlemen,' said Cucurullo. 'Is there any way by which I could send a message to my master?' he asked in a low voice.

'Either of the turnkeys would sell his soul for a dodkin, and blow up the castle for a ducat, Legate and all,' answered the sergeant in the same tone.

'I would willingly give a ducat if I might see my master.'

'I will bargain with him for half that, but it will have to be after dark. We go off duty at Ave Maria this evening, but to-morrow we have the night watch. Come about the first hour of the night, and you will find the little postern ajar in the left half of the gate. Push it open and come in.'

With this friendly promise Cucurullo had to be satisfied; and, indeed, he had good reason to congratulate himself, for if he had chanced upon one of the other sergeants he might have had a very different reception, though the whole garrison hated the Legate heartily. The guard for the month at the main gate was divided into three watches that took turns, being on duty there for twelve hours and off for twenty-four; this did not mean, however, that they were at liberty during all that time, for there was other sentry duty to be done about the castle.

Having taken leave of his new friends, the hunchback went back to the inn, debating with himself whether he should remain there until the following night, or seek a lodging in a more remote and quiet part of the town. But, on the whole, he resolved to trust the innkeeper—or it would be nearer the truth to say that he trusted to the power his deformity exercised over a man in whom he would not otherwise have placed much confidence. If he took a room elsewhere, he would be forced to make acquaintance with the owners of the house, and he was convinced that such a Governor as Monsignor Pelagatti must have his spies everywhere; it was safer to stay where he was already known, and was looked upon as a bringer of luck, than to go where he might find less superstitious people.

He therefore took the cheapest room in the inn, announced his intention of waiting till his master was set free, and by way of inspiring confidence he paid for three days' lodging in advance. His object in seeing Stradella was to get definite instructions in the first place, and, secondly, to take him a dish of meat and a supply of such food as would keep some time without spoiling. Stradella would probably bid him ride post to Rome and bring back an order from Cardinal Altieri which would set everything right; but it would scarcely be possible to cover the distance and return in less than ten days, at the very least, during which time it was only too probable that the musician would fall ill from lack of food and from the possible dampness and closeness of his prison.

The hours passed slowly enough in the solitude of the little upper room in which Cucurullo spent most of that day and the next, and the intervening night; for he thought it wiser not to be seen much in the town, being what he was, a mark for men's eyes wherever he went. He would have read if he could have found a book, for he was a good reader and writer, and often copied music for his master, for he could engross handsomely; but there were no books in the inn, not even the works of that 'poor Signor Torquato Tasso,' who had been so long shut up as a lunatic in Ferrara in the days of the Marquis Alfonso Second. The only book Cucurullo had been able to find was a small volume with a very strange name, for its title was *Eikon Basilike*; but Cucurullo did not understand a word of it, and the innkeeper said he thought the book must have been forgotten by two rich English gentlemen who had lately spent some days in his house.

At the appointed hour Cucurullo crossed the drawbridge of the castle, pushed the small postern, and went in. A hanging iron lamp, fed with mingled olive-oil and tallow, dimly lighted the great archway, where the sentry was pacing up and down. Sergeant Hector came forward as soon as the hunchback appeared, and closed and bolted the postern after him before speaking. The other men of the watch were presumably dozing in the guard-room, from the open door of which no light appeared.

'This way, my dear friend,' whispered the sergeant. 'The man is waiting.'

He hurried Cucurullo along the dark way towards the inner court, laying a hand on his crooked back by way of guiding him; but the truth was that since he had met Cucurullo his luck at play had been surprisingly good, and he would not miss the chance of refreshing it again at the magic source of fortune.

They passed the foot of the main staircase, went on a few steps farther, and then turned into a narrow passage. The glare of a lantern flashed in Cucurullo's eyes.

'Here is the gentleman,' the sergeant said in a low voice. 'This is our head gaoler,' he added, turning to Cucurullo. 'I have agreed that you should pay three silver florins in advance for the visit.'

'Cash,' said a voice that was unnaturally hoarse, possibly from the dampness of the underground labyrinth to which the man's business often took him.

Cucurullo was wrapped in his wide cloak, under which he had slung on himself the bottles and provisions he was bringing. He had prepared some loose money in his breeches pocket, and immediately produced the three coins. The turnkey was holding the lantern in such a position that it was impossible to see his face, but a grimy hand shot out into the yellow glare to take the money.

'Come,' said the hoarse voice; and as the speaker turned to lead the way, Cucurullo heard the jingling of his keys.

The sergeant was already gone, and the hunchback followed his guide along the passage, which descended by a distinctly perceptible grade. It was clear from this that the prisons must be below the level of the water in the moat, and already the moving light showed that the walls were dripping with moisture. Presently the passage emerged into a sort of crypt, in which huge masses of masonry supported low arches that in turn carried the cross vaulting. The floor, if it was anything but beaten earth, was slippery with a thin film of greasy mud.

At last the turnkey stopped before one of half-a-dozen doors, all studded alike with rusty iron nails, and each having a lock, a bolt, and a square aperture at the height of a man's head, strongly barred. Cucurullo now saw the gaoler's ugly features for the first time.

The door opened, creaking loudly on its hinges; and as the turnkey held up his lantern to see into the cell, Cucurullo, peering past him, caught sight of his master's face. It was ghastly pale, his sunken eyes had dark half-circles under them, and his unshaven chin and cheeks looked grimy in the yellow light.

'Is it morning?' he asked, in a dull voice.

Cucurullo slipped past the gaoler and spoke to him, and instantly the light flashed in his eyes and he smiled, for the first time since he had been arrested in Ortensia's room. Cucurullo took his hand and kissed it with devotion, as Italian servants often do in great moments.

Neither had yet spoken when the heavy door creaked and was slammed, and they were suddenly in the dark. The key turned noisily in the lock, twice in quick succession, and the additional bolt rattled as it was pushed into its socket.

'Good-night, gentlemen,' said the preternaturally hoarse voice of the turnkey through the square hole in the door. 'I will bring you your dinner at noon!'

Cucurullo sprang to the grated aperture, only to see the ruffian stalking off into the gloom with his lantern.

'Hi! Listen!' he cried. 'Come back, Sir Gaoler! You shall have a ducat———'

The man stood still, and turned his face towards the door of the cell with a sardonic grin.

'Now that I have you and your ducats under lock and key I shall take them at my leisure, Sir Fool!' he answered. 'I only agreed to let you in; I did not promise to let you out.'

Thereupon he turned again and stalked away, much to Cucurullo's consternation; and in this manner the fourth and last of the runaway party that had arrived at the inn from Rovigo disappeared in Ferrara, somewhat to the surprise of the innkeeper, but not to his loss, since Cucurullo had paid for his lodging in advance.

CHAPTER X

Stradella and Ortensia had fled from Venice on Thursday evening and had reached Ferrara at midnight on Friday. It was therefore on a Saturday morning that the musician was imprisoned, and on Sunday night Cucurullo was caught in the trap and locked up with him. It was late on that same afternoon that the Bravi took leave of Pignaver in the church of the Frari, and they did not leave Venice till the next day; for since they were to be paid for their time they could really not see any reason for being in a hurry. Moreover, they travelled like gentlemen, and though the proceeds of the emerald ring had already amply furnished them with the means of replacing many useful articles which adversity had forced them to sell or pawn, yet some further preparation seemed necessary, if they were to make their journey in a manner becoming to their rank.

As for travelling night and day, that was quite out of the question, for they would have thought it very foolish to trust implicitly to the information about the runaways which Pignaver had got from the Venetian police. Where such grave responsibility was laid upon them, it was right that they should rely only on what they themselves could learn with certainty. The consequence was that they did not reach Ferrara till Wednesday afternoon, having spent a night in Padua and another in Rovigo; and they were of course persuaded that Stradella and Ortensia were by that time already in Florence, if they had taken that direction.

So far, the Bravi had only spoken of their business when it was necessary to compare notes about the information they gathered. Having undertaken to murder both the lovers on the one hand, but also to deliver both of them safe and unhurt, Ortensia to the Senator and Stradella to the enamoured lady, the subject presented certain complications which were too tiresome to discuss until a final decision became necessary; and for that matter, Trombin and Gambardella fully intended to obtain the full five hundred ducats from each side.

'You and I were certainly meant to be lawyers or bankers,' Trombin had observed at Rovigo over a bottle of very old Burgundy; 'for whichever of two cards turns up, we must win half the stakes.'

'Both must turn up at the end of the deal,' Gambardella had answered with decision, 'and we must win everything.'

'Under Providence,' Trombin had replied, 'we will.'

Having said this much they had dismissed the subject, and their conversation during the rest of the evening had been of artistic matters, politics, literature, women's beauty, and whatsoever else two tolerably cultivated gentlemen might discuss with propriety in the presence and hearing of a landlord and his servants. As soon as they had arrived, they had learned without difficulty that the runaway party had passed through the place and had safely reached Ferrara, whence the carriage they had hired in Padua had duly returned.

The Bravi preferred to ride post, sending their luggage on with their servant, six or seven hours in advance of them. The serving-man they had hired in Venice had been a highway robber for several years, as they were well aware, and in an ordinary situation he might have made away with his masters' valuables, if entrusted with them; but he knew who Trombin and Gambardella were, and what they had done, and his admiration for such very superior cut-throats was boundless. Anything of theirs was safe in his hands, and therefore safe from robbers on the road, for he had not long retired from the profession, and had the thieves' pass-words by heart from Milan to Naples, and farther. As a servant, he had parted his hair in the middle and resumed his modest and unobtrusive baptismal name of Tommaso; but he had always been known to the gang as Grattacacio, that is, 'Cheese-grater,' because it was told of him that he had once done good execution with that simple kitchen instrument on the nose of a sbirro who had tried to catch him, but was himself caught instead.

The worthy courier arrived at the inn in Ferrara on Wednesday before noon and took the best room in the house for his masters, who, he said, would arrive at their convenience during the afternoon; as in fact they did, looking very magnificent in fashionable long-skirted riding-coats buttoned tight across the chest and under the broad linen collar, high-crowned felt hats with magnificent feathers, boots of the new fashion, cut off below the knee, and handsome silver chains instead of shoulder-belts for their rapiers.

Grattacacio had announced them as two Venetian gentlemen travelling for their pleasure, and when the innkeeper asked their names, the man answered that they had received titles of nobility from the King of France, and were called respectively Count Tromblon de la Trombine and Count Gambardella. When in Venice, he said, they dropped these appellations and took their seats in the Grand Council as nobles of the Republic. For the rest, Grattacacio continued, they were gentlemen of exquisite taste and most fastidious in their eating and drinking. Burgundy was their favourite wine, and they could not drink French claret if it was more than twelve or less than eight years old. They abhorred the sweet Malmsey which the Tuscans were so fond of, but if there was any old Oporto in the cellar they were connoisseurs and could appreciate it.

The landlord received them with all the respect due to such a noble pair of epicures, and long before they arrived preparations were making in the kitchen to cook them a dinner worthy of their refined taste and portentous appetites.

So far as their other pretensions went, they had really seen some service in the French Army, but their highest title to distinction was that they had narrowly escaped being hanged for selling information to the Dutch, and as soon as they had fled it was discovered that they had taken with them all the loose gold in the regimental chest, and the two fleetest horses in the Field-Marshal's stable.

The landlord, who did not know this, bowed to the ground as they dismounted under the archway, and at once led them to the best rooms, with which they expressed themselves well satisfied. For whatever their real names might be, they had been originally brought up as gentlemen, and they did not abuse everything that was offered them in order to make innkeepers believe that they lived magnificently at home. When they saw that they were given the best there was to be had, no matter how poor that might be, they accepted it quietly and said 'Thank you' without more ado; but if they perceived that the best was being withheld for some one else, they were a particularly troublesome pair of gentlemen to deal with; for nothing abashed them, and nothing seemed to frighten them, and they were always as ready to beat an innkeeper as to skewer a marquis according to the most rigidly honourable rules of duelling. As for the law, it might as well not have existed, so far as they were concerned. They never needed it, and when it wanted them they were never to be found—unless they were under the powerful protection of a prince or an ambassador, of whom the law itself was very much afraid, and who promptly demanded for them a written pardon for their last offence. For those were the only conditions under which Bravi could have exercised their profession as they did throughout Italy in the seventeenth century.

Trombin detained the innkeeper a moment when he was about to leave the two to their toilet, after the day's ride.

'Some acquaintances of ours must have spent a night here last week,' Trombin began. 'Do you remember them? They were the celebrated Maestro Alessandro Stradella and his young Venetian wife. They have with them a middle-aged serving-woman. Can you recollect when they left here?'

The landlord scratched his head and pretended to be racking his memory; for it would have been quite easy to say that the party had left on Saturday, on their way to Bologna. That was the answer the gentleman expected, and the innkeeper generally found that it served best to tell people what they expected to hear. But, on the other hand, there was the question of truth, if not of truthfulness. Who could tell but that such fine gentlemen might have with them an introduction to the Legate, who might tell them the story. If this happened, the two travellers would be angry at having been deceived, since, if the imprisoned man was really Stradella, they would naturally wish to help him to regain his liberty.

This reflection carried the day; the innkeeper therefore decided in favour of truth, and he told the tale of Stradella's arrest, and of the mysterious disappearance of the other three members of the party. The two Bravi listened in silent surprise, glancing at each other from time to time, as if to note some point of importance.

'Something must be done at once!' cried Trombin, when the landlord had told all. 'This is an egregious miscarriage of the law! Something must be done at once!'

'Something must be done at once!' echoed Gambardella very emphatically, though in a much lower tone. 'Are you quite sure that you do not know where the lady went, Master Landlord? Or have you only forgotten?'

He had fixed his evil black eyes on the innkeeper's face, and there was something in his look and tone that suddenly scared the stout Romagnole, who was no great hero after all; he backed against the door as if he expected Gambardella to spring at him.

'Indeed, Signor Count,' he cried in a rather shaky voice, 'if it were my last word, I know nothing more of the lady and her woman! They left the house immediately, but I do not know whether they turned to the right or the left from my door, for I did not see them go out.'

'Have you made any inquiries in the town?' asked Gambardella in the same tone as before. 'No? Then you had better set about it at once. Do you understand? That young lady is the niece of a friend of ours, who is a Venetian Senator, and if any harm comes to her through your having allowed her to leave your house unprotected, you may be held responsible. I fancy that the Legate here must be anxious to oblige the Republic in such matters!'

This was no doubt arrant nonsense, but nothing seemed laughable when Gambardella assumed that tone.

'Something must be done at once!' cried Trombin, and turning suddenly to the landlord he opened his round blue eyes as wide as possible, and drew his breath sharply in through his pursed lips with a soft sound of whistling.

He looked like a colossal angry cat, and was at least as terrifying as Gambardella. The landlord faltered as he replied to both the Bravi at once.

'Certainly, my lords, certainly—I will have inquiries made—I will do my best—it was really not my fault——'

'It may not have been your intention, but it was, in a measure, your fault,' answered Trombin, allowing his expression to relax, 'though it may have been only a fault of omission, and therefore venial, which is to say, pardonable, Master Landlord, in proportion to the gravity of the consequences that may attend it. And now we will make ourselves ready for the succulent dinner which, I have no doubt, your wise care is about to set before us, for your house has an excellent name, but we would have you know that our appetites are at least as good, and our understanding of the noble art of cookery much better. It is not becoming to speak of any actions we may have to our past credit in war, but we can at least boast without reproach that we have eaten some of the best dinners cooked since Lucullus supped with himself!'

This tirade, delivered with the utmost rapidity and punctuated with several smiles that showed the speaker's sharp and gleaming teeth, partially reassured the innkeeper, who took himself off at once; and as he had been frightened he proceeded at once to restore his self-respect by frightening the cook, cuffing the scullions, and threatening the drawer with an awful end if he should shake the bottles and disturb the ancient sediment when he brought the Burgundy to the gentlemen's table.

When he was gone, the Bravi did not at once talk over the unexpected news, for Grattacacio was with them, coming and going, bringing hot water, shaving them as well as any barber, unpacking their linen and clothes, and waiting on them with such a constant prescience of their needs as only a highly trained body-servant can possess. For the truth was that he had begun life as a bishop's footman, and had risen to be valet to a cardinal, before he had taken to the road after robbing his master of some valuable jewels; but his hair was now growing grey at the temples, and his nerve was not so good as it had been, and as he had escaped hanging till now, he gave up risking it any longer. Accordingly he had parted his hair and called himself Tommaso once more, and he was now looking out for a good place with a not too decrepit prelate; for he had been used to boast that no valet in all the Roman Curia could put on a bishop's sandals at High Mass with such combined skill and unction as he, nor carry a cardinal's scarlet train at a consistory with such mingled devoutness and grace. As for serving Mass, it had been a second nature to him, and even now he could rattle off the responses without a mistake, from the first 'sicut erat in principio' to the last 'Deo gratias' after the Second Gospel.

Trombin and Gambardella did not discuss the situation until this highly accomplished servant of theirs had accompanied them to the dining-room, to push their chairs under them as they sat down, and to assure himself that the table-cloth was spotless and the glasses not only clean but polished. Then he left them to their dinner, which, as he well knew, would last at least two hours.

The dining-room was spacious and airy, having two large grated windows that overlooked the square, and there were several small tables besides the long one at which the 'ordinary' was served every day at noon. The Bravi were now the only guests, and were installed near one of the windows, for the day was warm. From the middle of the vaulted ceiling a huge bunch of fresh green ferns was hung, not as a substitute for flowers, but to attract and stupefy the stray flies that found their way in from the kitchen, even at that early season of the year.

Trombin was the first to speak, after the preliminary appetisers had been placed on the table and the glasses had been filled.

'The situation strikes me as amusing,' he said. 'I have always felt that destiny possesses a sense of humour which makes the wittiest French comedy lugubrious by comparison.'

'You are easily amused, my friend,' answered Gambardella gloomily, and picking out a very thin slice of Bologna sausage for his next mouthful. 'We were looking forward to a pleasant journey to Florence or Rome, our expenses being liberally paid; instead, we find that all the people we wish to meet are here, barely two days from Venice, and as if that were not enough, they must needs melt away like snow in the street and disappear underground, so that we must turn sbirri to find them. I see no sense of humour in the destiny that brings about such silly circumstances.'

'You were always a melancholic soul,' Trombin observed. 'As for me, I cannot but laugh when I think that we shall have to rescue our man from the danger of being hanged as a counterfeiter, in order that we may conveniently cut his throat.'

Having expressed his view of the case Trombin swallowed half a glass of wine at a draught, while his companion sipped a few drops from his.

'I do not call it melancholy to like good things and to wish that they may last as long as possible,' Gambardella said, rather sourly. 'What could have been more delightful than to ride all the way to Rome or Naples in this way, travelling only on fine days, and stopping where one can get a bottle of old Burgundy and a slice of a decently cooked capon? Talk of sending people to a better world, my friend—it would give me infinite satisfaction to skewer this fool of a Legate for having interfered with our plans! A pretty job it is going to be, to get a man out of a dungeon under the Lion Tower.'

'Which one is that?' asked Trombin, looking through the grated window at the gloomy castle on the other side of the square.

'It is at the northeast corner at the head of the street they call Giovecca. You cannot see it from here. When we have dined we will stroll over and look at it, if you like, but you might as well try to rescue a prisoner from the Bastille!'

Gambardella sniffed his wine discontentedly and then sipped it. He was a grave man and business-like; he could drive as hard a bargain for a life as any Bravo in Italy, and do his work as neatly and expeditiously, when it was plainly laid out before him; but he had no imagination, and his idea of rescuing Stradella was evidently to get him out of the castle by some simple trick such as poor Cucurullo had tried in order to see his master.

'This seems to be a good inn,' observed Trombin thoughtfully, after a pause. 'I had as soon spend a ducat a day here as in a worse house. Now this Burgundy is of the vintage of the year fifty-one.'

'Undoubtedly,' assented Gambardella, sipping again as he did about once a minute. 'It has the "rose" bouquet like that of forty-six, but is a little younger. To think that if we could only get that fellow out of prison we could have him to dinner, and he would sing for us this evening! It is maddening to think that he may lose his voice in a damp hole through the idiocy of that thrice-confounded Legate!'

'It is indeed,' agreed Trombin. 'I wonder what has become of the lady.'

'I thought you were thinking of the girl,' said the other discontentedly. 'It would complete the situation if you should find her and fall in love with her yourself!'

'That is possible. It has pleased Providence to make me susceptible, whereas you are designed by nature for a monastic life. Our friend's description of his niece calls up an enchanting picture! The "Bella" of the late Titian, but younger and slimmer! Heaven send such a sweet creature to cheer my declining years! I do not wonder that the Maestro lost his heart and carried her off. And at this very moment she must be hiding somewhere in Ferrara, perhaps not a quarter of a mile from here! In a convent, no doubt, in some gloomy old house full of yellow-faced Carmelite or Franciscan nuns, with her glorious hair and her matchless complexion! I can see her in my imagination, a gilded rose amongst cabbages, a luscious peach in a heap of turnips.'

'For goodness' sake stop raving!' interrupted Gambardella. 'Why should she be in a convent, I should like to know?'

'Where else could two respectable women without money go? They could not possibly travel, and no one in the town would take them in without baggage or cash. I tell you they went from here to a convent and asked for shelter and protection. It is the most natural thing in the world. It is what the girl's middle-aged serving-woman would certainly think of first.'

'You may be right,' answered the other, his tone changing. 'Drink more wine, for it always stimulates your imagination, and you may imagine a way of getting Stradella out of the Lion Tower. I think you are right about the girl. We will make inquiries at the convents after dinner.'

Trombin filled his glass, which was quite empty, drank half the contents and set it down.

'In the first place,' he said, 'we had better try simple persuasion with the Legate. If you agree, I will go and see him late in the afternoon. He may make some little difficulty about receiving me, but that will only be in order to impress me with his greatness. Besides, you will give me a letter of introduction which I shall ask to present in person.'

'I?' Gambardella looked at his friend across his glass with an expression of inquiry.

'Certainly,' answered Trombin. 'I could not ask such a favour of any one who knows me better, could I? If any one can vouch for me, you can.'

Gambardella condescended to smile faintly, and suggested an outline of the letter.

'"I have the honour to introduce to your lordship's good graces the very noble Count Tromblon de la Trombine, who is here at great personal inconvenience for the express purpose of cutting Alessandro Stradella's throat, and will be much obliged if your worship will at once order the Maestro to be let out for that purpose." Would that do? I could sign Pignaver's name to it!'

'You have no imagination. I will make a rough draft, which you will then write out much better than I could. You shall see. While I am at the castle, you may make inquiries at the different convents.'

As their servant Tommaso had foreseen, they sat at table two hours, and on the whole, though they were highly experienced epicures, they were not dissatisfied with the dinner. Gambardella even admitted that one more day in Ferrara would not be intolerable, but that was as much as his second bottle of Burgundy could bring him to say. At dessert, Trombin called for writing materials and quickly drafted the letter of introduction he wished his friend to write out for him. The latter watched him, and from time to time picked out a fat red cherry from a quantity that floated in a large bowl of water, and ate it thoughtfully.

An hour and a half later the Legate returned from his daily airing, which he generally took on a handsome brown mule, accompanied by his private secretary or by the captain of the halberdiers of the garrison. He came home early, though the weather was warm, for he was beginning to be a little rheumatic, and he established himself in the sunny room which he used as his study. He had not been seated ten minutes in his high-backed chair, with a red cotton quilt spread over his knees and tucked in round his legs, dictating letters to his secretary, when word was brought him that a Venetian gentleman desired to be received, in order to present a letter of introduction from a high personage.

Monsignor Pelagatti had an almost exaggerated respect for high personages, though he was now considered to be one of them himself. Even kings may be snobs, when they are not very big kings, and much more, therefore, the lay governor of a papal province who had climbed to distinction from a steward's office in a Roman patrician's household. The Legate sent his secretary downstairs to bring up the visitor with all the ceremony due to the bearer of an important letter.

In a few minutes Trombin entered the sunny room, and the Governor, who had dropped his red cotton quilt and kicked it out of sight under the table, rose to receive him. Trombin's round cheeks were rounder and pinker than ever, his long yellow hair was as smooth as butter, his bow was precisely suited to the dignity of the Legate, and his manner inspired confidence by its quiet self-possession. His right hand held out the letter he brought, which Monsignor Pelagatti received with a gracious smile after returning his visitor's bow, at the same time inviting the latter to be seated on his right, where the secretary had already placed a comfortable chair.

'With your permission,' said the Governor politely, before proceeding to read the letter.

Trombin bowed his acquiescence from his chair and smiled again. The succulent dinner and rich Burgundy seemed to have made him sleeker and pinker than ever, and he watched the Legate's face with a pleasantly benevolent expression.

But Monsignor Pelagatti's jaw dropped as he read the missive, and his shrivelled lids seemed to shrink back from all round his little red eyes till they looked as if they were starting from his head, while Trombin watched him with quiet satisfaction.

The letter purported to be from the acting Chief of the Council of Ten in Venice, and was really a miracle of official style in its way.

The writer took the liberty of introducing a gentleman to whom he entrusted a delicate business, the noble Signor Trombin del Todescan. His high regard for the Legate, and his desire to avert all unpleasant consequences from so friendly and distinguished an official, had led him to treat directly and privately of a matter which would otherwise have to go through the hands of the Venetian Ambassador in Rome. The Legate had accidentally imprisoned a distinguished musician who had lately been the guest of the Republic, a matter which, in itself, might not be thought to have great importance. But the Maestro Stradella was on his wedding journey, and his young bride was no less a person than the noble lady Ortensia Grimani, the writer's niece. As for Bartolo, the counterfeiter, he had just been caught at Treviso, and, at the time of writing, was safely lodged in the Pozzi, either to be tried in Venice or sent to Rome, as might hereafter be agreed between the respective governments. Under the circumstances the Legate would see the propriety of setting the Maestro at liberty without delay, and of extending every courtesy to him and his young wife, who must be in despair at his arrest. The letter concluded by saying that if the Legate 'did not feel justified' in complying with these requests, the noble Signor Trombin del Todescan had instructions to proceed to Rome with the utmost haste and to place the matter in the hands of the Venetian Ambassador there, on behalf of the noble lady Ortensia Grimani, unjustly deprived of her husband, a Spanish subject, within the States of the Church.

The letter left nothing to be desired in the way of clearness, and the Legate's consternation was considerable. He had actually made a mistake which could not be glossed over by the simple process of condemning an innocent person to fine or imprisonment without appeal. He had never done such a thing in his life, and it was not pleasant to feel the coming humiliation of being forced to revoke an order given in court and to restore property he had summarily confiscated to the Treasury.

He felt himself shrinking in his chair, while the noble Signor Trombin del Todescan, the secret envoy of the Venetian Republic, seemed to grow bigger and more imposing every moment.

'I need not say that I am delighted to be set right, after making such a grave mistake,' said Monsignor Pelagatti humbly. 'The circumstances were very suspicious, as I hope your lordship will explain to the most illustrious Chief. Our information seemed very exact, and as I was in correspondence with the police of Venice in regard to the capture of Bartolo, I could not doubt but that the Republic would be pleased with the news that I had taken him, as I believed I had.'

'The Chief is persuaded of your worship's good intentions,' Trombin answered blandly. 'I can promise your worship, in his name, that the matter shall not be mentioned again. Will you be so good as to order Signor Stradella to be set at liberty? I will conduct him to the inn myself and see to his requirements. I am informed, however, that the Lady Ortensia and her serving-woman left the house immediately after the arrest on Saturday morning, and have not been seen since. Your worship doubtless knows where I can find them.'

'Certainly,' answered the Legate, proud to show that nothing escaped his vigilance. 'They went directly to the Ursuline nuns and asked to be taken in. The Mother Superior very properly sent to ask my permission before agreeing to let them stay, and I granted it. The most illustrious Chief will be glad to know that her ladyship, his niece, has enjoyed the protection of a religious order throughout this lamentable misunderstanding.'

Monsignor Pelagatti dictated and signed the order for Stradella's liberation, and then bade his secretary accompany the noble Signor and see that there was no delay, and that his property was duly returned. Trombin expressed the thanks of the most illustrious Chief of the Ten in appropriately flowery language, bowed, as before, with precisely the right show of mixed regard and condescension, and left the Legate to meditate on his ill-luck in having chanced to make a mistake in such a foolish manner that he could be forced to set it right.

He had no intention of changing his method of dispensing justice, however, for it was a simple one and had hitherto done him credit. It consisted in never admitting that he could be wrong, and in punishing the prisoner whom he had picked out as guilty from the first, regardless of anything that might turn up afterwards. One swallow, he now observed with truth, did not make a spring, nor could one mistake prove a system wrong. The exception proved the rule, he argued to himself, and as he considered that all his mistakes were exceptions, his rule must be practically infallible.

Meanwhile Trombin waited under the great archway while the gaoler fetched Stradella and his man, and two porters soon brought their valises and other belongings. The secretary disappeared for a short time and returned with the leathern purse containing the confiscated money, which, as he informed Trombin, must be counted out to the full satisfaction of the Maestro. The Bravo continued to smile blandly, and while waiting he walked up and down the covered way to the admiration of the halberdiers of the watch. They recognised in him the fighting man, the compact and well-proportioned frame, the easy stride, the assured bearing, and the quick eye; and, moreover, they had already understood what was happening, though they were not Sergeant Hector's men, who would only relieve them at nightfall. But all the soldiers hated the Legate alike, and rejoiced that for once he should be driven to acknowledge a mistake and give up a prisoner.

Stradella and Cucurullo came up from the dungeon in a miserable state, unwashed, unshaven, their clothes stained with the slimy ooze of their prison; their hair was damp and matted, their eyes blinked painfully in the light, and their grimy cheeks were of a ghastly colour. But they were not otherwise much the worse for having spent several days and nights underground, for the supply of provisions brought by the hunchback had sufficed to keep up their strength, and Stradella's constitution, in spite of his pale and intellectual face, overflowed with vitality, like that of all really great singers. As for Cucurullo, he had been inured to hardship and misery in his childhood.

They came forward together, and before Trombin could meet them the turnkey had disappeared again. Trombin took off his hat and bowed to Stradella, and the secretary thought it wise to make an obsequious obeisance.

'Signor Maestro,' the latter said, 'his worship the Legate charges me to offer you his best apologies for the painful mistake which has occurred, and to restore to you your property, confiscated through an error which his worship deplores and trusts that you will condone.'

In spite of his wretched plight there was much dignity in Stradella's bearing as he answered this speech.

'Present my compliments to Monsignor Pelagatti, sir,' he said, 'and pray assure him that I accept the excuses which you make with so much politeness.'

'I thank you, illustrious Maestro,' said the secretary, bowing again. 'Allow me to add only that the mistake has been rectified by this gentleman of Venice, the illustrious and noble Signor Trombin del Todescan.'

Trombin and Stradella once more bowed to each other with great ceremony.

'It has been my privilege to render the slightest of services to the greatest of musicians,' Trombin said. 'If you will allow me, Maestro, I shall have the further honour of conducting you to the inn, where your property and money can be restored to you with more privacy than in this place.'

'Three hundred and ninety-one gold ducats, Signor Maestro,' said the secretary. 'I have them here, and the porters are already gone on with your luggage.'

The halberdiers stood up, and the sentinel on duty saluted as the little party passed through the gate. The porters were halfway across the square, Stradella walked between Trombin and the secretary, who had placed himself deferentially on the left, and Cucurullo brought up the rear, sorrowfully surveying the stains and mud on the back of his master's clothes, only too clearly visible in the bright afternoon light. No more words were exchanged till they all reached the door of the inn, where the host was awaiting them, for he had seen from a side window the porters bringing back Stradella's luggage, which he instantly recognised, and the rest was plain enough. The Count Tromblon de la Trombine was evidently a great personage, and it had been enough that he should demand the instant release of the musician to produce the present result. The innkeeper was proportionately impressed.

He accordingly bowed to the ground, presented his condolences to Stradella on the unhappy accident, and led the way to a spacious and well-furnished room on the first floor, to which he had already sent the luggage.

It was not till he was gone and Cucurullo was unpacking his master's things that Trombin, who desired an opportunity of exchanging a few words alone with Stradella, led him to his own room. He carefully closed the door before speaking.

'A word of explanation, Maestro,' he said, 'for all this must seem a little incomprehensible to you. First, let me tell you that the Lady Ortensia has spent the time of your imprisonment in the convent of the Ursuline nuns with her serving-woman. That is the first piece of news you wish to hear, I am sure.'

The young musician drew a deep breath of relief, for his gnawing anxiety on Ortensia's account had been far harder to bear during his confinement than any bodily hardship, and he had not at first thought it safe to ask any questions of his liberator. The mere fact that the latter had been introduced by the secretary as a Venetian gentleman had filled him with apprehension, and even now he believed that Trombin had probably been sent by Pignaver.

As if understanding what passed in Stradella's mind, the Bravo volunteered an explanation.

'A friend of mine and I are travelling southwards on important business,' he said. 'Before we left Venice the town was ringing with your exploit, as it has echoed with your praises these three months past. My friend Count Gambardella and I are amongst your most ardent admirers, Signor Maestro, and I may say in confidence that we have a private grudge against the Senator Pignaver. You may imagine our delight on hearing that you had carried off his niece! Quite naturally we have asked after you at each posting station on the road. You understand the rest. My friend and I venture to hope that you and your bride will honour us with your company at supper.'

'I cannot find words for my thanks, sir,' answered Stradella, wondering whether he were not in a dream, still sleeping on the stone seat in his cell. 'I can only hope to show you some day how grateful I am. You have saved my life!'

Trombin smiled pleasantly, but said nothing.

CHAPTER XI

Gambardella knocked at the door of San Domenico twice in quick succession, and then again once after a short interval. For reasons known to himself he had not hesitated to begin his inquiries for Ortensia at the old Dominican convent then occupied by the nuns of Saint Ursula, and it was at once apparent that his knock inspired confidence. Instead of drawing back the small sliding panel in the weather-beaten door to see who was outside and to ask his errand, the portress opened the postern on one side almost immediately, without showing herself, and Gambardella slipped in unchallenged and shut it after him.

He found himself in a high and vaulted vestibule which received light from the cloistered garden round which the convent was built, and he was at once confronted by the portress, who seemed much surprised when she saw that she had admitted a fine gentleman.

Gambardella bowed respectfully before he spoke.

'Reverend sister,' said he, 'I have the honour to be a friend of your Order, and if I am not mistaken I am known to your Mother Superior, of whom I come to ask audience, if she will receive me.'

The lay sister hesitated. She was an elderly woman with flaccid yellow cheeks, watery eyes, and a more than incipient grey beard.

'I think the Mother Superior is resting,' she said, after a moment.

'So late in the afternoon, sister? I trust that her Reverence is not indisposed?'

'Besides,' continued the portress, without heeding him, 'you only said that you thought you were known to her. Pray can you tell me her Reverence's name?'

Gambardella smiled gently. Probably it was not the first time he had been obliged to argue with a convent door-keeper, that is, with the most incredulous and obstinate kind of human being in the world.

'Unless I am mistaken,' Gambardella answered, 'her Reverence's name, in religion, is Mother Agatha, and she was formerly Sub-Prioress of your house in Ravenna.'

'I see that you are well-informed,' the portress answered, somewhat reluctantly. 'I will find out whether she is resting.'

She turned from him to go into her dark little lodge, through which she had communication with the interior of the convent; but Gambardella called her back.

'One moment, sister! You need make but one errand of it. Pray let her Reverence know that a Venetian gentleman of the name of Lorenzo Marcello sends her this token and begs the honour of a few words with her.'

Therewith Gambardella drew from his finger the brass ring he always wore and placed it in the portress's hand. After repeating the name he had given, she nodded and went within. While he waited, Gambardella looked through the iron gate that separated the vestibule from the pleasant cloistered garden, and his melancholy face was even more sad than usual, and his singular eyes more shadowy.

'The Mother Superior will receive you in the parlour, sir,' said the portress, coming back, and her tone showed that she now accorded the visitor high consideration.

He followed her through the lodge, which only received light from its doors when they were open. Across one corner a dark brown curtain was hung, which presumably hid the portress's pallet-bed. She led him through a whitewashed corridor, lighted from above, into a wide hall from which a broad staircase led upwards, and which had several doors, besides two open entrances. The portress opened one of the doors and shut it as soon as Gambardella had entered.

He walked up and down the long gloomy room while he waited; the two grated windows were far above reach and opened upon a blank wall opposite. The bare stone pavement was damp, and the furniture consisted of a dark walnut table, once polished, a long straight-backed settle placed at one end, and twelve rush-bottomed chairs arranged round the sides of the room with great regularity. Above the settle hung a painfully realistic crucifix; on the wall at the opposite end a large barocco picture represented Saint Ursula in glory with the Eleven Thousand Virgins of Cologne. Opposite the windows there was a bad copy of a portrait of Paul III., the Pope who first established the order. Judging from the parlour, it could not be said that the Ursulines of Ferrara were living in reprehensible luxury.

In three or four minutes the door opened again and the Mother Superior entered. She was taller than most women, and very lean; her black gown and the black veil that almost reached the ground hung in straight folds, and her wimple and gorget framed a dark face, thin and expressive, with noticeably symmetrical features and ardent black eyes. It was impossible to guess at her age, but she might have been thirty.

She bent her head slightly, in acknowledgment of Gambardella's respectful bow, and looked at him during several seconds, as if she were recalling his appearance to her memory. Then she slowly walked away to the settle, seated herself in the middle of it, and pointed to a chair at a little distance. He sat down and waited for her to speak.

'Why have you come?' she asked, in a low tone that sounded resentful.

'Is it a crime to see you after ten years?' asked Gambardella with a good deal of sadness, and watching her face intently.

'Unless you have changed greatly, it is at least a sin,' she answered deliberately, and she met his eyes with eyes suddenly fierce.

'I have changed greatly, and not for the better,' he said simply, but he could not face her look. 'It is neither to confess to you nor to ask your forgiveness again that I am here, for you have no more right to a confession than I have to your pardon.'

'That may be,' answered the nun, her tone relenting, 'but such as my forgiveness can be, while I can still remember, you have it.'

Gambardella was visibly moved at this unexpected concession. He was seated too far from her to touch her hand, but he put out his own humbly towards the hem of her black skirt, then brought it back to his lips and kissed it with reverence, as the very poor and wretched sometimes do in Italy to express deep gratitude. She watched him, and there was the faintest suggestion of a smile on her tightly closed lips. After a little pause, during which their eyes met once, he spoke.

'I have come to inquire about a young Venetian lady and her serving-woman, who took refuge with you last Saturday,' he said, with perfect assurance, though he had no proof that the two were in the convent.

The Mother Superior's face darkened.

'What are they to you?' she asked sternly.

This was a question which Gambardella was not prepared to answer truthfully, and he had not foreseen it. He vaguely wondered what the woman who had once loved him so well would say and do if she knew that he had sunk to the condition of a paid Bravo, and had taken money from one person to cut Ortensia's throat and from another to deliver her up a prisoner, and was just now wondering how he could satisfy both his patrons.

Until now he had seen a humorous element in his two abominable bargains; but in the grim presence of his own past things looked differently. The terrible eyes of the high-born woman he had loved and betrayed long ago, when he was still called an honourable gentleman, were upon him now, and he feared her as he had assuredly never feared any man in all his wild life. She understood her power, and waited for him to speak.

But his fear only roused his faculties, and if he felt remorse when he thought of what she had once been and of the life she was leading now, by his fault, he knew well enough that as soon as she was out of his sight he would feel nothing but a dim regret that would hardly hurt.

'I take a vicarious interest in the Lady Ortensia,' he said after a little reflection. 'A friend of mine, who is travelling with me, is also a friend of the man with whom she has run away, and who has been locked up by mistake, as I dare say you have heard from her.'

'She has told me something,' the Mother Superior said coldly.

'I will tell you the whole story,' he answered.

He narrated the circumstances of Ortensia's flight substantially as they were known to the Senator, and in as few words as possible, and she listened without interrupting him.

'I know this Pignaver,' he said in conclusion, 'and I know positively that he has engaged two Bravi to follow the pair and murder them. At the best, he might be satisfied if Stradella were murdered and the girl brought back to him. Those fellows may be even now in Ferrara, waiting for a chance to do the deed. Our object is to unite the lovers and protect them on their journey till they are beyond the reach of danger. Do you see any great harm in that?'

'They are not married,' objected the nun.

'I am sure they mean to be, as soon as possible,' Gambardella answered. 'You know what the girl's life will be if you send her home, as I suppose you mean to do. You can guess the sort of existence she will lead when her uncle has her safely imprisoned in his house. I have heard it said that he intended to marry her, and if that is true he will deliberately torment her and perhaps starve her till she dies. He is as vain as he is cruel, and she has not a relation in the world to interfere with his doings.'

'Poor girl!' The Mother Superior sighed, and looked down at her folded hands.

'And even if you insist on keeping her here, where I admit that she is safe,' Gambardella continued, 'Stradella's life will not be safe when he is out of prison. For I will answer for it that he will not leave Ferrara without her, and his murder will be the first consequence of your refusal to let her join him.'

'But they are not married,' the nun said again. 'I cannot let her go to him. It would be a great sin! It would be on my conscience!'

'You will have his death on your conscience if you are not careful! But there is a very simple way out of the difficulty, if you will agree to it.'

'I will agree to nothing that is not right,' said the Mother Superior, in a tone that excluded any compromise, 'and I tell you frankly that I do not trust you. It would be strange if I did.'

'I do not ask you to trust me,' Gambardella answered. 'I shall merely show you your duty, and leave you to do it or not, as you please!'

'My duty?' The nun was both surprised and offended.

'Yes,' replied the other, unmoved. 'Your objection is that they are not married. Marry them, then! That is plainly your duty, if anything is!'

The Mother Superior looked at him quickly, as if not believing that he was in earnest, for she had been convincing herself that it was he who had carried off Ortensia, pretending to be Stradella.

'It must be a very easy thing for you,' Gambardella continued. 'You have your own church here, and your own priest, who will probably obey you. If you are afraid of committing an irregularity, you need only send a request to the Archbishop, explaining that a runaway couple, for whom you can vouch, wish to have their union blessed. No good bishop would refuse such a slight favour as a dispensation from publishing banns. My friend and I will bring Stradella here early in the morning, and you will send the bride into the church from the convent. They will go away man and wife, and before noon we shall all be many miles on the road to Bologna and Rome. Could anything be simpler than that? or more perfectly right? or more honourable for you under the circumstances?'

The nun had listened attentively, and when he had finished she nodded her approval.

'I believe you are right,' she said, though her tone betrayed some surprise that she could approve anything which he suggested. 'I will take it upon myself to promise that our chaplain shall be waiting to-morrow morning after matins, and that the bride shall be ready in the sacristy. Poor child, she is poorly provided for her wedding! But I will find a veil for her.'

'She will be grateful, and Stradella too. I have no doubt but that my friend has already obtained his liberation.'

'What is your friend's name?' asked the Mother Superior, showing some curiosity for the first time since the interview had begun.

Gambardella hesitated a moment, for the simple reason that he did not know the answer to the question, and that 'Trombin' alone was evidently not a name, but a nickname. The mere fact that the friends had both once had a right to sit in the Grand Council by no means implied that they had known each other, even by sight. To gain time Gambardella smiled and asked a counter-question.

'Why do you wish to learn his name?' he asked. 'You can never have known him.'

'That is true. It was idle curiosity. I do not care to know.'

'It is no secret,' Gambardella answered, having in the meantime thought of a name that would do. 'My friend is Gaspero Mastropiero, a Venetian gentleman of fortune and a great patron of musicians. And now,' he said, rising as he spoke, 'nothing remains for me but to thank you for seeing me, and to take my leave. Will you give me back my ring, Reverend Mother?'

He stood before her, holding out his hand with the palm upward to receive the token, and he laid a little stress on the title as he pronounced it. But there was no irony in his tone, for, young as she still was, it had been conferred upon her quite as much for her holy life as for her high descent, in an age when noble blood had great weight in such matters. He was certainly not speaking ironically; perhaps, amidst the tatters of his honour, some rag still covered a spot that could feel shame, and the monstrous deed, in doing which he had entrapped the nun to help him unawares, seemed foul beside the purity of her intention and the saintliness of her own life.

The emphasis he gave to the two words was, therefore, at once respectful and sad, and did not offend her. She had put on the old brass ring herself when the portress had sent it up to her with his message; she took it off now and gave it back to him, careful that not even the tips of her fingers should touch his palm. Then she led the way, and he followed her.

'May you never put it to a worse use than to-day,' she said, stopping and letting her eyes meet his for a moment. 'Good-bye.'

'Pray for me,' he said instinctively when he opened the door for her.

She said nothing, but she bent her head a little as she passed out, perhaps meaning that she would do what he asked. He watched her tall retreating figure as she went up the middle of the staircase, till she turned past the dividing wall at the first landing and disappeared without having once looked back. Then he himself went away through the high corridor and the dark lodge, and the portress let him out in silence.

He did not go back to the inn at once, for the distance was very short, and he judged that Trombin could hardly have procured Stradella's liberation in so short a time. He wished to be alone a little while, for, in spite of what he had come to be, his interview with the Mother Superior had disturbed him strangely. He had thought himself far beyond that bitterness of remorse and that sickness of shame which she had made him feel, and he wished to forget both before he met his companion to discuss the execution of the deed they had promised to do together, and could not now put off doing much longer. The nun's burning eyes still haunted and reproached him, and her shadowy figure rose before him with the thin white face in which he could still trace the beauty that had once enthralled him. It was the bare woof of beauty that remained, for grief and penance had worn away the warp, leaving only the lines on which the exquisite fabric had been woven; but what was left of the woman was still there, breathing and living, while her soul had grown great in strength and spiritual honour till it towered above his who had once loved her, and made him afraid to meet her look.

It could not last long, he knew, but while it did he must be alone. He walked far out on a road that led through the rich damp plain, and it was not till the sun was sinking low that he began to retrace his steps.

When he reached the inn he found Trombin and Stradella together, and his friend introduced him with some ceremony as Count Gambardella. The musician, who was fully informed of the latter's errand, pressed his hand warmly, and looked at him, evidently expecting news of Ortensia.

'The lady and her serving-woman are well, sir,' Gambardella said at once, 'and I trust that to-morrow may end your difficulties happily.'

'I hope so indeed,' Stradella answered.

He looked pale and careworn, but no one would have guessed from his appearance that he had just spent four nights and the better part of five days in the most noisome dungeon in Ferrara. He wore the same black velvet coat with purple silk facings which he was wearing when Ortensia saw him for the first time. It fitted him well and showed his athletic young figure to advantage, for the fashion was not yet for the 'French' coat which Louis Fourteenth afterwards made universal.

Gambardella measured him with his eye, as Trombin must have done already. He wore only the short rapier of a civilian gentleman, but he might be a good fencer and able to give trouble to a single adversary, and he looked strong. Neither of the Bravi knew what physical fear meant, but it was of no use to risk a useless wound, and men of Stradella's type could be more conveniently despatched by stabbing them in the back than by going through the form of a duel.

'I have not been able to see the lady herself,' Gambardella continued, 'but the Mother Superior of the Ursulines was so good as to receive me, and after some demur she agreed to let the Lady Ortensia and her woman leave the convent early to-morrow morning.'

'Not till to-morrow?' Stradella could not hide his disappointment.

'To-morrow, and then only on one condition, which I took it upon me to promise that you shall fulfil.'

The musician looked sharply at the speaker.

'I trust that you have not promised for me more than I may honourably do,' he said.

At this Trombin instantly pressed down the hilt of his rapier and made the point stick up behind; he pursed his mouth and opened his eyes till they glared like an angry cat's.

'I would have you know, Signor Maestro, that it is not the custom of Venetian gentlemen to promise anything not honourable, either in their own names or for others!'

Pignaver would have apologised at once if either of the Bravi had taken that tone, but the Sicilian singer was made of better stuff than the Venetian Senator.

'Sir,' he answered quietly, 'I am not a quarrelsome man, and, moreover, I am deeply indebted to you for my freedom. But there is a lady in this case. Let me first know what Count Gambardella has promised in my name; for if, as I hope, it pledges me to nothing unworthy of the Lady Ortensia or of myself, I shall be doubly in your debt; but if not, which heaven avert, I shall be at your service for a quarrel, without further words.'

While he was speaking he met Trombin's ferocious stare steadily, and when he had finished he turned to Gambardella. The Bravo liked his tone and manner as much as he had despised Pignaver for his repeated apologies. It would be shameful to stab such a man in the back, Trombin thought; as shameful and unsportsman-like as an Englishman thinks it to shoot a fox or to angle with worms for fish that will take a fly.

'The Mother Superior,' said Gambardella, paying no attention to what had just passed, 'is a saintly woman. She requires that before taking away the Lady Ortensia, you shall be duly married in the church of San Domenico, early to-morrow morning. This, sir, I ventured to promise in your name, and no more, as one man of honour speaking for another.'

'You could not have done me a greater service!' Stradella cried, surprised and delighted. 'I am sorry that I ever questioned your good judgment, sir!'

Trombin's fierce expression relaxed into one better suited to his round pink cheeks, and peace was immediately restored. But the Bravi exchanged glances which meant that they were perplexed by the undeniable fact that they were beginning to like the musician, quite apart from their admiration for his genius.

Before supper they consulted together in the privacy of Trombin's room over a thimbleful of Greek mastic, which they drank as an appetiser. They were agreed not to lose sight of the young couple again, and not to hurry matters to a termination. What could be more delightful than to make the journey to Rome together with the greatest singer in the world and his bride, acting at once as an armed escort and as friends ready to save the happy pair all trouble about small details from day to day? Stradella had declared that he meant to reach Rome without delay, while he was sure of a warm welcome and of the protection of Cardinal Altieri, in case Pignaver sent any one in pursuit.

'Rome,' said Trombin thoughtfully, 'is a convenient place for doing business. The streets are narrow, and there are many wells in the courtyards of the old houses.'

'It is true that we have never had any trouble in Rome,' Gambardella answered. 'Commend me to narrow streets for business. I hate your great squares, your promenades, your gardens, and your belvederes! Shall you ever forget that summer's evening on the Chiatamone in Naples?'

'I feel that I am still running away,' Trombin said. 'But Rome is quite different. It is true that we have not yet decided which of the two it is to be. But I have just thought of a way of getting both the fees.'

'For a man of imagination, you have taken a long time to think of it!'

'It is this. We will deliver up both in Venice, Stradella to the lady, and the girl to her uncle. The lady will believe that the girl is dead, for she will never see or hear of her again, and she will pay us in full. The Senator will pay half down when he gets his niece back, and after the lady has enjoyed the Maestro's company for a few days he can be done away with, and Pignaver will pay the balance. What do you think of that as a solution, my friend?'

'There is much to be said for it,' Gambardella admitted.

He nodded and sipped his mastic, which was not an easy operation, since he could not go on filling the small glass as he would a tumbler of wine; but he ingeniously set it to one corner of his mouth, well out of the way of his nose, and by turning his head on one side he succeeded in sipping it to the end without spilling a drop.

'It is a monstrous thing to interrupt such a career as Stradella's,' he continued, for his companion had said nothing. 'But five hundred ducats are a great deal of money, and beggars cannot be choosers! Nevertheless, if you can think of some plan which will accomplish the same result by saving the Maestro and putting the girl out of the way instead, I should prefer it. A woman more or less makes no difference, but there is only one Stradella!'

'I will do my best,' Trombin answered, 'but you cannot have everything.'

The Bravi and Stradella supped in a room apart for greater privacy, because a large party of noisy Bolognese merchants had arrived on their way to Venice, and were eating in the dining-room. Cucurullo and Grattacacio waited on their masters, the dishes being brought to the door by a scullion.

There were wax candles on the table in handsome candlesticks, for a mere brass oil-lamp was not good enough for such fine gentlemen as Trombin and Gambardella when their pockets were full of money; and in the middle of the board a magnificent majolica basket was filled with cherries and green almonds.

The two servants eyed each other with a certain mutual distrust, for Grattacacio had at once discovered that his colleague was one of those poor creatures that have not even the spirit to cheat their masters, and Cucurullo's quietly penetrating intelligence detected under Tommaso's accomplished exterior the signs of a still more accomplished scoundrel. For the present, however, the two treated each other with much civility, and their three masters were admirably served at supper.

They drank to one another in the old Burgundy, and Trombin proposed the health of the bride, repeating in her honour one of Petrarch's sonnets in praise of Laura. He said that as he had never seen her he could only compare her beauty to that of the angels, and her virtues to those of the blessed saints, whom he had not seen either, and had no expectation of seeing hereafter; similarly he likened the Maestro's voice to that of a seraph, on the ground that its like would never be heard on earth.

Stradella laughed a little, for the first time in five days, and emptied his glass to Ortensia. He was no match for his companions at eating and drinking, as he soon found out, and he was satisfied long before they were; but the good old wine had brought back the warmth to his face and hands, though he had drunk but little, and presently he went for his lute. He tuned it and then played softly while Trombin ate candied fruit and Gambardella cut himself shavings of fresh Parmesan cheese, which he nibbled with salt, and both drank wine, listening to his music with delight.

It was worth hearing, indeed, for under his masterly touch the instrument sang, laughed and wept, and whispered love-words at his will; now, one high string pleaded its passionate melody to a low and sighing accompaniment that never swelled to reach it; and now, the nineteen strings sounded together as a full orchestra, bursting in triumphant harmonies, and almost deafening to hear; again, the deepest string began a fugue that was taken up by the next above and the next, and traversed all, gathering sonorous strength as the parts increased from two to three, from three to four, all moving at once to the grand climax, and then sinking again and falling away one by one, softer and softer to the solemn close.

Stradella was profoundly happy, and he had but one way of expressing his happiness to himself, which was the most beautiful way there is, for he made the art he loved his means of telling the world his joy.

Later, when the window was open, and the young moon was shedding a gentle light upon the broad square, he began to sing softly, wondering that he should have any voice left after what he had suffered; but great singers are not like other men, at least as to their throats, and after a few trials the rich notes floated out deliciously, as effortless and as true, as soft and as strong as ever, in those marvellous love-songs of his own that thrilled all Italy while he lived, and long afterwards.

The Bravi had turned their chairs to listen, for he had gone to the window. They had finished their Burgundy, and most of his share to boot, and peace had descended on their restless souls; and if, from all the delights the world held, they could have chosen one for that May evening, they would have asked for none but this, to sit and listen to the greatest of living singers and musicians, deeply in love, and singing more for himself than that any one might hear him.

'It is absolutely impossible,' said Trombin gravely to his companion, when Stradella paused at last.

'Absolutely,' assented Gambardella.

'What is impossible?' the singer asked carelessly.

'To sing better than you,' answered Gambardella with a short laugh.

CHAPTER XII

Quite out of sight in the choir, more than sixty nuns and at least as many of their girl pupils were still chanting matins when Stradella and the two Bravi entered the Church of San Domenico, followed by Cucurullo. The latter's fellow-servant had left Ferrara at dawn with his masters' luggage, to ride ahead and order rooms and dinner at Bologna for the whole party. Stradella had secured a travelling-carriage on which his effects were already packed, and the harnessed horses were standing ready to be put to.

Gambardella dipped his fingers into the nearest holy-water basin and held them out dripping for Stradella to touch before he crossed himself, as the others also did; then all followed him up the side aisle to the door of the sacristy, where they waited till the singing ceased. The priest's deep voice spoke a few words alone, the nuns and pupils answered, and so again, through the short Responsory; and after a moment the soft shuffling of many felt-shod feet on the stone pavement was heard as the sisters and girls left the hidden choir in orderly procession.

The sacristan opened the padded swinging-door and saw the four men waiting. He was a small man with a round red nose and he took snuff plentifully, as the state of his shabby black cassock showed.

'If the gentlemen will put themselves to the inconvenience of coming in,' he said, 'they will find all ready and the lady waiting.'

He spoke with obsequious politeness, but his eyes looked with sharp inquiry from one to the other, trying to make out which of the three gentlemen was the bridegroom; that is to say, which of them would tip him after the ceremony—for in such matters, as he well knew, much may be guessed from the face and apparent humour of the giver.

He was relieved to see that Stradella now took the lead, and that every line of his handsome young face betrayed his joyous anxiety to be married as soon as possible.

Between the church and the sacristy there was a damp and gloomy vestibule, at the end of which the sacristan opened another swinging-door and Stradella suddenly saw Ortensia standing in a blaze of light, covered from head to foot with a delicate white veil shot with gold threads; for the early sun poured in through two great windows and flooded the sacristy, gleaming on the carved and polished walnut wardrobes, blazing on the rich gold and jewels and enamel of the sacred vessels and utensils in the tall glass-fronted case, and making a cloud of glory in the bride's veil. It covered her face, but in the splendid light it hardly dimmed her radiant loveliness.

Beside her, but half a step farther back, stood Pina, in her grey dress, as quiet and self-possessed as ever. Near them stood a tall old priest who had a thin and gentle face.

Stradella sprang forward with outstretched hands, forgetting everything except that Ortensia was before him. But he had not yet reached her side when the priest was between them, laying one hand on his shoulder and quietly checking him, though smiling kindly, as if he quite understood.

The Bravi had started when they first caught sight of the Venetian girl, for neither of them had expected such rare beauty; and with the added illusion of the gold-shot veil and the all-generous sunshine, it was nothing less than transcendent. Trombin and Gambardella looked at each other quietly, as they always did when the same thought struck them.

Meanwhile the tall old priest made the young couple kneel before the little altar on one side of the sacristy, where two praying-stools had been placed in readiness. Pina knelt down a little way behind her mistress, and Cucurullo took his place at the same distance behind his master; but Trombin went and stood on Ortensia's left and Gambardella on Stradella's right, as witnesses for the bride and bridegroom respectively.

Thus it was that the runaway couple were duly married and blessed in the sacristy of San Domenico on that May morning, little dreaming why it had all been so cleverly managed for them; but it was clear that Stradella had been prepared for the event, since he produced two wedding rings of different sizes and gave them to the priest to bless.

'I will,' he said, in answer to the latter's question.

'I will,' said Ortensia in a low tone, but by no means doubtfully.

'Ego conjungo vos,' the priest went on; and the rest was soon said, the Bravi dropping on their knees at the benediction.

Then the sacristan brought out the register and laid it on the broad polished table on which the vestments were folded, placing pens and ink and the sand-box beside it; and the priest first wrote a few words, to say that he had married the couple by a special dispensation from the Archbishop of Ferrara; and Stradella and Ortensia signed their names, and after them the Bravi, who indeed merely wrote 'Trombin' and 'Gambardella,' but managed to make their signatures almost illegible with magnificent flourishes. The priest bade Pina and Cucurullo sign too, as they said they could write, and the hunchback wrote 'Antonino Cucurullo' in a small neat hand like a seminarist's, and Pina set down her name as 'Filippina Landi.'

The priest, who had watched the signing, looked at her in some surprise.

'Are you married or unmarried?' he asked quietly.

'Unmarried,' answered Pina in her hard voice, and she turned away.

For Landi was a patrician name; and though Jews, when baptized, usually took the surname of the noble under whose auspices they were converted, it was quite clear that Pina was not of Semitic race.

Stradella had taken Ortensia's hand and kissed it when the little ceremony was over, but that was all, and neither could find words to speak. Pina took off the beautiful veil, folded it on the polished table, and rolled it up to carry away, for the Mother Superior wished Ortensia to keep it. Then the serving-woman produced the two brown cloaks in which she and her mistress had fled from Venice, and they put them on, and all left the church together after thanking the priest; and Stradella gave the sacristan two silver Apostolic florins, which was the largest fee the fellow had ever received in his life.

When they were all in the street, the Bravi took off their hats and asked to be introduced to the bride, and Stradella presented them with some ceremony, greatly to the surprise and delight of some ragged children who had collected round the church steps; for Ortensia made a court courtesy, and the Bravi bowed to the ground, sweeping the cobble-stones with their plumes and sticking up their rapiers behind them almost perpendicularly in the air.

'Count Trombin, Count Gambardella,' said the musician to his wife, introducing the pair. 'These gentlemen have liberated us from our respective prisons and have been kindly instrumental in bringing about our marriage.'

'We owe you both a debt of undying gratitude, gentlemen,' said Ortensia, blushing a little under her brown hood.

'It is an honour to have served your ladyship,' Trombin replied, with another grand bow.

Ortensia slipped her arm through Stradella's and pressed his surreptitiously against her side, as if to say that she would never let him go out of her sight again; and she wished, as she had never wished for anything in her life, that she were alone with him already, to throw her arms round his neck and tell him the very things he was longing to tell her.

Behind them the Bravi walked in silence, their hands on the hilts of their rapiers and their eyes fixed on the happy pair, each absorbed in his own reflections.

Trombin thought, in the first place, that Ortensia was one of the most beautiful young creatures he had ever seen; and he flattered himself that he had seen many. Gambardella, on the other hand, wore his most sour look, for he was disgusted to find that the impression left by his interview with the Mother Superior was not so ephemeral as he had believed it to be; and being angry with himself he wished that the whole business were finished, that Stradella were dead and Ortensia safe in her uncle's hands, or that Ortensia were already killed and that Stradella had been delivered to his Venetian admirer bound hand and foot and gagged, according to contract, so that Gambardella might apply his mind to other matters.

But Trombin was not thinking only of the lady. The humour of the whole affair struck him as delightful in the extreme, and he smiled to himself, showing his sharp white teeth, when he thought of the tricks that had been played on the Legate and the Ursuline nuns in less than twenty-four hours. It was most especially amusing to think how that cut-throat Gambardella, the weight of whose sins would have staggered the Grand Penitentiary himself, had played Old Morality to the Mother Superior, and had actually been the one to suggest a proper marriage as the only virtuous solution of the difficulty.

There was not much time for such reflections, however, for the distance to the inn was short, and when they reached it the young couple's travelling-carriage was ready and the horses were saddled for the Bravi, who were already dressed for riding. So there was nothing to hinder them all from starting at once, since the score was already paid.

In less than half an hour after they had left the church, the whole party was well outside the city gates and on the road to Rome.

CHAPTER XIII

A month had passed since Stradella and Ortensia had fled from Venice, and after their adventure in Ferrara no hand had been raised against them on their way to Rome. They had at first lodged in the ancient hostelry at the Sign of the Bear, which still stands, and is not only called the Orso inn as it was hundreds of years ago, but has given its name to the street in which it is situated. It stands at the entrance to that part of the city which was in old times dominated by the Orsini, who undoubtedly got their name from some ancient stone or marble bear that was built into the outer wall of their stronghold; but whether the old inn was called after the image itself, or after the Orsini badge, no one can tell.

Stradella and his wife lodged for a few days in that large upper room, of which the beautiful loggia may still be seen from the new embankment; but in those days, and much later, another row of tall houses stood on the opposite side of the street, between the Orso and the river, making an unbroken line as far as the Nona tower at the Bridge of Sant' Angelo, and completely cutting off the view. It was the best of the Roman inns, even when Rome had more hostelries than any city in Europe. Philippe de Commines lodged there, and Montaigne, and many another famous man who visited Rome before and after Stradella's time.

It was there, in that upper chamber, that the happy lovers first tasted peace and rest after the trials and fatigues of their long journey; for though they were man and wife it is but right to call them lovers, who loved so truly till they died. It was there that they first learned to know and understand each other, and to see why they had loved at first sight and had fled together, wresting their happiness violently from an adverse fate, when they had been alone scarcely one whole hour in all during their brief acquaintance, and had kissed but twice.

For as they lived those first days together they found all they had dreamed of, each in the other, and more too; and every fresh discovery was a sweet new world, till many worlds made up the universe of their new being that circled round love's sun in a firmament of joy. Love had been great from the first, but now he grew to be all-powerful; there had been hours when one or the other might have been persuaded to draw back for some weighty reason, but no reason was strong enough to part them now, not even the great last argument of death himself.

Surely, say you, the course of true love should have run smooth for them, if ever. But know you not that the gods envy no small thing, nor are angry at any humdrum happiness of common men? Know you not that the god of war spares the coward and slays the brave? That in the race for fortune Jove often trips the swiftest runners and lets the dull plodder creep past the winning post alone? Know you not that whom the gods love die young?

Ortensia and Stradella knew none of these things. He had grown famous almost without an effort when scarcely more than a boy, and fame did not desert him; and now that he had overcome obstacles and passed through danger to be happy, he believed with child-like faith that such happiness, once got, must be safe from outward harm, since it dwelt in the heart, where no one could see it, to envy it as men envied worldly glory. As for Ortensia, she neither thought of the future nor remembered the near past, but lived only in each present dazzling day.

For a whole week they scarcely showed themselves, though Stradella's return was known in Rome, and he received many invitations to rich men's houses and requests for new compositions, and pressing offers of money if he would but sing at mass or vespers in this basilica or that. If he had needed gold, he could have had it for an hour's trouble, or for an effort of a few minutes which was no effort at all. But for the moment he had enough, and nothing should disturb the first days of his golden honeymoon.

Trombin and Gambardella also lodged in the Orso, but in rooms far from the happy pair, whom they chose to leave in peace for the present, never asking to see them nor inviting them to their well-spread table. Indeed, any such invitation might have come better from the other side now, for never did a young runaway couple incur a heavier debt of gratitude than Stradella and Ortensia owed to the two cut-throats who meant to murder them, and were even then living under the same roof and on the best of everything with money advanced to them for that very purpose.

But the time and the conditions were not now suited for the deed, which might have been done easily enough a dozen times between Ferrara and Rome. Moreover, the Bravi had not yet come to a definite agreement as to the plan they should pursue, and Trombin's scheme, which seemed the best, was far less easy to carry out than a common murder, and very much more expensive; for it meant kidnapping both Stradella and his wife, and taking them all the way back to Venice as close prisoners, without exciting suspicion by the way, so that the inns at which they had all stopped on their journey southwards would have to be scrupulously avoided on their return.

There was no hurry, however, for they had not spent the two hundred ducats advanced to them; or, to be accurate, they had played at the French Ambassador's gambling-tables with a part of the money and had won a good deal. For in those days every foreign ambassador in Rome claimed the right to keep a public gambling-room in his embassy, for his own profit, which was often large, and was always a regular source of income. But the Bravi had already written to Pignaver as well as to the lady for more funds, on the ground that forty days had passed without affording them the opportunity they sought, and at two ducats a day their account thus came to eighty ducats, already gone for unavoidable expenses. Since they were paid twice over, it was quite natural that their expenses should sometimes be doubled.

Meanwhile they watched their prey closely, and without any apparent intention of disturbing the peace of the lovers' paradise they were very often just strolling out or coming in exactly when Stradella and Ortensia were passing through the gate in one direction or the other. In this way Trombin saw Ortensia almost every day, and all four generally exchanged a few friendly words before going on their way.

The beautiful Venetian and her husband were in the habit of going out together either early in the morning, when they were sure not to meet any of Stradella's fashionable acquaintances, or late in the June afternoons, when all society congregated in certain fixed gathering places and nowhere else, such as the gardens of the French Embassy, which was established in the Villa Medici, or in the vast grounds of the Villa Riario, which is now called Corsini, where Queen Christina of Sweden had finally taken up her abode, and was giving herself airs right royally as the chief living patroness and critic of all the arts and sciences. To her, too, and to her court, Stradella had sung more than once when he had last been in Rome, at which time she had lived there little more than a year. Again, the precincts of the Vatican were to be avoided, and the news-mongering Banchi Vecchi, where every smart gossip in town resorted twice or thrice in the week to replenish his sk of facts and anecdotes, true and untrue, and where he could buy the sensational account of the latest execution, or elopement, or fraud.

The young couple avoided all such places carefully. Stradella knew the city well, and led Ortensia to many lovely spots unknown to fashion, and into many dim old churches, more than one of which had echoed to his own music on great feast-days, from the Lateran and Santa Croce and Santa Maria in Domnica, far away beyond the Colosseum, in the wilderness within the southern wall of the city, to the fashionable Santa Maria in Via, and San Marcello and the Pantheon.

Sometimes, if they had turned and looked into the distance behind them, they might have seen Trombin's pink cheeks and well-turned figure not very far away. For he was a susceptible creature, as he often confessed to his companion, and the very first sight of Ortensia on the morning of her marriage had made a deep impression on him. It was not only her face and her hair, which resembled that of the late lamented Titian's Beauty; there was something in her figure and walk that made him half mad when he watched her; hers was not the stately stride of the black-eyed plebeian beauty, balancing her huge copper 'conca' on her classic head, still less was it the swaying, hip-dislocating, self-advertising gait of some of those handsome and fashionable ladies who frequented the Villa Medici on Sunday afternoons, and progressed through a running fire of compliments from pale-faced young gentlemen of wealth and noble lineage. Perhaps, after all, it was not Ortensia's walk in itself, but also every movement of her beautiful body that made the Bravo's pulses throb; it was not her step only, with all the mystery the moving draperies could mean, but the grace in the half-turn of her head too, the undulating motion of her hand and wrist and half-bent arm when she fanned herself, the resistless seduction in her flexible figure when she turned quickly to Stradella, while leaning on his arm and still walking on, to ask some new question, or in pleased surprise at something he had just told her.

The end of their first days of peace at the Orso came one afternoon quite suddenly in the queer round church of San Stefano Rotondo, which is not like any other in the world, and is entirely decorated, if the word may be so misused, with representations of the awful tortures undergone by early martyrs. If Stradella himself had ever been there, he would not have taken his wife to see such sights, but the church was not more often open then than now, and the two went in from pure curiosity.

As they entered the vast circular aisle and turned to the right, they came suddenly upon a group of fashionable people listening to the explanations of an imposing gentleman with perfectly white hair, who indicated the points of interest in a picture with a heavy stick made of a narwhale's ivory horn. He was describing minutely and realistically the sufferings of a virgin martyr, and his chief hearer followed what he said with absorbed interest.

Stradella instantly recognised the ex-Queen of Sweden. There was no mistaking the daughter of Gustavus Adolphus, with her square face and red cheeks, her disagreeable eyes and her black wig, her short green skirt and her mannish bearing. She was forty-four years old at that time. The fine-looking old man was Bernini, the sculptor; at her elbow, and not much above it in height, stood a misshapen youth with the face of a sad angel, the poet Guidi; he was evidently pained and disgusted by the lecture. Three other gentlemen stood at a little distance behind the Queen, but there was nothing to distinguish them from ninety-nine out of a hundred other fine gentlemen of fashionable society who wore extremely good coats, cut and curled their hair in the latest style, and proved that they were not absolute fools by holding their tongues when men like Bernini or Guidi were speaking.

At the sharp click of Ortensia's little heels on the stone pavement the Queen turned her head and instantly recognised Stradella, who bowed low as she nodded to him, and extended her hand in a gesture that bade him wait. He had no choice, and she looked at the picture again and listened with evident satisfaction to the great sculptor's explanation of the unpleasant subject. Guidi, however, tried not to hear; he also knew Stradella, who had set some of his verses to music, and he exchanged a glance of intelligence with him, wondering who his lady companion might be.

Stradella was already bending to whisper in her ear and tell her who the lady was, and that it was impossible to run away. Ortensia had never seen a queen before, and looked at her critically. Queen Christina, she thought, was anything but a fine-looking woman, though she looked intelligent, and Ortensia remembered scores of Venetian ladies who were much more queenly in appearance.

When Bernini had brought his poor little martyr to her last gasp, he added that, while he declined to disparage the work of a late fellow-artist, he considered Pomarancio's paintings beneath criticism; he then paused and took snuff. The Queen smiled sarcastically at his last words.

'Without speaking well of you, Cavaliere,' she said, 'I consider you as agreeable as you are famous.'

Bernini shut his snuff-box with a sharp snap and bowed low, though he quite understood the rebuke. Meanwhile Stradella led Ortensia forward, and the Queen turned to them as they came up.

'I am overjoyed to see you, Maestro,' she said, graciously giving him her hand to kiss while he touched the ground with one knee, and Ortensia executed a ceremonious courtesy. 'And who is this lady?' the Queen asked almost at once.

'My wife, Madam,' answered Stradella proudly. 'We are lately married.'

'Surely you are not a Roman, my dear child?' the Queen said inquiringly.

'No, Madam,' answered Ortensia, meeting the penetrating gaze of the disagreeable eyes without any nervousness. 'I am a Venetian, and was born a Grimani.'

The Queen smiled still more graciously at the ancient name, though she was a little surprised that a Grimani should have married a singer. Bernini and Guidi greeted Stradella while the Queen exchanged these few words with his wife, and the three gentlemen also came forward and pressed his hand, asking him questions about his journey, his marriage, and his present lodgings.

'What?' cried young Paluzzo Altieri. 'Lodging at the Orso? At an inn? My uncle will never allow that, nor her Majesty either!' He glanced at the Queen, who was still talking with Ortensia. 'You are the Pope's guests in Rome, Maestro, and I shall see that you are treated as such! Where will you be pleased to lodge, my dear Stradella? The whole Altieri palace is at your disposal, and you have but to choose your apartments———'

'Surely,' interrupted the Queen, who was listening now, 'I have a prior right to lodge a great artist in my house! Will you come and stay awhile with me, my dear?' she asked, turning to Ortensia again, with a sudden smile.

Ortensia was not at all overcome by the invitation, as the Queen perhaps expected that she would be, and she answered with demure caution.

'Your Majesty is too kind,' she said, without committing herself.

'Very well, my dear Altieri,' the Queen went on at once, as if Ortensia had already refused the proffered hospitality, 'I yield, but to His Holiness only, not to you!'

She laughed that strangely hard ringing laugh of hers, that reminded northern men of the sound of sharp skates cutting the smooth ice of a frozen river, where leafless birches and frost-bound banks send the notes echoing away between them till they are lost in the distance.

'The Pope owes your Majesty thanks,' the young courtier answered, bending his head a little, though he could hardly take his eyes from Ortensia.

Her Majesty Christina was out on one of her sight-seeing expeditions, in which old Bernini felt himself highly honoured to play guide, though she sometimes, as now, insisted on seeing sights which he would not willingly have shown her, and on hearing explanations which he would willingly have omitted. For though she set herself up as a profound critic and a super-refined æsthetic, her real nature was at once coarse and slightly Sadie, and she took pleasure in tales of bloodshed and suffering which would have disgusted a healthy-minded woman of ordinary sensitiveness. Indeed, as her Italian contemporaries knew her during those long years she spent in Rome, she was very far from being the royal Christina of the playwrights and poets. Her knowledge of art was not that of the critic, but of the professional dealer in antiquities, and though her opinion on the beauty of anything, from a picture to an inlaid cabinet, was often mere nonsense, she was never mistaken as to the price of the object. She was not an amateur, but an expert, and though anything that was really fashionable pleased her, she would buy nothing that had not an intrinsic value. In those first years of her permanent residence in Rome she was rich, for in voluntarily abdicating the throne she had reserved to herself a liberal income, which afterwards dwindled to very little, and she kept up a considerable state in the Palazzo Riario, that overlooks the river from the Trastevere side. There was hardly an artist or a literary man in Rome, or a student of science or a musician, who did not regularly pay his court to her, and dedicate to her something of his best work. Not rarely, too, she gave her advice; Bernini should finish his last statue in such and such a way, Guidi should avoid one rhyme and introduce another, on pain of her displeasure. Bernini yielded politely, because of all Italy's artists of genius he was the most thoroughly cynical in following the fashion of his time; Guidi obeyed because a dinner was always a dinner to a starving youth of twenty, and a rhyme was no great price to pay for it; but he quietly enclosed her suggestions in quotation marks, thereby disclaiming any responsibility for them.

The young Paluzzo Altieri was nephew to the Cardinal who governed Rome as the 'real' Pope, while the octogenarian Clement X., who was called the 'nominal' Pope, spent most of his days more or less in his bed. The Cardinal and all his relations had been adopted by him as 'nephews,' and as he was the last of his race he had bestowed on them and their heirs all his vast private possessions instead of enriching them out of the treasury, as many popes did by their families.

Alberto Paluzzo Altieri was good-for-nothing, and like most really worthless young men he exercised an extraordinary charm on every one who knew him, both women and men. For to be a real good-for-nothing, without being a criminal, implies a native genius for wasting other people's time as agreeably as one's own, and for helping rich men to get rid of their money with infinite pleasure and no profit at all, and for making every woman believe that she can certainly convert and reform the prodigal by the simple process of allowing him to fall in love with her, which, of course, must elevate him to her moral and intellectual level.

There was nothing very remarkable about Alberto except that charm of his. He was dark, he had straight black hair, and tolerably regular features, like many young Romans; he was neither tall nor short, nor exceptionally well made, and of the three young gentlemen who accompanied the ex-Queen on her sight-seeing excursion, he was the least ostentatiously dressed. But he had a wonderfully pleasant voice in speaking, with the smile of a happy and phenomenally innocent boy, and his bright brown eyes had the most guileless expression in the world. At the present time it amused him to be Queen Christina's favourite, perhaps because she was a genuine queen, or possibly because her cold-blooded murder of Monaldeschi was still so fresh in every one's memory that there was a spice of danger in the situation; but in any case he was prepared for the first pleasant opportunity of changing his allegiance which might present itself.

When he saw Stradella's young wife it occurred to him at once that such a chance was within his reach, and he was not satisfied till he had made the musician promise to move from the inn to the Altieri palace on the next day but one; for Alberto was the eldest son, and neither his father, who was old, nor his mother, who was a slave to her perpetual devotions, ever attempted to oppose his wishes in such matters. Was he not a model son? Could anything surpass his sweet-tempered affection for his parents? Why should he not have what he liked? Good-for-nothings are often their mothers' favourites; but Alberto had long ago won over his father as well, and not him only, but his uncle also, the Cardinal, who ruled Rome and the States of the Church like a despot. The great man was really not sorry that one of his own family should occupy the most important position in Queen Christina's household; for it is the instinct of all ex-sovereigns to meddle in politics, and it was not possible to predict what such a woman might do if she were bored.

Ortensia was a mere girl still, but her eyes had been opened of late, and she did not fail to notice the impression she had made on the young man; she was far too much in love with her husband, however, to care for such admiration, or even to be pleased by it, and somehow the present case seemed to be of bad omen.

The Queen and her party had already been long in the church, for they had begun their round on the other side of the entrance, and were just ending it when Stradella and his wife appeared; now, therefore, after a few more words, they took themselves off amidst much bowing and scraping on the part of all except the Queen herself. She smiled to Ortensia, and nodded familiarly to Stradella, making a beckoning and inviting gesture to him over her shoulder with her right hand as she turned away. Alberto looked quickly at the musician, not so much taking him for a possible rival as for a convenient successor; but the faintly contemptuous smile that flickered in the musician's face as he saw the careless signal assuredly did not mean that he was either flattered or attracted. Ortensia saw the gesture too, and resented it; but a moment later she smiled to herself at the thought that such a woman as the Queen could ever win so much as a second thought from Alessandro.

The two had seen enough of San Stefano, and were glad to escape from the nightmare of horrors depicted on its walls; but before going out they waited a few minutes in the vestibule to allow the party time to get out of sight.

'So that is the famous Queen Christina!' Ortensia said, expressing her surprise and disappointment as soon as they were alone. 'Pina looks more like a lady!'

CHAPTER XIV

After supper on the next evening Stradella and Ortensia were sitting for the last time in the beautiful loggia, in the soft light of the young moon that would soon set behind the Vatican Hill. The air was wonderfully dry and warm, as it is in Rome sometimes in June when there has been no rain for three or four weeks.

On the following morning they were to move to the Palazzo Altieri, where Don Alberto had caused to be prepared for them the apartment that is entered by a small door on the left, halfway up the grand staircase. They had been talking of the change.

'It will seem more natural to you to live in a palace again,' Stradella said in a laughing tone. 'You must have had enough of inns by this time!'

'The happiest days of my life have been spent in them,' Ortensia answered with a little sadness. 'I am wondering whether it will ever be the same again.'

'As long as we are the same there can be no difference, sweetheart. I am glad you are to be more worthily lodged. Don Alberto was always a very good-natured fellow and more or less a friend of mine, and he is taking the greatest pains to make us comfortable in his father's house.'

'I wish he would not take such infinite trouble to stare at me all the time!'

'Why should he look at anything else when you are in sight?' laughed the singer. 'Do I? And just consider what a pleasant change it must be for him after being obliged to gaze at the Queen by the hour together in visible rapture! The vision must pall sometimes, I should think! I really do not blame him for showing that he admires you, and he is not the only one. There is our friend Trombin, for instance, who stands in adoration staring at you and puffing out his round cheeks whenever we meet.'

'Oh, he only makes me laugh,' Ortensia answered; 'he is so funny, with his little pursed-up mouth and his round eyes! I am sure he must be the kindest-hearted creature in the world. But Don Alberto is quite different. I am a little afraid of him. I feel as if some day he might say something to me——'

'What, for instance?' asked Stradella, amused. 'What do you think he may say?'

'That he thinks me—what shall I say?—very pretty, perhaps!'

'He would only be saying to your face what every one says behind your back, love! Should you object very much if he told you that he thought you beautiful?'

'I do not wish to be beautiful for any one but you,' Ortensia answered softly. 'I wish that every one else might think me hideous, and never come near me!'

'And that I might seem to every one but you to sing out of tune!' laughed Stradella.

'At all events they would leave us alone, if they thought so! But I did not mean it in that way. I think you do not care whether men make love to me or not!'

She was not quite pleased, and as she leaned her head back against the wall he saw her pouting lips in the moonlight.

'I like to be envied,' said Stradella.

As he made this singular answer he bent over a mandoline he had been holding on his knee and made the point of the quill quiver against the upper strings with incredible lightness, so that the tinkling note seemed to come from very far away and could not interrupt the conversation.

'I do not understand,' Ortensia said, after a moment, and she lifted her arms and made her clasped hands a pillow between the back of her head and the wall.

'The beauty of anything is its immortal part,' he said; 'its real value is as much as people will give for it, neither more nor less. Do you not understand me yet?'

'Not quite. Why do you talk in riddles? I am not very clever, you know!'

'You are beautiful, dear. I have often told you so, and other men will if they get a chance. But as one of nature's works of art I doubt whether you are more beautiful than almond-blossoms in spring, or the dawn in the south on a summer's morning. Do you see?'

'No. Is it a parable? What will you compare me to next?'

Stradella was making sweet far-off music on the instrument. It came a little nearer and then died away into the distance, when he was ready to speak again.

'You may have almond-blossoms by hundreds in March for nothing,' he said, 'and any one may see the dawn who is awake so early! They have perfect beauty, but no value. No one can really envy a man who brings an armful of flowers home with him, or who sees the dawn of a fine day, yet both are quite as lovely as you are, in their own fashion, though they are common. But you have their beauty, and besides, you are of immense value, not to me only but to the whole race of men, because you are not only beautiful, but also a very rare work of nature, far rarer than pearls and rubies.'

'Then it was all a pretty compliment you were paying me!' Ortensia smiled. 'Of course I could not understand what you meant!'

Stradella laughed low, and the mandoline was silent for a while.

'The way to make compliments is to find out what a woman most admires in herself and then to make her believe it is ten times more wonderful than she supposed it could be. No one has ever told that secret yet, but it has opened more doors and balcony windows than any other.'

'That was not your way of opening mine, dear!' laughed Ortensia. 'I am afraid you needed no secret at all to do that.'

Again he touched the mandoline, but it was not mere tinkling music now, making believe that it came all the way down the long street from the dismal Tor di Nona by the bridge. It was that love-song he had made for her in Venice, and had sung to her when Pina left them together the first time; a measure of the melody trembled through the upper strings, and then his own voice took up the words in tones breathed out so easily that the highest never seemed to be high, nor to cost him more effort than ordinary speech. Of all instruments the violoncello can yield notes most like such a voice, when the bow is in a master's hand.

In Rome, at night, he may sing who will, even now: if he goes bawling out of tune through the silent streets, though it be not from drink but out of sheer lightness of heart, the first policeman he meets will silence him, it is true; but if he sings well and soberly he may go on his way rejoicing, for no watchman will hinder him. It is an ancient right of the Italian people to sing when and where they please, by day or night, in the certainty that tuneful singing can never give offence nor disturb even a dying man.

So the great master of song sat in the high balcony on that June night and let his voice float out over moon-lit Rome; and presently Ortensia slipped from her chair and knelt before him, her hands clasped on his knees and looking up to his face, for his magic was more enthralling now than when it had first drawn her to him.

When he reached the end he kissed her, the last long-drawn note still vibrating on his lips, and she felt that they were cold and trembling when they touched hers.

'Yes,' she whispered, drawing back just enough to see his eyes in the moonlight, 'that was the key to my window. When I heard that song I knew you loved me already, and that I must love you too, sooner or later, and for all my life. It is not my poor beauty that is rarer than pearls and rubies, love, but your genius and your voice. I know what you mean now! I like to be envied by other women because you are mine, with all you are, you, and your fame, and everything!'

'Do you see?' Stradella laughed softly. 'You should not be angry with people who stare at you, any more than I am with people who listen when I sing! And I am no more jealous because Don Alberto admires you than you should be because Queen Christina likes my singing, as she says she does.'

'Tell me, Alessandro, is that a black wig she wears, or is it her own hair?' asked Ortensia, pretending to be serious.

'In confidence, my love, it is a wig,' Stradella answered with extreme gravity.

'So much the better. I am glad she admires your singing; but if it were not a wig, perhaps I should be less glad. Do you think Don Alberto's fine black hair is his own, dear; and are his legs quite real?'

'Without doubt.'

'Then I think you ought to be just a little less glad that he stares at me, than if his legs were padded and he wore a wig as the Queen does, and were forty, as she is, with bad teeth and a muddy complexion like hers! You know you should be just a very little less pleased, dear!'

In the moonlight he could see her smiling, for her face was close to his, and she had laid her hands on his shoulders, while she still knelt at his knees.

'But that would mean that I was jealous, dear heart,' objected Stradella. 'Why am I to be jealous because he admires you, unless you like him too much? Most women say that a man is a brute to be jealous at all till they have run away with some one else! Your uncle, for instance, is really justified in being jealous of me.'

'Really?'

Ortensia laughed and kissed again before saying anything more; and just as their lips touched, the silver light began to fail, and the young moon dropped behind the Vatican Hill, and when they separated it seemed quite dark by comparison. Now any one can easily find out how long it takes the moon to set after she has touched the shoulder of a hill; and hence the exact number of seconds during which that particular kiss lasted can easily be ascertained. But time, as Danish people say, was made for shoemakers; and Ortensia and Stradella took no account of it, but behaved in the most foolishly dilatory way, just as if they were not a plain, humdrum, married couple that should have known better than to spend the evening in a balcony, alternately sentimentalising, kissing, and singing love-songs.

That was the last evening they spent at the Sign of the Bear, and though they had talked idly enough in the loggia under the light of the young moon about such very grave subjects as jealousy and envy, they afterwards cherished ineffaceable memories of that sweet June night.

For there had been an interlude in the comedy of their troubles, wherein love had dwelt with them alone and in peace, making his treasures fully known to them, and guiding their footsteps while they explored his kingdom and his palace; and they both felt instinctively that the interlude was over now, and that real life must begin again with their change of lodgings. Stradella was a musician and a singer, without settled fortune, and he must return to the business of earning bread for them both; moreover, he was famous, and therefore could not possibly get his living obscurely. The Pope's adopted family would vie with the ex-Queen of Sweden, the Spanish Ambassador and the rich nobles, to flatter him and attract him to their respective palaces. Alberto Altieri, who had lost his heart to Ortensia's beauty at first sight, would organise every sort of fashionable entertainment for the young bride's benefit, and would do his best to turn her head by magnificent display. Hereafter, till the summer heat drove the Romans to the country, no evening gathering in a noble house would deserve mention if Stradella and his wife were not there, as no concert would be worth hearing unless some of his music was performed. The young couple would be continually in the very vortex of fashion's whirlpool, and though they would not resent the distinction, and might even enjoy the gaiety for a few weeks, they would have but little time left for each other between morning and midnight.

It was apparent on the very first night they spent in the Palazzo Altieri that Don Alberto was not the only young man in Rome who wished to please Ortensia. Soon after the second hour of night, which we should call about ten o'clock in June, Stradella and Ortensia heard music in the narrow street below their new quarters; and as the sounds did not move farther away, it was almost immediately apparent that the singers were serenading Ortensia. It was no ordinary music, either; there were half-a-dozen fine voices and four or five stringed instruments, played with masterly skill—a violin, a 'viola d'amore,' and at least two or three lutes.

Stradella put out the light in the room and opened the outer shutters a little, for they had been closed. The moon was shining even more brightly than on the previous night, but the rays did not fall as they fell on the loggia at the inn; the roofs of the low houses opposite were partly illuminated, and the belfry of San Stefano, and of the little church of Santa Marta and the Minerva much farther away; but that side of the irregularly built Altieri palace and the street below were almost in darkness. Looking down between the shutters, Ortensia and Stradella could only see deeper shadows within the shade, where the serenaders were standing, and they were sure that the latter could not see them at all. They listened with delight, their heads close together, and each with one arm round the other's waist.

'They are men from the Pope's choir,' Stradella whispered, 'or from Saint Peter's.'

The first piece was finished, and the musicians exchanged a few words in low tones, while one or two of them tuned their instruments a little. A moment later they began to play again, and as Stradella recognised the opening chords of one of his own serenades, a rich-toned voice began the song.

Ortensia's arm tightened a little round her husband, and his round her, and their young cheeks touched as they listened and peered down into the gloom of the narrow street. Suddenly there was a stir below, and the sound of other feet coming quickly from the Piazza del Gesù; and though the serenade was not half finished, another choir and other instruments struck up a chorus, loud and high, almost completely drowning the first.

Stradella uttered an exclamation of surprise. The newcomers sang and played quite as well as the first party, if not better, and the music was Stradella's too—a triumphal march and chorus which he had composed when last in Rome for the marriage of the Orsini heir. It had been intended to drown all other sounds while the wedding procession was leaving the church, and it now fulfilled a similar purpose most effectually.

For a moment Stradella imagined that it was only meant as a surprise, and a reinforcement to the first party, and that the whole company of musicians would play and sing together. That would have been indeed a royal serenade; but half a minute had not passed before things took a very different turn, for the party in possession of the street charged the newcomers after a moment's deliberation; the twanging of strings turned into a noise of stout sticks hitting each other violently and smashing an instrument now and then, and steel was clashing too, while the voices that had lately sung so tunefully now shouted in wild discord.

Suddenly a flash of bright light darted through the dim confusion as a dark lantern was opened, and the glare fell full on the face and figure of Don Alberto Altieri, who stood hatless, sword in hand, facing an adversary who was quite invisible to the couple at the window. The instant the light was seen, the others of the two parties ceased fighting and retired in opposite directions.

'Sir,' said a voice which Stradella and Ortensia instantly recognised as Trombin's, 'I see that you are at least as young as you are noble, if not more so, and I shall therefore not press my acquaintance upon you so far as to take your life. But I shall tell you plainly, sir, that I am a fencing-master by my profession, and if you do not immediately dissolve into air, or, to put it better, melt away with all your company, I will lard you, in the space of thirty seconds, with fifteen flesh wounds in fifteen different parts of your body, not one of which shall be dangerous, but which, being taken in what I may call the aggregate, shall keep you in your bed for a month, sir. And moreover, sir, as you do not seem inclined to lower your guard and go away, there is one!'

The long rapier flashed in the light of the lantern, and instantly Don Alberto's sword fell from his hand. Trombin had run him neatly through the right forearm, completely disabling him at the first thrust.

The Bravo at once stooped, picked up the weapon and politely offered him the hilt, but he could not take it with his right hand, and grasping the blade itself with his left, he just managed to get it into the sheath.

'At least,' he cried, furious with humiliation and pain, 'that gentleman with the lantern there, who employs you, will answer to me for this in broad daylight, when my wound is healed.'

'With pleasure, sir,' answered the voice of Gambardella. 'But as one gentleman to another, I warn you that I am also a fencing-master.'

The instant Don Alberto was wounded his musicians had taken to flight, and he had now no choice but to follow them, which he did with as much dignity as he could command, considering that he was hatless, wounded, and altogether very badly worsted, for he had understood that he had fallen in with Bravi, probably employed by a rival. As soon as it was evident that he was going away, the lantern was shut and the street was dark again, Trombin's musicians tuned their instruments, and in two or three minutes the triumphal march rang out again, louder and higher than ever.

In the dimness above Stradella and Ortensia looked at each other, though they could hardly see one another's faces.

'Your two admirers mean business!' said the musician with some amusement. 'Trombin will seem less ridiculous the next time you see him staring at you!'

'How can you laugh!' asked Ortensia gravely, for she had never before seen men face each other with drawn swords.

She had always been taught that duelling was as wicked as it was dangerous, and her uncle Pignaver had shared that orthodox opinion; nevertheless, though she would not willingly have acknowledged it to her confessor, she was glad that Trombin had driven the lady-killer from the field, and she only wished that Stradella might have done it himself. As for the Bravi's serenade, she did not resent it at all, nor did her husband; it was a friendly entertainment, and nothing more, on the part of the two wealthy Venetian gentlemen to whom the young couple already owed an immense debt of gratitude. When the chorus was ended, Stradella clapped his hands.

'Bravo!' cried Ortensia, and the word sounded clearly in the momentary silence.

'At your ladyship's service!' answered Trombin in a laughing tone, for the jest she unconsciously made in using the single word seemed to him full of humour.

Gambardella's dark lantern sent its searching ray up to the window at that moment, and showed the heads of the two young people close together, for the shutters were now wide open; an instant later the light went out and the music began again. It was a madrigal this time, airy and changing, and sung by four men, one of whom had a beautiful male contralto, which is a rarity even in Italy. Stradella recognised it instantly, for he had often sung at the Lateran and knew the man.

'They are of the choir of Saint John's,' he whispered to Ortensia.

There was rivalry between the Lateran and the Vatican in the matter of music then, as there has been in our own day, and it was no wonder that the musicians themselves had joined in the fray when Don Alberto drew on Trombin and Gambardella.

The serenade continued, and the two Bravi enjoyed it quite as much as Ortensia herself; but it was not likely that Don Alberto would be satisfied to go quietly to bed after being wounded under the very walls of his father's palace by a professional cut-throat who had been doubtless hired to protect a rival serenader. There was a guardhouse of the watch not far away, at the foot of the Capitol Hill, and thither he hastened, after twisting his silk scarf round his forearm as tightly as he could to staunch the blood.

In less than a quarter of an hour he came back with a corporal's guard of the night-watchmen, armed with clumsy broadswords, but each carrying a serviceable iron-shod cudgel of cornel-wood which, according to old Roman rhyme, breaks bones so easily that the blows do not even hurt: 'Corniale, rompe le ossa e non fa male.' The corporal himself carried an elaborately wrought lantern of iron and glass, ornamented with the papal tiara and crossed keys.

Now the Bravi did not know Alberto Altieri by sight, and they had treated him as if he were of no more account than several hundred other young noblemen, sure that he would have his scratch dressed and go quietly to bed like a sensible fellow who has had the worst of it. Therefore when the watch came in sight suddenly, from behind the corner of the palace that juts out sharply towards San Stefano, the serenaders did not connect the appearance of the patrol with their late adversary, who had disappeared in the opposite direction; on the contrary, they went on singing and playing, well aware that night-watchmen never interfered with such innocent diversions, but would generally stop on their round to enjoy the music. Even now, when they came straight towards the musicians, the latter only made way quietly, supposing that they wished to pass. It was not till Gambardella recognised Don Alberto's face by the light of the corporal's lantern that he understood, and drew his rapier just in time to save himself from being arrested.

'The two Bravi faced the watch side by side'

'Run, while we hold the street!' he yelled to the musicians, who did not wait for a second invitation, but fled like sheep down the Via del Gesù.

Trombin's blade was out almost as soon as his companion's, and the two Bravi faced the watch side by side. Their hats were drawn well over their eyes, and they had clapped on the little black masks most people carried then, so that they were in no fear of being recognised. The corporal, who seemed to be a determined fellow, swung his stick like a sabre, to bring it down on Gambardella's head, but it found only the empty air in its path, and at the same time the officer's left hand was so sharply pricked that he dropped the big lantern, which rolled on its side and went out. Meanwhile

Trombin had parried the blow his nearest adversary had struck at him, and in return had instantly disabled him by running him through the right forearm, precisely as he had done by Don Alberto.

A moment later Gambardella opened his dark lantern, and held it in his left, so that he and Trombin became almost invisible to their adversaries and had them at a great disadvantage. Furious, the corporal struck another wild blow with his staff, but Gambardella dodged it even more easily than before, being behind the lantern that dazzled the other; and as the iron-shod stick hit the ground after missing its aim, the officer felt the Bravo's blade run through the muscles of his upper arm, like a stream of icy water, followed instantly by burning heat. With a hearty curse he backed out of the way of another thrust and bade his men draw their broadswords and finish the matter.

But this was more easily said than done. The half-dozen men obeyed, indeed, so far as drawing and brandishing their clumsy weapons was concerned, but the street was narrow, the lantern dazzled them, and the two long rapiers with their needle points and solid blades pointed out at them in the circle of light, ready to run in under the awkward broadsword guard with deadly effect.

The corporal swore till Cucurullo, who was looking out of another upper window, expected to see him struck by lightning, and all the people who were now at the windows of the low houses opposite the palace crossed themselves devoutly; but it was of no use, as long as those two gleaming points kept making little circles slowly in the light. There was not a man in the corporal's guard who would have gone within an arm's length of them.

Seeing that they already had the best of it, the Bravi began to advance by regular short steps, moving the right foot forward first and then the left, as if they were on the fencing ground, their rapiers steadily in guard; and the watchmen fell back, fearing to face them. But that was not enough; for though the two might drive the little band in that way from street to street, if they but lowered their points a moment their adversaries would spring in upon them, even at some risk.

'We are mild-tempered men,' said Trombin at last, 'but we are both fencing-masters, and it will not be prudent to irritate us, or, as I may say, to drive us to extremities. You had better go your way quietly and let us go ours.'

'If you do not,' said Gambardella, who was excessively bored, 'we will skewer every mother's son of you in five minutes, by the holy marrow-bones of Beelzebub!'

This singular invocation arrested the attention and disturbed the equanimity of the watchmen; they could stand being sworn at by every saint in the calendar, by every article of the Nicene Creed, and, generally, by everything sacred of which their corporal had ever heard, but they did not like men who invoked relics of such horrible import as those which Gambardella had named. Nor were their fears misplaced, for as they hesitated for two or three seconds before turning to run, the Bravo made a spring like a wild cat, struck the corporal violently on the nose with the iron guard of his rapier, jumped back one step, and then, lunging an almost incredible distance as the corporal staggered against the wall, ran the man behind him through the fleshy part of the shoulder. On his side, Trombin advanced too, pretended to lunge and then suddenly struck the man before him such a stinging blow with the flat of his rapier that the fellow howled and fled, whereupon Trombin encouraged his speed by prodding him sharply in the rear. In a moment the confusion was complete, and the watchmen were tumbling over each other in their hurry to escape. Then the lantern was suddenly shut, and the two Bravi faced about and ran like deer in the opposite direction.

CHAPTER XV

Don Alberto did not care to tell how he had been wounded, and kept the matter between himself, his doctor, and his own man, giving out that he had been thrown from his horse and had broken one of the bones of his forearm, a story which quite accounted for his wearing his arm in a sling when he appeared after keeping his room during five days. It was natural, too, that Stradella and Ortensia, who had recognised him by the light of the lantern, should say nothing about the matter, and the Bravi did not know who the young man was; so there was a possibility that the whole affair might remain a secret.

Trombin, however, was anxious to discover the name of the adversary he had wounded, and Gambardella was not unwilling to help him, though he considered him quite mad where Ortensia was concerned.

'You have no imagination,' Trombin objected, in answer to this charge. 'Can you not understand the peculiar charm of being in love with a lady of whom I have agreed to make an angel at the first convenient opportunity, and whom I have further promised to deliver safe, sound, and alive to her uncle in Venice?'

'I wish you joy of your puzzles,' answered Gambardella discontentedly.

'I derive much solace from the pleasures of imagination,' Trombin observed, following his own train of thought. 'In me a great romancer has been lost to our age, another Bandello, perhaps a second Boccaccio! An English gentleman of taste once told me that my features resemble those of a dramatist of his country, whose first name was William—I forget the second, which I could not learn to pronounce—but that my cheeks are even rounder than his were, and my mouth smaller. Under other circumstances, who knows but that I might have been the William Something of Italy? My English friend added that the painted bust of the dramatist on his tomb was quite the most hideous object he had ever seen, so I do not tell you the story out of mere vanity, as you might suppose. My misfortune is that I am generally driven by a sort of familiar spirit to do the things I imagine, instead of writing them down.'

'And pray what do you imagine you are going to do next?' inquired Gambardella.

'It has occurred to me that I might carry off the lady myself,' Trombin answered in a thoughtful tone.

'And leave me to manage the rest?'

'You will have no trouble. I shall take the road to Venice, of course, and after a month or two I will hand the lady over to Pignaver, for I dare say she will soon tire of my company. As for you, you will only have to follow her husband, for he will go after his wife as fast as he can, of his own accord, and when you both reach Venice together, I shall be waiting and we will lead him into a trap and give him up to his pretty adorer! The rest will be as I said. She will not be able to keep him a prisoner very long, and when he leaves her house we can settle the business.'

'And of course you will expect me to help you in carrying the young woman off?'

'Naturally! Should you feel any scruples about it?'

'No,' Gambardella answered, in an indifferent tone, but he changed the subject and went back to the question of the rival serenader's identity. 'It might be as well to think of more practical matters,' he said. 'The excellent Tommaso has not found out anything about the man you wounded last night, though he has already ascertained exactly where the ex-Queen of Sweden keeps her jewels!'

'Intelligent creature! He really has a good store of general information! I dare say he will take them some day and leave us without giving notice.'

'It must be very convenient to be born so low in the world as to be able to steal without disgrace,' observed Gambardella thoughtfully. 'I suppose such fellows have no sense of honour.'

'None whatever,' said Trombin, with equal gravity. 'As you say, it must make many things easy when one has no money.'

This conversation had taken place under the great colonnade before Saint Peter's, late in the afternoon, when the air was pleasantly cool. Bernini's colonnade was new then, and some of the poorer Romans, dwelling in the desolate regions between the Lateran and Santa Maria Maggiore, had not even seen it. It might have been expected that it was to become the resort of loungers, gossips, foreigners, dealers in images and rosaries, barbers, fortune-tellers, and money-changers, as the ancient portico had been that used to form a straight covered way from the Basilica to the Bridge of Sant' Angelo; but for some inexplicable reason this never happened, and it was always, as it is now, a deserted place.

The Bravi, who were men of taste, according to their times, admired the architecture extremely, and often walked there for half an hour before it was time to hear the Benediction music in the church, which was always good and sometimes magnificent.

This afternoon they were strolling not far from the bronze gate that gives access to the Vatican; a dozen paces or more behind them, within call but out of hearing of their conversation, walked the excellent Tommaso, otherwise known as Grattacacio, the ex-highway robber, about whom they had just been talking. The last words had barely passed Trombin's lips when they heard the man's footsteps approaching them rapidly from behind. They stopped to learn what was the matter.

'A young gentleman on a mule is coming, with several servants,' Tommaso said quickly. 'He has his right arm in a sling. Perhaps he is your man.'

The two friends nodded carelessly, but drew their hats a little lower over their eyes as they turned and walked back, skirting the inner side of the colonnade so as to watch the party that was coming straight across the Piazza in the sun from the direction of Porta Santo Spirito. As soon as they saw the face of the young man who rode the mule they recognised Trombin's adversary, who wore his broad-brimmed hat far down on the left to screen him from the sun, thus exposing the right side of his face to their view. They went on quietly, as if they had hardly noticed him, and he paid no attention to them. When he and his three servants had almost reached the bronzed gates, the Bravi despatched their man after him to find out his name from the groom who would hold his mule, while they themselves remained where they were, walking slowly up and down, a dozen steps each way.

'I see a golden opportunity rising in the distance,' said Trombin. 'It illuminates my imagination and lights up my understanding.'

'It will probably dazzle mine, so that I shall see nothing at all,' observed Gambardella with his usual sourness.

'Possibly,' Trombin answered pleasantly. 'I shall therefore hide my light under a bushel, as it were, and thus spare your mental eyes a shock that might be fatal to them. For my present inspiration is of such a tremendous nature that an ordinary intelligence might be unsettled by it.'

'Could you not communicate the nature of it in small doses, as it were?' asked Gambardella, mimicking him a little. 'One can get accustomed even to poisons in that way, as Mithridates did.'

'To oblige you, I will attempt it, my friend, but I shall endeavour to lead you to guess the truth yourself by asking questions, instead of presenting it to you in disjointed fragments. Now consider that youth whom I ran through the arm the other night, and answer me. Do you suppose that he was serenading Pina, the serving-woman, or Ortensia her mistress?'

'What a question! It was Ortensia, of course.'

'But was he serenading the Lady Ortensia out of ill-feeling towards her, or out of good-feeling?'

'Out of good-feeling.'

'What is the good-feeling of a handsome young man towards a beautiful young woman usually called, my friend?'

'Love, I suppose. What nonsense is this?'

'It is the Socratic method, as recorded by Plato. I learned something of it when I was a student at Padua. Now, you have told me that the young man feels love for the young woman, and you appear to be right; but what do you think he hopes to get from her in return, love or dislike?'

'Her love, no doubt.'

'You answer well, my friend. Now tell me this also. Will he get her love without the consent of her husband, or with it?'

'Without, if he gets it at all! I am tired of this fooling. It bores me excessively.'

'You will not be bored long,' answered Trombin with confidence. 'Answer me one question more. Do you suppose that the young man will have any success with the Lady Ortensia, unless he can separate her from Stradella by some stratagem?'

Gambardella looked sharply at his wordy companion.

'I begin to take your meaning,' he said.

'You have a good mind,' Trombin answered, 'but it works slowly. You are on the verge of guessing what my inspiration is. Let us, for a large consideration, be the means of carrying off the Lady Ortensia for this rich young man, and when we have done so and received his money, let us execute the plan we have already made. For it will be easy for us to persuade her to do anything we suggest, because both she and her husband are under the greatest obligations to us, whereas the young man would have to employ violence and make a great scandal. But here comes that excellent Tommaso.'

'You are certainly a great man,' said Gambardella, looking at Trombin with admiration.

It was clear from Tommaso's face that the intelligence he brought was important, and as he stood hat in hand before his masters he looked up and down the colonnade to see if there were any one in sight and near enough to listen.

'The gentleman is Don Alberto Altieri,' he said, almost in a whisper.

Trombin at once puffed out his pink cheeks, pursed his lips, and whistled very softly, for he was much surprised; but Gambardella seemed quite unmoved, and merely nodded to Tommaso as if well satisfied with the latter's service. Then the two strolled on again, and their cut-throat servant followed them, just out of hearing of their conversation, as before; for he was much too wise to try any common trick of eavesdropping on a pair of men who would just as soon wring his neck and throw him into a well as look at him. His highest ambition really was to be promoted to help them in one of those outrageous deeds that had made them the most famous Bravi of the whole century, who had received pardons from popes and kings, from the Emperor Leopold, and from the Venetian Republic itself, under which passports they travelled and lived where they pleased, still untouched by the law.

'This is a delicate business,' observed Gambardella, for both had heard the gossip about Don Alberto and Queen Christina.

'It will be the more amusing,' answered Trombin. 'When I reflect upon the primitive simplicity of the business we undertook for Pignaver, and compare it with the plan we have now conceived and shall certainly execute in a few days, I cannot but congratulate myself on the fertility of my imagination, or, as I might say, upon the resemblance between my mind and that of the novelist Boccaccio. But I feel the superiority of my lot over his in the fact that I am generally the chief actor in my own stories.'

'The Queen will be useful,' said Gambardella.

'Bless her for an admirably amusing woman!' cried Trombin fervently. 'She has the mane of the lion and the heart of the hare!'

'The mane happens to be a wig, my friend,' sneered the other.

'In more senses than one,' retorted Trombin, 'but the hare's heart is genuine. She was afraid of poor Monaldeschi. You knew it, I knew it, and Luigi Santinelli knew it. She ordered us to kill him because she believed he was selling her secrets to the Spanish, and was going to poison her in their interests. She is always fancying that some one wants to poison her. Oh, yes, my friend, a most diverting character, for she thinks of nothing but herself, and her Self is a selfish, hysterical, cruel, cowardly woman!'[1]

'I detest her for that business at Fontainebleau,' answered Gambardella.

'Precisely. So do I, though she amuses me. To strangle a superfluous woman is sometimes unavoidable, and there are occasions when it is wisdom to stab an unnecessary male in the back. But to put an unarmed gentleman to the wall, so to say, in broad daylight and deliberately skewer him, being three to one as we were that day, is a thing I shall decline to do again for all the gold in India, Mexico, and Brazil!'

'Unless it be paid in cash,' suggested Gambardella.

'Cash,' answered Trombin enigmatically, 'is one of the forces of nature.'

FOOTNOTES:

[1] For Trombin's view of Christina's character and Monaldeschi's murder, I am indebted to the admirable and trustworthy work of Baron de Bildt, a distinguished Swedish diplomatist, entitled *Christine de Suède et le Cardinal Azzolino* (Paris, 1899). The writer points out the singular ignorance of the truth about Monaldeschi displayed by Browning and the elder Dumas.

CHAPTER XVI

A week later fashionable Rome was gathered together at the Palazzo Riario to a feast of poetry and music. Christina had just founded the Academy which survives to this day in that state of mediocrity above which it has never risen in nearly two hundred and fifty years, for the idea had suggested itself to her when she found how easy it was to attract starving talent to a good dinner. 'Feed the hungry' is a good motto for those who aim at being patrons of the fine arts, like the ex-Queen in Rome, or Pignaver in Venice; the only condition is that the hungry shall be clever or witty starvelings who can pay for their dinners with their brains. However, when men of talent cease to be hungry they generally become snobs, and will take the fly of the season with as much voracity as any trout in May.

The literary and musical receptions at the Palazzo Riario took place in the portico that opened upon the gardens in those days; for the whole palace was afterwards rebuilt by the Corsini, and many parts of it were changed. Christina had been in Paris and had seen Louis Fourteenth dance as Alcibiades in Benserade's ballet, a sight to rejoice the gods of Olympus, who must certainly have laughed even louder at the bewigged King's mincing steps than they did at Vulcan's limp; for with many gifts, the Sun-King possessed no more sense of humour than Don Quixote, who stood on his head before Sancho as a proof that love was driving him mad. The ex-Queen was already dreaming of a wonderful pastoral play, in which Don Alberto Altieri was to appear as Endymion, and she herself, the elderly and slightly bedraggled virgin queen, would play Diana. There was Guidi to write the verses, Stradella should compose the music, and Christina herself would get most of the credit for the work.

In the meantime, though she had nothing so complete to offer, she invited the Romans to hear such poetry as she could provide, and some excellent music; and Bernini, who could make anything look like anything else by means of whitewashed wooden columns, coarse draperies stiffened and whitened with wet plaster, and caryatides modelled in plaster and pasteboard, had improvised a Temple of Art for the performance. In the midst of this sanctuary, amongst laurels and roses, he had placed the clay model of his bust of Christina herself, in a wig like the French King's. He afterwards cast it in bronze, and considering that he must have done his best to make the portrait pleasing, it is appalling to think what the original must have been.

The little temple stood just outside the portico, facing inward like a stage, on which the performers appeared in turn, the audience being gathered under the portico. Beyond it, the beautiful gardens stretched away in terraces and grades to the high distance. Christina herself sat on a sort of throne, facing the clay image of herself, while her courtiers and satellites were grouped behind her. Her intimate friend Cardinal Azzolino sat on her right, because Cardinal Altieri, who should have been there, had not come, and half-a-dozen other cardinals in scarlet occupied the huge gilt arm-chairs on both sides, each having one or two of his especial parasites behind him in readiness to do his bidding or to laugh at his jokes, as the case might be. There were not more than fifty other seats in the portico, and they were all occupied by the ladies of Rome, who came to applaud the performances of their countrymen and to laugh at the hysterical 'Minerva of the North,' who paid the poets and musicians, and went into such convulsions of appreciation when their works pleased her that the stability of her huge black wig was in danger. The ladies' chairs were not close together, but scattered about, as in a drawing-room, and almost every lady had her own little court of admirers or parasites according to her age and looks. Many of the younger ones were standing, or strolling about, in the intervals of the entertainment, each closely attended by one or two fine gentlemen; but as soon as a recitation of verses began, or a piece of music, they all stood still where they were, and the hum of voices instantly gave way to profound silence.

Ortensia was there too. She had come with her husband, and had been graciously received by the Queen, who evidently knew nothing of Don Alberto's serenade; but Stradella had then left her to join his musicians, for he was to direct a part of his new oratorio as well as sing an air in it himself, and Ortensia necessarily stayed behind with the audience. Don Alberto Altieri at once came forward to take care of her, and nine-tenths of the Roman ladies present immediately asked of their attendant gentlemen who the handsome young woman in straw-coloured silk might be, whose hair had 'quite the Venetian tinge,' and whom 'dear Don Alberto seemed to know so well.' The result was that the occasion was Ortensia's first real appearance in Roman society; and before her husband was ready to go home, she had made the acquaintance of nearly all the great ladies present.

The young man was delighted to show off his power and popularity before her as he led her about, being convinced that it could not fail to make an impression on her; for wherever he turned he was met by smiling faces, and she was followed by eyes that envied the distinction conferred upon her by the nephew of 'both the reigning Popes,' as the Romans called Pope Clement and Cardinal Paluzzo Altieri. At the same time, the gossips were beginning to wonder what Queen Christina-Minerva-Diana would say to her favourite's conduct if she saw anything of it, though Don Alberto kept well behind her as he piloted Ortensia from one great lady to another.

Then, all at once, the two had disappeared unnoticed. A dark young girl with sad eyes and a sensitive though slightly irregular mouth had just appeared on the stage, dressed as one of the Muses; that is to say, she wore an ample garment of purple silk, of no particular shape, but cut low at the throat and having wide sleeves which displayed a pair of rather nervous white arms; her black hair was knotted low at the back of her neck, and she wore a wreath of fresh bay laurel that was very becoming to her young face. She was one of those strangely talented creatures, still found in Italy, and most often amongst the people, who have the gift of improvising very creditable verses and music on any subject that is given them, or even upon a set of rhymes, after concentrating their thoughts for a time which rarely exceeds two minutes, and is often only a few seconds.

Don Alberto, who knew the programme of the entertainment, had man[oe]uvred skilfully. The girl appeared on the stage, lute in hand, and began to approach the wet clay bust of Christina with the mournfully inspired air of a Cassandra going up to the altar and image of Apollo; at the same moment Don Alberto found himself with Ortensia before an open door on the left side of the portico, a little farther back than the hindmost of the audience. Every one was watching the stage.

'An "improvisatrice,"' the young man whispered quickly. 'Tiresome rubbish! I will show you the statues while it is going on.'

Ortensia obeyed his gesture and passed through the door into a large hall where a quantity of fragments of antique statues were lying on the stone floor, or were propped upright against the walls, while half-a-dozen of the best were already set up on Corinthian capitals, or ancient altars, which served as pedestals.

Don Alberto had quietly closed the door behind him when he followed Ortensia into the hall. It was the first time he had succeeded in being alone with her since the night of the serenade.

'I trust you will accept my humblest excuses, dear lady,' he said as they both stood still, 'for having unwillingly broken off my little serenade the other night. I had intended it as a welcome to you and your husband on the first night you spent under my roof, but I had not thought of bringing a brace of cut-throats with me, as my rival did! They were too much for me—I wish I knew his name!'

Don Alberto laughed pleasantly and looked at her, waiting for an answer. At the word 'cut-throats' she made a slight movement of surprise, and was on the point of indignantly attacking him for applying such a word to the friends who had brought about her marriage with Stradella; but she checked herself, hardly knowing why.

'I was very tired that night, after moving to the palace,' she said calmly. 'My husband spoke of a noise in the street, but I must have been more than half asleep.'

But Altieri had seen her start and did not believe a word of what she said. He was partially satisfied, however, since she chose to take no notice of a scandalous affray which might easily have reflected on her own good name. He laughed again.

'As it was such a miserable failure, I am glad you were not awake to hear it,' he said. 'It was intended as a welcome, as an expression of my profound and devoted admiration, in which I hope you will believe now, though you were asleep that evening!'

'Your admiration is exaggerated, sir,' Ortensia answered with a light laugh, 'but if, by devotion, you mean friendliness to my husband and myself, I accept it for him and for me with all my heart!'

'I am grateful to your ladyship,' said Don Alberto in the same jesting tone, 'but, with your leave, I distinguish, as they taught me to say in the schools when I was nearly entrapped into a fallacy by a clever antagonist!'

'But I am neither your antagonist nor clever,' objected Ortensia, fencing gaily; 'therefore you need not make any fine distinctions!'

The young man changed his manner and tone with really dramatic effect; his face grew suddenly grave, his voice was sad, and he gazed into Ortensia's eyes with a wistful lover-like expression that women rarely resisted.

'You are unkind,' he said. 'You know what such words mean to me, and you say them willingly, meaning to hurt me—as you do!'

It was so well done that Ortensia was deceived, as well she might be, seeing how young she was, though years counted not then as they do with us, and every girl of fourteen was taught to be on her defence against men of every age and station.

'I did not mean to be unkind,' Ortensia said incautiously.

'Then pity me!' he cried with a sudden burst of real or affected passion. 'Are you blind, or are you cruel? Or are you only heartless? I do not believe that you were not at the window the other night! Your lips say one thing, your eyes another! You were looking down, you saw me wounded by that villain, and you listened to his master's serenade till I came back with the watch, only to be defeated a second time by a brace of hired fencing-masters! No! It was not out of friendship for your husband, I confess it frankly, it was for love of you, it was because you have turned my blood to fire and my heart to flame——'

'Hush!' Ortensia laid one hand warningly upon his arm, and at the same time she drew herself up with great dignity, and her face was proud and cold. 'I give no man the right to speak of love to me——'

'Wait!' interrupted Altieri. 'Wait, forgive, pity if you can, but hear me out! Far be it from me to slight your honour, soul of my soul, heart of my body!—for my own is gone, and you are in its place, and without you I should surely die! No—do not fear me! See, I stand back from you, you cannot even reach me with your hand as you did just now. But I must speak, and you shall hear me. I know your story, for the Venetian Ambassador has told all Rome how you lived in your uncle's house in miserable slavery, and how he meant to force you to be his wife, and that rather than submit to such an outrage you ran away with your music-master—we all know the truth about it, from the Pope, and my uncle the Cardinal, and the Queen, to the little page who carries Princess Colonna's train at a papal audience! There is nothing more romantic and adventurous in all the tales of Boccaccio and Bandello, and whatever the Senator Pignaver may attempt by way of revenge you may be sure that Rome will protect you. But now that you are free, now that the world lies before you and at your feet, will you not choose a man worthy of your birth and name?'

'A lover, sir?' asked Ortensia indignantly.

She had slowly moved backwards while he was speaking, till she leaned against the pedestal of a colossal bust of Juno.

'Heaven forbid!' said Don Alberto. 'I mean a husband——'

'You seem to forget that I am married,' Ortensia replied, with rising anger.

'I would quarrel with any man who dared suggest that you do not believe it,' said Don Alberto gravely.

'What do you mean?' She started, and a quick flush rose to her cheeks, but subsided instantly, leaving her pale.

'It takes more than a mere sacristan's trick to make a real marriage,' answered Don Alberto enigmatically. 'Do not be indignant, dearest lady! Let me speak. You were married in the sacristy of San Domenico at Ferrara. Do not be surprised that I know it. The Legate there, Monsignor Pelagetti, is afraid of getting into trouble for having imprisoned Stradella by mistake, and he has sent my uncle a full and precise account of all that happened. The Mother Superior of the Ursulines informed him of what had been done in the sacristy. Her intention was good, no doubt, but it is very uncertain whether the result is valid!'

'And why should it not be?' Ortensia was very angry. 'There were honourable witnesses, too! What can any one say against my marriage?'

'One thing is that the witnesses were not as honourable as you thought them, my lady! The two gentlemen who helped you have turned out to be two of the most famous Bravi in Italy——'

'Bravi?'

'Yes. Their pockets are full of pardons for the atrocious murders they have committed for money, and they are as well known in Rome as Romulus and Remus! As for the woman who signed the register after them, she is a runaway nun, whose mere presence as a witness would discredit any ceremony!'

'A runaway nun? Pina? What folly is this? She has been with me since I was seven years old!'

'And she is forty now! There was time for a great many things to happen to her before you knew her. Has she not one thumb unlike the other? You see, I am well informed, for the Cardinal knows everything; and if he says that your marriage is not valid, you may be sure that he is not speaking carelessly or without full information.'

Ortensia was now very pale, and her breath came quickly as she leaned against the pedestal of the Juno.

'It is not possible!' she cried, staring at Altieri in horror.

'It is more than possible that the priest may not have been a priest at all,' he answered, 'and that the whole scene was cleverly prepared to trick you. But the rest I know beyond a doubt and can prove. Your two friends are well-known Bravi and are at present lodging at the Orso inn, where you were, and your serving-woman is Filippina Landi, who escaped from a convent in Lombardy with a young Venetian and was abandoned by him. She was arrested in Ferrara some nineteen or twenty years ago and confessed the truth under torture, but was soon afterwards pardoned by the intervention of your uncle, the Senator Pignaver.'

'My uncle?' Ortensia almost forgot her new anxiety in her surprise.

'Yes, dear lady. Your uncle was, in fact, the young Venetian who had carried her off out of the convent, promising to marry her! It was no doubt in order to be revenged on him that she helped you to run away.'

Ortensia's hand strained upon the corner of the pedestal till Altieri could count the small blue veins and purple arteries that showed through the white skin. She was terrified by what he had told her, for it explained Pina's whole manner and conduct too well not to make what Altieri had said about the marriage seem vaguely possible. But if she had been deceived, so had Stradella; of that she was more sure than of anything else, and if it had been possible she would have gone to him instantly to tell him what she had heard.

Altieri saw how much disturbed she was and came towards her, for they were now half-a-dozen steps apart. He meant, no doubt, to offer her some consolation in her new trouble, unless he was going to fall on his knees and implore her pardon for having caused her such uneasiness. As a professional love-maker either course was open to him. But Ortensia stopped him with a gesture, keeping down her emotion.

'Listen,' she said, 'for I have something to say. You meant to shake my faith in my husband, but you have made a mistake, and instead you have done us both a great service. If, as you pretend, we are not validly married, nothing can be easier than to obtain a proper marriage in Rome, and we shall do so at once; but as for the rest, you are profoundly mistaken about me. I left my uncle's house because I loved Alessandro Stradella, and for no other reason, and while we both live we shall love each other as dearly as we did from the first, and I pray heaven that our lives may end together, on the same day and in the same hour. Do you understand? As you have seemed a friend to us both, be one in earnest, for you are wasting your time in playing at being in love with me!'

She smiled at the last, as cleverly as any skilful woman of thirty could have done, offering him the chance of laughing away the barrier his ill-considered declaration had made, and of taking up pleasant relations again, as if nothing had happened to disturb them; for she had regained her self-possession while she was speaking, and had determined to profit by what he had told her rather than to suffer by the facts he had revealed, if they proved to be true.

He was quick to accept the means of reconciliation, whatever his own intentions really were.

'I will indeed be your friend,' he said, with amazing earnestness, 'since you give me no hope of ever being anything more, and are willing to forgive the madness of a moment. Henceforth, command me what you will! In pledge of pardon, may I have your hand?'

She let him take it; he dropped on one knee as he touched her fingers with his lips, and then rose lightly to his feet again.

'Now let us go back,' she said, 'for we have been too long away.'

He led her out of the hall by another door and she found herself quite in the farthest recess of the portico and behind all the assembled company, just as the dark-haired Muse was finishing her last improvisation in an attitude of inspired wonder before the hideous bust of the Queen. At the last line of her sonnet she took the laurels from her head, and with a graceful movement that showed her nervous but well-shaped white arms to great advantage she placed the wreath upon the damp clay effigy of the great Christina's portentous wig; then, cleverly kicking the train of her long purple silk robe out of the way behind her, she backed towards the side exit, stretching out her hands and bending her body while still keeping her upturned eyes on the bust with an air of rapt adoration, like a Suppliant on an Etruscan vase.

Every one applauded enthusiastically, knowing that applause was expected in payment for having been invited to such a feast of the soul; but the wise Muse paid no attention to the sounds. To the last her gaze was on the bust, even when she lifted the dark velvet curtain with one hand and backed out with a sweeping courtesy that looked very well.

A good-looking young man of the people, dressed in his best Sunday clothes, was waiting for her at the head of the wooden steps. As she met his glance, she jerked her thumb backwards over her shoulder towards the stage and the Queen.

'May an apoplexy seize her,' whispered the Muse, with a strong Trastevere accent, 'her, and her friends, and all the family! You shall take me to supper on Monte Mario to-night! There we shall breathe! Bring the guitar, too. Old Nena is waiting to help me dress. No—no, I say—not here!'

For the handsome young fellow had caught her just as she was beginning to descend the steps, and he planted a very substantial kiss on the nape of her neck before he let her go; which was no great harm after all, since they were to be married in a fortnight or so, before the Feast of Saint John.

It was Stradella's turn after the Muse had disappeared, and while the improvisatrice was going down from the stage on one side, four liveried footmen were bringing up chairs on the other, with music-desks for the little orchestra, which immediately made its appearance. There were not more than a dozen musicians in all, and they ranged themselves in an orderly manner on each side of the laurel-crowned bust, in the order of the pitch of their instruments, the violins and flutes being in the middle, while the bass viol was at the extreme left, and the bass cornopean on the right. Next came a small chorus of eight singers, who took their places, standing behind the seated musicians; and last of all, amidst much clapping of hands,

Stradella himself appeared in front, and bowed low to the Queen, standing a little on one side so as not to hide the bust from the audience.

He looked very handsome as he stood there, dressed in black velvet and black silk, with a low collar of soft linen that showed his strong white throat, and having his lawn wristbands turned back over the cuffs of his coat.

As he bowed Queen Christina smiled graciously, and waved her hand to him in greeting, whereupon the applause became still louder.

Don Alberto had found a seat for Ortensia, and stood beside her, as the other cavaliers stood each beside the lady of his choice. Altieri thought it good policy to pose himself as Ortensia's official adorer from the first, at such a very select gathering of Roman society; for few would care to try their chances against him after that. Ortensia herself was dimly conscious that if she could keep him in his place, as she had done to-day, his admiration would protect her against other would-be worshippers.

While the music lasted she never took her eyes from Stradella, whether he was turned from the audience towards his musicians to direct them, beating time in the air with a thin roll of ruled music-paper, or when he faced the audience and sung himself, to the accompaniment of only four stringed instruments.

'Admirable!' whispered Alberto, bending low to Ortensia's ear. 'It is supreme genius, nothing less!' he whispered again, as she took no notice.

But Ortensia did not even hear him, and sat quite still in her chair, gazing with fixed eyes at the man she loved, and listening to his music as in the entrancement of a spell. Don Alberto looked down thoughtfully at her beautiful motionless head, though his ears were open too, for he loved music; but just then he was even more in love with the beautiful Venetian, and though he had been worsted in his first attempt, he was by no means ready to give up the siege. He was wondering what treasure could be found in all Rome that could induce Ortensia to take her eyes from her husband while he was singing or conducting his own music.

But when it was finished and the applause had died away, and he had bowed and left the little stage, she could not wait a moment.

'Take me to him,' she said to Don Alberto, rising from her seat.

'He will come here himself in a few minutes,' objected Altieri.

'Take me to him,' she repeated more imperiously. 'If you will not, I shall go alone.'

There was nothing for it but to obey, and Don Alberto led her quickly out of the portico to the carriage entrance at the back, then through a vaulted passage, and up a flight of half-a-dozen steps to the room to which the performers retired, and which had another exit towards the garden and the back of the stage.

When Don Alberto opened the door Stradella was just within, evidently about to come away, and he started in surprise when he saw his wife enter. The other musicians were standing in groups of three and four, with their instruments in their hands, for the place was completely bare of furniture; there was not so much as a table on which to lay a fiddle or a flute, but across one corner a piece of tattered canvas had been hung to cut off a dressing-room for the improvisatrice, who had already got into her own clothes and was gone away with old Nena and the handsome young man.

Stradella met his wife with a happy smile and nodded a greeting to Don Alberto, who remained in the door-way.

'Can you take me home at once?' Ortensia asked. 'Or must you go in?'

Stradella saw her look of distress as he took her outstretched hand in both of his.

'I am not wanted, am I?' he asked, looking at young Altieri. 'My wife wishes to go home, you see——'

'I will make your excuses to the Queen,' Don Alberto answered readily. 'My carriage is waiting and shall take you to the palace and come back for me.'

'How kind of you!'

Ortensia thought he was already beginning to fulfil his promise of friendship to her. He had, in fact, brought the couple to the Palazzo Riario in his own carriage, for there were no hackney coaches in Rome in that century, and people who owned no equipage were obliged to have themselves carried in sedan-chairs, from one end of the city to the other if necessary, unless they preferred to ride on mules or donkeys, which was not convenient in full dress.

In five minutes Stradella and his wife were driving rapidly over the cobblestones towards Ponte Sisto, and Ortensia was telling the astonished musician what had taken place between her and Don Alberto, with all he had told her about Pina, Trombin, and Gambardella.

CHAPTER XVII

Two days after the affair at the Palazzo Riario, Don Alberto sauntered out of his palace gate before the sun was high, and as he was merely going for a stroll to breathe the morning air he was alone. As a matter of fact, the air smelt of cabbage, broccoli, and other green things, for a hawker of vegetables had set down his three baskets at the corner of the Via del Gesù, and was bawling his cry to the whole neighbourhood at the top of his lusty voice. There had been a light shower before dawn, and the wet cobble-stones sent up a peculiar odour of their own, which mingled with that of the green stuff. Don Alberto did not like it and turned to his left, towards the Palazzo di Venezia, which was then the Venetian Embassy.

Where the street narrows between the Altieri palace and the church, a serving-man in grey overtook him and spoke to him.

'Excellency,' the man said in an obsequious tone, his hat in his hand, 'I pray the favour of a word.'

Don Alberto stopped in some surprise, for he had not noticed any one but the vegetable hawker in the deserted square when he had left his own door a moment earlier.

'What do you want?' he asked suspiciously, and stopping to face the man.

It was Tommaso, the ex-highwayman who served the Bravi, and the expression of his eyes was not reassuring.

'Your Excellency does not remember me,' he said. 'How should the Most Illustrious remember a poor valet? I served the Bishop of Porto for seven years, and often accompanied him to the palace here when he visited His Eminence Cardinal Altieri, who is now our Most Holy Father, Pope Clement. Your Excellency was only a boy then, and once did me the honour to speak to me.'

'What did I say to you?' asked Don Alberto incredulously.

'I should not dare to repeat such a word,' answered Tommaso in a humble tone, 'but your Excellency kicked me at the same time, and with great strength for one so very young, for I tumbled downstairs.'

Don Alberto's lips twitched with amusement.

'I believe I remember you by that, you scoundrel,' he said with a smile. 'And what do you want of me now? Shall I give you another kick?'

'May that never be, Excellency! I can feel the first one still!'

Don Alberto laughed at the comically significant gesture that accompanied this speech, and felt in his pocket for his purse.

'I suppose you want a paul to drink my health,' he said.

'That is too much for anything so common as a kick, Excellency, and too little if you will accept my service.'

'I have servants enough,' answered Altieri, slipping his purse into his pocket again. 'But since you think a paul is too much for one kick, I shall give you a florin's worth for nothing at all if you pester me with any more nonsense. So now be off, and waste no time about it!'

Tommaso suddenly drew himself up and squared his broad shoulders, which made him look rather formidable, for he was an uncommonly strong and active fellow.

'If you say the word,' he answered, dropping his obsequious manner, 'I will give Maestro Stradella's wife into your hands within a fortnight.'

Don Alberto started visibly. His high-born instinct was not quite dead yet, and he slightly moved his right hand as if he would lift the ebony stick he carried; but Tommaso had one of cornel-wood and iron-shod, and he also made a very slight movement, and he was square and strong and had a jaw like a bull-dog. Don Alberto's instinctive desire to knock him down disappeared suddenly.

'And how do you propose to accomplish such an impossible feat?' asked the young noble with some contempt.

'That is my affair,' answered Tommaso quietly. 'What will you give me when I have shut the lady up safely and shall bring you the key of her prison? That is the only question, but please remember that I must risk my neck, while you will only risk your money.'

'If you think I will give you any money in hand for such a silly offer, you take me for a fool,' retorted Don Alberto.

'I ask nothing in advance. How much will you give me in cash for the lady when I hand her over to you? I am in earnest. Name your price.'

'What is yours?'

'A thousand gold florins and the Pope's pardon,' said Tommaso boldly. 'You could not buy her like in Venice, if you had your pick of the latest cargo from Georgia!'

'You shall have the pardon and a thousand in gold,' Don Alberto answered, for he was much too fine a gentleman to bargain with a cut-throat, especially as the money would come out of his uncle's strong-box. 'I do not believe that you can do what you offer; but if you succeed, how shall I hear from you?'

'On the Eve of Saint John you will find me waiting for you with two saddled mules behind the Baptistery of the Lateran, when the bells ring the first hour of the night. Bring your money and I will take you to the house and to the lady and leave you the key.'

'I would rather you should come here,' said Don Alberto, suspecting a trap.

'Bring a guard with you if you think I mean to rob you,' answered Tommaso. 'Bring a squadron of cavalry, if you like! Besides, you know that there will be thousands of people about the Lateran all night on Saint John's Eve, eating and drinking on the grass to keep the witches out of their bodies for the rest of the year!'

'That is true,' Don Alberto answered. 'I will be there.'

'But if your Excellency should accidentally see me in the meantime,' continued Tommaso, 'your Excellency had better not notice me, nor be seen to recognise me.'

He had resumed his obsequious tone, and was already bowing to take his leave.

'I have one thing to tell you,' said Altieri. 'If you fail, I will have you locked up in Tor di Nona for prying into my affairs and making an infamous proposal to me, and it may be a long time before you get out.'

'At the pleasure of your Most Illustrious Excellency! I shall not make the least resistance if I fail.'

'You had better not,' returned Altieri, haughtily enough, as he turned away and left Tommaso bowing to the ground.

'Your Most Illustrious Excellency's most humble and dutiful servant!' said the man.

Then he went off in the opposite direction, passed the Altieri palace, turned to his right, and in due time reached the Sign of the Bear, where his masters lodged. He found them in Trombin's room, sitting near the open window with their coats off, and eating fruit from a huge blue and yellow majolica basket that stood between them on the end of the table. There were oranges, ripe plums, and very dark red cherries in handsome profusion, and the serving-girl, who cherished a secret but hopeless admiration for Gambardella, had brought a pretty bunch of violets in a coarse Roman tumbler.

Both the Bravi were of opinion that a little fruit taken in the morning was cooling to the blood in spring. Trombin had cut a hole in the top of an orange and was solemnly sucking it—a process for which his small round mouth seemed to be expressly formed—and his pink cheeks contracted and expanded like little bellows as he alternately drew in the sweet juice and took breath. Gambardella could not have sucked an orange to save his life, because his long nose was directly in the way; he ate cherries slowly, and looked like a large brown bird of prey pecking at them with his beak.

'Come in,' he said between two pecks, as some one tapped at the entrance.

'I have seen him, sirs,' Tommaso said, after shutting the door behind him. 'It is a thousand gold florins in cash, on the Eve of Saint John. I am to meet him behind the Baptistery of the Lateran at the first hour of the night and take him to the house.'

'Well done!' said Gambardella.

Trombin nodded his approval, for he was still at work on his orange, and was well aware that if the contact were broken for purposes of speech before the fruit was dry, the perfection of the satisfaction would be seriously compromised.

'Tommaso,' Gambardella continued, 'I think you know Rome well. Are you aware that in the Via di Santa Sabina there is a small house which is almost always uninhabited, except in the month of October, when the owner goes there himself to see his wine made? Do you happen to remember that house?'

'No, sir,' answered the ex-highwayman, whose admiration for his employers' wide knowledge increased daily. 'But I can easily find it, for I know the road. It is a lonely place.'

'A very lonely place,' said Trombin, at last detaching himself from the shrivelled yellow shell which was all that was left of the orange. 'It is so lonely that I may say there is never any one there, and there is rarely any one within hearing after dark. No thief goes near that road at night, Tommaso, because there is never any one to rob. Most people are fools, Tommaso, and suppose that robbers lurk in lonely and unfrequented spots, where they could not possibly find a purse to cut. Therefore, as we are no fools, Tommaso, but very intelligent persons, we feel quite secure in such places. Do you fully understand my meaning, Tommaso?'

'I have practised a part of what you preach, sir,' answered Tommaso with a grin.

'No doubt. Very good, Tommaso. When you have found the house, go on some distance farther, say a hundred steps or so, and you will see a door in the wall, which evidently gives access to the vineyard. The door was painted red when I last saw it. Perhaps you will find it ajar, but if not, knock two or three times with the head of your stick, not roughly or noisily, but in a sober fashion; and then wait awhile, and if nobody comes, knock again. If you cannot get in to-day, go back to-morrow and the next day. The best time is a little before noon, when the man is not yet at dinner.'

'Or asleep,' suggested Tommaso.

'Precisely. When he lets you in, you will know him because he has a reddish beard that is turning white on the left side. He cultivates the vineyard, and the owner takes half the produce; but for a consideration the man lets the small house in the Via di Santa Sabina to persons who are fond of vineyards and solitude. The only condition is that the shutters of the windows looking on the road must not be opened, lest the owner should pass that way.'

'I understand, sir,' said Tommaso, grinning again. 'I dare say the man is deaf at night.'

'Only at night, Tommaso, but then completely so,' answered Trombin. 'You will say that a gentleman of fortune desires the use of the little house for a week, with the keys, from the twenty-first to the twenty-eighth of June.'

'At one Apostolic florin a day,' put in Gambardella.

'But you must on no account let him know our names,' said Trombin. 'You can give him two florins in hand as earnest money——'

'One is quite enough,' interrupted Gambardella.

'Be guided by your judgment, Tommaso,' said Trombin, beginning to cut a hole in another orange. 'I take you to be a sensible and economical person, but we must not lose the use of the house for the sake of a florin or two. For I dare say you have guessed what we need the house for.'

'Partly, sir, partly. No doubt I am to take the young gentleman there on the Eve of Saint John.'

'Yes, amongst other things, you will do that. But indeed, Tommaso, you yourself will be surprised at the extraordinary number of things you will do on that evening, all to your great advantage. It is not in my power to tell you everything now, my good fellow, because I am going to enjoy this orange in my usual way, by means of suction. But you shall know all in good time, all in good time, Tommaso!'

Therewith Trombin opened his round eyes to their fullest extent, clapped his lips to the aperture he had cut in the peel, and grasping the fruit firmly with both hands, he began the long and delicious process of extracting the juice.

'And as you will have to receive the thousand gold ducats from Don Alberto,' said Gambardella, speaking to Tommaso, 'you will have a very substantial guarantee in hand. For though we shall never be far from you on that evening, we shall not be able to hinder you from running away and robbing us if you choose to do so.'

'What have I done to deserve such an insinuation?' asked the ex-highwayman indignantly, for he felt that his honour was assailed.

'Nothing whatever,' answered the Bravo calmly, 'and I insinuated nothing that should shock your sensibilities, my good man. The profession has two branches, to one of which we belong, while you have followed the other. We take lives, you take purses, and you should not feel any more hurt at my suggesting that you might take mine, than I should if you suggested that I might cut your throat.'

'That is true, sir.'

Tommaso spoke almost humbly, for he felt that if it should occur to the Bravi to exercise their 'branch of the profession' upon him, he should have no more chance of life than a kitten amongst bloodhounds. He was strong and active, no doubt, and could use most weapons fairly well, but he had neither the endurance of his terrible masters, nor their supreme skill in fencing; as for taking them unawares, they never rested without bolting their doors, and when they walked abroad they never heard footsteps behind them without looking round, nor passed the corner of a narrow street without drawing towards the middle of the road far enough to allow room for sword-play. A poor fellow like Tommaso, who had spent his early years as valet to a churchman, would make but a poor figure against such men in a fight; he was proud enough to be allowed to help them, almost without a thought of profit, and their money would be as safe in his hands as it would be in Chigi's bank.

"'The profession has two branches. We take lives, you take purses'"

He was ready to obey them blindly, too, which was what they wanted, for the plan they had at last decided upon was a complicated one, and would certainly miscarry if anything went wrong during the night in which it was to be carried out; on the other hand, they did not trust him enough to tell him what they meant to do, though he had to trust to their promises that Ortensia should be already a prisoner in the little house in Via di Santa Sabina when he should bring Don Alberto to the door; and he knew that, if they failed, his only chance of safety would lie in instant flight, before young Altieri could have him laid by the heels in prison. Neither the money nor the papal safe-conduct would be forthcoming until the young noble had actually seen Ortensia in the little house.

After the last words he had spoken, Tommaso quietly prepared to shave Gambardella, while Trombin was finishing the second orange. He had brought hot water with him in a bright copper can, and he now proceeded to tie a large towel round Gambardella's neck, after which he made a rich lather of Spanish soap, which he conscientiously rubbed into the Bravo's hard brown cheeks and sinewy throat; last of all, he stropped his razor with the air and flourish of an accomplished barber and set to work.

Trombin finished his orange and looked on.

'Did you ever cut a man's throat while you were shaving him, Tommaso?' he asked idly.

'Only once, sir,' Tommaso answered quietly, and he turned Gambardella's head a little on one side, in order to get below his jaw.

'Why did you do it?' inquired Trombin, dipping the tips of his large pink fingers into a bowl of water and carefully rinsing his lips.

'It was to save my neck, sir. The man was one of the cleverest sbirri I ever had after me, but he did not know me by sight. It was in the March of Ancona, at a small village near Fermo. He had tracked me all the way from Modena, and he came to the inn on the evening of the third day. He sent for the village barber before he had supper; but the barber was a friend of mine and was hiding me, and he let me go in his place. I told the landlord of the inn that I was the barber's new apprentice, and so I was admitted to shave the officer in his own room. You see, sir, both our horses were worn out, but his was still far better than mine, so it was safer that he should go no farther. That is the whole story, sir. I was over the frontier before morning.'

Gambardella smiled while Tommaso went on shaving him, and Trombin laughed as if the jest were very good.

'It was not strictly in your branch of the profession, Tommaso,' he said, 'but under the circumstances you acted with great tact. Nevertheless, even in an extreme case, avoid shaving Don Alberto in that manner, for there is no telling what the consequences might be if he were found with his throat cut in the little house in Via di Santa Sabina!'

CHAPTER XVIII

Cucurullo had his own opinion of what he saw during those days, and he kept it to himself for some time, though he and Pina talked together a good deal in the evenings over their late supper, in the little room next to the kitchen. The woman had interested the hunchback from the first, and when any one roused his interest he pondered much upon that person's character and ways, and asked questions with considerable cunning. On the other hand, Pina, who was not given to exhibiting much liking for any one, seemed to have taken a fancy to her fellow-servant—either out of pity for his deformity or from natural sympathy. They treated each other with a good deal of formality, however; Cucurullo, who was a Neapolitan, addressed her as Donna Pina, as if she were a lady born, and she usually called him 'Sor Antonino,' as though he were at least a clerk or a small shop-keeper.

'Tell me,' he said, one evening when they were eating the salad left over from their masters' supper, 'what is your opinion of this young gentleman who admires our mistress?'

'What opinion can I have?' asked Pina, picking up a small leaf of lettuce on her two-pronged iron fork; for she ate delicately, and her fine manners were Cucurullo's despair.

'This is a wicked world,' he sighed, rather enigmatically.

'If you mean also that Don Alberto is one of those who make it so, I am inclined to agree with you,' Pina answered. 'I have seen other young gentlemen like him.'

'You have had great experience of high life, Donna Pina. That is the reason why I asked your opinion. This young gentleman may be like others you have known, but besides that he is very powerful in Rome, and can do what he likes with impunity. He is so much in love with our mistress that he no longer understands, as we say in the South. He has lost his senses.'

'But he has his wits left,' observed Pina sharply.

'And he owes a grudge for that scratch in the arm,' added Cucurullo thoughtfully.

'He does not know who gave it to him.'

'Therefore he means the Lady Ortensia to pay him for it.'

'Yes,' Pina answered. 'That is just like a man. Because he was hurt in serenading a lady, it must needs be her fault, and she must give satisfaction! First, he would like to carry her off to some lonely castle he must have, somewhere in the mountains, and at the end of a week, or a month, he would turn her out of doors and say it served her right because he had been wounded under her window. Yes, Sor Antonino, you may well say that I have some experience of high life!'

Cucurullo heard the bitter note that rang in the last words, and he partly understood, for he had known her long enough to guess that she had a sad story of her own.

'We ought to watch the signs for the masters,' he said. 'They see nothing, hear nothing, and think of nothing but each other. One of these days the young gentleman will lay a snare and they will step into it like a pair of sparrows.'

'What can we do?' asked Pina in a dull voice. 'Whatever is fated will happen.'

'That is heresy, Donna Pina,' said Cucurullo gravely, for he was much shocked to hear a fellow-servant express such a highly unorthodox sentiment. 'It is a heresy condemned by the Fathers of the Church, and especially by Saint Thomas.'

'He never lived my life!' objected Pina with a sharp little laugh; and she poured out two fingers of sour white wine and drank it.

'If the Maestro had thought as you do when I was thrown overboard, I should have drowned,' said Cucurullo quietly.

'When did that happen?' asked Pina, interested at once.

'It was on a small vessel coming from Naples to Città Vecchia, five years ago, after my mother died,' said Cucurullo. 'I was coming to Rome because I hoped to get some clerk's work, having had some little instruction, and the Maestro was one of the two or three passengers in the cabin. He was hardly known then, being very young, and indeed he was running away from a Neapolitan princess who was too much in love with him. Well, at first the captain was glad to have me on board, and the crew made much of me, believing that the hunchback would bring them luck and a quick passage. But we had not got as far as Gaeta when a storm came up and we were driven out to sea. It grew worse and worse for two days and nights, and our sails were torn, and other accidents happened, which I did not understand. Then the crew and the captain began to look askance at me, and I heard them say among themselves that I was the wrong kind of hunchback and had the Evil Eye; and just when it seemed as if the weather were moderating, and the sun had shone out for half an hour, the clouds in the south-west got as black as ink, and one could see the white foam driving towards us below them. Then, when the captain saw that there was no time to be lost, he ordered the men to throw me overboard, saying that I was Jonah and Judas Iscariot in one, and that nothing else could save the ship. They took me by my arms and feet and swung me twice and then threw me clean over the side; but I had already shut my eyes and was beginning to say the De profundis as well as I could. I had hardly finished the first versicle when I struck the water, and I was indeed crying unto the Lord out of the depths, for I cannot swim, and my end was clearly at hand.'

'How awful!' cried Pina in a low voice.

'I never was in greater danger,' said Cucurullo gravely, 'and my mouth was already full of salt water. But I did not say then "whatever is fated will happen," Donna Pina, for I was anxious to say the second versicle of the Psalm before I was drowned, and I tried what I could to keep my head up long enough for that. Then, just as a big wave was breaking, I saw something flying through the air, and as it was a dark thing I was afraid it was the devil coming for my soul, because my mother, blessed soul, when she was dying, had recommended me to pay three Carlini which she owed for milk, and I had wickedly forgotten it. But I have since paid it. However, it was not the devil, but Maestro Stradella, who had thrown himself into the sea, as he was, to save my life, only because he had spoken two or three times to me on the voyage. The ship was not going on fast, but though one of the sailors threw him a rope he could not catch it, for he was holding up my head and telling me not to be frightened, as well as he could amongst the waves, and not to catch hold of him, for he would save me. Then the passengers and sailors took a great board ten ells long that was on the deck, and served for landing, and they threw it over; and somehow the Maestro got me to it and we climbed upon it, while the ship was getting farther and farther away, and the black squall was coming nearer and nearer.'

'The master swims like a water-rat,' said Pina. 'I remember that night in Venice, when the Signors of the Night were after him!'

'Ah, you should have seen him in the sea, God bless him!' answered Cucurullo. 'He had the strength and the long wind of a dolphin. When the squall came upon us we held each other fast, sitting astride of the plank, for it was a very heavy one, and did not sink with us. Then came the rain. Lord, how it rained, Donna Pina! You have never seen rain like that!'

'I remember how it rained that night when the master climbed into our balcony! That was enough for me!'

'Imagine ten times that, Donna Pina. The wind had blown the plank round, so that we got the rain in our backs, but even then I had to keep my mouth shut to hinder the water from running down my throat! And it must have lasted two hours, but the sea went down like magic in that time, and there was only a long, smooth, swelling motion, and the wind came from another quarter and carried us with it. That was how we were saved.'

'The ship came back and picked you up, I suppose?'

'After the squall we did not see the ship again, though the clouds rolled away and the sun shone brightly. She went to the bottom of the sea, Donna Pina, and was never heard of again, but we drifted for many hours, half dead with cold, and were washed upon the Roman shore.'

'And what was fated, happened,' said Pina with a smile. 'For if you had not been thrown overboard you would have been drowned with the rest, Sor Antonino!'

Cucurullo smiled too, very quietly, and helped Pina to the last drumstick left over from a cold chicken.

'Well, well, Donna Pina,' he said, 'that is your way of believing, I dare say, but I have told you what happened to me; and now you will understand better why I should be glad to serve the master with my life, if I might.'

'You are a good man,' said Pina in a thoughtful tone. 'If there were more like you, this would not be such a bad world as it is. What you say about Don Alberto is true, and if I could see any way of being useful in watching him I would do all I could. Are the two Venetian gentlemen who helped us in Ferrara still in Rome? I do not know what they are, and sometimes I was afraid of them, but they would be strong allies if they knew that our lady was in danger and if they were willing to help us.'

'They are still in Rome, for I saw them only to-day, going into the Gesù. They must be very devout gentlemen, for I often see them in churches, and their servant has been valet to a bishop, and understands the ceremonials perfectly. It is a pleasure to talk with him. He can tell the meaning of every vestment and of every change in a pontifical high mass, and I think he knows half the Roman Breviary by heart, and all the Psalms!'

Pina was not so sure about the piety of the Bravi and their servant, and as she nibbled her last bit of bread, she looked thoughtfully across the clothless deal table at the hunchback's trusting and spiritual face. In the dramatic vicissitudes of her own youth she had not learned to put her faith in men, nor in women either; and if there had ever been a gentle and affectionate side to her strong nature, it had been trodden and tormented till it had died, leaving scarcely a memory of itself behind.

As he sat on the kitchen chair, Cucurullo's head was not much above the edge of the table, and she looked down at him, meeting his sad eyes as they gazed up to hers. She liked him, and was glad that he did not know what was passing through her mind; for she foresaw trouble in the near future, and was afraid for herself. In some way she might yet be made to pay for what she had done in wreaking her vengeance on Pignaver. Cardinal Altieri might protect Stradella and Ortensia if the Senator tried to have them murdered, but if he demanded that Pina, his household servant, should be arrested and sent back to Venice to be punished for helping the runaways, who would protect her? At the mere thought she often turned very pale and bent nearly double, as if she felt bodily pain. For of all things, she feared that most. Sooner than suffer it again she would betray Ortensia into Alberto Altieri's hands, as she had almost forced her into Stradella's arms in order to be revenged on Pignaver himself.

'I have been thinking,' she said after a long pause. 'It would be well for you to go to those Venetian gentlemen and beg them to help us, if they will. You need not say that I suggested it, Sor Antonino.'

'Why should I speak of you at all, Donna Pina?' asked the hunchback, a little surprised.

'Exactly! There is no need of it, and you are very tactful. You will find out if they suspect anything, for after the affair of the serenade I am sure that they must have watched Don Alberto anxiously, to be sure that he had not found out who wounded him.'

'Perhaps I had better talk to Tommaso first. We are on very good terms, you know.'

'By all means, talk with him first.'

A distant handbell tinkled, and as Pina heard it through the open door she rose to her feet, for it was Ortensia's means of calling her.

Cucurullo thought over the conversation and reasoned about it with himself most of the night, and, so far as Pina was concerned, the more he reflected the farther he got from the truth. For he was grateful because she was kind to him in their daily life, and he could not possibly have believed that she was no more really attached to Ortensia than she was to the Queen of Sweden, and was even now meditating a sudden flight from Rome, which should put her beyond the reach of justice, if the law ever made search for her. In his heart he was sure that she must be as devoted to her mistress as he was to Stradella, though it was true that Ortensia had never saved her life. But Cucurullo saw good in every one, and thought it the most natural thing in the world that a faithful servant should be ready to die for his master.

On the following day he lay in wait for Tommaso near the main entrance of the inn, where the Via dell' Orso meets the Via di Monte Brianzo, which then bore the name of Santa Lucia.

It was long before the man appeared, and then he seemed to be in a great hurry, and did not see Cucurullo till the latter overtook him and spoke to him, for the hunchback had long legs and could walk quite as fast as any able-bodied young man.

'I have been waiting a long time in the hope of seeing you this morning,' he said.

'And now I am in such haste that I have no time to talk with you,' replied the other, going on.

'We can talk while we are walking,' suggested Cucurullo, keeping pace with him easily. 'How are the masters, Tommaso? Quite well, I hope?'

'Oh, perfectly well, thank you,' answered Tommaso, increasing his speed. 'I am sorry that I am in such a hurry, my friend, but it cannot be helped.'

'Do not mention it,' said Cucurullo, breathing quietly. 'I generally walk briskly myself.' Thereupon he quickened his stride a little.

'You certainly walk surprisingly fast,' said the ex-highwayman, who now had to make an effort himself in order to keep up with his companion.

The people in the street stared at the two in surprise, for they seemed to be walking for a match, and it looked as if the hunchback were getting the better of it.

'I trust,' he said in a quiet undertone, 'that Count Trombin is in no apprehension owing to his having wounded the Pope's nephew under our windows the other night?'

'Not at all,' answered the other. 'So you saw it, did you?'

'I saw it with satisfaction, for I was at the window, and I recognised the Count's voice at once. What do you think, my friend? Will that young gentleman come serenading again?'

'How can I tell?' Tommaso was by this time a little short of breath.

'You might have heard your two gentlemen say something about it,' Cucurullo said. 'Am I walking too fast for you? You said you were in a hurry, you know.'

'Yes,' Tommaso said, rather breathlessly. 'I was—that is—I am in—in a moderate hurry!'

'My reason for going with you is that I want your valuable advice,' Cucurullo went on, still keeping up the tremendous pace without the least apparent difficulty.

'About what?' gasped the highwayman, ashamed to be beaten by a hunchback.

'Your gentlemen have already helped my master and mistress so much, that even without the Maestro's knowledge I should like to ask their protection for his wife. That is, if you approve, my friend. I want your advice, you see.'

'You will have to—to walk slower—if you—want to get it!'

Tommaso was by this time puffing like a porpoise, for he was not as young as when he had been the terror of the Bologna road, and he had been living on the fat of his masters' plentiful leavings for weeks, with a very liberal allowance of the white wine of Marino. Moreover, knowing what he did of the Bravi's intentions, Cucurullo's suggestion seemed at once highly comic and extremely valuable. But Cucurullo himself, good soul, was pleased at having forced Tommaso to slacken his pace and listen to him.

'I come of my own intention, dear friend,' he said, 'because I am in constant anxiety about the Lady Ortensia. For Don Alberto is nephew to both the Popes, as they say here, and it would be an easy matter for him to carry her off into the country; the more so as she and my master are living in his own palace, and it sometimes happens that the Maestro goes out alone to a rehearsal of music, leaving only me and Pina to protect his lady, and what could we do if Don Alberto came at such a time with a band of men and simply carried the lady downstairs to his own coach and drove away with her?'

'My dear friend,' answered the other, who had now recovered his breath, 'I do not know what you could do. Am I a prophet, that you ask me riddles? The book of wisdom is buried under the statue of Pasquin, as these Romans say! If such a thing happened to me, I should consider the safety of my own skin, which is worth more to me than many other skins, even than the skins of lions for which His Holiness pays a great price, they tell me, when travellers bring them from Africa! For you might as well resist the Tiber in a flood, as try to hinder the Pope's favourite nephew from doing what he likes! Not that the Pope, or even the Cardinal, knows what he does; but he has a golden key to every door in Rome, a papal pass for every gate of the city, and a roll of blank pardons, duly signed and sealed, for any misdeed his servants may commit! What could you or I do against such a man?'

Having had his haste fairly run out of his legs, Tommaso was now inclined to be talkative, though what he said led to no particular conclusion, except that it would not be safe to interfere with Don Alberto's plans. The truth was that he saw magnificent possibilities for his masters in Cucurullo's request for protection, and he had not the smallest intention of risking a mistake by answering for them, still less of discouraging Cucurullo's hope that they would protect Ortensia.

Cucurullo answered a little despondently.

'I know it,' he said. 'All you say is true. And yet when I remember how your gentlemen wounded him and then drove the watch before them like sheep, and yet never so much as showed their faces, I cannot help hoping that they will do something for us.'

'Hope by all means, my dear friend, for, as you say very well, my masters are no ordinary fine gentlemen, made up of curls and lace collars, and paste buckles and satin, and drawing-room small-swords of about the size and temper of a silver hairpin! Why, most of these young dandies are no better than girls, and are not half such men as some priests I have known! Either of my masters could skewer a round dozen of them while the bells are ringing for noon, and sit down to dinner at the last stroke as cool as if I had just shaved them and smoothed their clean collars over their coats! But after all, dearest Cucurullo, they are only two, and I might bear them a hand with my cudgel, and we should be three—only three men against the whole army of the Pope, horse, foot, and artillery, besides the Swiss Guard and the five or six hundred sbirri in plain clothes whom the Cardinal maintains in the holy city! It would not be a fair fight, my friend!'

Cucurullo smiled at Tommaso's voluble statement of the odds, for the hunchback was not without a certain sense of humour.

'No doubt you are right,' he said, 'but if Don Alberto tried to carry off my master's lady, he would avoid the publicity of an escort of three or four thousand men! Indeed, I doubt whether he would take more than two or three of his servants with him, for whom you three would certainly be a match.'

'A match!' cried Tommaso, suddenly indignant. 'We would make sausage meat of them! We would mince them as fine as forcemeat in five minutes! Their bones would be nothing but a cloud of dust before you could count ten! A match, indeed! My dearest friend, you do not know what you are saying!'

'I do, but you have a greater command of language than I,' answered Cucurullo quietly. 'When I said that you would be a match for them, I meant that you could destroy them in an instant.'

'I see,' said Tommaso, pacified. 'But if you think I can talk, you should hear Count Trombin! Now listen, most worthy friend. If you desire it, I will speak with my masters for you; for the truth is, they are two very noble cavaliers, and would ask nothing better than to help a lady in distress, and I will meet you where you please, and tell you what they say. Or, if you prefer to speak with them yourself, go back to the inn now, and you will find them upstairs eating their morning dish of fruit. Do as you please, but perhaps I shall be able to speak to them at a moment when they are particularly well disposed. When they have dined well, for instance, they are always in a pleasant humour. They often give me a Giulio then.'

'You will do me the greatest service, my friend,' Cucurullo said. 'Pray speak for me with your gentlemen, telling them that I came to you entirely on my own responsibility. That is important, for I would not have them think that my master would approach them through his servant, which would be beneath their dignity and unworthy of his good manners.'

'I shall be most careful,' answered Tommaso blandly. 'But listen to me again. If, for instance, my gentlemen should desire to meet your gentleman and his lady in some quiet out-of-the-way place, in order to talk over the circumstances at leisure, do you think there would be any objection?'

'Why should there be?' asked Cucurullo in surprise. 'Are they not the best of friends?'

'Indeed they are!' replied the other with alacrity. 'I wish you could hear how my masters talk of the Maestro Stradella's genius, and of his voice, and then of his noble air and manner, and of the Lady Ortensia's beauty and modest deportment! It would do your heart good, most estimable friend!'

'It is a pleasure even to hear you tell me of it,' Cucurullo answered, much delighted, for he worshipped Stradella, and thought him perfection now that he was at last properly married, and there was an end of his love-scrapes, and of carrying letters to his sweethearts, and of silk ladders and all the rest of it.

'I have not told you half,' said Tommaso readily. 'And now, as I have an important errand, and my gentlemen are waiting to be shaved, I shall say good-bye. Will it suit you to meet me this afternoon about twenty-three o'clock, at the Montefiascone wine-cellar in the Via dei Pastini? It is a quiet place, and there is a light white wine there which is cooling in this warm weather.'

'I will be there,' Cucurullo answered with a friendly nod by way of taking leave.

Though they had slackened their pace to an ordinary walk that suited Tommaso's breathing powers, they had covered a good deal of ground in the five or six minutes during which they had been talking, and they were close to the Church of the Minerva, not far from the Altieri palace. As it was quite clear that Tommaso wished to go on his errand alone, Cucurullo turned into a narrow street when he left him, and walked slowly, picking his way over the uneven pavement. It was an unsavoury lane, that ran between tall houses, from the windows of which everything that was objectionable indoors was thrown out; and as His Eminence the Cardinal Vicar's sweepers were only supposed to pass that way once a week, on Thursdays, and sometimes forgot about it, the accumulations of dirt were pestiferous. Rome in those days was what all Naples was twenty years ago, and still is, in parts; it was full of the most astounding extremes of splendour and incredible poverty, of perfect cleanliness and abominable filth, and the contrast between the stringency of the law and the laxity of its execution was often not less surprising. Under the statutes, a man could be punished with torture and the galleys for owning a dark lantern, for carrying a pointed knife in his pocket, or for wearing a sword without leave; but, as a matter of fact, the detailed manuscript accounts of scores of crimes committed in Rome in the seventeenth century, and later, show that almost every one went armed, that any one who could dress like a gentleman wore a rapier when he pleased, and that dark lanterns were commonly used in defiance of the watch, the sbirri in plain clothes, the Bargello who commanded both, and the Governor who was his only superior in matters relating to public order.

I have digressed a little, both to explain the affair of the serenade under the Altieri palace, and to prepare my readers for what followed, and especially for the lawless doings of Trombin, Gambardella, and Don Alberto, which came to a climax during the night of Saint John's Eve, in spite of the many admirable regulations about lanterns and weapons which should have made the city a paradise of safety for unprotected females. But, after all, progress has not done much for us since then, for the cities are always growing faster than the police possibly can, so that it is in the very greatest capitals that the most daring crimes are committed with apparent impunity in our own time.

Cucurullo picked his way through the dirty side street, and was just emerging into a broader and cleaner one, when some one overtook him and tapped him on his hump, though he had not noticed the sound of footsteps behind him. He stopped, and saw a man in dusty and shabby black clothes, whom he took for a sbirro.

'Good-morning, Master Alessandro,' said the man with some politeness.

'That is my master's name,' answered Cucurullo, 'not mine, and he is not deformed. Therefore, if you are jesting with me, I beg you to pass on in peace.'

'Your pardon, sir,' the man said, lifting his hat, 'have I not the honour of addressing Signor Alessandro Guidi, the poet, for whom I have a message from Her Majesty the Queen of Sweden, whose servant I am?'

'No,' replied the other, pacified at being taken for the misshapen bard. 'I am only a servant like yourself, and my name is Cucurullo.'

The man seemed reassured and much amused, for he was a Piedmontese.

'Cuckoo-rulloo-cuckoo what?' he asked, laughing. 'I did not catch the rest!'

Cucurullo fixed his unwinking blue eyes on the speaker's face with a displeased expression, and after a moment the man turned pale and began to tremble, for he saw that he had given grave offence, and to rouse the anger of a hunchback, especially in the morning, might bring accident, ruin, and perhaps sudden death before sunset. He shook all over, and the blue eyes never winked, and seemed to grow more and more angry till they positively blazed with wrath, and, at last, the fellow uttered a cry of abject fright and turned and ran up the dirty street at the top of his speed. But Cucurullo went quietly on his way, smiling with a little satisfaction; for, after all, it was something to command kindness and hospitality, or inspire mortal terror, by the deformity that afflicted him. Possibly, too, in his humble heart he was pleased at having been taken for such a social personage as a scholar and a man of letters; for he had always been very careful to keep himself very clean and neat, and if he had any vanity it was that no one could ever detect a spot on his clothes. For instance, he always carried with him a little piece of brown cotton, folded like a handkerchief, which he spread upon the pavement in church before he knelt down, lest the knees of his breeches should be soiled, and he treasured a pair of old goatskin gloves which he had bought at a pawnshop in Venice, and which he put on when he cleaned his master's boots or did any other dirty work.

After he had parted from Tommaso, the latter went about his business, though not in breathless haste. His errand, as he had called it, took him amongst the dealers in coaches, new and second-hand, who had their warehouses near the Massimo palace and in the neighbourhood of Saint Mark's, and in other regions near by, from which the public conveyances started and where private carriages could be bought or hired.

The Bravi, who were practical men, judged that a former highway robber should be a good judge of such vehicles, and had commissioned Tommaso, who had stopped and plundered hundreds of them on the Bologna road, to find one that would suit their purpose. It was to be perfectly sound, not large, comfortably cushioned and provided with solid shutters to draw up outside the windows. There were to be good locks to the doors, with keyholes inside and out, and a boot for luggage, also provided with a safe fastening. It was no easy matter to find exactly what the Bravi wanted, without paying a high price for a perfectly new carriage, and it was a prime necessity that the one Tommaso was to buy for them should be able to stand a rather unusual journey without once breaking down.

They also needed good horses of their own, for there were several reasons why they could not hire a team from the post for the start, and they meant to trust to luck for exchanging or selling theirs at the end of the first stage. Tommaso was a capital judge of horseflesh, as they had found out on the journey from Venice, and they confidently left the whole matter in his hands while they occupied themselves with graver affairs, or sought relaxation in the pleasures which the city afforded.

CHAPTER XIX

Ortensia had told her husband everything that had passed between her and Don Alberto, and Stradella's first instinct was to seek him out, insult him, and force him into a duel. Ortensia saw the big vein swelling ominously in the middle of the white forehead, the tightening of the lips, and the unconscious movement of the fingers that closed upon an imaginary sword-hilt; she saw all this and was pleased, as every woman is when the man she loves is roused and wants to fight for her. But Ortensia did not mean that there should be any bloodshed, and she soothed her husband and made him promise that he would only watch over her more jealously than ever, and make it impossible for Don Alberto ever to be left alone with her again. If he would promise that, she said, she should feel quite safe.

He promised reluctantly, but said that he would not stay under Altieri's roof another day; he would not owe such an obligation to a man who had attacked his honour, he would not tolerate the thought that his wife was actually dwelling in the house of the wretch against whom she asked his protection. But Ortensia besought him to do nothing hurriedly, lest he should cause a scandal which would do more harm to her good name than Don Alberto's foolish declarations, which could be kept a secret.

'He began to look about for lodgings'

Stradella yielded to her entreaties at first, for he saw that there was some sense in what she said; but his pride could not bear such a situation long, and with every day that passed he became more anxious to leave the palace.

He began to look about for lodgings when he went out alone in the morning, and he saw more than one that would have suited him; but none of them would be free until the Feast of Saint John, which was then the quarter-day in Rome, on which leases began and expired. He wanted a dwelling with a hall large enough for rehearsing with his orchestra, and having a loggia looking towards the south, like the one at the Orso inn.

And now it happened, on that same morning when Cucurullo went to find Tommaso, that Stradella himself had gone out to see another house of which he had heard; and Don Alberto, who was well informed of the movements of the little household, judged the moment favourable for visiting Ortensia, since he had observed that Stradella was usually away at least an hour, and often much longer, when he went out early; and if Cucurullo should return sooner, it would not matter.

Ten minutes after the hunchback had left the palace Don Alberto knocked at the door of the small apartment halfway down the grand staircase. Pina opened almost immediately, not suspecting anything, but started in surprise when she saw who the visitor was.

'I desire to speak with the Lady Ortensia,' said Don Alberto suavely.

'The master is gone out,' Pina answered, 'and my mistress would never receive a gentleman's visit alone, sir.'

'The matter is urgent and concerns the Maestro,' Don Alberto explained, and at the same time he made the gold pieces in his pocket jingle, as if quite accidentally.

'The Maestro will be at home in two hours,' said Pina firmly, and making as if she would shut the door.

'I am too busy to wait so long,' objected the young man. 'My dear good woman, do you know who I am?'

'Perfectly, sir. You are Don Alberto Altieri, His Eminence's nephew.'

'Well, then, you need not make so much trouble about letting me in, my dear, for this is my own house, and a lady may surely see her landlord on a matter of business!'

Thereupon he took out a gold florin and tried to put it into Pina's palm in a coaxing way and with a smile. But she shut her hand quickly and held it behind her back, shaking her head. Don Alberto was not used to servants who refused gold. He tried flattery.

'Really,' he cried, 'for a girl with such a sweet face, you are very obstinate! If you will not take an Apostolic florin, I will give you the Apostolic kiss, my dear!'

He tried to kiss her, trusting that a middle-aged serving-woman could not resist the Pope's nephew when he called her a sweet-faced girl. But she kept him at arm's length with surprising energy.

'You are mistaken,' she said in a low voice, lest Ortensia should hear her within; 'I am neither young, nor pretty, nor quite a fool!'

Don Alberto suddenly seized her wrist unawares and held it fast.

'No,' he answered, 'you are not a fool, but you are Filippina Landi, a runaway nun, and though you once got a pardon, you are in Rome now, and I can have it revoked in an hour, and you will be lodged in the Convent of Penitent Women before night, to undergo penance for the rest of your life.'

Pina shivered from head to foot and turned very pale. He dropped her wrist, and, as if she were overcome by an invisible power, she stood aside, hanging her head, and let him pass in. For more than a minute after he had disappeared, she stood leaning against the marble door-post, pressing her left hand to her heart and breathing hard.

Don Alberto knew the small apartment well, for he had once lived in it with his tutor, before the Cardinal had left the palace to take up his quarters in the Quirinal. He went directly to the large sitting-room, from the windows of which Ortensia and Stradella had listened to the serenade and had seen the fighting; he tapped at the door, and Ortensia's voice bade him enter.

She was seated in one of those wooden chairs with arms and a high flat leathern back, which one often sees in Rome even now, chiefly in outer reception-halls and ranged in stiff order against the walls. The shutters were drawn near together to keep out the heat and to darken the room a little. She had a lute on her knees, but her hands held a large sheet of music, from which she had been reading over the words of the song before trying it. She did not look up as the door opened and was shut, for she supposed it must be Cucurullo who had come to ask a question. Don Alberto stood still a few seconds in silent admiration. She had evidently been washing her hair, for it was loose and was combed out over her shoulders in red-auburn waves; and the shorter locks at her temples and round her forehead floated out in little clouds full of rich but transparent colour. The morning was warm, and she was still clad in a loose dressing-gown of thin white silk trimmed with a simple lace. Never, in many misspent days, had Altieri seen a more radiant vision. When she had read all the words of the song, she laid the sheet on the table beside her, and spoke without looking round, for, as her chair was placed, the door was a little behind her, and she was sure that it was Cucurullo who had entered, since she had not heard the slight sound of Pina's cotton skirt.

'What is it?' she asked quietly.

'A thief, dear lady,' answered Don Alberto, smiling; 'one who has forced your door to steal a sight of you——'

At the first word she had risen, turning towards him as she rose, and laying the lute on the table at her left, which was between her and the door.

'How dare you come here?' she cried, indignantly interrupting his pretty speech.

'I dare everything and—nothing,' he answered; 'everything for the happiness of seeing you and hearing your voice, but nothing else that can displease you! See, I do not move a step, I stand here your prisoner on parole, for I give you my word that I will not run away! I will stand here like a statue, or kneel if you bid me, or lie prostrate at your feet!'

'I bid you go, sir! I bid you leave me, for you have no right to be here!'

'No right? I have the right to live, sweet lady! The meanest creature has that.'

'I do not bid you die,' Ortensia answered with some contempt. 'I only tell you to go!'

'And so to die most painfully, for I cannot live without seeing you! Therefore I will do anything but go away before my eyes have fed me full of you and I can bear another day's fasting!'

'Then, sir,' said Ortensia proudly, 'it is I that will leave you; and if you mean in earnest not to displease me, you will not stay here.'

She made two steps towards the door of her own room, before he moved; then he sprang nimbly forward and placed himself in front of her, at a little distance.

'I ask nothing but a kind word,' he said earnestly, 'or if you will not speak it, give me one thought of pity, and I shall see it in your eyes! You love your husband, and I respect your love—I admire you the more for it, upon my soul and honour I do! Did I not promise to be a true friend to you both? Have I broken my promise because I am here now, only to see your dear face for a few moments and bear away your image to cheer my lonely life?'

'Your lonely life!' Ortensia smiled, though scornfully enough.

'Yes, my lonely life,' he answered, repeating the words with grave emphasis. 'What would yours be, pray, if you were forced to be for ever a central figure amongst men and women who wearied you with adulation and never ceased from flattering except to ask favours for themselves and their relatives? And if, with that, you loved Stradella as you do, and he was another woman's husband and would not even look at you, nor let you hear his voice, would your existence not be lonely, I ask? In the desert of your life, would you not hide yourself in the hermitage of your heart, with the image of the man you loved upon your only altar? Would you not feel alone all day, and lonelier still all night, though the whole world pressed upon you, even at your rising and your lying down, to call you beautiful and gifted beyond compare, and a divine being on earth, and in return to beg a benefice for a graceless younger son, or a curacy for a starving cousin of a priest, or the privilege of providing the oil for the lamps in the Vatican? That is my life, if you call it a life! It is all I have, except my love for you—my honouring, respecting, venerating love!'

He spoke his words well, with changing tone and moving accent, but the one great gift he had received from nature was his wonderful and undefinable charm of manner; and surely of all marketable commodities, from gold and silver coin to coloured beads and cowry shells, there is none that can be so readily exchanged for almost anything in the world its possessor wants. Ortensia felt it in spite of herself, and while she was not touched by his attempts at eloquence, she was more inclined to laugh than to be angry at what he said. There was something in him and in his way that disarmed and made it almost impossible not to forgive him anything in reason.

'If my husband were only here,' Ortensia said, 'this would be as amusing as a comedy, but a lady cannot go to the play alone. Will you wait till he comes home? Then we will listen to you together, and you will get twice as much applause, for it is really very good acting, I must admit!'

A professional love-maker always knows when to stop being serious during the early stages of the game, and when to leave off laughing later on; for there is nothing so sure to weary and irritate an average woman as perpetual seriousness at first, when she has not yet made up her mind and perhaps never may, nor is there anything more ruinous than to jest about love when she herself feels it and bestows it. The reason of this must be that if you are too grave while she is still undetermined, she will believe that you are taking her love for granted, which is an unpardonable sin, whereas after she has unfolded her heart and given you the most precious part of herself, she trembles at the merest suggestion that you may not be in earnest.

Don Alberto was a professional love-maker, and at Ortensia's last speech he laughed so readily and naturally that she could not help joining him.

'The truth is,' he said presently, 'the Queen is going to have a little comedy performed by her friends, and I have been giving you some bits from my part. If you really think I do it well, I will wait for the Maestro, as you say, and he shall hear it too, for his opinion is valuable.'

'If you had told me the other day at the palace that you were only rehearsing, it would have been better,' Ortensia said, still smiling.

'No,' answered the young man, 'for I can only judge of my own acting when it carries so much conviction with it that it is mistaken for truth. Is that not sound reason?'

'Sound reason, but poor compliment, sir! In future, pray choose some one else for your experiments. I have heard a Latin proverb quoted which says that the experiment should be made on a body of small value! You hold me cheap, sir, since you try your experiments on me.'

'I hold you dearer than you guess,' answered Don Alberto gaily. 'But I am no match for you in argument. Giovanni Fiorentino tells the story of a lady who played lawyer to defend her lover against a money-lender to whom he had promised a pound of his flesh if he failed to pay. I think you must be of her family, and a Doctor in Law!'

'If I have won my case against you,' retorted Ortensia, 'there is nothing left for you but to retire from the court, acknowledging that you are beaten.'

'Beaten as a lawyer, but successful as an actor,' laughed Altieri, 'and a good friend at your service, as ever. Will you give me your hand, lady?'

'What for, sir? I was sorry I did, the other day. I should have boxed your ears instead!'

'Do it now!'

With a careless laugh he dropped on his knees, just at her feet, folding his hands like a penitent; and laughing too, in spite of herself, she lightly tapped his left ear. He instantly turned the other towards her.

'Remember the gospel,' he said. '"If thine enemy smite thee on one cheek——"'

Again she laughed, but she would not touch him a second time, and she turned away. He sprang to his feet, and there was a flash of light in his eyes, and his hands trembled; for he was behind her, and the temptation to catch her in his arms was almost too strong for him. At that moment the door opened without any warning knock.

'The master is coming up the stairs,' said Pina quietly, and instantly she disappeared again.

Don Alberto started, but Ortensia was calm.

'Stay here and say you have come to see him,' she said, and before he could answer she was in her own room and the door was shut.

Don Alberto was himself again in a moment, for no experienced woman of the world could have done the right thing with more instant decision than Ortensia had shown. He understood, too, that he had so thoroughly frightened the wretched Pina that she was henceforth his slave, on whom he could count as safely as Stradella had depended on her in Venice. With the instinct of an old hand he glanced quickly round the room to see that no object had been displaced in a way to excite suspicion, and he then sat down in a straight chair, folded one knee over the other, and waited for Stradella's coming.

The musician entered a few moments later and stared in surprise as Don Alberto rose to meet him with outstretched hand and a friendly smile.

'Your servant told me that you would not be back for some time,' said Altieri, 'but I insisted on coming in. Pray forgive the intrusion, for the matter is very urgent.'

Stradella had taken his hand rather coolly, but he did not mean his visitor to see that he was displeased, and he now politely pushed a chair forward, and took another himself.

'I am glad to find you here,' he said, 'for I also wished to see you in order to thank you once more for the use of this apartment.'

'But you are not going away?' cried Don Alberto in astonishment.

'Not from Rome. But I have at last found a dwelling which will just suit us, and we mean to move on Saint John's Day.'

'On Saint John's Day!' repeated Don Alberto, with still more evident surprise. 'Really! Indeed! I assure you that I did not expect this, my dear Maestro, and I am almost inclined to think it a breach of friendship. Are you not well lodged here? Are the rooms too small for you and your lady? Or do you find them hot, or noisy? I do not understand.'

'Pray put it down to an artist's foolish love of independence,' Stradella answered with suavity. 'It is one thing for you rich nobles to accept favours from each other; you can return them; but we poor musicians cannot, and so we set a limit to what we think we may fairly receive.'

'You give what we never can,' objected Don Alberto, 'for you give us your genius and its works, and I suspect you have some reason hidden away of which you do not care to speak. I can only tell you how sorry I am that you should leave this house, where I had hoped you would live whenever you came to Rome, and where you will always be welcome if you wish to return.'

'It is impossible to be more courteous, and I wish I could express my gratitude as well as you have worded your most kind invitation.'

The musician bowed rather formally from his chair as he spoke, but Don Alberto was not pleased.

'Come, come, my dear Stradella,' he said familiarly, 'one would take us for a couple of courtiers making compliments at each other. We used to be good friends and comrades a year ago. Have you forgotten that carnival season, and how we supped together on ten consecutive nights in ten different eating-houses, with those two charming ladies from Genoa? Ah, my dear fellow, how you have changed! But you were not married then!'

'And never thought I should be! But I am not as much changed as you think, and I dare say you will soon come to find it out. You spoke of some urgent business that brings you here——'

'Yes. It is an important affair for you. His Holiness wishes you to compose a high mass for Saint Peter's Day, for the united choirs of the Sistine Chapel and Saint Peter's.'

'But the feast is on the twenty-ninth of this month!' cried Stradella in surprise. 'The time is much too short! Less than three weeks for composing such a work! I cannot possibly undertake to turn out anything worthy in that time!'

'I give you the message as my uncle the Cardinal gave it to me,' Don Alberto answered with assurance, though he had invented the commission on the spur of the moment, quite sure that he could easily make it a genuine order, though it would never be executed if his own plans for carrying off Ortensia on Saint John's Eve succeeded.

'May I have a day in which to consider my answer?' asked the musician.

'If you like. But you will only lose twenty-four hours, since you will have to do what the Pope asks! A commission from the Sovereign is a command, you know. Besides, you must have a great many scraps of compositions and odds and ends of masses among your papers, a part of a *Credo* here, an *Agnus Dei* there—things you can string together and finish in a few days. The only part that must be new will be the Offertory for the day, unless you happen to have that too.'

'But the whole can never be harmonious if I do it in that way——'

'What has that to do with it, my dear friend?' asked Don Alberto. 'What has conscience to do with art, pray? If you do the work the Pope will be pleased, and you will be several hundred crowns the richer; but if you refuse to do it, His Holiness will be angry with you and the Cardinal, and the Cardinal will make you and me pay for the reproof he will receive! As for the music, nothing you write can be bad, because you have real genius, and the worst that any one may say will be that your mass for Saint Peter's Day is not your very best work. Therefore, in my opinion, you have no choice, and it is quite useless for you to take a whole day to consider the matter.'

'I suppose you are right,' Stradella answered.

He was not suspicious enough to guess that it was all an invention of Don Alberto's, and the latter had a very persuasive way with him.

'And now that it is all settled,' Altieri said pleasantly, 'I will take my leave. For during the next three weeks your own time will be more valuable than my company! My duty and homage to the Lady Ortensia, and good-bye; and if you will change your mind and stay here, I shall be much more in your debt than you in mine.'

'Thank you,' answered Stradella, rising to show him out.

When Ortensia had hurriedly left the room her intention had been to prevent any immediate trouble, but not to hide what had happened from her husband for more than a day or two. She was even more angry with Pina than with Don Alberto himself, for she could not but believe that the nurse had taken a bribe to admit him, and had then acted as if her mistress were in love with him, or at least willing to receive him alone in a toilet that could only imply great intimacy. The woman's sudden appearance and her face at the door recalled too well how she had come back suddenly, on the day of the last lesson in Venice, to warn the pair that Pignaver was near, and Ortensia could not bear to think that she could ever have been caught with young Altieri in such a situation as to make the warning positively necessary for her own safety. Indeed, she was so much ashamed of it now that she blushed scarlet, though she was alone, and wondered how she could possibly tell Stradella what had happened.

He found her sitting before her mirror near the window, and from her chair she could see the reflection of the door through which she had entered. When the handle turned she put up her hands and pretended to be arranging her hair, and in the mirror she saw her husband's face and understood that he was not angry, though he was by no means pleased. He came behind her, kissed her hair and then her forehead, as she bent her head backwards to look up into his face.

'Don Alberto has been here,' he said.

'Yes?' The interrogation in her tone might mean anything, and denied nothing.

'He came to tell me that the Pope wishes me to write a solemn mass for the feast of Saint Peter, on the twenty-ninth, and of course I was obliged to agree to do it. But Pina should not have let him in. Do you think she would take money? After what he told you about her I cannot help trusting her less.'

'Do you believe that what he told me is true?'

'It agrees well enough with what she said when she came to see me in Venice,' Stradella answered. 'Do you remember? Or did I never tell you? She made it a condition of our flight that we should take her with us, because, if she were left behind, your uncle would have her tortured, and she said she could bear anything but that. She said it in a way that made me sure she had already suffered the question, as Don Alberto has now told you is really the case.'

'It all agrees very well together,' Ortensia announced, shaking her head. 'Poor Pina! Perhaps Don Alberto threatened her, for I suppose he has power to do anything he pleases here in Rome.'

'I will go and ask her,' Stradella said. 'That is the simplest way.'

'No! Please——' Ortensia showed such signs of distress that her husband was surprised.

'Why not? Do you think it would be unfair, or would hurt her feelings? Then call her here, and ask her yourself before me. She will probably confess the truth.'

'She would be more likely to conceal it, since you have not the power to use threats!'

'Possibly, but I doubt it. The woman is a coward, and if you speak sharply she will be frightened. I do not like to think that when I am out of the house and my man is out too, anybody may get in. You are not safe in such conditions. Any ruffian who knew her story could force his way to you! No, no, love—we must speak to her at once!'

He was already going towards the door, but Ortensia rose quickly and overtook him before he could go out, catching him by the hand and holding him back.

'You must hear me first,' she cried in great anxiety, leading him to a seat beside her.

He had followed her without resistance, too much surprised to object. If any reason for her action suggested itself it was that she wished to spare Pina's feelings, probably out of affection for the nurse. But Ortensia took one of his hands and pressed it against her eyes as she began to speak, for she thought she had done something very wicked in concealing from him that she had really seen Don Alberto.

'I do not know why Pina let him in,' she said in a low voice, as if making a confession, 'but he found me there, in the next room, and he had come on purpose to see me, and not you.'

She went on and told Stradella everything she could remember, which, indeed, was most of the conversation, including Don Alberto's jesting pretence that he had been acting.

'I did not want to make trouble,' Ortensia concluded tearfully. 'I meant to tell you to-morrow—are you very angry? You can call Pina now, if you like——'

Stradella had risen and was pacing the room, evidently in no very gentle temper, though he was far too just to blame his wife for what had happened. After a few moments Ortensia rose and went to him, and as he stopped she laid her hands upon his shoulders, looking up into his eyes.

'You are angry with me,' she said very sorrowfully. 'I did the best I could. He would not go away.'

Instantly he took her in his arms, lifted her clear of the floor, and kissed her passionately, again and again; and at the very first touch of his lips she understood, though she could almost feel his anger against Altieri throbbing in the hands that held her.

'I have borne enough from that man,' he said, letting her stand on her feet again, and he slipped his right arm round her waist, and made her walk up and down with him. 'He will take no answer from you, he forces himself upon you when you are alone, he thinks that because he is the Pope's nephew no one dares to face him and say him nay!'

He was very angry, and at each phrase his hand unconsciously tightened its hold on Ortensia's waist, as if to emphasise what he was saying; and though he said little enough, she felt that his blood was up, and that it would be ill for Don Alberto to meet him in his present mood. A Tuscan would have dissolved his temper in a torrent of useless blasphemy, as Tuscans generally do, a Roman would have roared out fearful threats, a Neapolitan would have talked of the knife with many gestures; the Sicilian did not raise his voice, though it shook a little, and he only said he had borne enough, but if his enemy had appeared at that moment he would have killed him with his hands, and Ortensia understood him.

'You must think of me too,' she pleaded wisely. 'If you make him fight you, one of two things will happen: either you will kill him, and then no power can save you from the Pope's vengeance, or else he will kill you—for you will not yield till you are dead!—and I shall have to take my own wretched life to save myself from him!'

'God forbid!' cried Stradella in a troubled voice, and pressing her to his side again. 'To think that I imagined we should be safer in Rome than anywhere else! I suppose you are right, sweetheart. If any harm befalls me there is no hope for you. But what am I to do? Can I take you with me each time I am obliged to go out about my business? And if not, where can I find any one whom I can trust to watch over you? As for Don Alberto, it is easy to speak moderately when he is away, but if I meet him and talk with him——' He stopped short, unwilling to let his anger waste itself in words.

'Trust no one, love,' said Ortensia softly. 'Take me with you everywhere. I shall be far happier if you never let me be out of your sight an hour—far more happy, and altogether safe!'

'But I cannot take you up into the organ loft when I sing, or conduct music in church! You cannot go with me behind the lattice of the Sistine choir! On Saint John's Eve, for instance, at the Lateran, I shall have to be at least two hours with the singers and musicians. Who will take care of you?'

'Surely,' objected Ortensia, 'you can trust your own man. Let him stand beside me while I sit on the pedestal of the pillar nearest to the organ, where you can see me. Or ask our two mysterious friends to guard me, for they would overmatch a dozen of Don Alberto's sort!'

She laughed, though with a slight effort; but she saw that he was inclining to the side of discretion, at least for the present.

'And if worse comes to the worst,' she added, 'we must leave Rome and live in the South, in your own country. I have always longed to go there.'

'Even to starve with me, love?' Stradella smiled. 'It is not in Naples that I shall be offered three or four hundred crowns for writing a mass! Thirty or forty will be nearer the price! Instead of living in a palace we shall take up our quarters in some poor little house over the sea, at Mergellina or Posilippo, with three rooms, a kitchen, and a pigsty at the back, and we shall eat macaroni and fried cuttle-fish every day, with an orange for dessert, and a drive in a curricolo on Sunday afternoons! How will that suit the delicate tastes of the Lady Ortensia Grimani?'

'It sounds delicious,' Ortensia said, rubbing her cheek against his coat. 'I delight in macaroni and oranges as it is, and I can think of nothing I should like better than to have you to myself in a little house with three rooms looking over the sea! We will give Pina a present and send her away, and Cucurullo shall cook for us. I am sure he can, and very well, and why should I need a maid? Let us go, Alessandro; promise that we shall! When can we start?'

'Not till after Saint Peter's Day, at all events since I have that mass to finish and conduct,' Stradella answered, humouring her. 'But it is impossible,' he added, almost at once. 'You could not live in that way, and I have no right to let you try it.'

'We shall be happier than we ever were before!'

'For a few days, perhaps. But the plain truth is, that I am only a poor artist, and all I have saved is a matter of a thousand crowns in Chigi's bank. I must earn money for us both, and there is no place where I can earn as much as I can here, under the patronage of the Pope——'

'—and his nephews,' said Ortensia, completing the sentence as he hesitated; 'and one of those nephews is Don Alberto Altieri, who pays himself for his patronage by forcing himself upon my privacy when you are gone out! That is the short of a very long story!'

Stradella stood still, struck by what she said, and he looked into her eyes; they met his a little timidly, for she feared that she had hurt him.

'You are right,' he said. 'I will go at once to the Cardinal himself, and say that I cannot undertake to write the mass for the Pope. Instead of taking a new lodging, we will leave Rome on the feast of Saint John.'

CHAPTER XX

The following days passed quietly, and Don Alberto did not again attempt to see Ortensia alone. He was, indeed, much occupied with more urgent affairs, for Queen Christina had noticed the signs of his approaching defection and was becoming daily more exigent. On his side, young Altieri only desired to be dismissed, and instead of submitting to her despotic commands in a spirit of contrition, he cleverly managed to obey them with a sort of superior indifference that irritated her to the verge of fury. She wreaked her temper on every one who came near her, and so far forgot her royal dignity as to box the ears of poor Guidi, the deformed poet, for pointing out a grammatical mistake in some Italian verses she had composed. But he would not bear the indignity of a blow, even from her royal hand, and on that same night he packed his manuscripts and his few belongings and left Rome to seek his fortune where he might. The ex-Queen had Rome searched for him the very next day by a score of her servants, and it was one of her grooms who had mistaken Cucurullo for Guidi, because he hardly knew the poet by sight, and thought that hunchbacks were all very much alike.

Don Alberto had not neglected to speak to the Cardinal about Stradella's mass, nor was he surprised at the careless way in which His Eminence acquiesced to the proposal and agreed that the composer should receive a handsome fee. The young man did not notice that his uncle's thin lips twitched a little, as if with amusement. The truth was that Stradella had come to him before Don Alberto, and had explained that it was materially impossible to do what His Eminence had so kindly proposed through his nephew. The Cardinal was well aware of the latter's passion for the musician's wife, and was not at all inclined to encourage it, judging that there was more political advantage to be gained by his young kinsman's continued intimacy with the ex-Queen than by a love-affair with Ortensia. For Christina was almost always engaged in some intrigue, if not in actual conspiracy, and though her dealings of this kind were as futile as her whole life had been, it was as well that the Papal Government should know what she was really about.

A week before the Feast of Saint John, Ortensia was already packing her own and Stradella's belongings for the journey to Naples. Though she and Pina had left Venice with no baggage but a piece of white Spanish soap, a comb, and a little yellow leather work-case, Ortensia now had enough linen and gowns, and laces and ribbons, to fill two respectable trunks, and Pina was well provided with all that a serving-woman needed in the way of clothes.

Nothing had yet been said between the nurse and her mistress about Don Alberto's last visit, but an explanation was inevitable. One day Pina asked if she might have a small box or a valise for her own things.

'We shall not want you in Naples,' said Ortensia quietly. 'You shall have your wages from the day when my uncle last paid you, and a present of ten gold florins for your long service; but I shall not want you any more.'

She had been folding some delicate laces while she spoke, and she did not look up till she heard a little choking cry from the nurse. Pina stood grasping the back of a chair to keep herself from falling, and her face was grey.

'Good heavens!' cried Ortensia. 'Are you ill? What is the matter with you?'

Pina could hardly speak; she slowly moved her bent head from side to side as if in an agony of pain.

'It is death!' she moaned. 'You are sending me to die!'

Ortensia went to her and took her by the arm energetically, as if to rouse her.

'This is absurd!' she cried. 'I know what you said to my husband before we fled from Venice, and it is of no use to pretend that you are going to die of grief if you leave me!'

But Pina only shook her head, and would not look up.

'And as for having been so very faithful,' Ortensia went on, in a tone of displeasure, 'it was only the other day that you took money from Don Alberto to let him see me when my husband was out and I was alone! Do not deny it!'

Pina looked up now, with something of a born lady's pride in her eyes and tone.

'I never took a bribe in my life!' she cried indignantly. 'Don Alberto threatened to have me arrested and put to the question, and I was afraid, and let him in. Yes, I was afraid. I am a coward, for I have felt pain. That was done to me once, to make me confess, and more too!'

She held out her broken thumb, and her hand shook; and Ortensia shuddered as she looked at it.

'He threatened to have my pardon cancelled, and to have me tortured again, and then sent to the Convent of Penitent Women for life! Do not be hard on me, for I was in one of those places of penance for three weeks before your uncle got me a pardon and took me to his house to be your nurse. Don Alberto frightened me—I was weak, cowardly—I let him in!'

'Poor Pina! Then it is all true? He told me your story, but I did not believe him.'

'It is all true. It was to be revenged on the Senator that I wanted you to run away. But even so, I have helped you to be happy, for I know you are. For the happiness you have had through me, forgive me! Do not leave me here at Don Alberto's mercy, for the sake of Heaven! He means to carry you off, I am sure he does; and if you escape him, he will visit it all on me!'

Her hands strained on the back of the chair till the knuckles whitened with the effort, while her body quivered as if she had been struck. Ortensia understood that she had told the truth, and that the mere thought of physical pain almost drove her mad.

'I will take you with me to Naples,' Ortensia said. 'You will be safe there. I am sorry for you; but how can I trust a woman who is so easily frightened?'

'Easily!' groaned Pina. 'You do not know what it is!'

But she took her mistress's hand and kissed it gratefully, with many tearful blessings.

'I must confess something else,' she said presently, 'though it is Cucurullo's business as well as mine. We have been so much afraid that Don Alberto would try to carry you off by some daring stroke that Cucurullo has secretly asked help of the two Venetian gentlemen, who are still here, and they have promised to watch over you and protect you as far as they can, even at the risk of their lives.'

'Cucurullo should not have gone to them without asking his master's consent,' said Ortensia, not altogether pleased. 'Do you know what Don Alberto told me? He said that Count Trombin and Count Gambardella are Bravi, the most famous in Italy!'

'It is not possible,' replied Pina, shaking her head. 'I do not believe it!'

'Don Alberto told me the truth about you, it seems,' Ortensia said rather coldly. 'Why should he have invented a story about the other two who signed the marriage register as witnesses? And besides, if he meant to carry me off by force, would he not very likely employ just such men to do the deed for him?'

Pina did not try to answer this argument, but her face showed her incredulity.

'I have told you what I know,' she said. 'If anything should happen, and if one of those two gentlemen should tell me to do anything for your safety, am I to obey? I must know that, for perhaps there will be no time to be lost.'

'I will ask my husband,' Ortensia said. 'Let us go on with our packing.'

Pina knelt down before the open trunk again. She had told her mistress exactly what Cucurullo had reported to her after his second interview with Tommaso, when the two men had met in the wine-shop of the Via dei Pastini. On that occasion the ex-highwayman had told the hunchback that his masters would be only too glad to protect Stradella and his wife against Don Alberto, to the last drop of their blood, and that Cucurullo was free to inform the musician of their promise or not, as he pleased. It would make no difference, they had said; henceforth Don Alberto should be watched continually, as a mouse is watched by a cat, or in fact by two cats; at the very first intimation that he meant mischief, they would send him to the permanent future abode of all mischief-makers; and as for the consequences of their action, if they were ever detected, they would take such a trifle as that upon themselves. Don Alberto might be the nephew of all the popes and anti-popes that had reigned, excepting those who were canonised saints, and who might therefore be offended by the statement that they did not care a cabbage who he was, not a farthing, not a fig! If he attempted anything against the Lady Ortensia or her husband, they would not only make him wish he were dead, but would at once oblige him by satisfying his wish. This, at least, was Tommaso's version of what they had said, and Cucurullo saw no reason to doubt the statement, since he had seen the two gentlemen demolish and put to flight a whole watch in a few moments in the affair of the serenade.

What the Bravi thought of their own situation on the morning of the Eve of Saint John is difficult to imagine; for they were in one of those exciting but equivocal situations in which modern financiers not infrequently find themselves. Their feelings might possibly be compared to those of Lord Byron when he had written offers of marriage to two young ladies on the same day, and both accepted him; or to those of an 'operator' who has advised one intimate friend to buy a certain sk at any price, and another to sell all he has, while he himself has not made up his mind as to what he had better do; or to those of a jockey who has taken money to pull a horse when he was sober, and has backed his mount when he was drunk.

The Bravi had, indeed, concocted a plan by which they hoped to win their money from three employers for doing three different things, each of which was contrary to the nature of the other two. And Gambardella might be satisfied if the attempt succeeded; but Trombin was not only his friend's partner in the whole scheme and intent on getting an equal share of the profits, he was also very foolishly in love with Ortensia on his own account, and was pondering how he might substitute himself for Don Alberto in the first act of the coming comedy, or drama.

The preparations were now completed, and the two cut-throats awaited the Eve of Saint John without the least qualm or the smallest fear for their own safety. Had they not three blank pardons in their pockets, for themselves and Tommaso, to be filled in with their names if necessary, or to be sold at a high price to some gentleman in trouble, if they did not need them?

Nothing was wanting. Tommaso had found the very carriage for the purpose and the horses for the first start, and he himself could drive them four-in-hand without a postillion, for he was as good a whip as any man who drove a papal stage-coach. He had seen Don Alberto again, and, besides the blank pardons, he had obtained the necessary order from the Governor of the city to pass out of any gate during the night. Don Alberto had, of course, ascertained without difficulty that Tommaso was only a servant who represented the two famous Bravi, and in the hands of such men young Altieri felt that the enterprise could not fail.

The little house in the Via di Santa Sabina was also ready, but he knew nothing of this arrangement, and was willing that the Bravi should keep secret the spot where he was to meet Ortensia, if they preferred to do so. When the evening came he meant that one of his own men, who had served him in a score of adventures, should follow him and Tommaso stealthily to the place of meeting and hold himself ready, within call, after Tommaso had gone away with the money that was to be paid on delivering up Ortensia.

Now before I go on to tell what happened on that memorable night, let me say that if any of the events I am about to describe seem improbable to a sceptical reader, he had better learn the Italian language and dive into one of those yellow manuscript accounts of similar affairs which were written out in the seventeenth and eighteenth centuries, and of which whole volumes can still be bought in Italy for a few francs. He will not go far without finding matter quite as surprising as what I shall put down in this tale, though in all likelihood much more unsavoury to his modern taste. Moreover, there is proof that a good many of those accounts are quite as accurate as what a fairly decent newspaper gives us nowadays for truth; and they are not, as a whole, more nasty, though they are differently worded, because in those days Boileau was calling 'a cat a cat, and Rolet a rascal,' and even people who were not poets called a spade a spade.

A little rain fell during the night before Saint John's Eve, but the morning of the twenty-third of June was clear and calm, and the air had cooled a little. In Rome, for those who do not fear a little sunshine, June is the most beautiful of all the months, and the loveliest June days are those that follow showery nights. Then all the trees of the great villas are in full leaf and all the flowers are in bloom: the gorgeous, stiff-necked, courtly flowers in the formal beds and borders of the Pope's gardens; the soft, sweet-scented, shapely carnations that grow in broken pots and pitchers outside the humble windows of Trastevere; the stately lilies in the marble fountains behind the princely palace, and the roses that run riot in the poor Jewish burial-ground halfway up the Aventine; the heavy-scented tuberose and the rich blossom of bitter orange in the high Colonna gardens, and the sweet basil growing in a rusty iron pail in the belfry of Santa Maria Maggiore, where the old bell-ringer eats the savoury leaves with his coarse bread and cheese, while he rests after ringing the bells for high mass and waits till it is time to ring them again at noon, and he waters the plant from his drinking pitcher. Then the wild onion is in flower that scares away witches and keeps off the Evil Eye, and from all the broad Campagna the scent of new-mown hay is wafted through the city gates. Then, though the sun does not yet scorch the traveller, the shade is already a heavenly refreshment; and though a man is not parched with thirst, a cold draught from the Fountain of Egeria is more delicious than any wine, and under the ancient trees of the pagan grove the rose-purple cyclamens and the dark wood-violets are still blooming side by side. The air is full of the breath of life, the deep earth is still soft, and all trees and flowers and grasses still feel the tender youth of the spring that is not yet quite gone.

Then, too, the gilliflowers are out, and on Saint John's Eve before Vespers the Canons used to bless thousands upon thousands of them, tied up in neat bunches, in small flat baskets, and the poor of Rome came to the door of the sacristy on the south side and received them to take home to their sick and infirm, with the blessing of Saint John and a reviving breath of blossoming nature. But on that day many tents and booths of boughs were also set up on the broad green that stretched away to the hedges of vineyards and vegetable gardens, where modern houses now are built. In each booth there was a little kitchen, a mere earthen fire-pot, such as the alchemists used of old, but larger, and there were tables made of boards laid on trestles with rude benches for seats, and there were little ten-gallon barrels of wine still unbroached, and piles of loaves covered with clean white cloths, and there was much green lettuce for salad, floating in tubs full of water, and there were also fresh onions without end, with their long stalks and big bunches of tiny flowers. For on the Eve of Saint John the Baptist all fairies good and bad, and goblins that are black or grey, and the white hobgoblins too, and the shadowy, unearthly lemures, have deadly power; and ghosts and wraiths go wailing through lonely church-yards, and the fountain sprites float on the water and laugh in the pale moonlight; the misshapen things of evil that haunt murderers' graves move strangely in the gloom; and though the air be still, the chains that dangle from old gibbets all clank together wildly when the blood-spectres hang upon them with wan hands and swing themselves to and fro; then the banshee shrieks amongst the ancient elms, and deep down in the crypt of far San Sisto, by the Latin Gate, the Shining Corpse rises from his grave against the south wall and glares horribly all night at his fellow-dead. No wonder that against such terrors the Roman people thought it wise to eat snails fried in oil, and to carry onions in blossom in their hands, and especially to fortify their quailing spirits with many draughts of strong wine from Genzano, and Frascati, and Marino, till the grey dawn forelightened above the Samnite hills, and a decent man might go home to sleep safely by daylight, and be waked only by the bells that rang out for high mass at ten o'clock.

So in the late afternoon all those excellent preparations had been made for resisting ghostly fear, and as soon as the sun went down the firepots in the booths would be filled with charcoal, and presently a marvellous smell of frying oil would pervade the air, while thousands upon thousands of little lights would be lighted, all made of big snail-shells filled with olive oil and tallow and each having a tiny wick in it. But the sun was not low yet, and the great bells were ringing to call the people into the Basilica for Vespers.

Fine coaches drove up to the transept entrance, one after the other, bringing cardinals and princes and Roman ladies of high rank by the score; and their gorgeously liveried footmen followed them into the church carrying fald-stools and kneeling-cushions as if for a great ceremony in Saint Peter's; and though it was a cloudless day in June two huge closed umbrellas, of the colours of each family, were strapped upon the top of every coach, but those of the cardinals were scarlet. Amongst the many arrivals came the blue and yellow liveries of Christina of Sweden, and with her was Don Alberto in a wonderful summer suit of pale dove-coloured silk, and he wore the collar of the Order of Saint Gregory; there were several other gentlemen in her train, and not a few ladies, so that she was royally attended. She herself wore a three-cornered blue French hunting-hat on the top of her immense black wig, and a short riding-skirt of green cloth, and boots like a man.

The reason why there was such a concourse of society at the Lateran on the eve of the feast was that Alessandro Stradella was going to sing an air himself, and direct a part of the service which he had composed for the occasion; and besides, a vast number of the common people were collected about the Basilica, both from the city and from the Campagna, to enjoy the customary feast of snails as a defence against witches and fairies, and they thronged into the church through the great east door to hear the music too, till there was no standing-room at all in the transepts and little in the nave and aisles for thirty or forty yards below the tabernacle, close beside which the old organ used to stand. For there was no loft then, and the instrument stood out in the church with its wide wooden balcony, draped all in red, which is the colour appropriate to the Apostles, and to Martyrs also, of whom Saint John the Baptist is counted one. The organ was a new one then, and, by the same token, I saw it when I was young, and the keyboard was strangely made; for there were two black keys together everywhere where we have one, the first being for the sharp of the natural below it, and the second for the flat of the natural above; and this meant that the ingenious builder had thought he could get rid of the 'wolf' and produce an instrument with the combined advantages of the even temper and the uneven; and any one who does not know what that means may ask a tuner to explain it for him or not, just as he pleases; but the old organ had double black keys, for I saw and touched them myself, and that was the very instrument to which Stradella sang on the afternoon of Saint John's Eve so long ago. It has probably been destroyed altogether, but Rome is a great place for treasuring rubbish and rombowline, and perhaps the old keyboard still exists, with stacks of wooden and metal pipes and bundles of worm-eaten trackers, all piled up together and forgotten in some corner of the crypt, or in some high belfry room or long-closed attic above the gorgeous ceiling of the Basilica.

It is a long distance from the Palazzo Altieri to the Lateran, and the Canons sent one of their coaches to convey Stradella to the church. He brought Ortensia with him, and found Cucurullo already waiting at the transept door.

'It is impossible to get in by this way, sir,' said the hunchback, coming to the window of the carriage. 'All Rome is here, from the Sacred College and the Queen of Sweden to the poorest notary's clerk, and it would take an hour to make your way through the crowd. Below the tabernacle the church is nearly half full of country people.'

'You will have to go in by the main door,' Stradella said to Ortensia. 'Cucurullo will take you as far up the church as possible, and will not leave your side till I come. As for me, I must go round by the sacristy. Get up behind, Cucurullo, and tell the coachman to take us to the other entrance.'

Cucurullo obeyed with some difficulty, for a crowd of young idlers of the poorer sort had collected to see the cardinals and nobles go in, and they pressed upon him to touch his hump for luck, which should be at least double on such a day; and most of them blessed him, lest he should look round angrily and cast the Evil Eye upon them. But as he was short he found it hard to reach the footman's hanging strap, till a couple of strong fellows lifted him bodily and set him on the footboard. He submitted kindly to the touches he felt, and thanked his helpers with a smile. Then the coach drove away.

Leaning back in its depths, Ortensia wound her arms round her husband's neck, and kissed him tenderly.

'I shall sing for you only, love,' he said. 'Even if you cannot see me, you will know that every note comes from my heart, and is meant only for your ears!'

'One day more, and I shall have you all to myself,' she answered softly.

The coach stopped again, and Cucurullo dropped from the footboard behind and came to the door. Stradella had now no time to lose, and he let Ortensia get out alone and go in with his man, and before she had disappeared he was driven away to the door of the sacristy. A few moments later he was in the singers' robing-room, hastily getting into the purple silk cassock and the spotless lace-trimmed cotta which he had to wear when he appeared in the organ-loft of a basilica, or among the singers of the Sistine Chapel. He brought these things, with his own score of his music, in a purple cloth bag which Ortensia had worked for him, and she had embroidered a lyre on it in silver thread, with the word 'Harmonia' in cursive letters for a motto.

Half the singers were already in the organ loft, and the Canons were in their places droning the psalms for the day antiphonally, and very much through their portentous noses, even as they do to-day. As the noise they made was neither musical nor edifying, Roman society was conversing without the least restraint, except from the fact of being packed rather close together in a comparatively small space. Here and there little openings in the crowd marked the positions of the Cardinals and their parasites, of Queen Christina with her court, and of two or three of the greatest Roman ladies, such as the Princess Orsini and the Princess Rospigliosi, whose husbands were Princes of the Empire as well as Roman nobles. They all talked pleasantly and jested, and even laughed, as if they were anywhere but in church, only pausing when the Gloria Patri was sung from time to time at the end of a psalm.

Far overhead the level beams of the lowering sun poured through the northwest windows. From the ancient mosaic of the tribune vault the still faces of heavenly personages looked down at the doings of a half-believing age with a sad and solemn surprise.

While they talked, the ex-Queen and many others glanced occasionally at the balcony of the organ, and when Stradella at last appeared a little murmur of satisfaction ran through the courtly throng, quite different in tone from the hum of conversation that had preceded it; and as he looked down the great singer saw many acquaintances who made signs of greeting to him, and the ex-Queen waved her painted fan high in the air, while a sprightly little Neapolitan duchess, who was in Rome for a visit and had known him a long time, actually blew him a kiss from the tips of her small gloved fingers. He smiled gravely, nodded once or twice, and disappeared behind the other singers.

From the other side of the balcony, where it ran round the organ to the rickety wooden steps, his gaze searched the distance, looking for Ortensia; and at last he saw her on the outskirts of the crowd of common people and peasants, leaning against the corner of the third pilaster from the main entrance on his left as he looked down the church. His eyes were good, and, besides, though she wore a large veil exactly like that of many of the other ladies, he was sure it was she because Cucurullo was beside her, unmistakable by his deformity, even at that distance and in the shadow that darkened the nave below. Stradella had a roll of music in his hand and, looking towards his wife, he held it above his head for a signal; he immediately saw her raise her hand and wave it a little, and Cucurullo held up his broad hat too. They had seen him and he was satisfied; and at that moment the Canons reached the end of the last psalm, and Stradella joined in the Gloria that followed it, still standing where he was and looking at Ortensia in the distance. He let his voice ring out to her, as different in tone from all the other voices in the loft as strings are different from wood and brass instruments, and every syllable he sang reached her ear; and now she raised her hand again to show that she had heard him, and he held up his little roll of music to return her signal, and then went to the front of the organ to direct the concerted piece that was to follow.

If there had been time, he would have stopped and looked back again, for as he turned he had the impression, without the certainty, that Trombin and Gambardella were standing at the edge of the crowd on the other side of the nave from Ortensia. She had told him of the step Cucurullo had taken, and he had not blamed his man; on the contrary, the thought that the two Bravi were perhaps near her now was comforting, and he wished that he were quite sure of having seen them. As he took his place at the desk to direct, he glanced to his right again, but the singing men close to him hindered him from seeing the body of the church.

He had not been mistaken, however, for the Bravi were there and just in sight, at some little distance behind Ortensia, near the pilaster next beyond the one by which she stood. They were both dressed in black, and though it was a warm afternoon in June, each carried a black cloak on his arm. Their long hair was parted and smoothed with even more than customary neatness, and Trombin's yellow locks were so wonderfully arranged that they might easily have been taken for a wig. His pink face wore a more than usually boyish and innocent expression, and as he stood beside his companion listening to what the latter was saying in an undertone, his eyes gazed steadily at Ortensia's graceful figure. Both men were evidently indifferent to the possibility of her turning and seeing them, and in fact they had taken up their present position in the hope of being seen by Stradella himself from the organ, acting the part of protectors to his wife.

'We have trusted each other in much more dangerous affairs than this,' Gambardella said, almost in a whisper, 'but I have never before known you to lose your heart to the subject of our operations.'

'"Subject" is good!' answered Trombin. '"Subject" is excellent! You speak like a teacher of anatomy! But, so far, you are right, for I cannot take my eyes from that adorable lady. My friend, do you notice the exquisite curve from the throat to the shoulder and from the shoulder to the elbow? And the marvellously suggestive fall of the skirt? And the reflection of the sunshine from overhead in her wonderful hair where it shows from under her veil? Answer me, have you ever seen anything more perfect in art or nature?'

'No, nor anything more complete than your madness,' answered Gambardella. 'If you speak a little louder she will hear you!'

'And turn her angel's eyes to mine!' whispered Trombin sentimentally. 'There is no poetry in your soul, my friend! You were certainly born without any heart, or, if I may say so, with a heart like a German prune, all dried up and hard, and needing to be boiled for hours in syrup to soften it! On the other hand, I may compare my own to the fresh fruit on the tree in July, delicate, juicy, and almost palpitating in the sunshine with its own sweetness!'

Gambardella smiled sourly and shook his head.

'You once had a good intelligence,' he said, 'but it is shattered. Are you capable of listening to me like a sensible being, while that lady is in sight? If not, come with me behind the pilaster, for I have something to say before we separate.'

As if admitting that he was helpless so long as he could gaze on Ortensia, Trombin allowed his friend to lead him away into the shadow.

'Now, listen,' said Gambardella. 'We are playing three games, and if you call yours one, it is the fourth, and the stakes are high. The smallest mistake or hesitation will lose us everything, as you know, and before long we shall be living in an attic again and supping on salt fish and olives. But if we win we shall have money enough to enjoy a whole year of luxury, and with a little economy to live comfortably for a much longer time.'

'I know it,' answered Trombin, on whom the stronger will of his companion made an impression. 'I shall keep my head at the right moment, never fear!'

'But in order that we may risk nothing, I had better play the first part of the comedy, since that is the most important to the success of the whole.'

The two cut-throats looked at each other steadily for some moments, as if neither meant to give way, and possibly they remembered their first meeting, a good many years earlier; for their acquaintance had begun in a sharp quarrel, in which they had almost instantly fallen to fighting, and it was not till they had fenced for nearly twenty minutes, without a scratch on either side, though each was trying to kill the other, that they had both lowered their rapiers in mutual admiration, and had forthwith made the alliance which had never been shaken since.

Yet, though they were so evenly matched in strength and skill, Gambardella was the more determined character, and in important moments like the present his decision generally prevailed; and so it ended now, for Trombin at last turned his round eyes away and nodded his assent.

'Very well,' he said, in a tone of resignation. 'Then I will wait for Stradella at the door of the sacristy. That was the original plan. Hark! He is singing now!'

The two came out from behind the pillar and stood still to listen; and Gambardella's eyes gazed steadily at the vast mosaic above the tribune, while his friend's look fixed itself again on Ortensia's graceful figure, and he feasted his sight, while his ears were filled with the most rare music that the world had ever heard in that day.

Only those who have listened to a beautiful voice singing in the Lateran towards evening can understand that, in spite of the grievous disfigurements of the barocco age, and the exaggerated modern decorations of the nineteenth century, the 'Mother of all Churches,' as the Basilica is called, can still seem the most deeply and truly hallowed place of worship in Christendom. There is a mystery in it at the sunset hour which is felt by all men, though none can explain it; the light glows and fades there as nowhere else, the shadows have a sweet solemnity of their own, and consummate art, or supreme good-fortune, has made the vast nave and colonnaded aisles responsive to the softest notes the human voice can breathe. First the full organ blares out triumphantly alone, and by and by the chorus, borne up by the master instrument, swells from a hundred throats in such tremendous harmonies that the marble pavement seems alive and thrilling under a man's feet; yet the words are not lost in a clashing din of senseless noise, for every one of them is complete and reaches the astonished ear unbroken and distinct. Then, in an instant, the enormous gale of sound is hushed and leaves no echo, and one voice alone is singing a low melody, divinely spiritual as an angel's prayer. It rises presently, full and strong, but every syllable rings out clear and perfect, even to the outer doors; it sinks to all but a whisper, yet each delicate articulation floats unbroken to the remotest corner of the outer aisle, till he who listens feels the word vibrating in his heart rather than in his outward ears.

Ortensia felt more than that, for the music was that of the man she loved so well, and the single voice was his too, and the prayer it sang was for her, and was in her heart while she listened; and, moreover, Alessandro Stradella was not matched in voice or genius by any singer of his age. It would be as hopeless to attempt a description of his singing on that day as to analyse the feelings that thrilled Ortensia. There are delights that must be felt to be believed, and only three are noble, for they have their sources in true love, and in supreme art, and in honourable fight for wife and child and country. Ortensia felt the first two of these together; but he who dies, not having known even one of them, had better not have lived at all.

As afternoon turned to evening, the straight golden beams overhead melted to a red glow that spread downwards and illuminated all the great church for a little while; then the light deepened to purple, and that softened to violet, and the candles about the high altar under the tabernacle shone out through thin clouds of incense like many stars. Again Stradella's voice was heard alone, and Ortensia sank upon her knees beside her pillar, though it was not yet quite time for kneeling. It was as if she could bear no more of such intense pleasure without praying to heaven that it might be hers hereafter to love her true love to all ages, and for ever to hear his voice singing to her in a place of peace.

The Bravi had now parted company, and Trombin had quietly gone out of the church, leaving Gambardella alone. The dark-faced man in black moved slowly and noiselessly as a shadow; he crossed the nave far down by the door, and walked up the outer aisle on the south side, till he could go no farther up for the crowd; then he turned to his right, making his way quietly through the multitude wherever the people were least closely packed, and he emerged at last not far from where Ortensia was kneeling, and with all the appearance of having come out of the thick of the press, which was exactly what he wished her to believe.

She was still kneeling, and Cucurullo was standing beside her, hat in hand. It was now so dark in the body of the Basilica that Stradella could not possibly see any one there, especially as he was dazzled by the many candles that illuminated the upper end of the church.

Gambardella bowed gravely and bent down to speak near Ortensia's ear.

'I have a message from the Maestro for you,' he said, almost in a whisper.

Ortensia had already looked up with a little surprise, which now increased.

'A message?' she repeated. 'We came here together, and he has not left the organ loft since!'

'Precisely,' answered Gambardella, unmoved. 'I was standing in the crowd just below, and when he had finished directing the motett he made me a sign to go to the steps at the back. I went, and he was already halfway down the ladder. He seemed much agitated. You must have noticed how strangely his voice thrilled in that last piece he sang.'

'Yes. Tell me what he said!'

Ortensia was already breathless with anxiety, and as she spoke she got upon her feet. Gambardella helped her.

'He had a note in his hand. It was a warning which some one had brought to him in the loft. Altieri's plan is to conceal a number of men in your apartment this last night that you are to sleep there. When all is quiet they are to gag you and your husband, and carry you downstairs to Don Alberto's carriage. If you attempt to go home to the palace the scheme will inevitably succeed.'

Ortensia stood leaning back against the pilaster very white. Gambardella continued.

'The Maestro asked me if I knew of any place of safety to which you could both go to-night before leaving Rome to-morrow. I told him that my friend and I have just hired a small house in a quiet part of the city, which is at your service, especially as we have not yet moved to it. He begged me to take you there at once before Don Alberto can leave the church, and possibly see you driving away with me.'

'But my husband——' interrupted Ortensia.

'My friend Trombin is already at the door of the sacristy, and will bring him to you as soon as he can get away. It will be nearly half an hour before the Benediction is over. But there is no time to be lost. Ah—I forgot! He wished Cucurullo to hasten to the palace and get his manuscripts and his lute, and any small necessaries for you that can be hidden under a cloak. Your man can get there, and be on his way back before Don Alberto can be at home. Even if the men are already concealed in the apartment they will not trouble Cucurullo for fear of betraying their master. As for your woman, Altieri has probably had her arrested and taken away.'

Gambardella had purposely told his story so that Cucurullo could hear it, and had glanced at him from time to time to be sure that he understood.

'Are you afraid to go alone?' asked the Bravo, not at all contemptuously.

'No, sir. I am not afraid. Where shall I find my master when I have got the things?'

'Do you know where Santa Prassede is, in that narrow street near Santa Maria Maggiore?'

'Certainly, sir. Shall I wait at the side door of the church? It is a lonely place.'

'Yes. Be there as soon as you can. The house is close by, but I could not easily make you understand which it is.' Gambardella turned to Ortensia. 'Will you come with me?' he asked. 'My friend and I have a carriage, and it is at the main door.'

Ortensia laid her hand on the Bravo's arm, not doubting that she was obeying her husband's wishes for her safety and his. It would have taken more than Don Alberto's rude assertion to make her and Stradella distrust the men who had helped them so efficiently in their flight. The two might be Bravi, as he said, but they were friends, and in such a case as this they were the very friends the young couple needed.

The three entered the inner aisle to avoid all possibility of being seen by Don Alberto, and hastened towards the main door. Though Ortensia was not timid, her heart beat a little faster when she thought of the danger from which she was escaping. It was already nearly dark in the church, but the twilight was still bright outside, and the carriage was standing quite close to the old porch; for the present portico was not built then, and the steep carriage road ended in a square patch of pavement before the doors.

Cucurullo glanced at the coachman and recognised Tommaso, who nodded to him with a friendly smile. Then the hunchback hurried away on his errand, leaving Gambardella to take care of Ortensia, who was already getting in.

'To Santa Prassede,' said the Bravo to the coachman, in a tone meant for Ortensia's ears.

Then he got in, shut the door, and seated himself beside her, bolt upright, with his rapier between his knees, and his hands clasped on the hilt. Ortensia glanced at him in the dim light, and noticed his attitude with satisfaction, and not without reflecting on the terror she would feel if Don Alberto were in his place. Nothing could be more reassuring than Gambardella's behaviour.

'I suppose the carriage will go back for my husband?' she said. 'The Canons lent us one of theirs to bring us to the church and take us home, but you will not trust to that, will you?'

'No, indeed! If you do not mind being alone in the house for twenty minutes I will go back with this carriage, or it can go without me and I will stay with you.'

'I shall not be afraid,' Ortensia answered rashly. 'On the contrary, I shall feel much safer if I know that you are going for my husband yourself, for there can be no mistake then.'

'Precisely,' Gambardella said. 'That will be the best way.'

'How kind you are!' Ortensia sighed, and leaned back in the deep seat.

She did not know Rome very well yet, and it was the hour when all the little snail-shell lamps were being lighted for the feast, and their glimmer still further confused her; besides, she was not quite sure where Santa Prassede was, nor in what sort of neighbourhood it was situated. In that wide region, then almost without inhabitants, and mostly divided into hedged vineyards and market-gardens, small groups of houses stood here and there, more or less alike, but generally in the neighbourhood of the ancient churches which had been built before the city was unpeopled in the Middle Ages. Ortensia was not in the least surprised when the carriage stopped before a decent-looking little house, after ascending a steep hill. Gambardella opened the carriage and got out to help her down.

'Are you quite sure that you do not mind being left alone here for a while?' he asked, as he unlocked the door of the house, and held it open for her to go in.

'If you can give me a light I shall not mind being alone at all,' Ortensia answered, and she went in.

He followed her at once, shut the door behind him to keep out the chilly breeze, and began the process of getting a light with flint and steel and tinder and one of those wooden matches dipped in sulphur, which had then been recently invented. By the sparks he made Ortensia saw that he was standing beside an old marble table on which stood a brass lamp with a three-cornered bowl that slid up and down on a stem.

The place had the peculiar odour of small Italian houses that are built of stone, that stand in vineyards or market-gardens, and that are rarely opened; it is a smell compounded of the odour of the worm-eaten furniture, smoke-stained kitchen ceiling and wall, and the dusty plaster within the house, combined with a faint sub-odour of growing things, from vines to broccoli, which finds its way through the cracks of badly fitting doors and windows.

When there was light at last, Ortensia saw that she was in a commonplace little whitewashed vestibule, from which a single flight of stone stairs led directly to the door of the living rooms above. Gambardella went up first, holding the brass lamp low down for her to see the steps. The room into which he led her had a Venetian pavement, and was sufficiently well furnished. The walls were painted to represent views which were presumably visible from the windows by day.

'Are you quite sure there is no one in the house?' asked Ortensia, who liked the prospect of solitude less and less as the time for being left alone came nearer.

'There is a bedroom at each end,' answered Gambardella. 'You shall see for yourself. Above this there is a sort of attic which can only be reached from outside by steps that also lead to a terrace on the roof.'

He showed her the two bedrooms, which had evidently been just cleaned and put in order, and looked very neat. Ortensia was reassured.

'And what is there downstairs?' she asked.

'A kitchen and a dining-room,' Gambardella answered. 'But I must be off if I am to fetch the Maestro. We shall be here in half an hour at the utmost.'

Just then a great bell not very far off tolled three strokes, then four, then five, and then one, and an instant later it rang out in a peal.

'It is Ave Maria,' Gambardella said. 'The Benediction is over by this time. You had better come down with me and hook the chain inside the front door.'

Ortensia followed him down the stairs again, and he carried the lamp. As he went she heard him hurriedly repeating the Angelus.

'"Angelus Domini nuntiavit,"' he began, quite audibly, but the words that followed were said in a whisper.

Ortensia repeated the prayer to herself too, partly by force of habit, no doubt, but partly because it was a comfort to say it with the kind-hearted friend who had once more intervened to help her and her husband in time of danger. Even the Bravo, who could say his prayers uncommonly fast, had not finished when they reached the foot of the stairs, and as Ortensia set the lamp on the corner of the yellow marble table she distinctly heard him say the first words of the third responsory.

'"And dwelt with us,"' she answered quietly and clearly.

He laid his hand on the lock of the hall door, and when he turned to her his eyes met hers with a look she had never seen. Both repeated the third Ave

Maria aloud, while he gazed earnestly at her pure young face, so sweetly framed in the soft folds of the veil. Then without waiting for the final prayer he opened the door, and as he shut it after him she heard him say something aloud, but the words were so strange and unexpected that she repeated them to herself twice while she was hooking the chain before she quite realised what they were, and understood them.

"'And Judas went out and hanged himself.'"

That was what he had said as he went away.

CHAPTER XXI

When Stradella came down from the organ-loft after the Benediction he was in haste to reach the sacristy before any of the choristers, as he did not mean to keep Ortensia waiting a moment longer than necessary. But to his annoyance a number of his admiring acquaintances had already made their way to that side; and this was the more easy, because the throng of common people who had pressed upon the fashionable company had already retreated down the church to the main entrance in haste to see the beginning of the witches' feast and the snail-shell illumination.

At every step the musician had to shake hands and receive civilly the congratulations that were showered upon him; and suddenly Don Alberto was beside him, and was drawing him away.

'The Queen insists on thanking you herself, dear Maestro,' said the courtier, smiling. 'I see that you are in a hurry, but royalty is royalty, and you must sacrifice yourself on the altar of your own fame with a good grace!'

Unsuspecting of harm as he was, Stradella yielded, and tried not to look displeased. While speaking Altieri had dragged him through the crowd towards Christina, who was standing up, evidently waiting for them, and looking particularly mannish in her three-cornered hat and short skirt. The only ornament she had put on was the magnificent cross of diamonds which she wore on her bosom at all times.

'One has to come to church to see you, Maestro,' she cried in a heavily playful manner. 'Do you know that you have not darkened my doors for a fortnight, sir? What is the meaning of this? But I forgive you, for your music has ravished my soul, falling like a refreshing shower on my burning anger!'

The metaphors were badly mixed, but Stradella bent one knee and made a pretence of kissing the unshapely hand she held out to him, and he muttered a formula expressive of gratitude.

'I am overcome by your Majesty's kindness,' he said, or something to that effect.

'To-morrow,' said the ex-Queen, 'I shall send you the medal and diploma of my Academy as a slight acknowledgment of the pleasure I have had this afternoon. At present Don Alberto is going to introduce me to the quaint Roman custom of eating snails in the open air. Will you join us, Maestro? But I see that you are still in your robes, and I have no doubt you look forward to a more substantial supper than a dish of molluscs fried in oil!

Good-night, my dear Maestro. *Vale*, as those delightful ancients used to say!'

She waved her hand affectedly as she turned to go. It seemed an age to Stradella before he reached the sacristy, and when he got there he was surprised to find Trombin waiting by the door of the choristers' robing-room. The Bravo went in with him, and began to help him out of his cotta and cassock.

'I came to tell you that your lady is already gone home,' Trombin said in a low voice. 'She felt a sudden dizziness and weakness, as if she were going to faint. Luckily I was not far off, and when I saw Cucurullo supporting her I went to his assistance, and we took her out to her carriage, which was waiting.'

Stradella looked at him anxiously, but the Bravo only smiled.

'Nothing serious, I am sure,' the latter said, in a reassuring tone. 'But she will be glad to see you as soon as possible, and if the Canons' carriage has not come back, my friend and I will take you home at once in ours; we have just bought one for our convenience.'

'Thank you,' Stradella answered, letting Trombin help him to pull his arms out of the tight sleeves of the purple silk cassock. 'You are very kind.'

He was evidently too anxious about Ortensia to say more, and in a few seconds he had got into his coat, and Trombin was arranging the broad linen collar for him as cleverly as any valet could have done.

Trombin was well aware that Tommaso was not coming back to the Lateran with the coach, since the bells were already ringing for Ave Maria, and the man was to meet Don Alberto behind the Baptistery in an hour— 'the first hour of the night'; but he pretended angry surprise at not finding the carriage waiting. The one provided by the Canons was there, however, and Stradella recognised it, which Trombin could not have done, amongst the crowd of equipages that were waiting for the numerous ecclesiastics who had taken part in the service. It was now all but quite dark, but the coachman had received orders to be near the door and ready, lest the famous singer should catch cold.

Stradella was in far too great a hurry to question him, and jumped in at once, glad that Trombin should go with him. The carriage drove away at a smart pace, long before the owners of the other coaches were ready to go home.

Before the gateway of the Palazzo Altieri, Stradella got out, and tossed a florin up to the coachman, who caught it with a grin, and drove away at once.

'A thousand thanks!' the musician said, shaking Trombin's hand.

'I have done nothing,' the Bravo answered. 'I hope to hear to-morrow that your lady——'

But Stradella was already gone, and was running up the broad staircase at the top of his speed. A moment more and he knocked at his own door, of which the heavy key had been in Cucurullo's keeping when they had all left the house together to go to the Lateran.

Pina opened the door in her usual quiet way, and was a little surprised to see Stradella alone.

'How is she?' he asked, as soon as he saw her face by the light of the hanging lamp in the hall.

'Who, sir?' inquired the woman, not understanding.

'My wife——' He sprang past her to go in.

'The Lady Ortensia has not come home,' he heard Pina say behind him, in a tone of such astonishment that he stopped before he had reached the door of the sitting-room.

'Not come home?' he cried in amazement. 'You are out of your senses!'

Pina had shut the front door, and she followed him as he rushed into the sitting-room after speaking. She had lit the lamp, and it was burning quietly on the table. The door of the bedroom was opened wide to let the air circulate, but there was no light there. Nevertheless Stradella ran on to the bed.

'Ortensia!' he cried, feeling for her head on the pillows, for he could not see.

Then he uttered a low exclamation of surprise and looked round. Pina was already bringing in the lamp, and he realised at once that she had spoken the truth. Ortensia had not come home; but even now no doubt of the Bravi crossed his mind, and he was anxious only because Trombin had said that she was feeling ill. The carriage must have broken down or some other accident had happened which would explain why Trombin had not found the conveyance waiting as he had expected. The thought of a possible accident was distressing enough, but it was a comfort to think that Gambardella and Cucurullo were with her, and would bring her home in due time.

In a few words Stradella repeated to Pina what Trombin had told him, and in his own anxiety he did not see that she was now very pale, and that her hand shook so violently that she had to set down the lamp she held for fear of dropping it.

'She will be at home in a few minutes,' Stradella said in conclusion, trying to reassure himself. 'I will go downstairs again and wait for her. Give me my cloak, Pina, for I am very hot, and it will be cool under the archway.'

Trembling in every limb, Pina got his wide black cloak and laid it upon his shoulders. He drew up one corner of it and threw it round his neck, so as to muffle his throat against the outer air.

'Pina,' he said, 'your mistress was feeling ill. She was dizzy, my friend said. We must have something ready for her to take. What will be best?'

'Perhaps a little infusion of camomile,' Pina answered, her teeth chattering with fear.

He could not help noticing from her voice that there was something wrong, and he now looked at her for the first time and saw that she was livid.

'I have a chill,' she managed to say. 'I have caught the fever, sir. It does not matter! I have some camomile leaves, and I will make the infusion while you wait downstairs.'

'You ought to be in bed yourself,' Stradella said kindly, but at the same instant it occurred to him that Ortensia had perhaps taken a fever too. 'Tomorrow I will try to procure from the Pope's physician some of that wonderful Peruvian bark that cures the fever,' he added. 'They call it quina, I think, and few apothecaries have it.'

This was true, though nearly forty years had then already passed since the Spanish Countess of Cinchon had first brought the precious bark to Europe, and had named it after herself, Cinchona.

Stradella was not yet by any means desperately anxious about his wife when he went downstairs again, as may be understood from his last words to the serving-woman. He was, in fact, wondering whether Ortensia herself had not a touch of the ague, which was so common then that no one thought it a serious illness. He went downstairs with the conviction that she would appear within a quarter of an hour escorted by Gambardella and Cucurullo, and he began to walk under the great archway, from the entrance to the courtyard and back again.

As soon as he was gone Pina went to her own little room, taking the lamp with her. First she dressed herself in her best frock, which was of good brown Florentine cloth; and then she took a large blue cotton kerchief and made a bundle consisting of some linen and a few necessaries. On that very morning Stradella had paid her wages, expecting to leave Rome the next day, and she took the money and tied it up securely in a little scrap of black silk and hid it in her dress. Lastly, she put on the same brown cloak and hood she had worn on the journey from Venice, took her bundle under it, replaced the lamp on the sitting-room table, and left the apartment by the small door which gave access to the servants' staircase; a few moments later she slipped out of the palace, unobserved except by the old door-keeper who kept the back entrance and let her out.

'I am going to the apothecary's for some camomile,' she said quietly, and the old man merely nodded as he opened the street door for her.

The Bravi had cared very little whether Pina was at home or not when Cucurullo came to get the objects for which Stradella had sent him at Gambardella's suggestion. One of two things must happen, they thought, for it was clear that Cucurullo would explain everything to her, if he saw her. Either she would come with him to Santa Prassede, and there she might wait with him all night, for all they cared; or else she would run away as soon as he left the house, for they guessed that she would be afraid. But things had turned out differently. When Cucurullo had reached the apartment Pina was not there, for she had just gone down the backstairs to get the evening supply of milk which the milkman left with the keeper of the back door. Cucurullo, not finding her, had picked up the lute, the case of manuscripts, and a small hand valise which was already packed for the journey with necessaries belonging both to Stradella and his wife, and he had gone off again before Pina had returned.

She did not miss the things till Stradella came, and she carried the lamp into the bedroom; but then she understood that some one had been in the house during her short absence, and it flashed upon her that Ortensia had already been carried off, though she could not have told why she connected such a possibility with what she took for a theft committed in the apartment. Insane terror took possession of her then, with the vision of being left behind at the mercy of Don Alberto, and she fled without hesitation, taking with her nothing that was not her own, and only what she could easily carry for a journey. As for Cucurullo, he had no time to waste, and thought that in any case she would be safe enough from Don Alberto's men, whose only business would be to seize her mistress. Being fearless himself, it never occurred to him that she would run away out of sheer fright.

Stradella paced the flagstones under the archway, waiting for the carriage, and as the time passed his anxiety grew steadily till it became almost unbearable. The tall bearded porter stood motionless by the entrance, resting both his hands on the huge silver pommel of his polished staff. He could stand in that position for hours without moving. At last Stradella spoke to him.

'Has Don Alberto come home yet, Gaetano?' he asked.

'No, sir.' The porter touched his large three-cornered hat respectfully, for the musician had that morning given him a handsome tip preparatory to leaving. 'His Excellency may not come home till very late,' he vouchsafed to add, with a faint smile.

Stradella saw that he was inclined to talk, and though he himself had no fancy for entering into conversation with servants, he made a remark in the nature of a question.

'I dare say his Excellency sometimes does not come home before morning.'

'Sometimes, sir,' answered Gaetano, grinning in his big black beard. 'But then he generally gives me notice, so that I need not sit up all night. He is a very good-hearted young gentleman, sir, as I dare say you know, for you are a friend of his. And since you have asked me if he has come home, and you are perhaps waiting for him, I can tell you that he will not be back to-night, nor perhaps to-morrow, for that was the message he sent me by his valet this afternoon.'

'Thank you,' said Stradella. 'But I am not waiting for him. I am expecting my wife and my man.'

He nodded and went back to his beat under the archway, and before he had walked twice the distance between the gate and the courtyard, all the bells of Rome rang out the first hour of the night. An hour had passed since Ortensia had let Gambardella out of the little house in the Via di Santa Sabina.

The peal was still ringing from the belfry of the Lateran when Don Alberto and Tommaso met on the green behind the church, not far from the closed door of the sacristy. They came from opposite directions, and Tommaso was leading two saddled mules. The young courtier had succeeded in making his escape from Queen Christina and her party, promising to join them at supper at the Palazzo Riario within an hour.

In the lonely little house in Via di Santa Sabina, Ortensia was sitting upstairs by the table, pale and upright in her chair, and listening for the slightest sound that might break the profound silence.

But she heard nothing. The three wicks of the brass lamp on the table burned with a steady flame, and without any of those very faint crepitations which olive-oil lamps make heard when the weather is about to change. There was not the least sound in the small house: if there were mice anywhere they were asleep; if worms were boring in the old furniture they were working silently; if any house swallows had made their nests under the eaves they were roosting. The stillness was like that of a solid and inert mass, as if all the world had been suddenly petrified and made motionless.

It seemed to Ortensia that she had never been quite alone for so long a time in her life; it was certainly true that she had never before been locked up in a lonely house at night without a human being within call. First, her feet grew strangely cold; then she felt a sort of creeping fear stealing up to her out of the floor, as if she had drunk hemlock and death were travelling slowly towards her heart, paralysing every limb and joint on its relentless way.

It was not senseless physical fright, like Pina's; it would not drive her to leave the house and run away into the darkness outside; if there were anything to face Ortensia would face it, or try to, but what terrified her now was that there was nothing, not a sound of life, not the breath of a night breeze amongst leaves outside, not the stirring of a mouse indoors. It was like the silence of the tomb.

Suddenly she heard bells, but they sounded far off, and all the windows were tightly closed. She crossed herself with difficulty, and whispered a 'Requiem aeternam' for all Christian souls, as good Catholics are enjoined to do at the first hour of night. But it was an effort to raise her hand to her forehead in making the sign; and suddenly, as if in answer to her prayer, she seemed to hear the Bravo's voice close beside her:—

"'And Judas went out and hanged himself.'"

With the energy of a healthy young nature that revolts against supernatural fears, she rose to her feet and went to one of the windows, of which there were two on each side, looking over the road and towards the vineyard respectively. She tried the fastenings of the first and moved them, but she could not do more, though she used all her strength. The frame seemed to be stuck beyond the possibility of being opened without tools. She went to the next, and the next, till she had tried all four; then her fear came back, for it was all more like a bad dream than a reality, and the certainty flashed upon her that the windows had been purposely fastened with nails or screws to prevent her from looking out.

Gambardella had promised to come back with her husband in twenty minutes. Three times that interval had now passed, and more too, and she was still alone. It was not possible that any one should have knocked for admittance without her hearing the sound, for the door of the sitting-room was open to the stairs, and the house was no bigger than a cottage.

She went back to her chair by the table, ashamed of feeling that she could hardly stand. It was not strange that her fear of her own situation should be stronger just then than her anxiety for Stradella, believing, as she did, that Don Alberto had made his plans for that very night, and thinking, as was natural, that his great power in Rome might even have sufficed to have her followed from the Lateran, in which case he could well hinder her husband and Gambardella from joining her, and she would be at his mercy just as if she had gone home to sleep in the palace.

Tommaso and young Altieri rode quickly away from the illuminated meadow, which was now full of people who either thronged the overflowing booths, or walked about on the grass laughing and talking, and waiting till those who were supping should make room for them. The riding mules of those times were swift and much surer of foot than horses, and it was not long before the two men reached the rickety wooden gate of the old Jewish cemetery.

Here Tommaso dismounted, and whispering to Don Alberto to do the same, he tied the mules' bridles to the gate-post, which was still sound. Then he led the way up the hill, and both men trod so cautiously that when they passed the little house Ortensia did not hear a footfall in the road through the closed windows. Tommaso did not stop at the house door, however, but led Altieri on to the next, which was placed in the long wall and gave access to the vineyard. It was not fastened, and both went in, Tommaso putting his arm through Don Alberto's to guide him and help him if he stumbled.

The rain on the previous night had softened the earth, and there was a path between the inside of the wall and the trained vines. They followed this, until they were twenty paces from the house, when Tommaso stopped.

'The lady is alone in there,' he said, pointing. 'Show me the money.'

Don Alberto was prepared. With his left hand he produced a heavy deerskin purse, and with the other he drew a long knife from under his cloak. It gleamed in the starlight, and Tommaso saw it not far from his throat; but with the utmost coolness he took the purse and tried its weight in his hand, before untying the strings to feel the coins. When he was satisfied, he tied the purse again and gave it back to Don Alberto, who at once returned his knife to its sheath.

'To satisfy you,' said the old highwayman, 'I have set a ladder against the window of the room where she is probably waiting, and I have made a small hole through the outer shutter, through which you can see her. You will then come down the ladder, and I will let you into the house by the back door, which is open. Before you go in, you will hand me the money, and I will leave you, after giving you a light. We had better make no noise, lest she should come downstairs.'

'Very well. Take me to the ladder.'

Tommaso now struck through the vines, skirting the angle of the house at some distance, till he came to the straight walk that led to the back door. Don Alberto was used to night adventures, and saw the ladder distinctly before he came to it. When they had reached it, walking on tip-toe, Tommaso planted his foot firmly against the foot of it, so as to hold it steady, and he pointed to a little ray of light that shone out through the hole in the shutter. Don Alberto nodded and went up very cautiously. It was one of those long ladders used by Italian vine-dressers and had heavy rungs very far apart. Tommaso had wound rags round the tops of the side pieces, so that they should make no noise against the wall. Don Alberto stopped when his head was on a level with the ray of light, and applying his eye to the hole he saw the beautiful Venetian sitting motionless by the table. Having satisfied himself that she was within and alone, he lost no time in coming down, and the rest happened as Tommaso had explained that it should, except that it did not prove necessary to strike a light; for the back door opened under the stairs, in the small vestibule, and the door above being open, the lamp in the sitting-room sent down a glimmer from above that was quite enough to show the way.

At the first sound of steps below Ortensia started to her feet, understanding instantly that some one had entered the house by stealth, since she herself had put up the chain at the front door.

For one fatal moment she hesitated and stood motionless. Then, as the footsteps mounted the little staircase at a run, she sprang to shut the door; but it was too late, for Don Alberto was already on the threshold. He caught her with one arm and almost lifted her back into the room, while with the other hand he slammed the door, turned the key, and thrust it into his pocket.

She was struggling wildly in his arms then, but he laughed, as ruthless children do when they have caught a little bird and can torment it at their will.

'Softly, softly!' he cried. 'You will hurt yourself, my sweet! There, there! You have scratched your pretty arm already!'

It was true. She had cut her arm against one of the chiselled buttons of his coat, just above the wrist, and the red drops ran down over his lace wristband. But she felt no pain and she fought like a tigress against his hold; so far she had uttered no sound, but now her voice rang out.

'Coward!' she cried suddenly, and with one mad wrench she had her hands at his throat, and her strong little fingers were almost crushing his windpipe.

He could not hold her now, for she was strangling him; to free himself he let go of her waist and caught at her wrists to tear her hands away. But her strength was like a strong man's in that moment, and he could not loosen her hold.

He felt that in another moment she would have strangled him outright, for his eyes were already starting from his head, and the room swam. With furious violence he twisted himself sideways and tried to hurl her from him. Even then she did not loosen her desperate grip, but as he swung her and himself half round, her head struck the wall of the room. Then her hands relaxed instantly, and as he reeled backwards in regaining his balance, he saw her sink to the floor, stunned and unconscious.

'Trombin advanced upon him slowly, looking more like an avenging demon than a man'

A crash like thunder broke upon the moment's silence that followed. The window opposite the table was wide open and shattered, the frame and shutters split to matchwood, the glass in splinters, and, almost as Don Alberto started and turned round, Trombin sprang into the room hatless, with his long rapier in his hand, his round blue eyes wide open and glaring like a wild cat's, his pink cheeks fiery red, and his long yellow hair streaming out from his head like a mane.

At this terrific and most unexpected vision, young Altieri staggered back towards the locked door. Trombin advanced upon him slowly, sword in hand, till he was within three paces, looking more like an avenging demon than a man. Yet when he spoke his voice was calm and steady.

'If it is agreeable to you to draw, sir,' he said, 'I will do you the honour of killing you like a gentleman. If, on the other hand, as I gather from your attitude, you do not think the moment propitious for fighting, I will throw you out of the window as I would a lackey who insulted a lady, sir. Pray choose quickly, sir, before I have counted three, sir, for I am in haste. One—two—three!'

The last word was scarcely out of his mouth when Trombin dashed forward, and, dropping his rapier at the same time, threw his arms round the courtier's knees; he flung him over his shoulder like a sack of flour, ran with him to the open window and dropped him out.

Whether he meant to kill him, or did not care what became of him, is not certain, but Trombin was a gentleman who generally kept his head, even when he seemed to be most excited; and it is certain that, instead of falling some four or five yards directly to the ground, Don Alberto found himself clinging to the ladder halfway down. It turned sideways with his weight, slowly at first, and fell with a clatter on the drip-stones, when his feet were already touching the ground. He was dizzy, the tumble had bruised his shins, and he had sprained his hands a little, but he was otherwise unhurt, and the blood on his wristbands and collar was from the scratch on Ortensia's arm.

For a few seconds he steadied himself against the corner of the house where he had fallen with the ladder. Then he began to make his way towards the door in the vineyard wall, and when he had walked thirty or forty yards he stood still, whistled twice, and waited for an answer. But none came.

He had, in fact, sent his own valet and a running footman to the Lateran to follow him and Tommaso, and to note the house they entered. The runner was then to hasten back to the Basilica, where Don Alberto's coach was waiting, and was to come to the house with it, or to the nearest point it could reach. The footman was the most famous runner in Roman lackeydom and boasted that he could always cover a mile in five minutes, up hill and down and over the worst roads, and in a shorter time on a smooth and level path. As for the coach, it could drive to the very door of the little house; for the Via di Santa Sabina had always been practicable for vehicles, because it led to the castle of the Savelli, which was then partly in ruins and partly turned into a Dominican monastery. So all was well planned, and Don Alberto's valet was to hide near the last door his master entered in case the latter needed help.

Yet when Altieri whistled softly there was no answer. He went on twenty paces farther and whistled again, with the same result. He reached the door in the wall, and whistled a third time, peering into the gloom amongst the vines. At last he went out into the road, determined to go away on foot and alone, rather than to risk another interview with the quick-tempered man who had thrown him out of the window.

He went away on foot, indeed, but neither alone nor unaided; for he had no sooner stepped out of the door than a most unpleasant and unexpected thing happened. To his surprise and mortification, not to mention the pain he felt, an iron hand caught him by the back of his collar and ran him down the hill at the double-quick, encouraging his speed with a hearty kick at every third step or so. He ran by the house in a moment, being positively kicked past the door, and he ran on to the gate of the Jewish cemetery, whence the mules had now disappeared, and the boot of his implacable driver almost lifted him off his feet. The hand that held him was like iron, and the foot felt very like it too. Down the hill he was forced to run, till suddenly, at the turn near the bottom, where the road is wider, he came upon his own coach on its way up.

Then the kicking ceased indeed, but the hand did not relax its hold, while the coachman stopped his horses at the sound of quick footsteps just ahead. An instant later Don Alberto's tormentor had opened the coach, flung him up inside, and slammed the door on him.

'Palazzo Altieri!' cried a voice the courtier had heard only once before. 'Be quick! Your master is ill!'

The running footman had already dropped to the ground from behind, and was at the open carriage window in an instant, springing upon the step for orders. But Don Alberto was exhausted and had sunk back in the cushioned seat, panting for breath and aching, not only in every joint, but elsewhere.

'Home!' he managed to say, as he saw the footman's head at the window.

There was just room in the road to turn, and a few seconds later the carriage was rumbling along over the bad road towards the paved streets of the city, while its only inmate slowly recovered his breath and made attempts in the dark to repair the disorder of his dress before he reached his palace. But that was not easy, for he had dropped his cloak in the struggle with Ortensia and had lost his hat in falling with the ladder; moreover, his collar and wristbands were covered with blood, and his usually smooth hair looked like a wild man's. Last, and perhaps least in his estimation, he had given a thousand crowns, in the shape of two hundred and fifty gold ducats of Naples, for the pleasure of being half-strangled by a young woman, thrown out of the window by her rescuer, and finally kicked downhill for a distance of at least two hundred and fifty yards by an unseen boot. As an equivalent for so much money these mishaps were unsatisfactory; but what the sufferer now most desired was to save some remnant of his dignity before his servants, and then to be avenged on those who had so signally frustrated his plans.

He was disappointed in the first of these wishes, at all events, for when he was helped from his carriage by the porter and the running footman at the foot of the grand staircase, he found himself face to face with Alessandro Stradella, who was as pale as his own collar and half mad with anxiety. One glance told the musician that Altieri had been worsted in an adventure, which, he was sure, could only be accounted for by Ortensia's disappearance.

'Where is my wife?' asked Stradella, standing in the way on the step.

Don Alberto was surprised and angry, and his shame at being seen in such plight, in his own house, overcame any prudence or self-control he had left. Besides, he felt himself sufficiently defended by his servants.

'Your wife?' he said, trying to push Stradella aside. 'She is in a little house near the Lateran, with her lover!'

'Liar!'

With the ringing insult, the Sicilian's open hand struck Don Alberto such a blow across the face that he staggered back against the carriage step, the blood spurting from his nose and lips.

But almost at the same instant Gaetano, the big porter, and the athletic footman threw themselves bodily upon Stradella, shouting for help at the same time. Stablemen and grooms came running from the courtyard at the cry, and the singer was overpowered in a few moments, though he struggled fiercely, not so much for his freedom as to strike Don Alberto again.

'Call the watch,' said the latter, staunching his blood with a lace handkerchief as well as he could. 'You are all witnesses. He can be taken to Tor di Nona in my carriage.'

Thereupon, with more dignity than might have been expected of a young dandy in such a condition, he turned and went slowly up the broad stone stairs, holding his handkerchief to his mouth. He expected his valet to meet him at his door, but the man was not there: as a matter of fact he was then lying on his back on a tombstone in the Jewish cemetery, bound hand and foot, and securely gagged; and while he contemplated the stars, he felt much too cool for his comfort. For Gambardella had come upon him lurking near the door in the wall, after Tommaso had passed with Altieri, and the Bravo had made short work of his liberty, returning to the door in the wall just in time to catch Don Alberto as he came out.

Don Alberto's commands were law at all times in his father's palace, and on the present occasion the wrath of the whole establishment was on his side. Moreover, to strike the nephew of both Popes in the face and call him a liar was an offence which would have sent the noblest patrician in Rome to a dungeon in Sant' Angelo, if not to the galleys of Cività Vecchia.

It was therefore not surprising that Stradella should find himself in Tor di Nona within the hour, solidly chained to the wall in a dark cell; and so he was left to reflect upon the consequences of his rashness, though not to regret it, if indeed his gnawing anxiety for Ortensia left him room to think of anything else.

CHAPTER XXII

When Trombin had dropped Don Alberto upon the ladder, to take the chances of a bad fall, he looked down to see what happened, and being satisfied that the courtier was not much hurt, he turned at once to Ortensia; for if young Altieri had broken his neck, it might have been necessary to hasten what was to take place next. As for anything the courtier might do on the spur of the moment, Trombin knew that Gambardella and Tommaso were in the vineyard, ready to stop any mischief.

Ortensia was lying by the wall where she had fallen, but was regaining consciousness, for her limbs stirred now and then, and as the Bravo looked at her she opened her eyes and turned her head.

'Coward!' she said faintly, as what had happened began to dawn upon her and the recollection of the furious struggle came back. 'Coward!' she repeated, closing her eyes as Trombin dropped beside her on one knee.

'I have thrown him out of the window,' he said quietly.

She opened her eyes wide now, stared at him and recognised him, though as in a dream. Then she tried to raise herself on her elbow, and instantly he helped her; and feeling the strength of his arm, she got upon her feet, though with more assistance from him than she knew. He led her to a stiff little sofa at the other end of the room, picked up Don Alberto's cloak, rolled it into a pillow for her, and made her lie down. She had almost lost consciousness again with the effort of walking so far.

He saw the deep scratch on her arm, from which a few drops of blood were still slowly oozing, and he fetched a basin with cold water and a towel from the bedroom, and bathed the slight wound, binding it up afterwards with his lawn handkerchief, for he was skilled in such matters. Ortensia smiled faintly, without opening her eyes; but he, with the strangest expression in the world, drew in his lips till his mouth almost disappeared; and he fixed his round eyes on the shapely arm he was dressing, and touched it with a sort of wonder. For there was a secret side of his character which even his friend Gambardella did not know, any more than Trombin knew his companion's own love-story.

When Trombin said that he was a susceptible creature, full of sentiment, he was telling the truth, though his friend had never believed it. He loved all women in general, and seemed able to love a number of them in particular in close succession. Gambardella saw this, and exercised his wit upon the weakness; but what he never saw and could not guess was that his fellow-cut-throat was as shy and timid as a schoolboy in the presence of his sweetheart for the time being, whether she were of low degree or of the burgher class, above which Trombin had never aspired till he had seen Ortensia. The reckless Bravo, the perpetrator of a score of atrocious crimes, the absolutely intrepid swordsman, would blush like a girl, and stand speechless and confused when he was alone for the first time with a pretty girl or a buxom dame whose mere side-glance made the blood tingle in his neck. Moreover, many women know that there are plenty of such men in the world; and I dare say that more than one man may read these lines who has faced the extremest danger without a quickened pulse, but has collapsed like a scared child before a girl of eighteen or a cool-handed widow of eight-and-twenty. Oddly enough, those are not the men whom women love least, explain it how you will.

So Trombin, who had talked of carrying off Ortensia with even more assurance than Don Alberto himself, and had just found her senseless on the floor after he had put her assailant to flight, could no more have had the boldness to kiss the white arm he was dressing so tenderly and skilfully than young Altieri had found courage to fight him when he had suddenly appeared through the window, rapier in hand and glaring like a panther.

Meanwhile Ortensia came quite to herself, looked at him quietly, and thanked him.

'Where is he gone?' she asked, for she had not realised what he had said when he had first answered her.

As he met her eyes Trombin's white forehead blushed, and he stepped back, taking away the basin and towel he had used in washing her wound.

'Out of the window, gracious lady,' he said, as he disappeared into the next room.

'Out of the window!' cried Ortensia in astonishment. 'Is he dead?'

'No, alive and well,' answered Trombin from the distance. 'But I hear something at this very moment,' he added, coming back empty-handed and trying the front window, as if he did not know that it was fastened with nails.

He laid his ear to the crack, and held out one hand to keep Ortensia silent.

'Yes,' he whispered an instant later, loud enough for her to hear. 'Yes—it is the sound of kicking and running—some one is kicking some one else down the hill—it is gone now!'

He stood upright again and looked round at Ortensia, whose face betrayed her anxiety, now that she was fully conscious.

'Who can it be?' she asked.

'Most gentle lady,' answered Trombin, 'I do not know, but I suspect, pray, hope, and inwardly believe that the patient, if I may so call him, was Don Alberto, and the kicker was very likely my friend Gambardella.'

'But you were to have brought my husband here! Your friend told me so!'

Ortensia's memory came back completely at Gambardella's name, and she slipped her feet from the sofa to the floor and sat up suddenly. Trombin was, of course, prepared for the question with a plausible story, but he could never count on his presence of mind when he was in love and alone for the first time with the object of his affections.

'Madam,' he answered, 'the truth is—or, as I may say, the facts in the case are——' he stammered and stopped, for the lovely Venetian had risen and was beside him already, her frightened eyes very near his, and her hand on his sleeve. His heart beat like a scared bird's and his head was whirling.

'Where is my husband?' cried Ortensia in wild anxiety. 'Something has happened to him, and you are afraid to tell me! For heaven's sake——'

It had never been in Trombin's nature to be rough with a woman. In the two or three cases in which he had been concerned in 'removing' a lady, obnoxious to her husband or relations, he had been accused by his companion of being soft-hearted; but while Ortensia was speaking he was in such a state of rapt adoration that he quite forgot to listen to what she said; and instead of answering when she waited for his reply, he took the hand that lay on his sleeve in his, with such a gentle and sympathetic touch that she did not resist, even when he raised it to his ridiculous little mouth and kissed it delicately, with an air of respectful devotion that would not have offended a saint.

Nor was Ortensia offended; but she was frightened out of her mind by his manner, for it was as if he were already condoling with her, and offering his faithful service, before telling her the awful truth.

'He is dead!' she cried, breaking from him and pressing both hands to her temples in mad grief.

She would have fallen against the table, if Trombin had not caught her and held her up. He understood instantly how she had mistaken his action, and what the question had been which he had not heard.

'No, no!' he cried energetically. 'He is alive and well! He insisted on going back to the palace to wait for Don Alberto when he came home from the Lateran to catch you in your rooms! Instead, the villain tracked you here and got in. It was Tommaso's fault for leaving the back door open to the vineyard, and Altieri fastened it inside, so I broke in through the window to save you! We had nailed all the windows fast for your safety!'

Ortensia leaned back against the table and looked straight at him. He could tell the most amazing untruths with perfect coolness, but just now he was so very near the truth that his worst enemy would have believed him. Untruthful people often have a shifty glance, but the truly accomplished liar is he whose clear and limpid eye meets yours trustfully and sadly, while he tells you falsehoods that would make the Father of Lies himself look grave. The immediate result of Trombin's words was that Ortensia could almost have thrown her arms round his neck in her joy.

'Take me to him!' she cried, forgetting everything else. 'Take me to him! Come!' She tried to drag him towards the door in her haste, but he quietly resisted her.

'We must wait for Gambardella,' he said. 'Besides, you will have to trust your husband to settle matters with Don Alberto without you. He is far more likely to be prudent if they meet alone than if you are beside him——'

Ortensia's face fell, for she saw that Trombin did not mean to let her leave the house at once.

'But Don Alberto can do anything,' she pleaded, with clear foresight of Stradella's temper and consequent danger. 'My husband will accuse him, and will be furiously angry! He will not hesitate to strike him, or to fight him in his own house! And then Don Alberto will have him imprisoned!'

It was, in fact, what was about to happen, and what Trombin himself expected. On the other hand, Don Alberto knew very well where the house was to which he had been taken by Tommaso, for he was a Roman, and every yard of the road was familiar to him. Within less than an hour it was more than likely that he would send a force of sbirri to besiege the house, men who would not hesitate to break down the doors if they were not admitted, and by no means so easy to frighten away as the clumsily armed watchmen whom the Bravi had put to flight. The only possible safety for the Bravi lay in leaving the place with Ortensia before such a thing happened. The post-carriage in which Trombin meant to carry her off that very night was waiting not far away in charge of a well-paid stable hand, and Tommaso and Gambardella had only to bring it to the door. The stableman was then to take back the two mules, and the coach would leave the city at once, by Porta San Lorenzo, while Ortensia would suppose that she was being taken to the Palazzo Altieri or to some new place of safety. The plan was well laid, for it would be easy for Gambardella to make Stradella believe that his wife had been spirited away by Don Alberto's agents, and that Trombin had followed on horseback in hot pursuit. Stradella would lose no time, and would certainly accept Gambardella's assistance in the chase; and in due time husband and wife would reach Venice separately and fall into the respective traps the Bravi had ready for them.

All this might succeed easily enough by the liberal use of money, and under the protection of the pardons and passports the two cut-throats had in their possession; but it was clear that no time was to be lost, and while Trombin's gaze lingered on Ortensia's lovely face, he was anxiously listening for his friend's knock below, and he did not even attempt to answer her last speech with reassuring words.

'We cannot move without Gambardella,' he said, speaking in a low tone now, lest any sound from without should escape his hearing.

It came a moment later, and Trombin hastened to the door at the head of the stairs; it was locked, however, and the key was in Don Alberto's pocket, as Ortensia quickly explained. But such a trifle as an ordinary door that was fastened was not likely to stop a man who had lately smashed in a strong window-frame with his fists and his shoulder. He drew back one step, raised his heel to the level of the lock, and smashed it as if it had been made of egg-shells. The door flew open and he ran down the steps to undo the chain. Seeing that her shadow kept the light from the stairs and the vestibule, Ortensia drew back on one side of the entrance, expecting that Trombin would come up at once with Gambardella. Instead, the two stood talking in low tones on the threshold of the front door.

In a few moments it was clear to Ortensia that some disagreement had arisen between the friends. Their voices grew a little louder, so that Ortensia could hear about half of what they said. It was clear that Gambardella was refusing to do something which Trombin insisted with rising temper, while the other grew colder and more obstinate every moment.

'Altieri's thousand crowns,' she heard Gambardella say distinctly; and then, in broken words, '... more than enough ... morning ... the Neapolitan frontier ... leave her here ...'

'Judas!' cried Trombin very audibly, and clearly in a rage.

'At your service,' answered Gambardella, 'and instead of thirty pieces of silver, I fling a thousand in your face! You shall not have her!'

Ortensia heard a sort of chinking thud, as if a heavy purse had fallen on the stones. This was instantly followed by a scuffle, and she knew that the two men had closed and were wrestling. The whole truth had flashed upon her through the few words they had exchanged, or enough of it to prove that young Altieri had not calumniated the men she had thought her friends when he had called them Bravi.

Her heart stood still for an instant, while she looked round for some means of escape. No sound of voices now came up from below, but only the shuffling of feet and the hard-drawn breath of men wrestling in the dark. She ran to the window and looked out, thinking that the ladder was still there, and then, seeing that it was gone, she peered into the gloom. Perhaps she could let herself down by her hands and then drop to the ground. At any moment one of the Bravi might come up again and seize her.

She listened for a moment before trying it. The sound of the struggle had ceased, and all was still again; very cautiously she crept to the door and listened again, but there was not a breath. She ventured to look down the stairs, keeping her body on one side, and she saw that the vestibule was empty, and now her quick hearing caught the sound of shuffling footsteps in the road outside; the noise was decreasing already, as if the two men were moving down the hill in their furious fight. The house was empty for a moment, Trombin had spoken of a back door opening to the vineyard, and she saw her chance.

She ran downstairs, almost falling in her haste, and as she reached the floor she stepped upon something that yielded with a chinking sound. It was the purse containing the thousand crowns in ducats, and she thrust it into her bosom without hesitation. A cool draught of air from under the stairs guided her to the back entrance, which was not closed, as Trombin had said it was, but wide open. She was out of doors in an instant, and in the starlight she could just see a broad path that led straight through the vineyard from the little house. She gathered up her silk skirts with both hands, and ran for her life.

Almost at the same moment Gambardella, who was the lighter man, threw Trombin heavily on his back in the dust, and at once proceeded to kneel on his chest.

CHAPTER XXIII

At sunrise Ortensia wearily climbed the steep ascent that led up to the Quirinal Palace, leaning on Cucurullo's arm, and wearing his short brown cloak to cover her dress as much as possible. A few words will be enough to explain what had happened in the night. After waiting two hours and more at Santa Prassede with the things he had brought, Cucurullo had come back to the Palazzo Altieri, suspecting an accident, or at least a misunderstanding. It was not till he had knocked again and again that the porter had opened the little postern in the great wooden gate, and seeing who was there had hastily explained that Stradella was in prison for having struck Don Alberto on the nose, at the foot of the grand staircase, and that, after this, he, Gaetano the porter, had not the courage to admit any one belonging to the musician's household. He was very sorry, and said so, being much afraid of the Evil Eye if the hunchback should be angry; but he was even more afraid of Don Alberto. Cucurullo, who had been prepared for trouble, bowed his head, and said he would wait outside till morning. Gaetano offered, as a great favour, to take the things he carried and hide them in his lodge, a kindness which Cucurullo readily accepted.

As for Ortensia, she did not know where she had been, and it was not till she had wandered for hours in the desolate regions between Santa Maria in Cosmedin, San Gregorio, and the Colosseum, that she at last struck into the Campo Vaccino, which was the open field under which the Roman Forum then lay buried. By the first faint light she recognised the tower of the Capitol, and in less than a quarter of an hour after that she found Cucurullo sitting on one of the stone chain-posts outside the Palazzo Altieri, his two long legs hanging down almost to the pavement, and his humped body looking like a large ball covered with a short brown cloak, and surmounted by a servant's high-crowned black felt hat with a wide brim. He was not asleep, for he hardly ever slept, and he knew his mistress's light step before he saw her at his elbow. In a moment he had explained what had happened, as far as he knew the truth, from the moment when he had left her getting into the carriage with Gambardella.

Her mind was made up in a flash; she would go directly to the Pope himself, and if he would not see her, she would insist on seeing Cardinal Paluzzo Altieri. He would not refuse her an audience, if she sent up her name with a message to say that she had found something of great value that belonged to him. As for taking any rest before going to the Quirinal, she literally had not where to lay her head; but she was young and strong, and would not realise how tired she was till the strain of her anxiety was over, and she was borne up by love, which is quite the most wonderful elixir in the world against all weariness of mind or body. Nevertheless she leaned on Cucurullo's arm as they climbed the ascent, for it was very steep, and the last part of it was the long flight of steps which still leads up from the Tre Cannelle and comes out close to the little church of San Silvestro, where the great and good Vittoria Colonna once met Michelangelo.

The doors of the Quirinal Palace were opened at sunrise, and two sentries of the Swiss Guard paced up and down before the entrance, their breastplates and halberds gleaming in the morning sun. They did not stop Ortensia, who saw their sergeant standing just within, very magnificent in his full-dress uniform; for it was the Feast of Saint John, and Midsummer Day, and one of the great festivals of the year, though not so solemn a one as that of Saint Peter which comes five days later, on the twenty-ninth.

The Swiss sergeant was gravely civil and answered Ortensia as politely as he could, considering how imperfectly he knew the Italian language. His Holiness? No. The Pope was far from well and had not left his room for a week. His Eminence? It might be possible in an hour. The Cardinal was an early riser, and was to pontificate at high mass in the Lateran. The sergeant could send a soldier to the major domo's office by and by, but no one would be stirring upstairs for at least another hour. The gracious lady seemed tired; would she wait in the sergeant's own room? It was at her disposal.

Ortensia accepted gratefully, and the big, fair-haired, wooden-faced Swiss opened the door for her, pointed to a sort of settle on which she could rest, and told Cucurullo to wait in the guard-room. The sergeant himself would call her as soon as the major-domo's office was open. He saluted her with stiff politeness and went away.

Even then she did not realise that she was tired, and instead of stretching herself on the settee, as she might have done, she sat bolt upright on the edge of it, staring at the door that had just been shut, as if she expected the sergeant to come back at once. Yet she was not conscious of the passage of time, and her intense anxiety centred in her coming interview with the Cardinal rather than in any present longing for the sergeant's quick return. In her mind she went over what she was going to say, and tried to put together the Cardinal's probable replies. She meant to ask for immediate liberty for her husband, or immediate imprisonment for herself with him. Nothing could be simpler; if the great man refused to grant either, leaving her at liberty, she would risk everything and appeal to the Venetian Ambassador.

She had not changed her position once in three-quarters of an hour when the door opened again, and the sergeant most respectfully invited her to go with him. His Eminence had been informed that she was below and wished to see her at once. She remembered nothing after that, till she found herself in a small sunny room hung with red damask and furnished in the same colour. The Cardinal sat in a high-backed chair at a magnificent polished writing-table, on which stood a crucifix having the sacred figure carved apparently from a single gigantic amethyst; the inkstand, pen-tray, and sand-boxes were also gilt, and made a glittering show in the bright sunshine that poured through the open window.

Cardinal Altieri was a grey-haired man with steely eyes set near together, the strong lean face of a fighter, and the colourless complexion of most high ecclesiastics, who are generally what the physicians of that day called 'saturnians.' He held out a large, hard, white hand, with a ring in which was set an engraved amethyst, Ortensia touch the stone with her lips, and he motioned to her to be seated in a comfortable chair at his left.

'I know everything,' he said quietly. 'I always do.'

The comprehensiveness of this sweeping statement might have made Ortensia smile at any other time. But she was staggered by it now, and forgot the speech she had prepared. On the face of it, to tell anything to a man who knew everything was superfluous. She reflected a moment, and he took advantage of her silence to speak again in the same calm tone.

'You sent me word that you had found something of value belonging to me, madam. I shall be glad to receive it, but, in the first place, I have the honour of returning to you some of your own property, which you left last night in a little house in the Via di Santa Sabina.'

As he spoke the last words he put down his right hand on the side away from her and brought up a long veil, a silver hairpin, and one white doeskin glove all together.

'That is all, I believe,' he said, with a very faint smile. 'If you left anything else there, I will order a more careful search to be made. I may add that there were stains of blood on the floor and one of the walls, and as you do not appear to be wounded, madam, the inference is——'

Before he could explain his inference, Ortensia stretched out her arm from beneath the cloak she wore, and showed him that it was bound up in a blood-stained handkerchief; for the small cut had been deep. With her other hand she took the purse from within her dress and held it out to the Cardinal.

'A thousand crowns in gold ducats,' she said, 'which your Eminence's nephew paid two Bravi for the privilege of giving me this scratch. But they cheated him and drove him away and then quarrelled, and fought about which should have me for his share. I escaped from the house while they were fighting outside, I stepped on this purse and I picked it up, being sure that the money belonged to you, and there it is! In return, I ask for my husband's liberty.'

She saw from his face that he was much surprised, and that what she had just told him had produced a decided effect in her favour; for it is almost needless to say that the account of the affair which Don Alberto had dictated to his secretary and had sent to his uncle late on the previous evening gave a very different view of the case. According to the young man, Ortensia had met him of her own accord, deliberately enticing him into an ambush from which he had barely escaped with his life, only to be insulted and struck in the face by her husband, who was, of course, acquainted with the whole plan.

The Cardinal examined the purse minutely, then opened it and looked at the contents. He guessed that the value of the gold must be about a thousand crowns, as Ortensia had said it was. During this time she quietly arranged her veil on her head, fastening it with the long silver pin, and then put on the glove he had restored to her. At last he looked up and spoke.

'Where one knows everything,' he observed, 'it is impossible not to be surprised at the lamentable ignorance in which most people live. For instance, if I had not this demonstration of the fact, which agrees well with my own knowledge, I should find it hard to believe that you and your husband could have been foolish enough to make friends with the very men whom your uncle the Senator Pignaver had sent to murder you.'

'We were deceived, Eminence,' answered Ortensia. 'I need not tell you how, since everything is known to you. All I ask is my husband's liberty.'

'Your husband, madam, appears to have broken my nephew's nose,' replied the Cardinal, with the utmost gravity. 'Moreover, Alberto is not only my own nephew by blood, but His Holiness's also, both in fact, as the son of the Pope's niece, Donna Lucia, and also by formal adoption. I doubt whether His Holiness will easily overlook such an offence. To break the nose of a Pope's nephew, madam, is a serious matter. I would have you understand that.'

'Then send me to prison with my husband!' cried Ortensia desperately.

The Cardinal slowly rubbed his pale chin with his amethyst ring, and looked at her.

'There may be an alternative to that somewhat extreme course,' he observed. 'Calm yourself, I beg of you, and I will see His Holiness as soon as possible. In the meantime, it would be well for you to take some rest.'

'Rest!' Ortensia exclaimed. 'How can I rest while he is in prison, unless I can be near him?'

'I cannot see the connection of ideas,' the Cardinal answered coldly.

He looked at her with some curiosity, for he had never been in love with anything but power since he had first gone to school.

He rang a gilt bell that stood beside the gilt inkstand, and a grey-haired priest, still unshaven and shabbily dressed, came at the call. His face was as yellow as common beeswax, and his little eyes were bloodshot. The Cardinal pushed the purse across the polished mahogany.

'Count that money,' he said briefly, and opening the drawer of the table he took out a sheet of paper and began to write, while the shabby secretary counted out the gold in the palm of his hand, as if he were used to doing it.

The letter was not long, and the Cardinal read it over to himself with evident care before folding it. He even smiled faintly, as he had done when he had returned Ortensia's things. He turned in the top and bottom of the sheet so that the edges just met, and after creasing the bends with his large pale thumb-nail he doubled the folded paper neatly, and then turned up the ends and slipped one into the other.

'Seal it with a wafer when you have done counting,' he said, tossing the letter to the priest, for he detested the taste of sealing-wafers, and, moreover, thought that the red colouring matter in them was bad for the stomach. 'How much money is there?' he asked, seeing that the secretary had finished his task.

'Two hundred and fifty gold ducats, Eminence,' answered the latter, and his dirty crooked fingers poured the gold back into the leathern purse.

When that was done, and the wet wafer had been slipped into its place and pressed, the secretary handed the letter to the Cardinal for him to address it. Instead of doing so at once, however, he turned to Ortensia, who had been watching the proceedings in silent anxiety.

'Madam,' the great man began, in a suave tone, 'knowing everything, as I do, you may well imagine that I am anxious to spare you the grief of seeing your husband condemned to the galleys.'

'The galleys!' cried Ortensia in extreme terror. 'Merciful heavens!'

The Cardinal went on speaking with the utmost coolness and without heeding her emotion.

'If what my nephew believed last night could be proved true, madam, your husband's neck would be in great danger, and you yourself would probably spend several years in a place of solitude and penance.'

Ortensia's horror increased, and she could no longer speak.

'Yes, madam,' continued the Cardinal inexorably, 'I have no hesitation in saying so. My nephew believed that you and your husband had purposely enticed him to a clandestine meeting with you, in order to have him thrown out of a window, at the imminent risk of his life, and otherwise maltreated by hired ruffians. It was little short of a miracle that he reached his home alive, and he had no sooner stepped from his carriage than your husband put the finishing stroke to the series of atrocities by breaking his nose. I do not say that this was a blow at the Church, madam, but it was a violent blow at the authority of the Pope's government. I take it that a blow which can break a man's nose is a violent blow. That is the argument for the prosecution.'

Ortensia stared wildly at the colourless face and the steely eyes that met her own.

'Happily,' the Cardinal went on, after a short but impressive pause, 'my nephew does not know everything. There are some arguments for the defence: that purse is a good one, madam, and the wound you have received is better; my own universal knowledge fills the lacunæ that are left, so far as concerns what happened at the house in Via di Santa Sabina. Two Bravi, who have undertaken to murder you, thought they could earn an additional thousand crowns by selling you to my nephew, whose admiration for you is unhappily a matter of notoriety. Their plan was then to drive him away, after which one of them was to carry you off, while the other remained behind to murder your husband. Fortunately for you they quarrelled, you made your escape, and your excellent good sense made you come directly to me, which, in the case of a lady of your noble birth, is a clear proof of innocence. Moreover, I know it to be true that the two Bravi were found fighting desperately in the street during the night, but when the watch fell upon them to separate them they turned their swords against the officers of the law and sent the cowardly pack flying, though not one of the fellows had anything worse than a pin-prick to show. Your former friends are very accomplished swordsmen, madam! That is the argument for your defence, and it satisfies me.'

'Thank heaven!' exclaimed Ortensia, whose face had relaxed while he had been speaking. 'Then my husband will be let out, after all!'

'That depends on His Holiness, not on me,' answered the churchman. 'It may depend on your husband himself. Your friends'—he emphasised the word with a cool smile—'your friends the Bravi are responsible for everything except my nephew's broken nose, but that is a serious matter enough. Bertini'—he turned to the secretary—'you may go. I wished you to hear what I have just said. Order one of my own chairs to be ready to take this lady to the palace in five minutes.'

Bertini bowed and left the room. It was not until the door was shut that the Cardinal spoke again.

'His Holiness expressed to me only last night his august desire to hear your husband sing, and regretted his inability to go to the Lateran for that purpose. His Holiness has now spent a good night and it may be hoped that he will be able to rise this afternoon. Your husband shall have an opportunity of singing to him before supper. That is all I can manage for him. He must do the rest.'

'Thank you, thank you!' cried Ortensia gratefully. 'Only———'

'What, madam?'

'How will he be able to sing, after such a night, if he is kept in prison? He will have a sore throat from the dampness, he will be worn out with anxiety, and weak for want of food! What chance can he possibly have of moving the Pope to pity?'

'I have attended to that, madam,' the Cardinal answered, tapping the letter that lay under his hand. 'The Maestro shall lack nothing which can restore his strength and his voice.'

He rang his little bell twice in quick succession, and at the same time he wrote an address on the folded paper. A man in black entered before he had finished. Then he scattered red sand on the writing, and poured it back into the sand-box.

'To Tor di Nona,' he said. 'Tell the messenger to gallop.'

The man was gone in an instant.

'You will find a chair downstairs,' the churchman said. 'The men are to take you to your apartment in my palace.'

'But if the porter———' Ortensia began to object.

'He will hardly venture to turn my liveries from my own door, madam. Go to your rooms and rest. You will find that your maid has left you. She fled in terror last night, and left Rome an hour ago in the coach for Naples. I saw no reason for having her stopped, but if she has robbed you I will have her taken. Your husband has a queer hunch-backed man-servant called

Cucurullo; he looks like Guidi, I remember, the young poet who ran away from our royal guest the other day.'

The Cardinal smiled vaguely, and rubbed his chin with his ring.

'He is downstairs,' Ortensia said. 'He is a good creature,' she added quickly, fearing lest the great man was about to tell her something to Cucurullo's discredit.

'An excellent fellow,' the Cardinal assented readily. 'I was going to say that if your husband wished to part with him, I should be glad to take him into my service. You will not suspect me of entertaining any foolish superstition about the good fortune which hunchbacks are supposed to bring with them, I am sure! That is ridiculous. Besides, I would not for the world displease the poor fellow, if my suggestion were not agreeable to him, as well as to your husband, madam, believe me!'

Even in her anxiety Ortensia was inclined to smile, for it was clear that the master of Rome believed in the deformed man's supernatural gift as profoundly as any beggar in the street who tried to touch the hump unnoticed.

'I will speak with my husband about it,' Ortensia said. 'Only let me see him,' she added, in a pleading tone.

'For the present, madam, I have done all I can, except to promise you that if His Holiness is well enough to hear the Maestro sing, you shall be present. Meanwhile, you must go home, and remain in your rooms till I send for you.'

He held out his ring for her to kiss, and she saw that she must go.

'I thank your Eminence with all my heart,' she said, and with a deep courtesy she turned and left the room.

Her heart was lighter than when she had entered it, for though she did not like the Cardinal, who was liked by few, she could not help believing that he was in earnest in all he had said, and really meant to give Stradella the only chance left to him of escaping some heavy penalty for his hastiness. But she longed to see him more than ever, and to repeat all she had just heard exactly as it had been said.

As she retraced her steps from the study to the stairs, accompanied by a servant who showed her the way, she looked about her in surprise, for she had not the slightest recollection of anything she now saw, and was amazed at the distance she had traversed without noticing anything. She could have sworn that she had gone up by an ordinary staircase, but instead, it was a winding one, and everything else she saw surprised her in the same way.

Cucurullo was standing beside the large sedan chair with the four porters who wore the Cardinal's livery of scarlet and gold. Two of them were to carry her, while one walked before and the fourth followed behind, both the latter being ready to take their turns as bearers at regular intervals.

When they reached the palace a quarter of an hour later, they did not even pause at the lodge, and it was with considerable astonishment that Gaetano saw Ortensia enter in such state, followed by Cucurullo, who smiled pleasantly as he passed.

Ortensia stepped from the chair at her own door and thanked the men, for she had nothing to give them; but the hunchback always had money, and when he had unlocked the door he handed them a silver florin with an air as grand as if he had been at least the seneschal of the palace.

Ortensia went on to the sitting-room, still almost unconscious of being tired; but she had hardly entered, followed closely by Cucurullo, when her knees suddenly gave way under her, her head swam, and she had barely time to stagger to the long sofa before she fainted away, utterly worn out with fatigue and emotion.

She came to herself before long, and Cucurullo was leaning over her and cooling her forehead and temples with a handkerchief soaked with Felsina water. But she only sighed as she recognised him, and then he saw that she fell peacefully asleep, just as she lay. He drew the blinds closer together to darken the room, and went off to shave himself and restore his usually neat and clean appearance, which had suffered somewhat during a whole night spent out of doors.

But Ortensia was outwardly in a far worse plight as she lay sleeping on the hard sofa, for her pretty silk skirt was soiled and torn at the edges, her little kid shoes were splashed with mud, covered with dust, and half worn out by her walking in rough places; the blood-stained handkerchief on her arm told its own tale, too, and her glorious hair was all disordered and tangled. Yet, somehow, she was not a whit less beautiful than when she had left the house with her husband on the previous afternoon fresh from Pina's skilful hands.

She was dreaming of Stradella now, after she had been asleep more than four hours, and the sun outside was high and hot. It was not a vision of terror, either, or of tormenting anxiety; she thought he had come back to her, and that it had all been a mistake, or a bad dream within the present sweet one; for he was just the same as when she had seen him last, his gaze was clear and loving, his touch was tender, and when his lips met hers——

She awoke with a startled cry of joy, and it was all true; for he was kneeling beside her, and she felt his kiss before her eyes opened to see themselves in his. It had all been a bad dream that had turned to a sweet one and ended in the delicious truth. He had not left her since she had rested there, on that same sofa after dinner, and they had not yet been to the Lateran—it was still yesterday.

Then she remembered, and put down her feet to the pavement as she sat up in his arms, and framed his face in her hands, pushing it a little away from her to see it better.

No; he was himself, his straight dark hair was neatly combed, his cheek was smooth and fresh and cool, his collar was spotless and lay over his dark coat just as it always did. She was either still asleep and dreaming, or she had dreamed every terror she remembered. To be sure that she was awake, she opened and shut her eyes several times very quickly, and then gazed at him in sweet surprise.

'She sat up in his arms and framed his face in her hands'

'Beloved, am I awake? I do not understand——'

Instead of answering her in words, he kissed her again, and the long thrill that made her quiver from head to foot told her that she was indeed awake.

Presently they began to talk, and each told what the other could not know, till there was nothing more to tell; moreover, Ortensia's tale was by far the longer, and Stradella's eyes darkened more than once at what he heard, but whenever she saw that look in his face, she kissed it away, and told him that they were safe now, if only he could sing to the Pope to-day as he had sung yesterday for her in the Lateran.

'But what can I sing?' he asked.

'"Lord have mercy on us!"' answered Ortensia, almost laughing. 'That must be the meaning of the song, at all events.'

'A *miserere*?' Stradella was surprised at the suggestion, for old men do not usually like dirges.

'No, sweetheart, I did not mean that! It must not be in Latin, but in Italian, an appeal from you, as a man who has committed a fault, to the Pope, as a sovereign, who has power to forgive it if he will.'

'Do you mean that I am to compose the words and the music between now and sunset?' asked the musician, somewhat startled.

'Why not? Did you not compose the greatest love song you ever wrote in a few hours, and for me? What is the use of being a man of genius, my beloved? Just for that, and nothing else!'

'But I am not a man of genius! And I have spent the night in prison!'

'You look as fresh as a May morning!' laughed Ortensia. 'Whereas I am all bedraggled, and scratched, and dishevelled, and everything I should not be.'

'I dressed while you were sleeping,' answered Stradella. 'There was plenty of time!'

'Do you mean to say that you had the inhuman cruelty not to wake me the instant you came home? And you pretend to love me! I shall never believe you again. But that only proves that you are a man of genius, as I said—you have not half a heart amongst you, you great artists! But I will have my revenge, for I shall go to my own room, and shut myself up and make myself fit to be seen, while you compose your song!'

'And who will dress your beautiful hair now that Pina has run away?' laughed Stradella.

'I will. And if I cannot, a certain man of genius, called Alessandro Stradella, may try his hand at it!'

She ran away laughing, but he caught her before she reached her own door, and though she struggled, he kissed her on her neck, just where the red-gold ringlets grew, low down behind her little ear. They behaved like a pair of runaway lovers, as they were.

But when he was alone his face grew grave and thoughtful, for he knew there was great danger still. He had been sent home under a guard, a prisoner still, and there were sentinels outside both doors of the apartment, who would be relieved at intervals all day, till the time came for him to be taken to the Quirinal. He might have been somewhat reassured if he had known that Don Alberto himself was also under arrest in his bedroom, by the Cardinal's orders; and he might have felt some satisfaction if he could have seen his enemy's injured nose, swollen to an unnatural size and covered with sticking-plaster, and if he could have also realised that it still hurt quite dreadfully; but, on the other hand, these latter palliative circumstances were likely to make the real trouble even worse, since that same nose was not to be classed with common noses, but as a *nasus nepotis Pontificis*, that is, nepotic, belonging to a Pope's nephew, and therefore quasi-pontifical, and not to be pulled, struck, or otherwise maltreated with impunity.

Nevertheless, Stradella forgot all about the injured feature and its possessor in a few minutes, when he had tuned his lute and was sitting by the table with a sheet of music and a pen at his elbow, for he thought aloud in soft sounds that often ceased at first and then began again, but little by little linked themselves together in a melody that has not perished to this day; and with the music the words came, touchingly simple, but heart-felt as an angel's tears.

Ortensia heard his voice through the door, and listened, half dressed, with a happy smile; for she knew the moods of his genius better than he knew them himself, and she understood that the song he was weaving with voice and lute would be worthy of him, as it is; for in the growth of music, the fine art, his masterpiece of oratorio are left behind and forgotten, being too thin and primitive for an age that began with Beethoven and ended in Richard Wagner; but his songs have not lost their hold on those simpler natures that are still responsive to a melody and vibrate to a perfect human voice.

It was late in the afternoon when Stradella had finished his work, and the last note and rest of 'Pietà Signore' were written down. The two had dined on the supper which Pina and Cucurullo had prepared for them on the previous evening, and in the warm hours Ortensia had fallen asleep again for a little while, still listening to the song and hearing it in her dreams. But when Stradella was sure that nothing more was to be changed, she opened her eyes wide and got up; and she came and knelt at his knees as she had done on that last night in the balcony of the old inn; and then he sang what he had composed, from first to last, in a voice that just filled her ears when it was loudest, and still echoed in her heart when it sank to a mere breath. When he was silent at last there were tears in her eyes, and she kissed his hand as it lay passive on the silent strings of the lute, while he bent down over her and his lips touched her hair.

They had not much time left after that, as it seemed to them, when they remembered it all and looked back on one of the happiest days in their young lives. The last time they kissed was when they were ready to go downstairs to the carriage that was waiting to take them to the Quirinal. Strange to say, Stradella felt a little faint then, and his heart was beating almost painfully, whereas Ortensia was quite calm and confident, and smiled at the two sbirri in black who were ready on the landing to escort the prisoners to the Cardinal's presence.

They were there at last, in a spacious room where everything was either white, or gilded, or of gold, the walls, the furniture, the big fireplace, the heavy carpet spread on the marble floor, where the Pope sat in his gilded chair, himself all in white, with a small white silk skullcap set far back on his silvery hair. His face was almost white, too, and the short beard on his chin was like snow, for he was over eighty years of age, thin, and in ill-health; but the face was kindly, with soft dark eyes that still had life in them; and the shadow of a smile flickered round the faded lips as Stradella and Ortensia knelt together at his feet.

On his left side stood Cardinal Altieri, erect and motionless in his purple cassock with red buttons, and his scarlet silk cloak. His face was grave and inscrutable.

'Holy Father,' he had said, as the pair knelt down, 'these are the prisoners who implore your pardon.'

That was all he said, and for some moments the Pope did not speak, though he nodded his snowy head twice, in answer to the Cardinal's words, and his gentle eyes looked from the one young face to the other as if reading the meaning of each.

'You sang to me a year ago, my son,' he said at length to Stradella. 'Go now and stand a little way off and make music, for though I am old I hear well; and do your best, for I will be your judge. If I find you have even greater mastery than last year, your skill shall atone for your rude handling of my nephew; but if you sing less well, you must have an opportunity of practising and perfecting your art in solitude for a few months.'

If Stradella had dared to glance at the kindly face just then, he would certainly have noticed how the dark eyes brightened, and almost twinkled. But Ortensia, being a woman, and still full of girlhood's innocent daring, was boldly looking up at the Pope while he spoke; and he smiled at her, and one shadowy hand went out and rested on the black veil she had pinned upon her hair.

'Go and stand near your husband while he sings to me,' he said. 'You will give him courage, I am sure!'

The two rose together, and Stradella took up the lute he had laid beside him on the floor when he had knelt down at the Pope's feet. He and Ortensia stepped back half-a-dozen paces, and the musician stood still, but Ortensia moved a little farther away and to one side. The windows were wide open to the west, and the rich evening light flooded the white and gold room, and illumined the figure of the aged Pope, the strong features of the tall grey-haired Cardinal beside him, and the two young faces of the singer and his wife.

Stradella's heart beat fast and faintly, and his fingers trembled when they touched the strings and made the first minor chord. As long as he lived he remembered how at that very moment two swallows shot by the open window, uttering their eager little note; the room swam with him, and he thought he was going to reel and fall. For a moment he saw nothing and knew nothing, except that he had reached the end of the short prelude on the lute, and that he must find voice to sing for his liberty and Ortensia's, if not for his life.

'Pietà, Signore——'

The first words broke from his chilled lips in a low cry of despair, so strange and moving, and yet so musical, that the Cardinal started visibly, and the Pope raised his white head and looked slowly down the room, as if some suffering creature must be there at the very point of death, and crying low for pity and forgiveness. Even Ortensia, who had heard all, could not believe her ears, though she knew her husband's genius well.

'Signor pietà——' he sang again.

Fear was gone now, but art poured out the appeal for pardon with supreme power to move, roused to outdo itself, perhaps, by that first piteous cry that had broken from the master-singer's lips. The plaintive notes floated on the golden air as if a culprit spirit were pleading for forgiveness at the gates of paradise, a wonder to hear.

Ortensia held her breath, her eyes fixed on the aged Pontiff's rapt face; for he was gazing at the singer while he listened to a strain such as he had never heard in all his eighty years of life; and his kind old eyes were dewy with compassion.

The last note lingered on the air and died away, and there was silence in the great room while one might have counted ten. Then the shadowy white hand was slowly stretched out in a beckoning gesture, and the Pope spoke.

'Come,' he said, 'you are forgiven.'

They came and knelt at his feet again, and he, leaning forward in his great chair, bent his head towards them.

'You were pardoned in my heart already, my son,' he said to Stradella, 'for I have been told the truth, and the provocation you suffered was great. Go free, and fear nothing, for while you dwell under our care in Rome you shall be as safe as I who speak to you. Go free, and use the great gift you have received from heaven to raise men's hearts heavenwards, as you have raised mine to-day.'

He gave his hand to Stradella and then to Ortensia, and they kissed the great ring with devout gratitude, deeply touched by his words. Then he spoke again, and still more kindly.

'Will you ask anything of me before you go?'

'Your blessing on us, as man and wife, Holy Father,' Stradella answered.

'Most willingly, my children.'

With fatherly tenderness he joined their right hands under his left, and then, lifting his right above their bowed heads, and looking up, he blessed them very solemnly.

I shall tell no more, but leave the singer and his young wife to their happiness. If any one would know the end that followed years afterwards, he will find it in chronicles that are in almost every great library. I shall only say that while those two lived they loved, as few have, and that Stradella's fame was greater when he breathed his last than it had ever been before; and in Italy he is not forgotten yet.

But whether Trombin and Gambardella will ever stroll into the story-teller's dreamland again, and act other parts, he himself cannot surely tell, nor does he know whether they will be welcome if they come. Their names are not in the chronicles, as Stradella's and Ortensia's are, as well as Pignaver's. The Venetian nobleman 'sent certain assassins,' and that is all we know; and as for the names and faces and figures I have given to the Bravi, I found them beyond the borders of truth in the delicious Gardens of Irresponsibility, where many strange people dwell together, who might be real, and may be alive some day, but who have not yet made up their minds to exchange the flowery paths of fiction for the stony roads and dusty lanes of this working-day world.

Milton Keynes UK
Ingram Content Group UK Ltd.
UKHW030904151124
451262UK00006B/1023